ZOMBIE FALLOUT 12

DOG DAYZ

MARK TUFO

Copyright © 2019 by Mark Tufo

All rights reserved.

No part of this book may be reproduced in any form or by any electronic or mechanical means, including information storage and retrieval systems, without written permission from the author, except for the use of brief quotations in a book review.

❀ Created with Vellum

ZOMBIE FALLOUT 12 - DOG DAYS OF WAR

Dedications:
To my wife Tracy,
I cannot thank you enough,
for the love you give.
(Yup that's a haiku!)
To my most awesomest beta readers, Kimberly Sansone, Patti Reilly and Vanessa McCutcheon. Every time I think I have a near perfect book you all prove me wrong. I mean it sounds like a bad thing but all your corrections are greatly appreciated by me and I would imagine the readers! And speaking of the readers, a huge thank you to all of you, because without your support, I'm most likely sitting in cube city pissing off all those around me. I can assure you those people are thankful you support me as well!
To the men and women of the armed forces your daily sacrifices never go unthanked in the Tufo homestead. Thank you for all that you do.

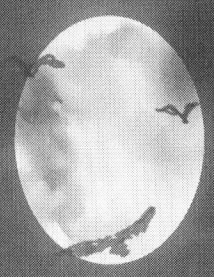

PROLOGUE

HOME. What a wonderfully strange place to be. Tracy was working, Nicole and Justin were in trade schools and Travis was in a more or less regular school. When I came back from missions, my primary duty became dog sitting–maybe one of the best things ever. I could usually be found on the living room floor wrestling with Henry, Riley, and Ben Ben for some prize they'd found. This, and being with my family; it was why I did everything I did. But it was strange, no doubt about it. We lived in a tightly gated community; armed guards patrolling was the norm. But when I was home, I made sure to stuff my camis far back in the closet; I lived the illusion of normalcy and my family followed me straight down the rabbit hole.

We never discussed the zombies, certainly never any of my missions, and even stranger still, we did not talk about all those we lost along the way. It was always there though, like an oily film coating an otherwise pristine lake in the mountains. You could only see it from a certain angle, but one match could set the whole thing ablaze making it look like something straight from the underworld. As part of my commission in Bennington's Corps, I was required to attend a counseling session once a week whenever I was on base. The counselor, Fred Scarborough, was overworked with a patient load that would have made him one of the wealthiest men in the free world–if we were still in a commercial market. I'd long ago learned all the key words to tell him so that he never delved any deeper into the many problems I carried around with me. I was just smart enough as to be dangerous, as the saying goes.

We were trying to move on with our lives as best we could and I was going to do my best to be that strong glue that kept our house of cards standing. If I could learn just one thing from the dogs, it was how happy they were to live in the moment. To just enjoy a game of tug-of-war, or to revel in the delight of the bacon grease I poured over their dog food. Of course, I suspected that they remembered past events and had learned from them, but they did not let those memories define them. The past did not have a stranglehold over their future like it did us lesser creatures.

"Henry, you think if I ever became a werewolf I could enjoy life as much as you?" I had the bullie's massive head in my hands and was looking straight into his eyes. He sneezed in response.

"Werewolf?" Tracy had just come in from getting a few supplies. "That's all we need. You already make big enough messes." The living room was a disaster; at some point Ben Ben had got ahold of a pillow and had savagely ripped it open. Probably my fault, considering I'd been shoving it in his face to keep him from licking me.

It was strange and it was wonderful here. Gary and Tommy came over all the time, BT much less so; if not for Lyndsey I'm not sure if I'd see him at all during our down times. I don't think it was anything he did on a conscious level, just that every time he saw me I would imagine he was forced to remember all we'd been through again, and, yeah…he was doing the same thing we were all trying to do. Just flat-out ignore the misery and death that pressed in on the fences we had built both literally and figuratively. This saddened me profoundly. BT was above and beyond my best friend on this planet and the thought that seeing me pained him? I mean, what do you do with that?

I think Bennington had a good idea establishing the line his raiders walked, as once we were inside the fortification, we were left alone. We didn't need to show up for revelry or report in to anyone until such time as we were given a mission. I liked it here; we were making a difference. I could not help but wonder how long the illusion would last.

1

MIKE JOURNAL ENTRY 1

Let the fuckery begin

"You have got to be shitting me!" I stood up quickly.

"You realize where you are, right?" BT asked, pulling on my arm.

"Sorry, sir," I spoke to the colonel, who looked bemused. He motioned for me to take the seat again but I waited a good long moment before I even felt remotely calm enough to do so.

"I realize what you've been through—what you've all been through, and I wouldn't ask this of you if it wasn't imperative."

"Ask? Or order?" If he offered a loophole, I was damned sure going to dive through it.

"At the moment, I'm *asking* because of the necessity of this mission."

"And if I don't acquiesce willingly?"

"Acquiesce? One way to look at it. I could send another team, but you know the area."

"Sir, the missus and I visited Times Square once and I got so lost I took her to the wrong Christmas tree."

"What?" BT looked at me. "How could you not know you weren't at Rockefeller Center?"

"Hey man, how the hell was I supposed to know they had more than one enormous tree and skating rink? I figured it had to be it. Seemed strange though; the tree did always look bigger on television. Figured it was the wizardry of the broadcast."

"Lieutenant."

"Colonel, we fought to get out here. We gave up so much…lost so much." I had to fight to keep the hitch out of my voice. "I don't know how I can possibly go back there."

"You won't be there for more than a day or two. Get you there in a C-130, bring you back the same way."

"Sounds wonderful. Did you tell my gunney here how we're off-loading ourselves and the equipment?"

"Wait…what?" BT asked.

"Well, when you fly into what was one of the most heavily populated cities in the world, it's best not to attract too much attention, so we're going to parachute out."

"Fuck you, Mike." Now it was BT's turn to stand.

"Him. His call." I pointed to the colonel.

"My kids, when they were toddlers, had more military decorum than the two of you combined. It's a good thing you all know what you're doing."

"Yeah, fantastic. First time in my life I wished I'd listened to my mother when she said I could be anything I wanted."

"Context, Mike, you left us hanging."

"I was seven, really liked bats. Told her I was going to be one when I grew up."

"Helpful," BT said.

My head sagged. "When do we leave?"

"Your unit is already waiting."

"I cannot believe we're going back to the East Coast." I

stood and shook the colonel's hand; he wished us luck. Our ride to the runway was waiting outside. Good thing too or I might have been inclined just to walk out the gate and into the Washington wilderness; me and my Yeti friends could start our own colony. BT glowered at me throughout the entire ride and for the first two hours of the flight.

"What makes you think the parachuting part of this was my idea? I heard his orders at the same time you did," I told him.

"They giving him four chutes like they did our Hummer?" Gary asked.

"What are you talking about?"

"Because of his size? I figured they'd give him four chutes so he would land safely."

"Would suck if we had a casualty on the flight over." BT was grinding a fist into his open hand, his teeth were gritted. Gary gulped and readjusted his headphones; I think I heard *Walk like an Egyptian* blaring through.

"You going to open that?" BT asked. I held a sealed manila envelope that contained our orders.

"Figuring if I didn't open it, it wouldn't be real. I'm heading back to the East Coast, and I didn't even have time to tell Tracy goodbye. I'm scared, man. I've got this feeling in my gut we're going to lose this cushy ride and we're going to once again have to fight our way back. BT, I don't know if I have it in me."

His face softened; for once I wasn't being a smart-ass or giving him shit. "We'll be alright, man. We do this, we go home. Same as it always is."

"If you say so." I said the words, but the farther east we went, the sourer my mood became. Saw the Rockies, the flats of Kansas, the Mississippi River and other landmarks as I spent a fair amount of time up in the pilot's area. More than once I thought about hijacking the plane and going to Mexico.

I couldn't help but wonder how many people down below were watching our passing. A few years ago, wasn't a person in the world that would have given a plane in the sky a second thought. Now though, this had to be a relatively rare event. Wouldn't doubt if more chupacabras had been spotted in the last month over airplanes.

"Lieutenant, it's neither vital nor desired that you stay behind my seat the entire time I fly this plane. I assure you, I can do my job at a high level."

"No problem, Major Eastman. I was just looking everything over, deciding if I could fly this thing or not."

The major laughed, thinking I was kidding. It was Major Jackson who clued him into the opinion he didn't think I was joking around.

"Go sit down, Lieutenant," a now uncomfortable Major Eastman ordered.

"How you doing, brother?" BT was mowing through a box of chocolate chip granola bars.

"I wouldn't think you'd want to be adding any more strain to the parachute you're about to use."

BT stopped mid-chew. "That's just mean, man."

"Sorry, just...the East Fucking Coast. We tried so hard to get there and then we tried so hard to get away. I can't believe we're going back."

"Get your seatbelts on back there!" Eastman said over the intercom.

I was in the seat nearest to the cockpit and could see in; a couple of the instruments were blinking red. A moment later I'd wished I'd sat farther away.

"Who the hell is painting us?" Major Jackson asked.

I wasn't overly versed in pilot lingo but I knew enough. Being painted meant there was a weapons system directed our way.

"Missile away!" Jackson said just as the plane pitched hard to the side. We were so far over, when I turned my head I was above and looking straight down at Corporal Rose. My seat belt attempted to cut me in half as it did its job admirably and held me in place. Didn't see what good that was going to do, though, if my distinct halves landed wetly on him.

There was a general cacophony among my charges as they tried to figure out what was going on. BT was to my left and above me; if his seat gave he was going to take out the whole row, finishing us off if the missile didn't do its job. The plane leveled off, then came the high pitched whine of the engines as we plummeted straight down. I was gripping the armrests, doing my best to keep my body in place. I was looking straight out the front window and I could see the contrail of something fast approaching.

"That what I think it is?" BT was looking at the same thing I was.

I tried to answer; it came out more like "Nyuh." The belt was dug so deep into my lap I could have used it to wipe my ass. Sorry.

We were somehow forced over even more, I figured if Eastman went any further, we were going to start flipping tail over nose till we hit the ground. The engines were screaming now; not only was that missile coming straight for us but the ground was approaching. I could just make out a large convoy of trucks and cars. I was getting a sick sort of fascination as they began to speed towards us. Seemed to me like Eastman was playing Kamikaze; if they got us, there was going to be some severe collateral damage on their part as this nearly forty-ton war machine rained down on them.

We were plummeting down and the missile was rocketing up. We're talking speeds too fast for humans to even gauge, but I swear I clearly saw "USA" proudly printed on the side of that missile as it blew past our nose. I was honestly surprised when I didn't hear the fin of that thing scrape paint off our fuselage.

"Pull up! Pull up!" Eastman and Jackson were fighting with

the controls. At first, I thought it was them yelling those words—ended up being me. Pretty sure they knew what to do. The plane's trajectory was changing at incremental degrees; the ground didn't give a shit. It just kept getting clearer and clearer. It had been like watching an old and often used VCR tape, but now it was high-fucking-definition. Another second or two and I'd be able to count individual leaves on the trees below us. Whoever had launched the rocket was entirely too busy attempting to escape what was going to be a huge man-made crater to launch another. That worked out in our favor, I guess.

A slim line of sky appeared at the very top edge of the window as the pilots fought to get us horizontal. I decided to shift my focus to that slowly expanding horizon.

"Talbot!" BT yelled. "If we die, I want you to know I love your sister and and…you're alright too! Plus…man I feel guilty about this….I used your toothbrush once."

I didn't think things could get much worse. I was wrong. I fought against the g-forces being applied to me to look over at him.

"I'm sorry, man. It was the night we came over for dinner. You know how Tracy loves to put onions in everything, then we were sitting out in the back enjoying the fire pit getting cozy…how could I kiss your sister with onion breath?"

"I want you to shut up about every part of that last sentence. Every part!"

"Even the onions?"

"Especially the onions!"

My last words were extremely loud now that the engines were working much closer to their regular load.

"Radio that in," Eastman told Jackson over the speakers. "Safe now. As I'm sure all of you already know, we had a surface-to-air missile fired at us. Looks like it was just the one. ETA to drop: forty-five minutes."

I figured that would be how long it would take for my

heart to calm down, just in time to start ramping up for the jump.

"My fucking toothbrush?" I had undone my strap so I could stand and be somewhat closer to face-to-face with the man sitting.

"I'm cleaner than you," he offered as a defense.

"You think that matters? I have to chant a mantra every time I use the thing my fucking self! I brush my teeth then put the thing away only to shove it in my mouth the next day–I can about taste the giant bug-germs crawling across it! The only thing that gets me through is thinking that they drown in the toothpaste!"

"Toothpaste isn't a disinfectant," he replied calmly.

"It is in my world!"

"Lieutenant, is there a problem?" A harried Major Eastman was looking back at us.

"You have no idea," I told him. "Might have been better off if the missile'd hit us. Can you imagine the size of the germs that live in his mouth?" I was pointing to BT. "Probably a whole new strain, germus-giganticus. No wonder I've been feeling like my teeth are shifting! They just shove them around to get inside all the crevices."

"You're losing your shit over nothing," BT replied.

"Nothing? Fine. If we're gonna go there, I've got something to confess."

"Careful, Talbot."

"No, no…this has been eating away at me. I want to get it off my chest. You know that night you made the gumbo?"

"Yeah…?" he answered cautiously.

"I don't like foods in sauces or stews; freaks me out because of my mother."

"I know that."

I paused. "Really, man? You invited me over for a pot of it! That's some pretty passive-aggressive shit right there."

"You're lucky it wasn't ham! I was trying to broaden your horizons, dumbass."

"I'm fine with the horizons I can see, thank you very much. Anyway, while you were in the living room I went into the kitchen, decided I was going to try the mumbo…"

"Gumbo."

"Whatever. Anyway, I took a spoonful, ended up with something that felt like an eyeball in my mouth–it was reflexive, man. I spit it out."

"And…" BT had undone his belt.

"It landed back in the dumbo."

"Gumbo! *And you spit in my food?*"

"It was an accident! And in light of recent events, I think that makes us even."

"I ate that for the next three days! We're hardly even." BT had a finger pointed straight down on my head.

"Don't put eyeballs in your damn food, then."

"There were no eyeballs in it!"

Ended up getting saved by Gary. "Since we're confessing, I think you should know something." He was standing next to BT.

"Can't wait to hear it," he replied, though he had not turned away from me.

"There was a fly on the lip of the cooker, and when I hit it with the fly swatter it fell into the gumbo." BT's mouth hung open. "I tried to fish it out, but it got swallowed up in the mix."

"See? Just one more reason to not eat sauced-over foods," I said in justification.

"There was a fly in there too? But…you ate, like, three helpings?" Now he was completely focused on Gary.

"Little extra protein never hurt anyone. I was trying to eat it before anyone else got to it; figured if I had enough bowls, percentage-wise I was sure to get it."

"I am so fucking glad I put a burger on the grill," I sighed.

"You realize how rude that was, right?" BT immediately swung his attention back to me.

"Next time make something everyone will enjoy and there won't be a problem."

"You were the only one! For a minute I felt bad about the toothbrush thing, but now I'm glad I drooled all over that thing, happy that those little bristles wrapped around each of my teeth, pushing and pulling away the gooey orts of food. Oh, and the *heavenly* feeling when I scraped it over my tongue, grinding out all the milky deposits in and under my taste buds…" He smiled broadly. "About the cleanest my mouth has ever felt."

"Next time you come over you'd better wear Depends, because I'm not letting you near the bathroom."

"Yeah? Well you better bring a bagged lunch because I'm not letting you in my kitchen."

"You two are kidding me, right? We just narrowly avoided getting blown out of the sky and you are about to be dropped into a hot zone, and you care about that crap?" Eastman was looking back at us, his mouth hanging open in astonishment as he watched our argument.

"Aw man, if we didn't argue after every time we almost got killed or were just about to, we'd never talk," BT said.

I fist bumped him before I started laughing. "We good?" I asked.

"Of course, man. I love you."

"Love you, too," I told him as I sat down.

"Fucking nuts," Eastman mumbled before turning back around.

"What about me?" Gary was still standing there.

"Yeah, you too," I told him.

It was relatively peaceful for the next few moments.

"Lieutenant, need you up here," Eastman motioned.

"You want me to fly this thing?" I asked when I got there. I was going for levity; he was all business.

"We've got a problem."

It would have been hard not to notice all the pulsing red lights on his dash.

"You're going to have to jump early."

"And?"

"Going to be right over the city."

"How much time?"

"Get them up…one minute."

"Everyone up," I said calmly, though my innards were churning as I went back to the passenger compartment.

My squad headed to the back; the other group with us stayed put. There were a few extra men on board; if I had to take a guess from the look of them, I'd say Navy SEALs. Whatever they were doing, we weren't on a need-to-know basis; at least, nothing was in the orders I'd received.

"You coming?" I asked the captain of the other group.

He looked at me but said nothing.

"You're really not even going to acknowledge I asked you a question?"

"Go on with your crayon-eating self," he said as a dig to all Marines everywhere.

"Hey, man—you've never lived until you've eaten the purple ones."

"Whatever."

"Your mother a cactus?"

"What?" He stood, knowing it was some sort of insult.

"I asked if your mother was a cactus because you're a prick."

"Sit down," BT told him. SEALs aren't big on other people telling them what to do.

It was Eastman that prevented a brawl. "Lieutenant! Get moving!" he shouted.

"You're lucky. I would have let him check how good your medical coverage is." I pointed to BT before we went back with the rest. Kind of bummed they weren't coming with us;

first, because I wanted to kick his ass, and second, they're great to have watching your back.

There was a red light that ran the length of the back of the airship. When it turned green, we pushed out our two Hummers and then I tapped each of the men in turn to follow.

"I fucking hate this." BT had adjusted his goggles and headed out. I gave one long look the way of the cockpit, wondering if the SEALs would try to stop me if I took the plane over before I decided to follow my group out. There was about three seconds of complete terror where your mind doesn't even have the capacity to think outside of panic. Let's face it; humans aren't meant to free-fall through the sky. We are far from aerodynamic beings. But then, as the chute deploys, there is a rush of endorphins and a general sense of well-being, promising that you are going to make it down safely.

I was looking around at the chutes, at our equipment, and at my squad; I had all of them accounted for. I then scanned the ground, suddenly realizing the stupidity of this jump. Building spires pointed up at us by the hundreds; looked like a booby-trapped hole in the ground someone might have encountered in Vietnam, a tiger pit, and we were very much in danger of being skewered. We had the much newer rectangular parachutes, which allowed us a fair measure of ability to maneuver, as opposed to the old-style circle ones that fell where they might. With that being said, landing in this minefield full of buildings was still going to hold its own unique set of problems. Already had a stiff cross breeze, and once we got lower and that breeze was channeled through those buildings, there was going to be something akin to a gale force to be reckoned with. We'd been going for stealth–quick in, quick out. That all ended when the second Hummer caught the corner of a skyscraper roof. In the abstract, action movie kind of way, it was pretty stunning; the rear of the Hummer collided with the side of the roof, even with the wind rushing past my ears I could hear and even feel the contact. The rear wheel and some of the body were ripped free, as were significant chunks of steel and concrete from the building. I watched as a cache of rifles, ammunition, a radio, and the ZADAR fell from the back. Wouldn't even be worth scavenging, once those items rode down the hundred-floor express elevator.

"You seeing this?" BT's voice came through my earpiece.

"Wish I wasn't," I responded.

"Stop watching the truck and look lower."

I did. The loss of the transportation and equipment paled in comparison to what was waiting at the bottom. Pretty sure those were zombies racing out of the surrounding buildings in large groups. At least I figured it was zombies; couldn't imagine that many people together, especially with no weapons.

"Hope this is worth it," BT said.

"Bennington thinks so...suppose that's all that matters. Alright, team! Hard to the left!" This was achieved by pulling on the left "brake" strap. It pulled the edge of the parachute down and caused it to bank that way. We were too low and moving too fast to clear the street completely, but I was going to use the wind to our advantage. Push us as far away from the gathering horde as was possible. "Shit, Halsey! Your other damn left!" Dumbass had turned right.

"You forgetting about the other Hummer?" Winters asked.

"You want to get it?" I asked him.

"Not so much, sir."

"Sir, this is Corporal Rose. My right brake line is tangled." She sounded concerned, but thankfully, not panicked.

I looked down and over to Rose, who was struggling with her line. Not much you can do when it is above you and beyond your reach.

"Go to your reserve, Rose—no time," I urged her. If she

landed awkwardly due to the bad brake line, it could equate to a death sentence. The landing wouldn't necessarily kill her, but a busted ankle could be enough right now.

I imagine for a seasoned jumper with five hundred or so jumps under your belt, deploying your reserve would be old hat. None of us were that. The thought of cutting free a relatively decent chute and deploying another is not a fun-filled prospect. That, and we were rapidly approaching the range where this wasn't a safe thing to do. She yanked on the quick release system; she fell away like a stone. I held my breath the entire time I waited for her reserve to deploy. I think it was an hour and a half later when it did.

"Parachute is four by four," Rose announced. I could hear the relief in her voice.

Besides trying to explain the totaling of the Hummer to the insurance company, Corporal Rose was now going to land a solid twenty seconds ahead of us. Normally not a huge deal, but this time...well, again we go back to potentially deadly. The odds she'd land unnoticed were as close to zero as possible. We would be landing right where the zombies were headed. Our escape window would shrink with each passing second. A perfect landing would entail pulling on the brakes at precisely the same moment to *cup* enough air with the edges of the chute so that you land no harder than if you'd stepped off a kitchen chair, your momentum stopped to the point you would be at a brisk walking pace. You could then pull the release and let the parachute go back down the sidewalk. If done correctly, it would be something James Bond would be proud of.

Out of the ten practice jumps we'd done, I'd stuck my landing four times; the best was Tommy at six. The worst was Halsey at a flat zero. It wasn't that he'd ever got hurt, he just tended to roll a fair amount. We always got a good laugh as he came up eating grass; sometimes I suspected he did it for that reason. Right now I wasn't interested in laughing, and I hoped he realized that.

The second Hummer and Corporal Rose landed at roughly the same time, though more than a couple of hundred yards away from each other. I was happy to note the heavy vehicle mashed or damaged more than a dozen zombies on landing, but that quick burst of joy was tempered with the fact that our ride was now entirely surrounded by the bloodthirsty bastards.

"Anyone have eyes on the extra supply bag?" I asked.

"Far off to our left, LT. Looks like a heavy wind caught it," Private Halsey said.

My eyes followed the likely trajectory; I gave it a fifty-fifty shot of not getting hung up on a building, which roughly translated to a hundred percent chance we'd never see it again. We were heading into a hot war zone with no rides, no extra ammunition, and no long-range radio.

"Winters, get on the horn with Major Eastman. Give him a quick sitrep."

We were seconds from landing when Winters got back to me. "He's well aware; no help is coming."

"Kind of what I figured all along, but no sense in not throwing a Hail Mary."

BT stuck his landing and released the chute like he'd done this a thousand times. He got his rifle up and was covering the rest of us. Rose was racing toward him, unfortunately bringing a bunch of her not-friends with her. Everyone else had varying degrees of success except for Gary, who landed decently but had trouble releasing his harness. He was being dragged back toward the horde; eleven firearms were chirping around him. I had a few seconds before I touched down and with my superior position, decided to use them to my advantage. I was firing nearly straight down into the skulls of the advancing enemy. Tommy was rushing to Gary, a large knife in his right hand.

My brother was being dragged backward at close to twenty miles an hour, doing everything in his power to halt his progress. He was going to have some serious scrape wounds and would be exceedingly lucky if he didn't break his skull skipping over all manner of debris littering the roadway.

"Hurry, Tommy," I said under my breath. I had seconds to brake myself or I was going to leave my own blood and teeth bits on the asphalt. I pulled one end of the chute so I was headed back toward them; felt a bit like a starling heading for a jet engine turbine, truth be told. I hit the brakes late, felt the reverberations all the way up through my spine. I unclipped and turned just as Tommy grabbed Gary's boot. It took him a few more seconds to stop the momentum and yank my brother backward. He swung that knife like one would a scythe at a notably dense row of wheat. The parachute flew free and entangled over a dozen of the closest zombies. They went down in a heap; one of the best methods I'd seen to halt their progress thus far.

"BT, get the rest of the team to safety. Let me know where you end up," I called over as I advanced towards Tommy and Gary, making sure to steer clear of them as I continuously fired suppressive cover.

Gary's right side was scraped raw. Besides being in a considerable amount of pain, he was going to need medical attention quickly to prevent his wounds from getting infected. Tommy had hefted him up into a fireman's carry and was fast coming back my way. This was all great and fine, but it left me alone to deal with the masses. Some of the zombies tore through the parachute or were trampled as the rest were coming. If I'd had an unlimited amount of belt-fed ammunition, my position would have still been overrun. Tommy had just passed me by. Gary looked and sounded like shit as he jostled past. He was groaning; his eyes were wide in fright and also half-closed in agony. It was not a good look. I gave

Tommy a few more steps before I joined him in his hasty retreat.

"Mike, I can see you…we're about a block up. Not going to believe this but we're in M&M's World. It's clear in here." BT sounded stressed out.

"Winters, you have a medic kit on you or did you leave it in the drop bag?"

"Got it on me, sir."

"Gary is in a bad way. Gonna need some work. That place defendable, BT?"

I knew the answer; this was Times Square and I'd been to M&M's World before. The entire storefront was one giant pane of glass, the better for the tourist and prospective shopper to see its colorful wares.

"Not so much."

"Winters, I'm not ordering you, but if you could find another place, we'll meet you there." I didn't want to drag an unwanted group of party crashers to BT's candy house.

"On my way. Sir, as soon as you pass M&M's World, take a left. I'm heading to Rockefeller Center."

"Copy that," I told him. Tommy had pulled ahead as I had turned to check out our pursuit. We had about a hundred yards on them, or I did; Tommy was about half that again. "Tommy, I'm going to slow them up as much as I can. Get Gary to Winters. I'll catch up."

"Don't like that, Mr. T," he replied, though he didn't slow down or offer another solution.

"BT, I'm close. Do not, and I'm ordering you, *do not* engage the enemy."

"Well how else are you going to look the hero if we step in to help? Don't give a shit what you say; you get in trouble and there are eight of us here that are coming to your aid."

"Just for once I wish you'd follow an order of mine, but thank you."

I tossed an expended magazine, put another in, hit the

bolt release and was back in business. I was backing up quickly while also firing; it was not a natural fighting routine and the results suffered for it.

"We're there," Tommy said.

"Mike, go. They're coming from across the street and Stenzel says from further up the street."

"All right you guys, sit tight. We'll see how Gary is and how to continue this mission. If there are peanut butter M&M's in there, I'm going to want some." I was on the move.

"Good luck," BT said as I dashed by.

The front glass doors of Rockefeller Center were utterly smashed out. I could make out Tommy staying low behind some debris. I was close when I stumbled off to the side; a shrieker was trying to get my brain to rupture. My eardrums popped from the pressure. Felt like a stroke victim as I tried to regain my equilibrium; I was doing my best to continue moving forward, though I was pulling hard to the left. Another shrieker joined the first. If I didn't know better, I would have assumed they were trying to locate us by echo, but that was absurd, right? Tommy grabbed me just as I was passing him. He pulled me down hard, placed his finger to his mouth. Whatever it was, was so close he didn't even make a soft *shushing* sound. A bulker burst through a shop to our right and straight through a large, concrete flower box that, at one time, had held a perfectly manicured bush but which was now littered with glass, a broken body, and some twisted, misshapen vegetation. He waited until it ran past before picking me up.

"How you doing, Mr. T?" he asked, gently brushing me off.

"A light coating of dirt is the least of my problems, and thank you. Let's check on Gary. Whoa," I said as we went through the entrance and into the opulence. Even though it was suffering from some neglect and wildlife were beginning to encroach, it still held on to a lot of what had made it special. Had I the time, I would have taken a grand tour, but getting Gary help and getting back to the team and getting this mission done, right now that was all that mattered. Even if I did want to steal Jimmy Kimmel's chair...Matt Damon would pay me a fortune for it.

2

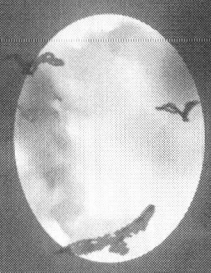

MIKE JOURNAL ENTRY 2

F‍ound Winters working on Gary behind the reception desk; he looked rough. Not Winters, my brother. Like he'd slid down the world's largest cheese grater, rough. He was in a lot of pain and bleeding from a dozen spots; well, more like a *weeping* of blood. He wasn't in danger of bleeding out, but with that much wounded area exposed to the elements, he was in danger of an infection, which we were ill-prepared to deal with.

"I'm going to need way more bandaging than I've got here." Winters looked up and over to me. I wouldn't necessarily say there was panic in his eyes, but *concern*, yeah, there was a lot of that. "And burn ointment–going to need a vat of that."

Gary was moaning; don't even think he was aware of it, as his eyes were closed.

"Would love to give him a shot of antibiotics, and not for nothing LT, a hit of morphine."

"Don't think I need to go out on a limb to say this, but all that stuff is in the supply bag, right?"

He nodded.

"And if we can't get it?"

"The morphine is for his comfort and to keep him quiet. The antibiotics, I think are pretty much life or death."

I stepped away. "BT, we have a situation here."

"Listening, Mike."

"Do you by any chance have eyes on our supply bag?"

"You mean that very same bag that's spread over a fair amount of Broadway?"

"Yeah, that one."

"What do you need?"

"Gary is going to need the med supplies."

"Entire street is enemy held, and I wouldn't even know where to begin to find what you need. Got some more great news. Just heard from Eastman; he lost comm with Etna. Says his radio suffered some sort of damage in the attack."

My heart, which had kicked into overdrive, began to slow back down. For a moment, I'd thought something had happened back in Washington. Trouble on our end I could deal with, as long as my family was safe.

"Mike?"

"Yeah, sorry; I'm here. Just thought…"

"No, near as I can tell everything is fine there. But we're alone right now."

"First priority is my brother, get him stable. If anything changes you know where to find me. Tommy, stay with Winters. I'm going to go a few floors up and see if I can find a medical office."

"I don't think going alone is a good idea, Mr. T."

"I completely agree, but Winters can't work on Gary and watch around him."

Tommy looked torn but nodded to me. I pulled the door open and nearly had a friggen' heart attack as three chairs tumbled down. Someone hadn't thought this problem out when they attempted to construct a barricade. The stench was pervasive; the darkness impenetrable as I poked my head in. I waited until I was all the way in the stairwell and had closed the door behind me before I turned my flashlight on. Besides some miscellaneous furniture, I was all alone on the first landing. I found the absence of brass strange, but then remembered this was downtown New York, not Dallas. I panned the light all around; there was some blood, but not enough to convince me there had been a slaughter here. Made it to the second floor with absolutely no trouble, actually, all the way to the fifth, before it began to get interesting.

As I moved my light up to the sixth floor, I noticed the glut of office furniture—as if the previous tenants had refused to pay their rent and management had evicted them by throwing everything into the stairwell.

"What the hell?" The obvious play would be to exit there on the fifth floor and see what I could, or go in and find another stairwell up, but I had to take a moment to see what had happened. We all make mistakes, and this was one of mine. I picked my way up to the next floor; I tried to be as quiet as possible, but every little noise was echoed and amplified within those narrow confines. I played my light across what I now considered a makeshift wall. I figured it was to stop whatever was downstairs from coming up; didn't realize it was the other way around until my flashlight glinted off the rheumy eye of a zombie peering back at me from the other side. After my initial surprise, I got back up to the small hole-through and got a better look. From what I could tell, the entire stairwell behind that one zombie was jam-packed with his brethren, and I'd just given them a reason to start their escape efforts again.

"Just another reason to dislike cats," I said softly as I quickly retreated. I was referring to how curiosity killed them, apparently, and how if I'd just stuck to my mission, gone and did what I'd set off to do, I might not have stirred the nest. I could hear furniture shifting from the press of bodies, but as of yet they had not got through. I was on the fifth floor, mistakenly thinking I'd left my troubles behind, when I literally stumbled over my first clue that not all was as it should be here. A gnawed-on femur had nearly tripped me.

Heard the telltale, low growl of a zombie; she was a large one, but not a bulker. From her movements, I had her pegged as a first-generation zombie, that of the slow, stiff-legged variety. I'd have plenty of time to scope out the surrounding area and get gone before I ever had to do anything about her. That was, of course, provided she was alone. Apparently, that was too much to ask. Her office mates began to come forth from their cubes. I lost a few precious seconds trying to figure out why they were even in them. Residual memory? Muscle memory? Overtime? When faced with absolutely nothing to do or eat, maybe they had gone back to a place they were familiar with. Weird and terrifying, as I now found myself faced with more than a dozen of the ghouls. Unlike the newer versions, these were in various stages of decay, torn-through faces, hanging flesh, bodies glistening wetly. Their grayish color added greatly to a tragic, haunting feeling. With arms outstretched, they advanced.

I quickly went over to the windows and began scanning the horizon. I'd been so intent on keeping an eye on the things that wanted to murder me, I hadn't been paying attention to what I was looking at.

"This is New York City. Shitload of people…has to be hospitals everywhere. Focus, man." I took as much time as I dared, truly studying the nearby buildings. Betty, the Big Zombie, was close. I was just about to move to a more private spot when I suddenly found what I was looking for. A large, white plus sign in a field of red, a block and a half away at the most.

"Rockefeller Medical Center." I moved to the north-facing windows; bought me an additional twenty seconds. Betty heavy-sighed as her midday snack left her in the lurch. "Holy shit." I was looking down at another medical center; must have passed it on the way in. I resigned not to be too hard on myself for the oversight.

"Sorry, Betty!" I waved to her as I headed out the exit. Had to sidestep a chair that fell free from up above. I could see the obstruction begin to swell; was only a matter of time and they were going to bust through.

"Mr. T, we have zombies," Tommy radioed.

"On my way." I was taking stairs three at a time. Our best bet now was to all head to the medical center. Rockefeller Center had been compromised. Seemed like I was never going to get that chair for Matt. Tommy was standing guard over Winters and Gary, his rifle up, switching from target to target, yet never firing. We had six shufflers, one of which I cracked in the back of the head with my butt stock, sending him flying. I won't swear it on a stack of bibles, but from the back, it sure did look like Matt Damon might add me to his Christmas mailing list for who I'd just hit.

"Moving isn't a good idea," Winters said. Gary was stripped down to his briefs.

"Gotta go. Good news–there's a medical center about a hundred yards from here," I said.

"I'll carry him," Tommy offered.

"Don't touch any of his wounds," Winters warned.

That was akin to not getting sand on yourself at the beach. How he was going to manage that was a mystery. Winters grabbed up his meager supplies and Gary's boots; everything else was going to need to be replaced as it was cut to shreds by the ground and finished off by the medic.

"BT, we're on the move. Leaving Rockefeller Center and heading not far, to a medical services area."

"Copy that," BT replied.

"All good where you're at?"

"Tough to say. Zombies aren't leaving–in fact, they look like they're having a giant meeting about what they plan on doing next."

"Getting better and better. Hey, are there clothes in that place?"

"Why? You planning on doing a little souvenir shopping?"

"Yeah. I'm sure the missus will be thrilled when I bring her back an M&M's t-shirt. Gary is without gear; he's going to need something."

"Sorry. How's he doing?"

"Road rash like a mother. As long as this place has some supplies, we should be all right, and then we'll just have to deal with his modesty. I'll never get him out of here if he doesn't have clothes. He's the only person I know that wears a bathing suit in the shower." BT laughed at that.

"We all have our issues," I said.

"Some more than others."

"And he only does that when other people are home," I clarified.

"Just so happens he's in luck! He's going to be as bright as a Mardi Gras drunk, but he'll have a t-shirt and some sweats. Don't see anything besides flip-flops for shoes though."

"Got that covered. Boots made it."

"Hurry up and find a way for us to regroup. Something is going to go down soon and I'd rather we were all facing it together."

"Get back to you soon," I told him.

We made it to the medical center without any mishaps, which, considering my track record, is pretty good. Although, even I should be able to travel a hundred feet without expecting a piano to land on my head. It wasn't much more than a medical tent like you'd see at a concert, a place for the overly fucked-up and super-dehydrated to get back on track. It did, however, have gauze plus burn and scrape medication in spades. The problem with the ointment, though, was it came in little foil travel packets. We were going to need to rip open a couple hundred of the things and squish them all over my brother. We'd do it because we needed to, but just because we hadn't encountered any problems getting here didn't mean we weren't bringing some with us and time would be of the essence. The Rockefeller zombies had seen us leave, and I would think had seen us enter this small facility. We wouldn't be able to hole up here indefinitely.

Winters tossed an armload of the A&D packets toward me along with a pair of sterile gloves. "Keep spreading this on him. I'm going to look for drugs." I could hear him in the back, pushing things all over the place. Tommy was keeping an eye on the door. "Got a couple of Z-packs…that's going to have to do. No painkillers, though. I don't think aspirin is going to cut it."

I was surprised he even found antibiotics in the little aid station; the thought he'd hoped to find opioids seemed crazy, especially in the heart of New York and without an armed guard.

"Talbot–need an update," BT called in.

"Have Gary at an aid station, got medicine and wrappings, no hard drugs for the pain. Have a few minutes… maybe…before we need to move again."

BT was quiet for a second. "Any medical personnel there? And before I get a smart-ass answer, I mean any *bodies*."

"Why? And, yeah, at least one. Younger guy in a white coat in the corner, what's left of him anyway."

"Check his pockets."

"I'd rather use your spoon! Bud, he's mostly a pile of goo. It's…disturbing."

"When I was on the force, about half the people we busted for popping pills were medical professionals. 'Physician heal thyself' and all that shit."

"More like, 'What's up, doc?'"

"That was horrible. Just check the body. Odds are pretty good he's got a little something on him."

"Tommy, I don't have another pair of gloves. Can you check that guy for pills?"

"Nice delegation," BT murmured.

"Being an officer has its perks."

Tommy didn't look thrilled about the prospect, but I only got two, maybe three, dirty looks as he fished around. He had to flip the man over to get to the side pockets. If I thought any of this was gross before, I was mistaken. There was a wet tearing sound as Tommy lifted the edge of the medic up, well, as he *tried* to lift the edge of the medic up. Ended up half his body stayed where it had been on the floor. Tommy was more or less just shuffling a moist skeleton into another twisted position. Instead of wrestling with the compost, he just pulled the white lab coat free. Winters was watching the whole thing; I think his jaw was less than three inches from hitting the floor.

"I've seen a lot of things, but I'm not sure anything is going to get any worse than that," he said as he came up beside me. "What's he doing exactly?"

Tommy came over with a brown bottle; it did not have a label on it, but it most certainly did have pills. He shook them at us.

"What are we supposed to do with that? Could be Viagra for all we know and I for one am not carrying a man around sporting a perpetual hard-on." Winters was busy dressing the wounds I had slathered. Tommy opened the container up and spilled a couple of pills onto the counter, getting ready to hand them to me. "We can't give unknown pills to him; they could be heart medication or something even more dangerous."

"What do they look like?" BT asked. I forgot I'd kept the channel open. I took a glove off and took one of the pills from atop the shelf.

"Got OP on one side and the number ten on the other."

"Give him one," BT said.

"Since when did you become a pill identifier?"

"I've seen enough OxyContin to know what you've got."

"This is Oxy?" I looked at the pill. "Tommy, how many do you have?"

"Twelve." He was looking inside the brown bottle.

"Don't even think about it Talbot. We're on a mission."

"Too late…the thinking part, anyway."

"Tommy, under no circumstances are you to hand that bottle over to the lieutenant."

"Buzzkill."

"There's water behind the counter; let's get that in him." Winters was wrapping Gary like a mummy. I got up and found the water. The pull was strong as I held that water and that pill; who wouldn't want to check out from our current situation? "Should have checked the damn body myself," I mumbled as I went back over, managed to get my brother to swallow that and the first couple of pills from the z-pack.

"That should keep him safe until we get him back."

"Got a group of shufflers coming," Tommy warned as he went back to his post.

"You clear over there? We're going to need to move again."

"That's a negative, we're hemmed in. The zombies look like they're making a grid search pattern. They've got a large main group in the roadway and they're sending out patrols to go into each building on the street. We might have to move soon, too."

"Winters, get Gary's boots on him. We gotta move out. BT, two blocks southeast of you is Nintendo World; we're heading there now. I want you to make a run for it; we'll cover your move. Tommy?"

"Got him." Tommy gently picked up Gary, who groaned in protest. I stepped out of the store. Upon seeing me, the shufflers quickened their pace.

"Times like this I wish I'd brought a sword."

"Or a crossbow." Winters was beside me.

"Can you imagine trying to load that thing fast enough to stop a horde?" I asked.

"Not really."

We started moving away. If we could keep a big enough lead on the shufflers, we could lose them, although, what was the use? As soon as we started shooting to cover BT's breakout, they'd find us. Rifles began to fire; there was an extended concentration of percussion as they fought to get free. Sitting idly by, waiting for my unit to show themselves, was exceedingly difficult. I was getting it in stereo through the radio as BT ordered the group forward.

We were by the Nintendo store; it was two floors, all windows. Oh, you have no idea how much I wanted to go in there, fill a rucksack with all manner of games, grab a few Mario knick-knacks…but if we set up shop on the second floor we'd be quickly trapped. So, there we were, just standing on the street, and I honestly didn't have a clue where to go. We had to wait for BT and the rest; getting split up in a city overrun by the undead was not an option. We were cut off from our home base and as of yet, we hadn't even begun the mission we'd been dropped down here for. If I went back to Bennington and told him we couldn't finish because of zombies, I had a feeling that wouldn't fly. We were on this operation, despite the zombies or because of them; either way, we had to finish.

"I see them." Tommy was pointing ahead; my gaze was still fixed on the second floor of the Nintendo store and the giant stuffed Donkey Kong. When I looked back, they were running full tilt; could see a brigade worth of zombies following them. Standing and fighting was not an option and from this angle, we didn't even have clear lines of sight to cover their retreat. I turned to look around, spotting for alternate escape routes when I saw the boy. He looked like a street urchin from a Dickens play; he stood at the end of the block, watching us.

"What fuckery is this?" I said, Winters turned. "You see that too?" I asked.

"Yeah…not sure I want to, though."

The boy started waving. Don't know why; he already had our attention. Then he made a motion as if to follow him.

Winters looked at me.

"No idea," I told him honestly.

"We're coming in hot," BT chugged out.

"Keep running past the Nintendo building. We're following a lead to the end of the block," I replied.

"Really?" Winters wasn't thrilled.

"Every building around here is nothing but glass panels and I don't want to end up bunkered in one. Tommy, come on."

The boy was gone when Tommy looked. "Where to?"

I started jogging. I didn't have an answer for him. We rounded the block; either we had taken longer than expected or the kid was phenomenally fast. He was nearly a block and a half away, still waving with his arms for us to follow.

"Any part of you think this could be a set-up?" Winters asked.

"Is what a set-up?" BT asked, he sounded close to being out of breath.

"A kid is leading us somewhere," I told him.

"Leading us where?"

"Don't know, and right now I'm not flush with options, and stop talking and do more running."

He grunted a deep, "Fuck off." Their gunfire had trailed off, as trying to slow down the vanguard by firing some shots into the group proved wholly ineffectual. Much better to flat out run.

A tall man came running out onto the street ahead of us, wrapped his arms around the boy's shoulders, and was leading him off the street. The boy was adamant as he pointed toward the four of us coming their way. Even from this distance, I could see the man tense up. He spoke something over his shoulder; three people came onto the road, all with handguns. In terms of firepower, we had it over them—or the ones showing, anyway–but that wasn't how I wanted this to play out. The man's evident surprise led me to believe the kid was acting on his own, trying to get us to safety, and that this wasn't some elaborate ruse. I was still running, but I had my hands halfway in the air, holding my rifle.

"Winters," I urged the sergeant to do the same. Tommy had Gary in his arms, so he wasn't pointing anything.

"Far enough!" the tall man shouted as we neared.

"No can do…about to have a few thousand zombies here."

He fired a shot over my head; might have been a good ten feet over, didn't care. I take extreme offense to any high-speed projectiles deliberately sent my way. I leveled my gun on him.

"Try it again! I'll fucking drop you in a puddle of your own making."

I had pulled up short as had Winters; even Tommy adjusted Gary so he could with one arm bring his rifle to bear. We had a standoff, but if bullets started flying the advantage was all ours; the pistols were out at about the extreme of any accuracy. Besides ourselves, the only other I cared about was the boy. I had no desire to see him become a casualty of war. I was happy the man had the wherewithal to push the boy behind him; it gave me an inkling of his character. Not enough I'd trust him with my life, but an advance, nonetheless.

"Heard…a…gunshot…" BT managed to get out during deep breaths.

"We're fine! Just get your ass moving."

"Who are you talking to?" the tall man asked.

"Backup, followed by not backup."

"What does that mean?" he asked, then I saw his eyes go wide. I would imagine he just saw the enormous black man round the corner with seven others of my team. That was fairly impressive in itself; his jaw dropped when he saw what was making them move so fast.

"Lyle! Get in the church now!" the man commanded.

"Dad, what about them?" He was pointing at us.

"What did I tell you son? Not every stranger is a friend you haven't met yet."

"My name is Lieutenant Michael Talbot! I'm part of a group out of Washington."

"DC?"

"State." I clarified.

"Long way from home."

"You have no idea. We're on a mission, got attacked. Our plane was forced down…we had to jump before we were ready and it's been a downhill slide ever since."

The man looked at the three he was with. "Follow us."

"Jason?" the lone female questioned him.

"What makes you think they're not going to come anyway? This way, if you're coming." And without waiting to see my response, they left.

"What are we doing?" Winters asked.

"Gonna go soak up some of that New York hospitality."

"This is what passes for hospitality on the East Coast?"

"This is actually pretty good. Only got shot at once. BT– we'll make sure to keep you in view. Just a little farther." I didn't really know how much more we had to go but he sounded like he was on his last legs; I had to give him some hope.

"Kirby, get your ass up here!" BT roared.

"Shit! Got a couple falling behind. Winters, Tommy, go. They went into the church. I'm going to help them. Go! That's an order!" We were next to Saks Fifth Avenue, and Lyle and Jason, with the others, had just gone into St Patrick's Cathedral. I was alone for the moment, and I was waving them on. "A hundred yards past me and into the church, BT. Do not stop. I'll pick up the stragglers!"

He didn't respond. We trained extensively for cardio, but there's only so far you can sprint-none of us were marathoners. Everyone was reasonably tight except for Private Kirby and Private Harmon. The latter had a limp and the former was doing his best to keep those closest to her from dragging her down. I climbed onto a car hoping for some height and a somewhat decent firing angle, but these shots were going to be close. Private Autumn Harmon had been the last to join my team; I'd be damned if she was going to be the first to die. She'd lost her hat at some point, and her long auburn hair was just about tickling the nose of the closest pursuing zombie. If his arms hadn't been pumping so much to gain speed, he could have reached out and yanked her head back. I had a window about the size of a dinner plate to shoot at. With a thudding heart and a moving target, I was taking my time lining up the shot. I hate to say "hesitating," because that is what gets people killed in combat.

BT and the others were a moment from passing me by. I let a bullet fly. The zombie behind Harmon was pushed to the side as I placed one high in his shoulder. His side dipped down and caused his feet to trip up; this was enough for him to take out the two closest behind him. They went down in a heap of arms, legs, and teeth. Kirby was reaching over to keep Harmon moving.

"Private, go! I've got her. Run!" He looked to me, to her, the church and the zombies...must have been a lot of math he was calculating. Finally, he did as I asked and sped up. I took three more shots, giving her a few feet, but she was tapped. I could see it in her eyes; she wanted to give up. Maybe not *give up*—no one willingly goes into the teeth of the zombies—but she was at the end of her abilities and her injury was taking its toll.

I jumped off the car and ran to meet her; felt like a relay racer waiting for the baton. I grabbed her by the side and we were off. She practically fell into me. "Hundred yards, Talbot...you've got this." I growled, cheering myself on. My team was waiting on the cathedral stairs, firing the second we came into view. I could feel the air pressure around us ripple as bullets whizzed past. Harmon screamed out and I felt her jerk back. The zombie behind had won the hard-fought prize of a chunk of her hair. Could almost guarantee if we got back to Etna she was going to end up with a bob and a comb-over to fix or hide the damage done. Might even go with a buzz cut, if the length of what I saw in that zombie's fist was any indication.

"Move, Private!" At this point, I was nearly dragging her. If I'd had the time, I would have scooped her up.

She had a response, but it was stuck in her throat along with her pounding heart and extreme fear. I stumbled as the back of my heel collided with what I suspect was a zombie's kneecap. I grunted as I pitched forward; if not for Harmon attached to my hip, I would have gone down. We were less than twenty-five yards from perceived safety. BT had shifted his angle so he could better help mine and Harmon's escape. It was going to be close for all of us involved to get into that church. Zombies were storming from every direction, converging on that one place. How they could be moving so fucking fast while they were so densely packed together defied some sort of law of physics, or some mathematical principle... I don't know. Let me see if I can describe an accurate picture: let's say St. Patrick's is high ground during an immense flooding from a Tsunami. This massive rolling tide of water has rushed in and is blasting through everything in its way until it finally concentrates and coalesces on that last remaining high spot that it has not had a chance to wash asunder. That was the zombies. We were in just as much danger of being cut off from the front of the church as we were being dragged under.

BT realized this, popped two more rounds my way before jumping back into position to get to safety. I took flight, hauling Harmon with me as we cleared the five steps leading up to the door. BT was next in line for our life or death relay race, mumbling, "Come on come on come on," and patiently reaching for the baton. He grabbed my side and shoulder and flung all of us through the massive door. A large rope had been attached to a handle inside; four people were manning it and pulled it closed the moment we were clear. Not quick enough, though, to keep two zombies from entering with us. There wasn't a thing I could have done as the three of us were sprawled out on the floor some ten feet from the entrance. Stenzel, Tommy, and Winters made short work of the interlopers. The sound of the shots reverberated throughout the cavernous structure for another ten seconds.

Harmon was lying back against the cool marble foyer, her chest rising and falling at an accelerated pace. I sat up, as did BT; I clapped him on the thigh.

"Thanks, man."

He nodded. I stood up with Tommy's help; BT was inclined to stay where he was a little longer.

"Umm...Lieutenant, we have a problem." Winters was looking behind me, not to the heavy door that was being pummeled; he was referring to something else.

I turned; was looking at roughly thirty people, all holding a variety of weaponry that, if used, would spell the end of us all.

"Hold off." I had my hands half-raised, talking to my squad rather than the group of armed people in front of us. "If I put my weapon down can we talk?"

"What about them?" The tall man motioned with his pistol.

"Them? No, they're holding on to their rifles. One of you gets an itch you figure needs scratching I'm going to make sure they can defend themselves and save my ass from getting shot. Hate getting shot; I consider it a rude gesture. But here, I'm going to offer some goodwill." I lifted my rifle, attached to its tactical harness, up and over my head and gently placed it on the floor, rising back up with my hands held halfway high.

"You're not going to follow suit? Remember, you asked me to follow you," I said to the man who seemed in charge. He looked left and right to the people with him before holstering his weapon.

"First off, I want to thank you for allowing us in. For those of you I haven't met, my name is Michael Talbot. I am a lieutenant in the Marine Corps; this here is my squad, and I'm in charge of them." BT scoffed at that. "We're on a mission that has gone slightly awry."

"Slightly?" the woman to the left of Lyle's dad replied.

The man halted her with a hand movement. "Jason," he extended his hand, "Jason Vorhees." He must have seen the expression change in my face. "I've heard it all–you don't need to add to it."

I diplomatically kept my mouth shut. "Before we start talking, do we need to worry about them?" The pounding on the door remained constant.

"Nothing is coming through there." Jason seemed pretty sure of himself. The doors looked stout, but I don't know if they were bulker-stout.

"Sgt. Winters, check on the private here. Sgt. Van Goth, I want you and a detail of four to keep an eye on the door." That left a few to keep an eye on them without having to say as much. "Gunney, I want you with me." BT was just getting up off the floor. I noticed Jason and a few others involuntarily step back a pace or two; it was kind of hard not to when faced with the larger-than-life man. Pretty much exactly the effect I was hoping for. We meant them no harm and I demanded the same from them; any intimidation I needed to employ to keep them in check, I would use.

"First off, little man, thank you for saving our butts." I smiled to Lyle and gave him a thumbs up. He seemed pretty pleased with himself, even though he got more than a few dirty looks from the rest of the survivors for bringing strangers into their midst. We headed toward the dais of the enormous gothic structure. There were towering columns and pointed arch ceilings that soared above us, completely remote from the troubles below them. Intricate stained glass windows brightly depicting the stations of the cross lined both walls. The pews had been moved up to the front, marking the borders of their sleeping section. Off to my immediate left was what looked like where they must eat, but judging by a general look at the population here, they were not getting enough. They weren't emaciated or lethargic, nor did they have that far-off stare of those consuming their innards to stay alive, but they were knocking on that door like they wanted to take a peek.

"How many here?" I asked curiously while we were walking. Wasn't quite sure how Jason would take it, like, whether I might be sizing them up.

He looked over his shoulder. "Are you who you say you are?"

"Who else would I be?"

"I think he's looking for confirmation that you're not an asshole…Lieutenant," BT finally added at the end.

"Listen, I'm not perfect and sometimes I probably head into less than decent territory. My wife can attest to that. But we're not here to cause your people any harm in any way. Just extremely thankful for the help." We had got to the dais and took a left heading back to the refectory and what looked like the priests' quarters.

Jason opened the door to a small room with a large dining table. The chairs were oversized and had high backs covered with a plush, purple velvet fabric. I could not get *gaudy* out of my mind. Kept it to myself as Jason said a small prayer then sat.

"The priest no longer here?" I asked once he was done.

Jason looked at me, a sadness in his eyes. "We were in the middle of a wedding when he turned. My daughter was marrying her high school sweetheart; they had just graduated college and were getting ready to move to Chicago. Both of them had good jobs waiting." He paused and looked off to the side, water beginning to fill in the wells of his eyes. "She had just said 'I do,' when Father Callahan collapsed. She went to help him and he…"

"We get it, you don't need to continue." I wanted to spare him the rehashing of a horrible memory and honestly, I wanted to spare myself from having to add another one to the arsenal of nightmares I already carried.

"Her almost-husband Calvin, he beat that priest to death with the crucifix. Then he said he was taking Penny to the hospital. That priest…he…" Jason gulped hard. "He'd chewed through her face. She was unrecognizable. By the time we rushed to the door and were heading out to our cars, the city was a disaster. People screaming as others attacked them. Could hear sirens, gunshots, twisting metal and screeching brakes from any number of accidents happening all around us. It was a war out there and it was impossible to tell who was fighting for which side. Doctors attacking homeless, children eating policemen…none of it made any sense. I'm ashamed to admit it, but, I froze. My poor Penny was dying in Calvin's arms and I locked up. He was running down the steps and I found myself backing into the church. I tell myself I did it to protect my son Lyle and my wife." He stopped to look directly at me, a haunted expression in his eyes. "But that wasn't it. I couldn't think of anything but the terror that was coursing through my body, gripping my heart."

"You know the moment that priest bit your daughter, she was dead, right?" I said, trying to ease his pain.

"I know that now; didn't know it then, and still I did nothing. Calvin looked back once at me and I swear he felt betrayed–though he didn't say anything, and then he just started running. I shut the church doors; locked them, too. Everything I've done since that day has been to try and make myself a better person, someone that wouldn't cave in the face of intense circumstances. Someone my son can be proud to call his father. My wife hasn't said more than two words to me since that day. We weren't exactly the poster-children for a perfect marriage; that just happened to be what ended it."

"Jason, listen. I realize how horrible all of this, all of that, is and was, but you can't blame yourself. This is all uncharted territory; there's no way any of us can know how we're going to react in a scenario that shouldn't exist, that doesn't even seem possible. Everyone in that church back there, whether you meant to or not, they're alive because you locked that door. Without a weapon of any sort you would have been lost with Calvin. A senseless loss in a world already overrun with them."

He nodded at my words, but I wasn't a skilled therapist. Not even sure if I had scratched the bright shiny surface of his misery.

He shook his head, trying to rattle the horrible thing from his mind. I don't know why he told me what he had; maybe the guilt was so pervasive on his part that he wanted everyone he came into contact with to know him for the coward he thought he was. I'm sure there's some sort of term for that, wanting loathing from others, but he wasn't going to get it from me. In terms of the atrocities I had seen humanity perform on itself and others, he was at the lower end of the shitty spectrum.

"Can you save them?" he asked. "Can you save them all?"

"How many do you have here?" BT asked.

"Eighty-two."

I hadn't noticed half that when I came in. "Where are the others?"

"Others?" Jason appeared to be exiting a dream.

"You said eighty-two; my guess had you closer to forty," I said, giving a quick glance over to BT. His eyebrows furrowed. It appeared to both of us that the man was on the verge of a breakdown. Why now, though? Had he just been waiting to recall his story to someone he didn't know? To finally pass the torch, as it were?

"Sorry. Started with eighty-two, have thirty-eight. Most were lost those first few days, trying to get home or gather supplies."

"Speaking of supplies, how is your food situation?" I probed.

"Had a bit of luck there. The previous weekend the church had a food drive, was going to give the donations to the local homeless shelters for Christmas. We ate pretty well for the first couple of weeks and then we began to realize that help wasn't coming and we couldn't safely get out. We began to ration at that point. We're down to a couple of spoonfuls of beans and half a bottle of water a day now. Most of the time, I give my portion to my son. Realistically, we can't make it much longer. That, in part, was why I told you to follow me. I'm desperate, *desperate*, to keep him alive."

MIKE JOURNAL ENTRY 3

"We might be able to help, Jason. I can't guarantee anything at this point, but if our plane can get repaired and we can get to it...then I can get you back to Etna. At that point, it's still up to the commander at Etna Station. We don't have the resources to take everyone in. It's a pay-to-stay type of situation, hence this uniform," I said, pulling at my camouflage utilities.

"Just my son. I don't care about myself, just him. If he can make it, I'll consider it a victory."

"Some might be turned away, but worst case scenario, they'll get cleaned up, new clothes, some food and the perimeter of the base is a relatively safe place. Personally, that's the best I can offer. I'm fairly low on the totem pole myself."

"Hey, Mike." Gary was at the doorway, leaning against the frame. I wanted to smile at his outfit, looked like a mascot for some minor league baseball team in his bright M&M's clothing, but it was easy enough to see he was in a great amount of discomfort.

"How you doing, brother?"

"It hurts, even through the haze of the pills. Winters wants to see you."

"He could have come here, you didn't need to do it."

"Hurts more to lie down."

I could understand that; weren't many parts of his body that weren't scraped raw. Lying on those bits would be like recuperating from a sunburn inside a sandpaper sleeping bag.

"Is he coming?" I asked.

"He wants to talk to you alone."

"If you'll excuse me." I stood and waited for Gary to move away; I didn't want to rub up against him accidentally. He was following, albeit very slowly. Winters was in the far corner of the church, talking into his handset.

"Roger that," he said before turning to me. "That was Major Eastman. They have more damage than they originally thought."

"Still no comm with Etna?"

Winters shook his head.

"ETA on repairs?"

"That's the thing…without parts, it's indefinite."

"Fuck. I told Bennington coming to the East Coast was a bad idea! Too far away from any help. Okay, so, what are our options?" I was thinking out loud. "There's got to be a radio station or television studio around here; would we be able to broadcast something to them?"

Winters was thinking on it. "We'd need to get a backup generator for power, but the communication satellites are still up there. No reason to think they wouldn't still be working. Etna monitors all bands. We still have a small continent's worth of zombies outside, though, before we can get anywhere."

"We'll add that to our list of growing problems. These people are starving; we're going to need to get them some food and water. How's Harmon?"

"I think she might be in shock. She's got a raw patch on

her head I'm sure is going to hurt for a while, but that'll heal long before she gets over this."

"Anything else I should be aware of?"

"I think that about covers it."

"Thanks." I went with him to check on Private Harmon. Corporal Stenzel and PFC Grimm were both with her and they were talking. They stopped when they saw me coming. I motioned with my head for the other two to leave. "How you doing?" I sat on the pew next to Harmon.

"Good to go, sir," she said without ever looking up.

"This isn't a psych eval, Private. I'm genuinely concerned about your well-being."

She was wringing her hands in her lap; she took a moment before pulling her head up to look at me. "Scared shitless, sir."

"About the normal reaction. It would be a lot crazier if you weren't."

"Like, so scared, I'm not sure I'm ever going to be able to leave this seat. I feel like I might be losing my mind."

"Again, normal response, Harmon. You did good out there." She rolled her eyes at me. "You're alive, right? I'm alive. We made it. Keep talking with your friends and remember 'almost dead' and 'actually dead' are two vastly different states of being. You can have some downtime when we get back, but sooner rather than later, I'm going to need you and your impressive shooting skills perched up high." I pointed to the balcony that overlooked the congregation. "You're going to be my sniper while we try to find a way out of here."

"Are you sure, sir?" She held up her hands; they were trembling.

"Anything I can help with?" Jason had come our way. The rest of the congregation, I use that word for lack of a better one, mostly ignored us. I think it had to do with the hunger or just the fact of having been stuck in here since the beginning. You could be bunkered in the Taj Mahal and still lose your mind not being able to go out. Or maybe they were still flat-out suspicious; at this moment it wasn't a puzzle I was overly worried about solving.

"Unless you have an easier way to get out of here so we can get to the NBC studio, probably not." I'd meant it more as an aside; his delay and hesitation in not responding had me thinking otherwise.

"There's a passageway from Times Square to Rockefeller Center." He licked his lips.

BT had assisted Gary and was now with our burgeoning group. By assist, I mean he walked behind him to make sure my brother didn't fall; he did not prop him up because there was no safe place to grab hold of him.

"Want me to have Winters give you another pill? Maybe you can get some sleep. You make me hurt just looking at you," I told him.

"Wouldn't be the worst thing," he responded.

"Harmon, can you go get him one? Thank you."

"I know that shortcut. A lot of folks use it when it's cold out. If I remember correctly, that's maybe a block away, though." BT thought back on the old haunts.

"One of the entrances is across the street," Jason replied.

"That might as well be a country mile," I said.

"Do you even know what that means? Or are you just making up some bullshit analogy?" BT asked.

"Country mile, right? They're longer because of trees and shit," I said.

"What I thought." BT looked triumphant.

"Archbishop Francis Joseph Spellman detested the cold," Jason said, seemingly out of the blue, but there was something else there.

"And?"

Again he was hesitant.

"Why are you stalling?" BT was looking down on the man with all his mass tensed and ready to pounce. I'm sure we could have forced it out of him, but I was hoping he'd give it up willingly.

"Do you understand why I don't want to talk?"

"I don't. If you've got an alternate way out of here, I think you should tell us. Your people are starving; the situation in here is not sustainable. Plus, if we get out of here and get a message to our people, we can evac you all."

"You yourself said they might not be able to take us all in. Then what?"

He'd just ten minutes ago said if his son was safe then nothing else mattered. "Still a fresh start," I answered. "I bet if I go and ask those people if they want to die here or try somewhere new, we'll get a lot of takers."

"But if you know the other way in you could…"

"We could what, Jason? The three people you had guarding us are all sitting down, doing their own things. Only one is even looking our way, and he put his pistol down beside him. I have eleven highly trained military people here with a variety of automatic weapons. I give one word and we own this building in less than ten seconds. Doubt me? Go on and take stock."

He stood. The woman who had seemed so cross at us in the beginning was asleep. The second guy was trying to read a book, but his head kept dropping and he nodded off, and the third who'd been somewhat cognizant of the situation was staring up at the stained glass, looking lost. My team, on the other hand, was alert, armed, and strategically placed almost entirely around them.

"As I told you before, I don't want to harm anyone and I'm not looking to take over your sanctuary. We're all very grateful you opened the doors. We are who I say we are, and there's a chance I can get help for all of us. Food and some clothing, at the minimum. But I can't do anything from here. Now I'll do my best to fight our way through the front, but, like you, I'm very protective of my people and that would not be my first inclination—not if there's a safer way."

He sighed. "You're right, I know you're right. We've just been isolated in here for so long we've become distrustful of everything on the outside. Come on, I'll show you."

We ended up in a large bedroom. I saw more red, crushed velvet there than I have in my entire life. The bed was enormous; looked like two kings sewn together.

"Not trying to go anywhere with this, but why would a man who has taken a vow of celibacy need a bed that could hold a harem?" I asked.

"Fuck, Talbot! You got all the class of a shitting gopher," BT said.

"Yeah, and country mile was a bad analogy," I replied.

"Archbishop Spellman had four dogs; the only time they weren't by his side was during mass," Jason filled us in.

"I think I like this Spellman guy," I said.

"Archbishop," Jason corrected me. "He used to complain about getting crowded out of his bed; he had this specially made. Funny, though, according to his memoirs, they still crowded around him."

"Can we get the tour moving?" BT seemed antsy.

"You alright?" I asked as Jason traversed the room.

"Not a big church fan. Last time I was in one was to bury a girl I'd shot; I don't like being reminded of it," BT said.

"Gotcha, brother. We'll get out of here soon enough."

Jason was standing next to a bookshelf full of tomes. If I had to guess, I'd say there was about a metric ton of paper and binding there. The entire unit swung outwards effortlessly.

The kid in me loved the idea of a hidden entrance like that. The cynic in me wondered what nefarious purposes it had been used for. Hanging from the back of the bookshelf was a skeleton key; it looked like it belonged to a Medieval castle in England, or maybe to that castle's dungeon. It was huge, about half the size of my forearm.

"I don't want to state the obvious, but if you guys are starving why didn't you go out through here to forage for supplies?" I asked.

"Oh, we did...did all right at first, too. Most of the places in the underground tunnel were offices and they had fridges and vending machines; held us over pretty good. But once we went through those stores and had to venture back out onto the streets, that's when we started losing people. It got to the point there were so many people who never came back we couldn't get anyone else to go looking. It was a death sentence; might as well have asked them to walk the final steps to the electric chair."

"Just like *The Green Mile*," BT said out of left field.

"Could you maybe reel yourself back in?" I asked my gunney.

"It was a good book and movie; pretty sure I could have played John Coffey."

"I could see that. He was a lot nicer, though. Wait a sec," I said to Jason, who placed the key into the lock. "What's on the other side?" I had my rifle nearly at the ready, as did BT.

"A fortified tunnel under 5th Ave."

"That's pretty impressive. How'd they pull that off? Ordinances, permits...I can't imagine anyone getting permission to do that," BT frowned.

"Archdiocese in the '50s could have put a casino in the church if they wanted," Jason told us. "Getting a small tunnel dug so that the Archbishop could go to his favorite bagel shop without getting snowed on was nothing. That was his outward reasoning, anyway. Actually, he hated his dogs' paws getting wet and cold."

"I hope that guy got sainthood," I replied.

"Archbishop," Jason said again.

"So, is this the way your people were going out?" I asked.

"Not all the time."

"Is there any reason to think there's anything…hostile on the other side of that door?" I asked.

"Not likely, but that changes once you get across the street and open *that* door."

I noticed he said "you" and not "us." I imagined if he hadn't been chasing his son he wouldn't have come out at all, and most likely, that was the first time he'd had direct sunlight hit him in a very long time.

"BT, what can we expect?"

"The tunnel is fairly long, goes from 5th to 7th. I'm thinking it's going to be dark. It's not some small passageway; it's like a mall down there, wide as a street. Plenty of places for people and things to hide."

"Hold off, Jason. We need to figure this out. It's gonna take more than two of us, and I still might opt for the more direct approach."

"Ammo, Mike; we didn't bring a bunch and we lost some. This was supposed to be a quick in and out mission."

"Yeah, I know that, but have you ever seen the movie *Descent*?"

"*Descent*? That the crazy cave movie? How does that apply?"

I didn't answer him.

"Oh…thanks for that," he said when he got it. "I would have been much better off had you not mentioned that."

"Me too." We went back out to the rest of the squad.

Jason was off tending to his flock while I sat with my team. I wasn't a fan of dividing our forces, but I didn't want to have a large group doing this, and I could not take Gary along.

"Gunney, I want to take you, Winters, you as well, because you're our comm expert. Anyone can get a broadcast out it's going to be you."

He nodded.

"Tommy?"

Of course, Mr. T, I mean, Lieutenant, sir."

I wanted Tommy because he was the most capable warrior in the group—especially in close combat—which looked like it might be the case. "Stenzel, I want you with us. Corporal Rose, that puts you in charge back here. I don't think there will be any trouble with the natives, but if you have an uprising, you put it down quickly."

"Deadly force authorized, sir?" she asked.

"It won't come to that, Rose, but use the zip ties if you need to. PFC Grimm, you're with us. The rest of you stay alert. And keep an eye on those doors; that the zombies aren't trying to break them in has me on edge. If something should happen, you get everyone into that tunnel. We clear?"

"Sir, I'd like to go as well." Private Harmon was looking directly at me. I held contact with her gaze. I wanted to give her some time to collect herself after her harrowing ordeal; I got the idea of getting back up the horse and all, but I couldn't afford to bail her out if she froze in combat. I didn't ask if she was sure because that would have shown the rest of the group, I doubted her ability, and once I did that, none of them would trust her. The stakes were too high to have reservations about a comrade in arms.

"All right. Grimm, you're sitting this one out."

"I'm ready to go, sir."

"I know you are and hold on to the gung-ho attitude. We're going to need it soon enough. We'll stay in constant radio contact. If you don't hear from us for over twenty-four hours, assume the worst. Hold out here until the zombies dissipate, then make a go for the airfield in Stewart Air National Guard Base. Understood?"

"Yes, sir," from the rest in varying shades of enthusiasm.

"Corporal Rose, I want you to set up a schedule for the secret door; I want it manned the entire time we're gone. I don't trust Jason to open it up if he feels we're in trouble, I'd feel much better if we had one of our own on the other side."

"On it, sir."

"Okay, those coming with, gear up and meet me in the Archbishop's bedroom in five."

"Sir, we'd all appreciate it if you came back." Corporal Rose had stayed behind to deliver the words.

"Just covering bases…it is fully my intention to do so. Keep everything in order here and we'll be back before you know it." I turned to the front; Harmon was in front of the altar on her knees saying a prayer. Her file had her listed as an agnostic; couldn't blame her, though. She was covering her bases as well. I went and knelt next to her; no sense in leaving a message unsent, even if I thought no one was home and wouldn't be picking up mail for a while. I got up wordlessly; she followed a moment later.

BT handed me an extra magazine. I nodded and put it away.

"Everyone check their lights?" I was doing my best not to notice how Harmon's light was shaking on the wall as she tested it.

BT looked over to me, skepticism regarding her mission readiness all over his face. Trust me, I had the same reservations. If I took her off this mission, there was a good chance she would be through. She'd *think* herself into the depths of doubt. But I had to balance what she was going through with the safety of the rest of the team. Leading people into combat situations was never really something I'd aspired to, and right now I knew exactly why. She shut her light off when she realized most of us had been looking.

"Deep breaths, people. We all have each other's back. Single file in the passageway, and we stay tight once we get into this mall tunnel or whatever the hell it is. Clear? I'll go first."

"Excuse me, sir, but I'll do it." Stenzel checked to make sure her gear was tight.

If I was a true officer, I would have put Harmon in the

lead as the lowest ranking among us. I just fundamentally could not put people in danger ahead of myself. It went against everything ingrained within me. I nodded curtly to her, my lips pressed tight; I did what procedure dictated.

"You ready?" Jason was fumbling with the key. He turned the lock; the light from the bedroom didn't penetrate more than a few feet into the well of darkness. Anything could have been ten feet away and we'd never know. My muscles tensed as I awaited the worst. Stenzel's light blazed down the majority of the small tunnel; I was happy to note there were no creatures from my childhood waiting to reach out and pull me into their nightmares, no red balloons and more importantly, no clowns. I was expecting that the tunnel would be this rough-hewn hole in the earth, the shovel marks of the laborers still visible–something more akin to what inmates in a maximum-security prison would dig to escape the confines their actions had landed them in. What I was looking at was a straight, tiled, sidewalk-sized walkway that, in better times, I'm sure looked downright pleasant. Stenzel went in, immediately followed by Tommy, then Harmon. I plucked the key from a reluctant Jason before I followed, then Winters and BT brought up the rear. I figured he should go last just in case he got wedged tight like a wine cork, and I said as much. He didn't think it was funny, which is funny, because everyone else did.

"Everything all right down there?" Kirby spoke through the radio.

"Good to go," Winters responded.

"Jason here is losing his shit with the door open," Kirby announced, I'm sure loud enough for Jason to hear. I liked that he didn't give a shit who heard him speak his mind.

We hadn't made it a quarter of the way across when the little bit of light afforded us from behind winked out of existence. Jason had shut the door; I shouldn't have expected anything more from him. He'd shown his true colors early on and had never deviated from that path. Didn't matter; it was plenty bright in there with all the flashlights bobbing up and down.

"What's that dumbass hope to accomplish? He can't lock his side without the key," BT grumbled. It wasn't the optimum set up. Once we opened up to the mall, we would have to shuttle the one and only key back to the church. I didn't want to keep it on any one person in case we got separated or, well, the alternative. No, the only plan that made sense was to send it back and keep a guard at the gate, so to speak, to let us back in.

"At the door," Stenzel whispered. "Don't hear anything." That didn't mean much; it wasn't like the zombies were known for their loud and boisterous rave parties. Still…something, though. As quiet as the door had opened in the bedroom, the converse happened here. There was an ear-grating squeal and the teeth gnashing sound of broken glass sandwiched between the bottom of the door and the floor, scratching deep grooves into the concrete.

"So much for a tactical entrance," BT came through my earpiece. I was more than half expecting to see the bright muzzle flashes of Stenzel's weapon; I was pleasantly surprised when that wasn't the case. Harmon looked frozen in place.

"Private, get the key, bring it back to Kirby." She didn't move. "Harmon."

She didn't answer me, but she moved to the front and did as I'd ordered, glancing up at me as she went past and back.

BT shut off his radio before he spoke. "Mike, I don't want to step on your toes here, but...."

"She'll be all right."

"She looks shell-shocked."

"This unit is her last shot; she left her medical training."

"Yeah, because she couldn't handle the sight of blood. I'm not thinking this was the appropriate substitute career."

"BT, if she doesn't make it here, Bennington will set her outside the gate."

"Don't start guilting me Talbot, I'm not Catholic."

"Not working? Baptists don't have guilt?"

"I'm not Baptist."

"Episcopalian?"

"You don't know, do you? We've had this conversation at least a dozen times." BT looked pretty mad.

"Seventh Day Adventist? Latter Day Saints...err, Mormon?"

He was shaking his head. "None of those and I'm more concerned with the added danger Harmon brings to this mission and to us, should she freeze up. Again. And LDS are Mormon," he added.

"Really? And I'm aware of what's going on, BT. I'll keep an eye on her."

He grunted before turning his radio back on; clearly, he wasn't a fan of my decision. We waited in silence for the couple of minutes it took Harmon to come back. More than once I thought it possible she might not.

"Stenzel, we're ready," I said as Harmon came up alongside me. I watched the corporal's light as it moved into the tunnel. There was a sharp intake of air.

"What's going on?" BT asked her.

"Sorry. There's a pizza restaurant out here."

"And?" I prompted.

"Standard fare, thinner crust, New York style."

"Corporal."

"Sorry sir, it's just, I haven't had good pizza in so long. The chow hall puts spaghetti sauce and a piece of American cheese on top of an English muffin and calls it pizza."

"I love that pizza," Tommy replied.

I couldn't defend his position; this was the same kid that ate rhubarb and mayonnaise Pop-Tarts.

"As good as having some authentic pizza would be, can we perhaps move on?" I asked.

"Reluctantly, sir."

"Understood. You can file a grievance when we get back to Etna."

"Duly noted. Just past the entrance to the restaurant there was a fight. Got six or seven dead zombies and maybe three or four people, hard to tell. There's blood and parts everywhere." Could hear the tinkle of brass being kicked aside or stepped on as she moved farther out.

Tommy was out next and was checking the hallway behind her. "Looks like an office here. All the glass and the doors have been broken out. Movement."

"Stenzel–move back," I said as I came out into the tunnel way. She was too far away if this was a trap and we needed to make a hasty retreat. BT was next out, his light trained toward Stenzel, watching her steady back-walk to us.

"See it?" Tommy asked. To be honest, the play of shadows with our flashlights made it difficult to see anything subtle. He kept his light trained on one specific part of the office window down by the bottom, while I looked like I was trying to paint the entire area with mine. Let's be honest; I was expecting to see hundreds of outstretched hands and gaping mouths moving toward us. I mean, we were in an underground tunnel in the city; should pretty much be par for the course. Instead, when I finally stopped looking for the massive attack that wasn't there, I saw something, though, I was having a difficult time saying what it was. It was right at the bottom of the window. I could just see something pop up for a second or two then dip back down.

Winters was moving alongside me. "You hear that, LT?"

"Shit." I raced over to the busted-out window. There was a zombie on the ground. At one time it had been a woman office worker; she had her headset wrapped around her neck and a large file cabinet had been overturned on to the bottom half of her body, effectively pinning her there for all time. She snarled at me as I reached my barrel in and blew her tattling brains out. "We've got to move." I couldn't see much after the muzzle flash except a bright yellow blob in my primary field of vision.

"What gives?" BT was keeping an eye on the area.

"This one was letting others know we're here."

"No shit?"

"No shit. And you want to know what's worse?"

"Not really."

"She's got gnawed-through body parts all around her."

BT put it together. "She rats us out and gets a piece of the take."

"Give that man a prize." I was looking deeper into the office space.

"That's some next level shit."

We knew about the shriekers and the fact that the zombies as a whole seemed to be gaining in intelligence, but BT was right. This was advanced gameplay, for sure. She was calling to others, offering them our plump flesh, then collecting a finder's fee.

"Onward or back," BT asked as I kept looking for any others inside.

"No choice; we have to keep moving. Being stuck in the church does us no good."

"Tommy, watch our back. Stenzel, you heard the man. Find us a safe route out." BT was moving back toward the door, Harmon was just coming out.

I saw Stenzel run the tips of her fingers along the pizzeria sign as she went by. "There's a bend up ahead."

"Advance slowly. Let us catch up," I told her.

"Got an odor up here sir, and it ain't fresh pizza."

"Going to have to let that go, Stenzel." I moved quickly to get alongside her.

"I don't want to." She said it softly, hoping the radio

wouldn't pick it up. We both rounded the corner at the same time; the eye shine staring back was startling. There were six pairs, but they were too far away to see what was attached to the glinting orbs staring back at us.

"That people, sir?"

"Doubtful."

"We shooting?" She had her rifle up against her shoulder.

"A little closer." I was fairly certain of what we were advancing on, but not entirely. I'd never be able to forgive myself if we took out a family seeking refuge in this subterranean corridor. "Make yourself known!" I yelled. Funny thing is…nope, don't like that. Ironic thing, maybe? They did exactly as I ordered. Three broke for us instantly. Stenzel was quicker than I was and dropped two in the span of three steps. By the time I blew out the top of the third one's head, the other three were coming, but we now had BT in the mix. It was a short firefight, but the rifle percussions in the enclosed space were exceptionally loud and the muzzle flashes excessively bright; I had two senses knocked down a few degrees. Even if my hearing was down to fifty percent, it would have been impossible to miss Tommy's warning.

"Horde to the rear!" Then the staccato burst of his rifle, maybe Winters' and Harmon's as well.

"Back to the church entrance?" I was caught in indecision. There was a chance that we were being herded into the mouth of another group to the front.

"Won't make it." I could hear the bounce in Winters' voice as he ran.

"Stenzel, BT, stay with me. Looks like we're going to have to make a path."

BT didn't have to say anything; I could hear his heavy sigh. He was right. Moving quickly through darkened corridors without having any idea of what we were getting into was not a wise move, but we were being forced, plain and simple.

We didn't have the luxury of picking our way through carefully.

A light from behind swept over us.

"Going to need to move faster, sir!" Winters said. He wasn't quite panicked but, yeah, there was an urgency there. Not sure he needed to say anything, as even over the exceedingly loud discharge of their firearms, we could hear hundreds of footfalls slapping along on the flooring.

"Mike." BT's flashlight was pointing into one of the offices on our left.

I turned my head to see zombies navigating around office furniture.

"Winters, Tommy, move! We got speeders streaming in from the side!"

BT stopped to place some decent shots into the throng.

"Contact!" Harmon shouted out; I thought my eardrum was going to rupture from the shrillness. She was sending three-round bursts downrange as quickly as she could pull the trigger. I was about to admonish her for her lack of trigger discipline, but it was effective fire.

Between the flashlights and the multiple muzzle flashes, the corridor was brightly lit. Unfortunately, it was not a view worth dying for.

"Mike, my man." BT was looking for some direction. Obviously, he didn't need help killing zombies; he had that part covered. The unspoken question was: where to? Backward was a literal dead end. To the right was a small coffee shop; we could head there and make a go at barricading ourselves in, but to what goal?

"Forward. Just forward."

It seemed the more I shot, the more bobbing heads of the dead I saw. It wasn't a dense pack like what was chasing us, but it didn't need to be; there was enough to slow us down and that was enough. As my bolt popped open, I reached down onto my utility belt to grab a fresh magazine. I kept advancing as I performed the much-practiced routine of reloading. Used to be a time where I would have needed to stop everything I was doing, pull the rifle from my shoulder, fumble for the magazine release button, look down to grab the new magazine, make sure it was oriented correctly, then breathe before popping it up and into the magazine well. After slamming it home, I'd still have to watch where my thumb was going so I could hit the bolt release; then I'd second guess myself to make sure the bolt hit home before deliberately bringing the rifle back up to my shoulder to begin firing again.

It was a quick sequence; on a good day, maybe that routine took ten seconds, not horrible. But now I could keep moving forward, the buttstock never leaving my shoulder, drop a mag to the ground, reload, and be firing shots in under four. When every second counted, that was a hell of an improvement. All great and fine if I was looking at an infinite amount of ammunition. It's times like this I wish I was in a sci-fi book and could get my hands on a plasma rifle or something that didn't generally run out of projectiles. I mean really; what could be worse than hordes of the undead? No time like the present to wish for omnipotence.

Winters and Tommy were coming up quick, even though they were going as slow as they could and doing as much damage as possible on their way in an effort to keep us from being overrun. It was us up front that weren't holding to our end of the agreement. Zombies were knocking each other away in a bid to get at us and it was jamming their progress; probably the only reason we hadn't been laid into yet.

"Bulkers!" BT warned. If he hadn't said anything, I would have assumed it was the NYC transit system back up and running.

"Got a door!" this from Harmon.

"Go! We'll follow!" I told her. I had no clue if we were heading into a broom closet, the bathroom, or Bloomingdale's; at this point it didn't matter. We'd lost the area; our only options were to take the exit or stay and die. On the spectrum of possibilities, that one rated fairly low. Either the zombies were into self-preservation or the bulkers had sent a message for them to clear a path, but we could see tendrils of openings tearing through the horde like a knife dragged over tight fabric; the zombies parted, allowing the heavier, more destructive bulkers an access route.

"Locked," came Harmon's breathless reply. We were pulling into a tighter and tighter semi-circle as she fought with the lock. The thundering of the bulkers was making the ground bounce. We were firing into them, but it wouldn't be enough. They were going to press us into the wall. Wouldn't leave much for the starving zombies, as we'd likely be vaporized.

"Move," BT told Harmon, bringing his weapon over his head. I heard the crunch of his rifle and the sound of metal hitting the tile. Had no idea if it was the door handle or parts of his gun. "It's open."

"Let's move, people, inside!" I ordered.

"Harmon! Get your ass in there!" Stenzel shouted, I turned in time to see her pushing the private through the opening.

"Go sir," Winters said. "We're right behind you."

Time for words was done. There could be no debating. I tapped BT's arm and motioned. He went in, and I was half a step behind him. Stenzel and Harmon had moved a few feet farther in.

"Stairwell," Stenzel said.

"Check it out–quickly," I told her. Once Tommy and Winters got in we needed to move fast. The door would not lock, and getting a door open, even if they had to pull on it, was not above the zombies' new skill set. The door was a stout steel one, set into a concrete and steel frame, and still, it shook. We could only hope that the bulkers would take a few minutes to clear away; right now they had a ton or more of accumulated weight pressing up against it.

"Stairs only go down." Stenzel's light was trained down the well. "It's clear."

Her definition of "clear" was a little different from mine. There were eight people on those stairs; they were in various stages of mummification. My guess was they had starved to death. Harmon let out a small scream that seemed to excite the bulkers, who were going to try and force their way through. Stenzel picked her way down cautiously.

"Lost my rifle." BT looked dejected as he showed me an amalgamation of parts that had at one time been a deadly weapon.

We were making our way down and he was still holding on to it. "You can probably leave that. Here, buddy." I handed him my 1911. Looked like a cap gun in his hands; I wasn't even sure he'd be able to fit his finger through the trigger guard.

"Might as well toss rocks." He was pissed.

"Door's open." Stenzel looked back.

"Hold on for some back-up. Tommy?"

"On it." He pushed past.

Winters was still watching the door to our back.

"Mike, you realize this is most likely a dead end, right?" BT asked.

He was right; if the door downstairs was unlocked, that was because the people in the stairwell hadn't seen any reason to lock it, meaning nothing was coming that way. So, if they starved to death because they couldn't go out the way we had come, well, that question answered itself.

"Got other plans?"

"If this wasn't a party line…" He left whatever he wanted to add unsaid.

"Looks like a maintenance tunnel," Tommy replied. "About thirty feet long, bunch of pipes, shelving, that kind of stuff. Clear otherwise. Got some other unfortunates in here too."

"Let's go, everyone down." It was what we needed to do, but being entombed with the dead was about as appealing as cuddling with Eliza. The bulkers made one final assault, then I could feel them moving away, which meant the smarter ones were going to take a crack at us.

We'd been in that small area for a few minutes and I'd looked it over a couple of times already, avoiding the four bodies huddled to the side as best I could, so I'd looked over at them ten times a minute, seen their decayed expressions at least thirty times. I was fairly certain there were no mystery doors to explore, no secret portals to another time and place. I had expertly painted us into a corner; just so happened that this paint job had teeth, lots and lots of teeth. The smell wasn't as bad as it could be, but the way those faces were pulled tight, their smiles forever engraved in cringing desperation…they seemed to sneer at us and the trap we had run headlong into.

"Sir, I can't pick up the church." Winters had his radio in his hand and was fiddling with some of the buttons. We had no comm outside of this area. We had light for another ten hours, no food to speak of, low ammunition, and no viable exit. All in all, it wasn't looking like the day had got off on the right foot. I didn't want to be the next set of mummies when some other hapless victims sprang the same trap we had.

4

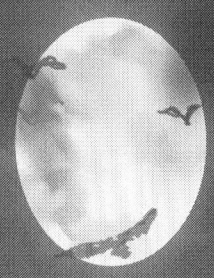

MIKE JOURNAL ENTRY 4

BT HAD DRAGGED me to the far end of the room. He motioned for me to turn off the radio. "That pipe looks good-sized," he said.

My gaze had been drawn to it from time to time, but by "good-sized," if he meant an infant could crawl through it easily, then, yeah, it was good-sized. Anything adult-shaped, not so much.

"Harmon will fit," he said. My gaze immediately went over to the private, who looked like she was having a difficult time holding on to the fraying edges of her resolve. The pipe was cast iron; couple of rounds would open it up.

"You realize that's most likely a sewer line, right? You bust that and it's full, we could drown in shit, BT."

He turned away from me, ripped his cap off and ran his hand over his head. "FUCK!" he yelled so loud I must have heard it a dozen times as it echoed back and forth. When he calmed down somewhat, he turned back to me. "You got anything useful in that mind of yours?"

"They're in," Tommy said as he pulled his head back through the door and threw the lock. All of our attention was directed to the door; we were all expecting a mad rush and the attempted twisting of the handle. What we got was worse, in its own way. We could hear what sounded like wet cardboard being rent. I think maybe my psyche was doing its best not to piece together what was happening; it was Winters who brought it to the forefront.

"Are they eating the mummies?"

The sound was nauseating; allowing the mind to create visuals the eyes could not see was infinitely worse. It provided a subconscious opportunity to be distracted, as my people began to talk quietly amongst themselves, just loud enough to drown out the slurpings and chewings but not loud enough to draw the attention of the enemy.

"What are the odds they finish their meal and head on out?" BT asked, I gave him a look he usually reserves for me. "Forget I asked."

The eating went on longer than any of us expected. Seemed to me the smarter zombies had kept this small prize secret from the waiting horde; it appeared that some zombies were a little more equal than others. I was starting to think it was a little like *Animal Farm* out there.

I did some tapping on the pipe, as did BT. We both concluded that yeah, there was fluid in there, but no, it wasn't full. That didn't necessarily mean anything because if it was running water, it could still fill this chamber up. It had been an hour since the zombies had tucked into their impromptu feast.

"How long does it take for them to eat?" I asked.

"What's your rush? We're dessert," BT replied.

"There's that, I guess."

Spirits were understandably low. We had no reason to think any help was coming and we were stuck fast; our seemingly only avenue of escape involved a shitty pipe and a Marine on the verge of losing her shit. Somehow it was fitting. Just when you think things can't get worse, they somehow do. We could hear movement outside the door; we would find out soon enough why.

It was Tommy who bent over first, holding his left ear, then the sound swept over all of us: shriekers, and a few of them, too, by the sound of it. They were out there singing their discordant notes. I'm not a frequent migraine sufferer, but like most, I'd gone through a few over the years. This was like those times, only some inconsiderate asshole kept manually forcing my eyelids open so they could flash a 15,000 lumens light into my corneas, thus burning imprints into my tortured brain. I was fearful I was going to snap my teeth off as I gritted down on them.

"Stenzel! Get the door!" I couldn't even consider opening my eyes wide enough to look through my red dot.

BT had grabbed Stenzel's rifle and was by my side, his pain so intense he was shaking. Stenzel cracked that door wide open. I don't think they'd been expecting that particular maneuver. BT and I opened fire; shriekers registered surprise as we fired into their heads, reciprocating their pain in spades.

"Karma's a bitch," I managed to get out as the pain abated. The other zombies began to crowd to the door while also letting the shriekers move away. We cut through them; the carnage enough that neither the aggressors nor the escapers could make progress. After I was through my second magazine and there didn't seem to be any viable targets, I had Stenzel shut the door.

"Can't tell you how much I appreciate that, sir," she said, leaning up against the wall.

We were all drained. I had my hands on my knees.

"What if they get more?" Harmon asked.

"From what I know, they're fairly rare. We dealt them a killing blow." BT handed the rifle back to Stenzel; she hardly looked like she was able to support its weight. I had a few of the flashlights turned off to conserve battery life. If it was depressing beforehand, now it was downright disheartening. My claustrophobia was beginning to make its presence known in full; it didn't help that BT stayed within an inch of me at all times. If that was how he reacted to his fear of tight places, it sure was a strange response. We were sitting with our backs against the wall; I was continually circling the limited options we had. Basically, they all involved opening the door and attempting to blast a hole through the zombies and escape to freedom. Unfortunately, the success percentage meter kept stopping at zero.

"Movement." Winters had his ear up by the door. We waited long minutes for an update. "Sounds like they're removing the bodies."

"Probably to get bulkers down here." BT had stood, but I noticed he did not step away. If we got out of this, I was going to need to have a private talk with him regarding personal space. He motioned to his headpiece; this was our signal to go to a private channel. He grabbed his radio and flipped it open to get to the embedded keyboard.

"If we die down here, no one is going to know."

"We will," I responded. He was less than amused. In fact, he made it over to the anger spectrum.

"Any ideas?"

I shook my head instead of responding.

"It's got to be the pipe. There's nothing else."

"I'm not sure she can fit, and if there is any significant bend, she won't be able to traverse it," I replied.

"Don't even tell me you're thinking of giving up."

"Just looking for something with at least some sort of odds we can hang a hat on."

"Why now?"

"Ha ha," I responded aloud, which sounded funny in the silent room.

"Whatever they're doing, it sounds like they're done." Winters looked over to me.

Was expecting to hear and feel the coming of the immense ones; I even hazarded the thought of letting one in to see if it could crash through a wall like the Kool-Aid man. Wonder how much property damage that thing had done over the years? That's how desperate I was; thinking about letting a six-hundred-pound behemoth into our small lair. I could imagine that going wrong in a dozen different fascinating ways.

"Come out," was whispered in my head–well, everyone's head. That was easy enough to tell, as all of us were looking around at the other, wondering what had just happened and who had said it. All of us still sitting, stood, as if choreographed. I placed my hand up to halt all the obvious questions I was about to be bombarded with and for which there was no possible way I could answer. "Come out," was repeated again and another five or six times on top of that. It was a soft insertion, without the harsh urgency of the shriekers. This coherent yet terrifying sentence was followed by a jumble of words that didn't fit together quite so nicely but still conveyed a powerful message:

"Eat."
"Hunger."
"Feed."
"Food."

"They fucking talk now?" BT could not contain himself any longer.

"Not coming out," I said aloud and thought it. I knew my track record; I could, on a limited basis, reach out and give them a message if they were close enough.

"Feed. Must."

Tommy was looking over at me; he could hear the dual messages I was sending.

"We're prepared to die in here. No chance we're going to let you eat us." This I kept on the mostly private party line.

I was convinced the zombie speaker sighed at the notion of us becoming wasted food.

"Starving." It was more of a feeling; I could *feel* its stomach cramps. If he was trying to elicit sympathy, not only was he barking up the wrong tree, he wasn't even in the right forest. I was about to tell it to fuck off, when something even stranger than what was already happening, happened.

"Half," the zombie said.

"Half what?" BT asked, but he was looking at me with his brow arched.

"Half eat, half go."

"Wait…we give you half and the rest of us are free to go?" I asked.

"You aren't seriously negotiating with them, are you?" BT might not have been the most distressed, but he was the one showing the most visual cues.

I held up my hand. "Hear it out," I told him. "Four. I'll give you four." It was either Winters or Harmon who gasped.

"Not one more."

"Which four you planning on giving?" BT asked.

"I'll volunteer." Harmon raised her hand.

"Stop, everyone stop. I'm not looking for volunteers and I'm not ordering anyone. We already have our takers." I pointed over to the four by the wall. It distressed me to no end to potentially use them so callously, but I had to believe that their higher essence was long gone from this place. There were long moments of silence interspersed with labored breathing from the stress we were all feeling.

"Four," was all it said; I was not sure what to deduce from this. "Open."

I looked around at my squad.

"Don't do it, Talbot." BT beseeched. "We can't trust zombies now any more than before they could talk. They're mindless predators."

Right now, *mindless* didn't seem fitting. "Open, then what?"

"I can't believe this is happening right now," he said, turning away.

"That makes all of us," I told him.

"Rest go. Eat later."

"Bird in the hand." Tommy was looking at the door.

"Open," it urged.

"We ready? Do not fire unless necessary. BT?"

"I'm cool man, I'm cool." He took in two big breaths of air then blew them out slowly.

I opened the door. I more than expected to be pushed back from the onslaught of zombies pressing through; there was just one. If I had to peg a label, I'd say it was a lawyer, once upon a time. His short hair, which was unkempt now, had probably been well cared for. He was wearing a suit that looked like it might have cost more than my entire wardrobe, such as it was. Not sure what that meant, as most of my clothes back in the day consisted of shorts, t-shirts and jeans. But still, even five-dollar Star Wars shirts from Walmart begin to add up. The dry cleaner was going to charge him an arm and a leg to get the blood, brain, piss and shit stains out of them, but it still might be serviceable. The zombie snarled at me as I moved aside.

"Four," it said in my head and attempted to vocalize. Sounded like a hissing snake might. It was sniffing at the air and occasionally sticking its tongue out like the reptile it seemed to be. I stiffened when it moved a step closer to me. It hissed again when I placed the barrel of my weapon square into its chest. The advantage shifted to him in the close quarters; all he needed was the smallest of nibbles to effectively win. There was something hugely different about this zombie, though. He had more than a survival instinct. I could feel it in his thoughts–again, nothing verbalized; it was a part of his being. He did not want to die. He would not be one of the mindless horde that sacrificed bodies for position. He looked over each and every one of us. There was a ravenous leer to his gaze; he looked like a serial rapist in a downtown bar who had just got in a large shipment of Rohypnol.

The lawyer licked its lips as it surveyed the menu. It sounds funny when I write it down; at the time it was terrifying, but when his gaze hit BT, he looked like Bugs Bunny when Lola Bunny strolled on by, eyes popping out, heart pounding hard in his chest, kind of thing. He growled at me when I pushed against him with my barrel, directing him toward the deal. Neither of us liked being this close. I was reminded that man's turn at the top was at, or already had come to, a crashing demise, and he didn't feel he was getting the respect he deserved as the usurper.

The zombie moved past all of us to look at his treasure. "Dead." There was displeasure in its voice. Got a feeling he would have preferred something more of the rare prime-rib variety.

"Them or nothing." I motioned for the door. He looked from us to the dead and back again. And then even once to the door. I had a feeling he was contemplating calling in for reinforcements. "Do it," I told him, the end of my rifle no farther than three feet from his head. "Might be the end of us, but you aren't getting any parting taste."

"What the fuck you doing, Talbot?"

"What part of you thinks I have a playbook for what is happening right now?" I answered him without ever taking my eyes off the zombie. Instinctually, I knew that if I was in any way distracted, it would take that as an opportunity and roll those dice in its head. And I didn't like that one bit. Yeah, this one was a self-preservationist; odds were it was friends with Deneaux.

"Go," it said. Out of the corner of my eye, I looked to Harmon; thought I might have to tell Winters to grab her if she decided to bolt, but she was holding steady.

"Then?"

"Eat later," it said again.

It didn't elaborate, and that was open to entirely too many interpretations. Maybe he'd let us get topside then they'd start the hunt again? Or maybe they get us out of this room then surround us? I was all about the former and the fighting chance it afforded us, not so much the latter; we'd be in a prison made solely from zombies.

"We're taking you. I think you're going to be our golden ticket out of here."

"Talbot, we're taking zombie hostages now?" BT wanted to know.

"Most definitely. This one is all about himself."

"Go," it reiterated.

"Tommy, turn its shoulder."

Tommy roughly forced it to face our exit. I traded weapons with BT and took my 1911 back. I placed the barrel firmly against the back of the zombie's skull. "We get out of here alive, so do you." I pushed it forward with the gun. It snarled. "Stay close."

"Um, sir, no disrespect, but no fucking way," Stenzel said.

"I'll take that under advisement. Now get the fuck over here, Corporal."

If we'd got packed any tighter, we would have been able to tell each other's preference for boxers, briefs, or commando status. All was fine as we got out, and even the stairwell was clear, but the exit door was jam-packed with zombies. The eye shine they produced bobbed around as they jockeyed for position.

"Tell them to move." I forced the zombie's head down, I was pressing the gun so tightly up against his skull.

We had a dozen or so theories about the zombie intellect, ranging from mindless brain eaters to a collective hive mind. "Dewey" here from Dewey, Cheatum, and Howe, well, he was a revisionist. He was going to force us to rewrite all the rules. Or so I hoped; I was banking our lives on it. If he was part of a collective, then his individual life meant nothing in the grand scheme of things. Survival of the colony was of utmost importance. It wasn't lost on me in the slightest that it would be a lawyer who was placing himself above all others.

"Live or die, Dewey. The choice is yours."

"Dewey?" BT asked.

"Tell you later."

"Live." A murderous clown born of hell, bent on rending the souls of the damned, would have had less malice in its tone.

I could feel a "push" order emanate from it. Nothing was happening–nothing that we could tell. It was all due to how congested the zombies were; there was no room for them to shift, like an emergency vehicle attempting to get to the scene of a particularly gruesome accident through the densely packed vehicles that had the misfortune of trailing behind. I'd been in some binds with zombies, but this time was the worst. We were pressed into single file; the zombies were as tightly packed as a Christmas toy encased in styrofoam. You know the kind. Ever open one of those things up only to realize its broken and not only is your kid bummed out, now you have to try and get it back into the box to bring back to the store? It's like the fucking thing grows once it's exposed to the air. I've had better luck telling my wife I was going out with the boys on our anniversary. Just so we're clear, that's an analogy and not something I'd ever be dense enough to try in real life. Not twice, anyway.

Every part of me was brushing up against something or someone. I'd never felt so personally compressed or compromised since my tunnel travails with Trip. Felt like ketchup frosting being piped through a squeeze bottle. I was barely holding on. I got progressively intense sensations from the zombies, not that they were going to break and run, but rather: "Fuck Dewey's orders, let's eat."

We were *crawling* along, a verb I wished I had steered clear of, as I could swear I had things creeping on me from the close proximity to the zombies. My skin itched and it was all I could do to not rip through it. Staying quiet and not doing overtly human things like scratching, coughing, sneezing–that was what was keeping us alive in the precarious position we found ourselves in.

Dewey was the boss, or a boss, at least, and he'd not be the first that had to suffer through a mutiny. The zombies begrudgingly yielded their space, and the farther we went, the more begrudged we were each inch. Our small steps were rapidly shrinking to shuffles. Harmon yelled out; I saw a wet tongue wrapped around some loose strands of her hair. I shoved Dewey's head so far down he was looking at his double vested buttons; we felt the slightest shift in pressure.

"Done playing. Get us out of here. Just keep remembering it's always going to be you first, and I got a feeling even your mother wouldn't miss you. Probably sued her for more play time when you were ten, am I right?"

"Mike, focus," BT said in hushed tones.

"Laser-guided," I told him, even if that wasn't mostly the truth. Laser something, but more like an array. My mind was scattered as I fought the demons in my head. I was more than slightly astounded that there was a significant part of me that wanted to blow Dewey's head clean from his body and then do as much damage as I could to the putrid meat bags around me, whatever that lead us to. The panicked terror was grabbing so deeply into the folds of my mind, it was doubtful I'd ever get another night of peaceful sleep that was not brought on by medication. Good thing my squad was in the same boat; we'd be able to force a volume discount.

It got marginally better when we made it out of that first corridor, and by marginally, I mean we'd gained enough inches of space around us that the zombies couldn't sample a taste of us simply by an errant lick, which had happened more than I'd care to remember. You can take the zombie out of the graveyard, but you can't…oh screw it; the analogy wasn't that good. Suffice it to say there was a rebel or two among Dewey's crew that wanted nothing more than to tear into us like a bag of steaming microwave popcorn. I can't even begin to say why they didn't. Fear of reprisal? Shunning by their mates? Couldn't have been Dewey's leadership alone. Not much of any of this was making sense. But as long as we escaped, it didn't need to. I don't overburden myself with all the "whys" of something; I prefer to leave the thinking to those more qualified.

"I see light." Winters had some tempered excitement; hard to get too thrilled about anything, given our current state. I'd been concentrating so hard on a one-inch square on the back of Dewey's head, I'd never even noticed that the flashlights were beginning to get drowned out. A zombie's foot found its way in between mine and I stumbled; I was thankful I did not have my rifle or I would have fallen over. As it was, I reached up with my free hand and wrenched down on Dewey's left shoulder. At the same time all of this was going on, the zombies had pressed in closer. Looked like our benefactor had other designs on how he wanted this to go down. The bullet I fired through his right earlobe and into a zombie in front of us looked to be enough to dissuade Dewey from pursuing this proposed change in our agreement.

Anger poured forth through our limited connection, I say limited because apparently, he could communicate with the zombies on a whole level we weren't able to detect.

"Can't believe I missed! I'll make sure that doesn't happen again. How about you, Dewey? You gonna make sure that doesn't happen again?" He didn't answer. I blew that ear off his head; there was a small cloud of cartilage debris and a smattering of blood. "I asked you a fucking question! Answer me, because the next one goes right into your brain bucket. Are you planning any more tricks?"

The "No" he gave me felt like it had been pried from the jaws of a pit bull who had sunk his canines deep into a raw t-bone.

"Got to admit, Dewey, that was pretty shitty of you. I kept up my end of the bargain and you decided in the middle of the whole thing to go and change it up? But then, you were a fucking lawyer, right? Your kind aren't happy with your fair share; you want everyone's fair share." I didn't tell him that when we got outside, I was fully planning on blowing his brains out. At that point, he'd be too dead to care about it. Seemed duplicitous of me to give him a hard time about changing the deal when I'd meant to all along; maybe I was mad that he'd tried first. He'd got pretty close to succeeding, too.

I could see the door that proudly announced we were about to exit onto 7th Avenue; we were about to be right by M&M's World again. It hadn't been that long, but by now it felt like almost a year had gone by. Although, that doesn't make sense; the saying is "time flies when you're having fun," and so far, there had been very little of that on this mission. Could see zombies on the roadway as we exited, and a fair number came outside with us.

"What gives, Dewey?" My intention had been to put one in his noggin then make a run for it; he'd obviously had enough foresight or intuition to realize my plan and now had a security team hemming us in.

"Free," he said at first then, "both" followed.

"Wily fuck, aren't you."

"What's going on, Talbot? Why they still around?" BT wanted to know.

"Dewey here is a pretty smart guy. I let him go, he lets us go."

"That's a bad idea," he replied.

"What's your alternative? You want to keep moving through this shuffling clusterfuck?"

"This a vote, sir? Because I'm going with no," Stenzel said.

"I'll let you vote, Stenzel, as long as you agree with me." I pulled my pistol back from Dewey's head; he turned slowly, his black eyes locked onto mine.

"Remember," he said. I think he was referring to the fact

that I had indelibly burned myself into his memory. Another enemy in an ever-expanding list of them. Dewey made sure that his shoulder bully-struck mine as he walked away; the zombies parted and he went back into the underground area. The zombies around us slowly moved backward, reluctantly yielding ground.

"Everyone good?" I looked around at a bunch of pale faces. "Great," I said before anyone could answer. "Let's move." Dewey was true to his word; the zombies turned to watch us go, but none made an overt gesture to follow.

"How long you think we have?" BT had come up beside me.

"Not as long as either of us would like."

"You realize you're a master of answering a question without actually giving anything of substance, right? How you missed your true calling of politician, I don't know."

"I swear too much."

"That the only thing holding you back?"

"Not really; no way would I be able to do all the hand-shaking and kissing of miniature germ factories. Can you imagine? Out there kissing Mr. and Mrs. Maguire's adorable bundle and the thing sneezes on me? I'd seize up, and you know that would be the picture the newspaper ran with. My opponent would be all over it; *how can you trust a man to do right by our community when he can't even stand babies?*"

"Is that how it would go down?"

"Pretty much, I've thought it out."

It was the first smile I'd seen on the man in a while, which, in turn, made me feel better.

"Let's move, people." We were double timing. I was amazed I was able to get my legs going; they felt like sticks of timber. We'd gone an entire city block without any problems–hardly something we could have done when people ruled Manhattan, so it was even more impressive now.

"We've got eyes on us, sir," Winters said.

I turned to look behind. He was pointing up. I noticed on every other building or so, there was a zombie, sometimes two, standing there, watching as we went past.

"How is this even possible?" BT wanted to know; we all did. He was just the first to voice it.

"Take them out?" Stenzel was sighting in.

"Not yet. When we get closer to our destination." Though I didn't know if this would work; they seemed to be stationed everywhere. No way we'd be able to kill enough of them to make a difference then melt away without giving our location to their ground forces. We were a city block from the NBC studios; there were still zombies either on fire escapes, roofs, or in windows, all just watching, and I would imagine relaying information back through the zombie mental hotline. Communication during a battle was paramount to a successful outcome. Knowing where the enemy was, calling in for help or extraction; all of it was vital, and if the zombies now possessed this strategic ability, everything had got significantly more complicated. Zombies like Dewey *had* to be in the minority; I was now weighing my decision to not kill him.

How many zombies could he directly influence? Was he a hundred-thousand-watt antenna, or merely a strong walkie-talkie? Could he bounce signals off others of his kind, giving him a network? Logistically, him and others like him would be a nightmare. If Dewey was unique, one of a kind, I had done a great disservice to humanity not blowing his brains out. Our lives were a drop in the bucket compared to the hell he could rain down upon the remaining survivors. The best thing I could do now was report back on my findings as I understood them. We were a couple hundred yards from the Rockefeller Center, our ultimate destination, when the zombies began to move.

"Looks like they finished lunch," I said. "We're going to move fast. Winters, you get us up and running; I'll get a quick message off to Etna, then we're going to make a run for the church." Winters looked like he'd swallowed a few eggs whole. "You've got this," I told him.

"It's not quite the same as setting up our equipment."

"I have faith." I smacked his shoulder.

"That's one of us," he mumbled as we entered.

"Stenzel, Harmon, stay at the front. Keep me informed about any gate crashers. Do not engage. Pull back to our location."

Stenzel nodded; Harmon paled. I knew she was dedicated, but I was concerned for her military readiness. Right now, it appeared as if BT was right and I should have left her behind. I knew deep down that would have been the worst thing for her, but now I was left wondering if bringing her had been the worst thing for us. We ran past a desk where, apparently, in better times, we would have met for a tour. We ended up climbing eight floors and into the Saturday Night Live studio. It was difficult to reconcile the juxtaposition of the terror we were in the midst of with standing in a place that had delivered laughs immeasurable over decades. I'd been a fan of the show since...forever. Some of my earliest memories revolved around Chevy Chase stumbling and bumbling over things; I smiled despite it all.

Winters took a cursory look at the massive cameras and then headed back to the studio booth where five chairs were stuffed along with a wall of equipment. He absently scratched the top of his head as he looked over the panels that made a commercial airplane's instruments look like Mr. Coffee auto-brew settings in comparison.

"No power," Winters mumbled. I didn't hover over him; what was the point? And anyway, I was too busy walking the same hallowed ground as John Belushi, Gilda Radner, Eddie Murphy and dozens, maybe hundreds of other comedians that had made my life more bearable.

"Tina Fey." BT was sitting in one of the seats reserved for the studio audience.

"Excuse me?" I asked him.

"Had a thing for her. She was my celebrity crush; I told Linda as much."

"You'd better shut up about that or I'll tell my sister."

"I will stick my finger in every bit of food you are going to eat for the rest of your life if you do that." He was boring through me with a tangible gaze.

"Fuck. No power," came through my earpiece. I could hear the frustration in Winters' voice as he worked. He was speaking to himself, maybe forgetting he was talking to everyone, as he mumbled his way through the problem.

"Always wanted to come here," BT said.

"Of course you did; how else were you going to stalk her."

"Don't turn something innocent into something sordid."

"Were you barred from here? Restraining order, maybe?"

I could see his jaw tighten as he became angrier.

"Hmmm…now that I think of it, my sister and Tina share some similarities. Have you ever screwed up and yelled out 'Tina!'? Oh fuck. I can't believe I asked that. Forget that I said anything."

"That's the thing, Mike, there are things you say that can't be unheard. Maybe if you gave your words more than a cursory glance before they exited your mouth, the world would be a better place."

"You did fuck up!" I was pointing at him.

I don't think I'd ever watched a blood vessel burst in real time; it was looking like that was about to change. Instead, he finally let out a pent-up breath. "You're an asshole. That's your sister you're talking about."

"Or Tina." I was saved from BT's wrath as Winters spoke.

"Sir, if you could come to the booth." His tone did not convey hope. BT followed.

"LT, this is Stenzel. We've got a small group coming down the road."

I turned my mic back on. "Get behind the reception desk; see if they go by."

"Roger that."

"Generator is dead." Winters looked up as we entered.

"Okay, then why do you not look particularly glum?"

"Glum? That's the best you could come up with?" BT asked.

"You a thesaurus now? This your way of getting back at me for the Tina Fey thing?"

A massive finger hovered a few inches from my face.

"Uh…there are solar panels on the top of this roof. It's possible we have enough juice to run this." Winters saved me from having my brains swirled by a sausage finger.

"Okay." I was hesitant; he was talking about power, but everything was off, near as I could tell. "Does it work?"

"I don't know but I'm going to switch it over and see. It either does or it doesn't."

I knew what he was saying; if the panels stayed dark there was nothing we could do to get them up and running, short of getting some fuel for the generator, wherever that was located. And it seemed like our allotted time was running out. I'd rather he had just done it without the set-up for a big reveal; those generally didn't go as you expected. I'd been on one blind date in my life. Paul and his girlfriend at the time had thought this girl and I would make a great couple. Now normally, this wasn't something I would do because of too many variables, but Paul and Candice had both said numerous times that she and the other girl, Wendy, could be sisters. And Candice–she was a looker and a sweetheart; I thought she might be the one Paul settled down with. Unfortunately, she jumped off the deep end with a religious cult; went from stable to nucking futs in the span of three months.

But back to the date. We were at the restaurant and Wendy was late, like, three beers late. Finally, Candice stood up and was telling us she was here; I turned and tried to find the girl that could look like her sister. I scanned a group of seven or eight people twice and the only family resemblance came from a middle-aged gentleman that could have been her uncle. When she said her hellos to Candice and Paul and barely gave me a look nor offered an apology for her tardiness, it was safe to assume where this night was going. Let's be politically correct for once and say that she didn't even have a great personality. After the meal, I ordered a shot of vodka and another beer. When they came I downed them quickly and stood.

"Paul, Candice, as always it has been a pleasure. Can't say the same, Wendy; I've had more meaningful and lively conversation with a goldfish."

"Where you going, buddy?" Paul asked.

"Heading home. Gonna go take a big shit and flush this night down the toilet."

Paul smiled, Candice fumed, and Wendy nearly choked on the cheesecake she was inhaling.

5

MIKE JOURNALY ENTRY 5

As I finished the thought, I saw a red light blinking. Now, as far as I know, red generally isn't a cherished color when it comes to electronics, and I was about to say something. Winters held his finger up. More lights slowly began to come to life. I could feel hope rising; Stenzel's news helped quell that.

"Not moving past sir. Congregating might be a better term."

"They coming in?"

"No sir; I think they're waiting on numbers."

"Same orders. Keep an eye on them and disengage the moment they decide to come in. Winters, you need to get me on the air quickly."

"No disrespect, sir," he started.

"You sure do get that a lot from your personnel," BT interjected.

I flipped him off and motioned for Winters to continue.

"If I knew enough to be a television producer, I wouldn't have been doing this Marine Corps gig. Get in front of a camera, and I'll let you know when I'm ready."

BT and I headed out. "How do I look?" I asked him.

"Does it matter?"

"I don't want to have a nose rocket hanging out."

"You're reporting back to base, not hosting a variety show."

Tommy had come back from checking out our perimeter. "No zombies, but this place had guests recently, within the last few weeks. It seems they have moved on."

"Any food?" I asked.

"I'm sorry about this," he said as he pulled out a dozen or so packets of unfrosted cherry pop-tarts.

"I'm sure you are." I turned my back on the small feast as I looked into the reflective lens of the camera, doing my best to look somewhat presentable.

BT ate his allotment like it was filet mignon. Tommy went and handed Winters a pack; he shook his head but pocketed the morsel anyway. I saw a light on the camera begin to blink; it was weird, but I got butterflies. I can't imagine many people had access to a television or even the ways and means to run one, but I was about to go live. Then I thought on the dangers of that. This would not be a secure transmission, and just how much did I want any eavesdroppers to know? I knew Etna would see this because they actively searched all bands, but did they do it all the time? And I had no idea if I could receive a response.

"On in three, two…" The light atop the camera went from red to green, Winters pointed at me, and I froze.

"LT! Zees coming in!" I could hear Stenzel and Harmon's footfalls echo throughout the vaulted antechamber as they were making a run for it.

"Now what?" I turned and looked into the booth.

"We wait for Etna to acknowledge you," Winters said.

"So, I just stand here like an idiot?"

"Make no mistake, Mike, you don't need to stand to look like an idiot," BT said.

"Tommy, will you make sure Stenzel and Harmon make it up here? BT, that moves you to the door."

"Just trying to get rid of me." He moved that way.

I was acutely aware that I was on the same stage as so many legends had been; I could almost hear their voices as they made millions laugh. I wasn't even aware when I said: "No Coke, Pepsi!"

"Sir?" Winters asked.

"Sorry, just remembering a better time."

"Not all that hard to do," I heard him say. "Wait, message coming through. Patching it out your way."

"This is Etna Station, Lieutenant Talbot. Hold one while we get Colonel Bennington."

"Better make it quick, we're in a bit of a rush."

Bennington's voice came on in less than a minute. "Lieutenant Talbot, good to see you. When we lost communication, we feared the worst."

"Did you lose any sleep, sir?"

"Excuse me?"

"Sorry. It's been a long few days."

"Stick to the sitrep."

"This is a party line, sir, not going to go into specifics."

"Understood."

"Our ride was attacked, lost comm, and they lost the ability to keep giving us passage. We were dropped off early."

"And your transportation?"

I had to bite my tongue. In the grand scheme of things, that plane was a much more valuable asset than any of the occupants within it; didn't ease the feelings of being downgraded.

"Safe, but not going anywhere without help. We've run into the next iteration of zees; they have the ability to communicate intelligently and can direct other zombies over an unspecified distance. That and they can talk with us." Like the rest wasn't terrifying enough.

"Your original mission, Lieutenant."

"Did you hear the part, sir, where I said we were dropped early from our target and encountered smart zees?"

I could hear Winters' gasp from where I stood.

"Your hardships notwithstanding, the mission is of paramount importance."

"No disrespect, sir, but even if we somehow escape our current predicament, what do I do with…"

"What you can, Lieutenant," he shot back. I almost forgot I wasn't on a radio and was so close to flipping him the finger I had to consciously stop the movement with my other hand.

"We have your ride's location and will be sending assistance. In the meantime, I expect you will be doing all you can to complete what you have been tasked with."

"Understood, sir." I gave Winters a cut motion across my throat.

"I don't think he's done."

"Yeah, but I am." I walked off-camera; a moment later the light turned red. "What does he mean he knows where the plane is?"

"Transponder?" Winters guessed.

"So they've known all along." Then I put it together. "But if they thought we'd crashed or been shot down, they weren't going to spend the resources to come and look for us. I've been in a couple of the shittiest armpits in the world, and I've never felt so abandoned as I do in downtown New York."

"I'm here, sir."

I looked at him with furrowed eyebrows. "I mean from Support."

He cleared his throat. "I knew that, sir." We heard gunfire; our attention turned to the stairwell.

"Where's Belushi and his samurai sword when you need it?" I quickly moved to where BT was. "See anything?"

"Nothing yet. What did Etna say?"

"Pretty much told us to stop slacking off and get what we were sent here for accomplished."

"I'd say you were full of shit but you look pissed." He was looking over the handrail and down the stairs, as was I. We could see muzzle flashes and hear the reports as Stenzel and Harmon made their way up.

"Winters! Look for an alternate exit!"

"On it!"

"Tommy…what's going on?"

"On the fifth floor. Zombies have stopped coming in. Stenzel and Harmon are with me."

"How many we talking about?"

It was Stenzel that replied, "A couple dozen came in, but twice that are outside sir."

"This shit is getting old. I wonder if they think that too."

"Don't start rolling down the inner highway now, Mike. There aren't going to be any peace accords down the line."

"Stop being a realist, BT."

"My bad."

Stenzel and Harmon came up first. "Sergeant is watching our back," Stenzel said, referring to Tommy staying back a few flights lower.

Winters was back within a few minutes. "South stairwell is empty."

"Tommy, let's go," I told him.

"Etna sir?" Harmon asked.

"They're coming. We still have some work to do though," I told her, not giving any indication of how frustrated I was.

BT clapped Tommy on the shoulder as the other came up.

"Anyone by any chance see, or, better yet, put a bullet in Dewey?"

Got some head shaking. "Unfortunate. Alright, let's do a gear check and get ready to leave. Winters, get on the horn with Corporal Rose, find out what's going on there and then fill her in."

"Yes, sir."

"One of these missions, I'm just going to forgo all the other shit we carry and just pack out ammo." BT was thumbing rounds into a magazine. "Seriously. Not once have I used the sleeping bag and bedroll we bring. Or that little infant shovel…what am I supposed to do with that thing? About the size of the spoon I use for breakfast. For fuck's sake, Mike, I carry extra underwear. I mean, sure, there are plenty of times when I want to shit my pants, but at that point, man, I'm not stopping to change my drawers."

"You all right?" I was smiling, but the look that BT gave me back was not one of jest. Humans aren't built to deal with continued, unrelenting stress; it starts to break down who we are at our core, infecting every other aspect of our existence. "We do this, BT, we go home, take some time, be with my sister. There is an end."

He wanted to question how I knew this, but he didn't ask, because yes, there would be an end, but I'd not said it would be a good one. The important part was to live the good life while you could, in spite of the enemy that was out there.

"Rose says the church is clear." Winters looked from me to BT, not sure he was thrilled with what he saw.

"Change of plans. We're not going back there. Tell them the primary meeting place is Central Park Zoo. If we're not there, they are to head to the Bio-Reference Labs and continue the mission."

"What should I tell her about the people in the church?" Winters asked.

"We're going to have to come back for them. I can't take them with us, not yet." This only compounded my problems. I knew what I'd promised Jason; how I was going to deliver was eluding me at the moment.

Winters did not look thrilled to relay the message.

"Let's go, people. We're out of here."

Didn't smell anything, or better yet, see anything, as we

quickly made our way down the south stairwell. We skipped the first floor and headed to the basement.

"Clear." Winters had first looked through the small safety window in the door then poked his head out to check.

"What are the odds any of these will start?" I was looking at ten long-abandoned cars.

"Not good," Harmon said. "My dad was a mechanic; worked with him a lot. If we had a new battery and could drain the old fluids, then yeah. Otherwise…" She left it there.

We could have ridden in style. I touched the front end of a late model Benz; the thing was stout, heavy enough that we could have used it as a dozer for the zees we were likely to encounter. We were cautiously making our way up the ramp that led to street level; we somehow had the good fortune to not encounter any zombies.

I nodded to Stenzel to take point. "I've got this," Harmon spoke up.

"Right behind you," I told her. I saw her shoulders heave as she took in a great gust of breath and then she soldiered on. BT pursed his lips and nodded slightly; impressed, I think, that she was marshaling.

I had an unshakable fear that the moment she stepped from the shadows of the parking garage and into the light of day, the alarm would sound and we would be once again sprinting for our lives. She had one foot in the light and was swiveling her head; she took another, then a third, until she was basking in the sun.

"All clear." Hadn't heard more magical words since I'd been with my wife, and I'm not telling you those words, though, how many guesses do you need? "Which way, sir?"

"Not the front."

"Helpful," BT said as he shouldered past.

"Don't worry, Mr. T. It was extremely helpful to me." Tommy was moving up front.

"Kiss ass." BT hip-checked Tommy.

We went two city blocks away from where the majority of the zombies we knew of were, and hopefully, far enough away from Dewey's influence. We stayed tight on the sidewalk, but it was impossible to stay hidden.

"How far to the zoo?" I asked. We all had handheld GPS units, but Winters, by default, was generally where our information came from.

"Little less than two klicks," he answered, pausing to check.

"That a mile?" BT asked.

"About," Winters clarified.

One mile. We could make that in about twenty minutes at our current, cautious pace. It was one mile closer, not to safety, but to getting out of this hellhole, and I was good with that, especially since we would meet up with the rest of the squad. We heard gunfire off to the east; this was followed by some garbled transmission.

"Winters!"

"Buildings are messing with the signal, sir."

I wanted to tell him to fix it, but short of demolishing all the scrapers, that wasn't going to happen.

"Contact…" came through loud and clear; everything else sounded like a television underwater, two rooms away.

"Forward or back?" BT looked antsy.

"Hold. We don't know what we're getting into or where they're going."

I had my hand up while I tried to catch snippets of the quick conversation going on.

"Kirby, watch our six!"

"They're coming from the side!"

I looked at the anxious faces of those with me.

"Lieutenant, this is Corporal Rose." They were close, if the quality of the transmission was any indication, even if the gunfire still sounded far away.

"Go, Rose." I gripped my rifle tight.

"We got company. Going to be coming in hot. You still want us to rally at the zoo?"

"Affirmative. Can you make it?"

"We've got some room, but they're converging–coordinated, even."

"Dewey," I hissed.

"Sir?"

"Nothing. We'll set up some support for your arrival. How's Sergeant Talbot?"

"Holding his own, sir. I'm going to be happy when he doesn't look like a giant smurf, though…tough to take him seriously."

"Just get all your asses there."

"Roger that, sir."

"Let's go! Double time." Eight minutes later we were standing in front of the zoo, and unfortunately, a turned-over and long-abandoned hot dog truck.

"Think the animals are gone?" BT asked as we hit the entrance.

"For all our sakes I hope that's the case." For obvious reasons; the big cats were scary, but monkeys were terrifying. They seemed to take the violence they doled out personally. Like each of them knew all about the fucked-up experiments we humans had performed on their kin over the years. I mean, why else would they bite fingers off and rip faces, along with genitalia, free from our bodies?

"Sir, we're coming down 64th; be there in five minutes." Rose sounded out of breath.

"Admin building to our left–looks like a fortress. We'll give them some cover here." It was a three-story brick building. The front entrance was of thickset, wooden double-doors. Tommy lifted Stenzel so she could go through a broken-out window. The father in me wanted to tell the woman, who was my daughter's age, to be careful of getting cut. I wisely held back; she might be young, but out of us all, she was, arguably, the best at her job. "Go," I told Tommy, who looked back at me once the corporal was in. He jumped up, grabbed the windowsill, and swung a leg to get in.

"Must have been closed the day the zombies came," Stenzel said. "Except for some dust, this place looks like it's just waiting for the next work day. Heading for the front door."

"We'll meet you there," I told her. "Rose, take a quick left when you get to the end of 64th; you'll see a tall brick building. We're leaving the front doors open for you."

"Yup," was her quick reply; not sure she had much more than that to give.

I was worried–and I mean *a lot*. Rose was my PT freak; she worked out regularly on her cardio, and if she was on her last legs, the rest of the group was going to be in trouble, especially my brother, who wasn't ever going to make a cross-country team even on his best days–and he was far from those.

"Need a volunteer." The last word hadn't even come out of my mouth when everyone there said: "I'm in" or a variant. "Tommy, you and I are gonna go out there and see if we can give them some cover."

"Sir, I'd feel better if you stayed here," Stenzel said.

"Me too," I told her as I followed Tommy out. We'd no sooner rounded the corner when we saw the rest of the squad humping it towards us with most of hell on their heels. They couldn't spare any time to turn and fire upon the enemy. I saw why Rose was struggling; she was hefting a fair portion of Gary's weight, nearly dragging him along. His mouth was open and his head almost thrown back in a scream. His bright blue outfit was coated in a fair amount of his own blood as he continually broke open his freshly scabbed wounds.

"I'll get him." Tommy was on the move; he didn't wait for me to tell him yay or nay. There wasn't much of anything I could do with my rifle; the two groups were too close and my angle, or my lack of angle, rather, made it impossible to shoot safely. Rose had her head down, concentrating on moving as fast as she could. Kirby and Springer were behind her, doing their best to give her a cushion and help when they could. I saw the relief flood into her face as Tommy came in from the other side and grabbed Gary into a fireman's lift. There was now only a hundred yards between them and me. I moved to the sidewalk and started blowing rounds into the zombies nearest them. When they got to twenty yards out, I took a few more shots and got ready to join them in their final sprint.

"Sir," Grimm shouted as he passed by.

I motioned for him to keep going. Springer, Halsey, and Kirby were next. Rose was keeping stride with Tommy and Gary. I fell in right behind them. I saw puffs of smoke from the zoo admin building; couldn't hear the shots because of the sheer number of feet smacking against the pavement. It was that loud; trapped between the buildings, the sound was amplified. By the time I made it up the stairs and in, I didn't have more than ten feet on the lead zombies, all of which were met with a hail of lead and a hearty, *Fuck You!* from me. I flipped them off as Stenzel and BT shut and barred the doors.

"That help?" BT asked.

"You betcha."

The six runners were in various states of catching their breath or reliving the horror. A couple were on the floor, chests heaving, ragged breaths shuddering through their bodies. Rose was close to the doors, doubled over, her hands on her knees. Winters was taking a look at my brother, who was sitting in an office chair. Gary looked miserable, and what I was about to say wasn't going to help.

"You've got five minutes. Don't get comfortable." I could feel the heated gazes upon me. "I know you're all tired. So am I, but we can't afford to stay here. We don't have the supplies to do it and help isn't coming until this mission is complete."

"Fuck this mission," PFC Kirby blurted out.

"If you think about it, it's really the mission fucking us,"

Harmon said. I was thankful for her bit of humor; it created the motivation I was going to have to work with.

Kirby was the first off the floor, and he helped the others.

"Still clear," BT informed me regarding the rear of the building.

"Rose, can you rig me a quick something on those doors?" I asked.

"I can give them a little welcome surprise."

"Three minutes." I was looking at my watch. In my mind, I was thinking how much I wanted to punch Bennington in the head. On one end of the spectrum, I completely understood the necessity of what we were doing. But the thought that these people under my command, most of them kids, were expendable in his eyes…well, that pissed me off to no end. If none of us came back, save the bio-engineers we were here to retrieve, I'm not sure he'd lose a single night of sleep. I knew that was an oversimplification on my part; as a commander, it was his job to put men and women at risk every day. If it furthered the advancement of the cause we were fighting for, then that was what had to happen. But as one on the front line, watching a team suffer, I tended to see things differently.

As far as I was concerned, the three minutes took an hour to pass; I'm sure for those whose legs and lungs still burned it was more like twelve seconds.

"Just about ready. No one sneeze," Rose said as she looked upon her handiwork. "That ought to give them a little what for."

We were out the back and heading through the zoo; I was happy to be on the move again. The zoo was its own special kind of hell. The animals that had not broken out on their own had met some terrible fates. Some, like the giraffes, had been overrun by zombies and stripped clean; massive, long-necked skeletal structures remained crumbled behind fences. In some of the enclosures, the starving animals had turned on each other, with no other food source. Starvation had forced them to become cannibals. The fight in the polar bear pen had been an epic one, if the dried blood splashes across the heavy Plexiglas of the now empty water pools was any indication. I was not thrilled that the grey wolves seemed to have found their way out; I wondered if they were going to be a problem further on down the line.

We were three quarters of the way through the zoo. I would have had my people make a mad dash for it, but there still might be animals here and I would not lose someone to a lion. That, and we were exhausted. Better to move at a cautious pace while also conserving and restoring energy. That changed when the admin building was breached; this we knew from the massive explosion.

I looked over to Rose, who shrugged. "I figured the more I used, sir, the less I had to carry."

"Can't fault that logic. Let's pick it up." With a traditional enemy, the blast would have sent them scurrying for cover and tentative to make another assault. With zombies, the opening was just a vacuum that needed filling.

When we got to the back of the zoo, we were faced with a nine-foot concrete retaining wall. I'm sure this posed no problem for the monkeys that vacated the area, but for us right now, we may as well have been Huns in China. BT gave Tommy a small boost; he didn't need it, but the others suspected something about the boy, and we were doing our best to limit the speculation and keep the talk to a minimum.

"Honey, they're home." Kirby did his best Jack Torrance voice; if I had to rate it, I'd have given him a solid seven. It was the facial expression that put it over the top. I've got to think he practiced it a lot in a mirror. Either that or he was certifiable, like his father, Peter. Man, I missed that crazy bastard. We lost touch after the Corps. The men I had known and fought next to were as close, if not closer, than brothers, but when the shooting finally stops, sometimes you don't want to be reminded of the past. I knew I was guilty of that.

Tommy was reaching down and snagging people like a crane would a stack of lumber. They might have had questions about him, but he was liked and respected and well, shit. When someone offers you a hand to get away from a bloodthirsty horde, you take it. The zoo was beginning to swell with zombies. We, as of yet, had not been discovered, but it looked as if they were not going to leave any stone unturned in their quest to find us.

"Does this seem a little excessive, even for them?" BT asked as he waited until everyone else was up and over.

"Clear on the other side," Stenzel said.

"Zombies like to eat, but, yeah…they're after us like a Jenny Craig dropout going out for all-you-can-eat shrimp. I think this has to do with Dewey, like, maybe he wants to keep his secret a secret for a little while longer."

"It's fucking weird when you make sense. Kind of like those pictures on the internet when a chameleon grabs a screwdriver."

"What the fuck are you talking about?"

"Little-known fact: chameleons will grab anything placed in front of them. But just because they have it wrapped in their grip doesn't mean they know what to do with it. Kind of like you with a valid thought."

"I wonder if Bennington will let me trade you out. I could probably get a sixth-round draft choice."

BT and I helped Gary up, trying to touch as little of him as we could. His teeth were clenched shut and he didn't yell out, but he was visibly uncomfortable. Gary had been gently let down on the other side when Tommy gave us the warning that we'd been spotted.

BT didn't need much help; a small jump and he had his elbow and underarm on the top of the wall. Tommy grabbed his pack and gave an assist.

"You ready?" Tommy leaned down and hauled me up.

I was standing atop the wall, looking over the sea of

several hundred zombies running toward the wall. Tommy had dropped down and into Central Park.

"I fucking see him." Dewey was standing on top of one of the huts that used to serve refreshments. I had him directly in my sights and was in the process of pulling the trigger, when a collision of zombies broadsided into the wall. I thought I saw a plume of blood exit from Dewey, but it was impossible to tell as I was now fighting the vibrations from the impact. I was teetering. That I was going over was not much in doubt; which way, however, was a life or death question. My calves were bunched as my front half-pitched far forward; I arched my back, flung my arms, and threw as much of my weight into going that way as possible. I wasn't trying to correct and stand back up; that ship had sailed. I gave not a shit about how I landed in the park, just that it was in the park.

I was both happy and dismayed when BT caught me. Happy that I hadn't landed on my head or shoulder or in some way that would have broken something and slowed me down. Dismayed, well, because he caught me like Richard Gere had carried Debra Winger in *An Officer and a Gentlemen*. Sure, it was a great scene and even the most macho of men secretly teared up when he swept her off her feet. I mean, that's what I've heard. I wouldn't know...I didn't see the flick. So there I was, cradled in his oversized arms; I even had my arms around his neck. The entire thing couldn't have lasted a second and a half before he roughly deposited me onto the ground, but now it had happened. I wasn't sure how my sister was going to react to the news; I'm sure she was going to be devastated. Tracy would take it in stride, probably even say she expected something like that from the beginning, the way I always gave him googly eyes. I mean...okay, but that was more due to the sheer size of the man.

"Thanks," I mumbled. I wanted to add something about the Bears, but I didn't want to make any more out of it than necessary. And given the circumstances, it was more likely my squad would be thinking about grizzlies and not the football team. I pulled my gear straight. "Winters, get us moving."

We had cleared the zoo and still no signs of zombies breaking through, but that would happen soon enough. That wall wobble had told me it wasn't going to hold against a sustained attack; our best strategy would be to not be around when it finally gave. We had a mile and a half to the lab and somehow Central Park was free from zombies. Got a partial answer a half mile later. Elephants. Yup, I said elephants. Three of them. A colossal male, an even larger female I figured was the matriarch, and either a baby or another, smaller type. The three of them were walking around, grazing, trumpeting, cavorting, normal elephant stuff. I was worried that our presence would bring them harm; I need not have been concerned. What I had failed to notice, but Grimm pointed out, were the stomped, smattered and splattered zombies all around us. It looked like at one time the zombies thought the elephants would make a grand meal and pushed their chairs up to the table only to be told they would not be served there. This part of the park looked like it had been paved with the flattened bodies of the truly dead.

The female elephant turned and eyed us warily as we were going to approach, about a hundred yards to the small group's side. Yeah, she knew what guns were and it didn't look like the experience had been a happy one. We kept moving. The bull took his cues from the female; he shook his massive head and stomped around then let out a loud trumpet blast in warning. If he charged, we would be forced to shoot; I sincerely hoped it wouldn't come down to that.

"Stop, everyone stop!" I ordered. "Turn and face the elephants, hands off your weapons."

"Do you know what you're doing?" BT asked as he raised his hands.

"The male looks like he wants to charge I don't want to

give him a reason to do it." Like the animal had heard my words, he took three quick steps our way.

"Hold!" I yelled when I saw more than one of my group's hands falter and begin to slide down to their rifle.

"Wasting time." BT looked over his shoulder to the way we had come.

"Saving lives." And I meant *theirs* and *ours*.

I raised my hands higher, that seemed to agitate the bull even further; the matriarch, though, she understood the gesture. She wrapped her trunk around the male's tail and gave it a pull, getting his attention. He swung his head to look at her; don't know what she said or how she said it, but he immediately deferred to her. He turned his back to us like we were never there. The small elephant stayed hidden behind the female, who made sure to continually watch us as we departed.

"Fuck me, you adding elephant whisperer to your resume?" BT asked.

"You know I am."

We'd been at a slight jog, but that last half mile there wasn't anyone in my squad not feeling the effects of what had been happening. We were down to a weary and wary walk. Had Halsey at point; the building was in sight and I was about to have us stop so we could reconnoiter the place before we just barged in. Three speeders burst forth from a bodega not ten feet from where Halsey was. He didn't even have a chance to register alarm as the first of them broadsided him. By then it was already too late; he gave an ear-piercing scream as his nose was completely bitten off. I've been shot by a bullet, by a crossbow–stabbed and cut so many times there was very little of me that had not suffered trauma–but in terms of pain, all of it was trumped by a bite. There is something so savage, so visceral and paralyzing in intensity about a bite. Halsey was in shock and survival mode as he tried to push the aggressor away and might have been able to do just that…if the other two hadn't dog-piled him.

It takes a moment for the mind to process exactly what it is seeing; yes, even though all of us had witnessed it dozens, hundreds, maybe thousands of times, you still don't expect it to happen and most definitely not to one of your own. Not someone you were talking with a minute ago. The four were on the ground; three fat parasites were systematically ripping into one of my men and there wasn't a damn thing I could do about it. Couldn't shoot them for fear of hitting Halsey, even though I knew he was dead already. This would not be something he walked away from, unless…I was thinking about the lab as I cracked my rifle against the skull of a zombie teenager. Its pale gray face turned to me; I'd ripped the skin most of the way up and off. The side of its jaw was laid bare; teeth were exposed along with the cartilage of its nose. It snarled at me once and made as if to go back in for another piece of Halsey. I cracked it again, and this time it stood. Winters delivered a point-blank round into its forehead.

BT had kicked one of the zombies like he was trying to make a sixty-three-yard field goal; it wouldn't have split the uprights but it was sufficient enough to launch the woman away, where someone put her down for good. The third made sure to wrap its arms and legs around a convulsing Halsey, using the dying man as a shield. Halsey's eyes were rolling into the back of his head and he was busy chewing on his tongue; the zombie kept moving its head to keep it clear from us while also moving in to take as big a bite as it dared. It was Stenzel who ended the détente as she snapped the blade of her knife into the temple of the zombie. Its arms and legs opened wide and it rolled over. It was staring straight up into space, its left arm moved ineffectively towards the offending insertion before falling weakly back to earth. By this time, all of our attention was on Halsey.

"Help me grab him!" I yelled.

"Sir," Winters started. I knew where he was going with this; we all knew the private was going to die. Really, the best thing we could have done for him was to end it quickly. But I felt like we had one more chance. That bio-building; we were here for a reason. Maybe they had a cure.

"The lab—we get him to the lab."

"I'll take him." BT draped the private over his shoulder and we started moving quickly.

We were at the front doors in a matter of minutes. I don't know what they were testing, but this place was a vault quality facility. Could see the hands of the government all over the drab-but-solid structure. I banged on the doors and then looked up to the camera.

"I know you can see me. I'm Lieutenant Talbot. We were sent by Etna Station to rescue you."

There was a long delay. "What's wrong with the man?"

"Bit. We need help."

"We can't help him." The voice didn't sound frightened to let us in; on the contrary, I'd say there was empathy. "I'm sorry."

I didn't understand. "But if we were sent to get you, and you work at a lab, you must have a cure."

"Cure? Now that would be something."

"Let us in."

"I'm afraid I can't do that—not with the infected man. You must understand; we cannot allow someone who is going to turn, in."

"He's not quite a zombie yet."

"That camera is infra-red and can also perform bio scans. I suggest you have your Gunnery Sergeant put him down before you have two casualties."

BT quickly but gently set Halsey onto the front stoop. The convulsions had stopped. Halsey took one final breath before his eyes clouded over. He sat up, his face a mass of hamburger, but the snarl on his lips and the predatory look in his eyes was all we needed to know.

"Forgive me," I told him as I shot him from a foot away. There was stunned silence from those all around me as his head smacked off the concrete and he was finally still. We heard the door click as the locking mechanism was released.

"Sir?" Harmon asked as she grabbed the door handle. All of my attention was still on my fallen private. My pistol holding hand was still raised; BT pressed it slowly down.

"Come on, man. We gotta go; more are coming."

"Shit."

As soon as we got in, the door locks reengaged. We found ourselves in a small corridor faced with another set of locked doors which promptly opened up.

6

MIKE JOURNAL ENTRY 6

"I'M SORRY ABOUT YOUR MAN." The person who stepped through the doors looked less like a scientist and more like the manager at a rundown nudie bar. He had a large gut, slicked mustache, and greasy hair that hung down to his shoulders. The only thing that even competed against this seedy persona was the flawless, white smock he was wearing.

"I'm Doctor Jeremy." He looked relieved to see us.

Then it dawned on me. "Are you related to…"

"Fifth or sixth cousin; I don't think he even knows." He attempted a faltering smile.

"What are you talking about?" BT whispered.

"Think hedgehog," and I left it at that.

"You are the weirdest fuck I have ever met." He followed me as I went and shook the doctor's hand.

We were safe for the moment. The doctor showed us where we could get cleaned up and eat, though you can hardly call a quarter packet of ramen a sustaining meal. But it was something. I penned a letter to Halsey's girlfriend and dreaded every second I'd spend giving it to her. I'd lost her significant other on my watch. It happened; men and women died all the time in war. That didn't make it any easier. I had just folded the letter up and put it in my pocket when there was a soft knock on the door to the room I was sitting in.

"Just got off the radio with your commander. They'll have a new plane at the airfield tomorrow; he expects us to be on the return flight. Again, Lieutenant, I am sorry for your loss. The rest of your people are getting some rest; I suggest you do as well."

"Thank you, doctor. Can you tell me why we're here? Was it worth it, at least?"

"Time will tell. It's always history that is the perfect scrivener of events, although, unfortunately, history is always tampered with by the humans recording it. They are inclined to write things down in a light that puts them or their cause in the right."

"How about we discuss the philosophy of historical bias another time, and you tell me why Bennington cost me one of my men and risked the rest of our lives, and I'll internally decide if admission was worth the price."

He put his hand to his chin and looked up before he spoke. "I do think it was worth it. What we have here isn't just research or a theory; we have a working weapon, a biological agent."

I pressed the bridge of my nose and paused; as a soldier, I didn't like anything that started with the word *biological*. "So how do we get all the zombies to head down to the local clinic to receive their treatment? Who's the poor bastard that has to administer those shots?"

He cocked his head slightly, not following the thread of my thinking. Not surprising, really; you have to be around me for a fair amount of time to thread around the tangents and pull it into something relatively cohesive.

"Why, you, of course. And others like you," he added quickly. "You see, the viral agent is added to bullets, much like how the Native Americans would dip their arrows into toxins created either from dangerous plants or poisonous animals."

"Great. We're going back to primitive weapons."

"I think you are failing to understand the basic principles involved here."

"Inform me."

"How difficult is a headshot?"

"A lot harder than hitting a target center mass."

"What if I were to tell you that a grazing wound on the arm of a zombie could now be its undoing?" I sat up straighter. "I thought that might pique your interest." He smiled.

"So, we just dip our bullets in some scientific mystery brew, then?"

"It's a little more difficult than that; the virus is hardy but not quite that stable. We have experimented quite successfully on hollow-tipped bullets. We fill in the hole then seal the bullet with a plastic cap. Once it strikes the enemy, the contents are introduced into the victim."

"How fast?" This was all great and fine, but if the virus took twenty-four hours or longer to make the zombie sick and then die, it was barely above useless. If we were firing, that meant we were usually a minute or less from being killed.

"Our first trials typically took three hours; we now have it down to ten minutes, and we think we can improve upon that, though, we have begun to run out of the necessary resources to keep testing and advancing."

Ten minutes was a vast improvement, but still contained some serious drawbacks.

"Lieutenant Talbot, I'm saying that we can get this to be nearly instantaneous and soon. Imagine the lives that can be saved if even the most superficial of shots will drop the enemy."

"Sounds great and all, but what of the safety to the personnel around this new miracle weapon?"

"Meaning?"

"Meaning, how toxic is it to the people that handle this

viral agent? What if a soldier is hit by friendly fire or, more likely, while they are putting rounds in a magazine and one of these plastic caps comes off and they get some on themselves? What then?"

"That would not be advisable."

"Not advisable like they will get a headache, or not advisable like all of their internal organs will liquefy and run out their assholes?"

"More the latter."

"Are you kidding me, doc? You want to send soldiers out there who, in most cases, are just kids, with a weapon that can kill them upon contact? You realize what goes on out there, right? Lots of running, dropping things, hurriedly getting magazines ready in the worst types of situations. I've seen men put bullets in their mouth as a placeholder as they pick up fallen rounds. What about an antidote?"

"There isn't one; we saw no need to work on that. The virus we have created, it mimics the one it is attacking. That is why it is so effective and ultimately difficult to treat."

"It can be done; I've seen it."

He looked at me like I was lying. "I don't want to discount what you may or may not have seen, but that is highly unlikely."

I left it at that. I had my son and my best friend as all the proof I needed and Avalyn too, maybe. He exited my room shortly after that. I should have slept like the dead; instead, I had my hands clasped behind my head and got into a staring contest with the ceiling tiles. Something wasn't right here. Was it just coincidence that Dewey existed in New York? Or had he been shot with one of these poisonous darts? Was there ever a viral agent with a hundred percent death rate? I suppose there were many, if left untreated. Rabies was one, plague was another, and I'm sure there were plenty of others; hell, viral infections killed millions. But didn't most deadly viruses only have a ninety-eight percent mortality rate? Or even eighty? What if Dewey was one of the two percent, or twenty percent, that had survived? Had he incorporated this new virus and twisted it around to make himself a better version? That stopped my mind in its tracks. Was Doc Jeremy effectively creating a super-soldier zombie? This thing that mimics its host before taking it down; how do we know our enemy so well? Isn't it always so, that things which herald a great change for good, also bring in or make way for a great evil as well? The balance remains. The two are too tightly intertwined to stand independently. I entertained the thought of shooting all of the people in this facility and then burning the place to the ground. I'd be executed for committing treason, but if I let them live, would I eventually be known as the man that effectively hammered the final nail into the coffin of humanity?

It was some hours later when there was a knock on my door; at some point I'd fallen asleep. Dreamt I was trapped in the subway and I was being chased by a billion or so rats. To me, it was even more proof that I was the Pied Piper in this story, although, instead of getting rid of the plague I was bringing it with me. Either that or my betraying mind was setting me up to think that. Can't trust the brain; it's always out doing its own thing and then you're left there, trying to assemble all the pieces into an understandable picture. Kind of a weird thing when one part of the brain is determined to confuse the other.

"You in there?" BT finally asked as I was running around with errant thoughts.

"Since when do you knock?" I was sitting on the bed tying my boots.

"Since the last time I walked in on you and you were trying to hula hoop. I've wanted to talk to you about that; first off, where'd you get the toy, and why were you trying to do it naked? Forget it…I'm sure you've got some half-assed explanation as to why you were, and in your mind, I'm sure it makes complete fucking sense, which means it will mean zero to me. I don't even know why I brought it up; now I have to relive that." He rubbed his eyes. "Fuck, now I don't even know why I'm here."

"Wanna see what I can do with a slinky?" I stood.

"Not a fucking chance. Oh yeah, Bennington is on the line for you."

"Why are you running that errand?"

"Because the rest of the unit is kids, man. I didn't want to take the chance of exposing them to something they'll never be able to forget. They're so young and impressionable–they'd have years for that to fester around in their heads. Plus, while we walk down the corridor I want you to tell me what you think about what they're doing here."

"You know?"

"Not sure what the security clearance on this place is, but they can't stop talking about it. I think they'd high-five each other every few seconds if they weren't so damn nerdy."

"What's nerdy got to do with it?"

"They'd miss and smack cach other in the face. Little pencil-necked geeks would be running around with wads of toilet paper shoved up their noses."

"You done?"

"Tell me I'm wrong."

"Never said that. As far as their weapon, I love the theory behind it, terrified of side-effects and practical use."

"Side-effects?"

"I think Dewey might be a side-effect."

BT stopped in his tracks. "Whoa there. You got anything besides that insane imagination of yours to back that up?"

"Not one iota–other than the fact that Dewey resides about a mile from this location."

"That's a leap, Mike, but it's not quite as mighty as some of the ones you've taken in the past. What are you going to tell Bennington?"

"Maybe to nuke New York; doesn't really matter what I think. He wants what they've got. He's just calling to make sure we get their asses on that plane."

"You seriously have a bad feeling about this?"

"A man-made virus rushed to the battlefield that hasn't been properly tested? I mean, what could possibly go wrong?"

I had not been expecting to have a video link to Bennington; when I went into the communications room, he must have read in my face the thoughts I'd been going over.

"Everything all right, Lieutenant?"

I didn't know what to say; all I had were gut feelings, nothing even close to evidence. *Conjecture*, I guess that's what the experts would call it. Bennington took my unwillingness to answer as an answer.

"Good. We have sent appropriate parts for Major Eastman and his crew to repair their plane. Your job is to get Doctor Jeremy, his team and their work aboard the replacement plane. You and your people will guard the other plane until such time as it is ready to take off again. Talbot, your demeanor is speaking louder than any of the words you have yet to voice."

"Colonel…this weapon they've designed; I'm not sure it has been tested properly or completely, I mean, for potentially devastating side-effects."

"And the reason for your concern?"

"You realize it's a virus, right?"

"I am well aware of the work; been following it for months now."

It dawned on me then. "So, if it hadn't worked up to par, these men would be staying here."

"You know the limitations we have at Etna; we cannot continue to grow without those coming in being able to offer something in return."

"Viruses mutate continually. You are going to take what they are using here and introduce it into the zombies. I think there needs to be more testing to check for potential problems."

Bennington didn't say anything but it was clear enough he was holding back some anger.

"Have you ever thought, Lieutenant, that perhaps it is best to leave the thinking for those that are capable of it, and that you should just do as you are told?"

"You realize it's my personnel that are out here sacrificing to make sure that this mission is completed, correct? And that now, I have to come back and sit down with Private Halsey's girlfriend to tell her he gave all? I think I have a right to be concerned with what we are fighting for and how we do it."

"I'll let you know what you need to be concerned with, Lieutenant. You get those scientists on the plane and I'll deal with the rest."

"You're making a mistake, sir."

"This conversation is done. You have six hours; get them to where they need to be." And with that, he shut off the feed.

"That went well," BT said from off to my side.

I must have been wearing my anger on my sleeve.

"Hey, man, don't direct that my way."

"If our loved ones weren't in Washington, I'm pretty sure we'd be hijacking a plane. I knew Bennington was a hard-ass; I never thought of him as an asshole, though."

"A hard-ass and an asshole are pretty close to each other, if you want to get technical," BT said.

"I suppose you're right. Let's get the eggheads of the apocalypse rounded up and ready to go."

The bio-engineers had known for a few days that we were coming to bring them to Washington, yet they'd done nothing to prepare for it, almost as if they couldn't think of two things at once. Although, who was I to fault them that? I was lucky if I could think of one thing at once, like, ever. But the fact that they were just now *packing* was mind-boggling. Like they never even considered that we might be coming in hot and would have to leave as quickly as we had arrived. I could somewhat understand their perspective, I suppose. They had not suffered through the zombie apocalypse like the rest of us had; they'd not fought through hordes to find refuge; they'd not watched loved ones be torn apart, unreachable, unsavable. They'd not had to relive the horror of constantly running, the shaking, spasming limbs that kept us awake for hours afterwards, despite utter exhaustion. That's not to say their existence had been easy thus far, but it had not been quite as intense as the vast majority of those still clinging to this side of life.

"Haven't these people ever heard of hard drives?" BT asked as we moved about the fortieth box stuffed with paperwork and files.

"Jeremy, we need to go," I said. The doc looked harried and afraid. At this exact point in time, I was under the impression he was regretting his decision to leave the facility. No part of me blamed him for that. I was beginning to wonder if they were packing everything in their desire to take as long as possible. With a deadline looming, I was pushing them as hard as I could. As a Marine, it was ingrained in me to hurry up and wait. I would much rather have left the moment Bennington started the timer, then sit and wait at the plane for five hours. In my mind, that was infinitely better than packing out for five hours then making the one-hour drive to get there in the nick of time. The odds everything was going to go off without a hitch were not in our favor. Four hours should be plenty of time—if we left now. At the two-hour mark, I forced their choice.

"We're not ready," he responded, short of breath.

"I get that this stuff is important, but if you put any more in the vans, there's not going to be any room for the rest of us."

I saw it, I swear I saw it in his face. He wanted to fill the van with gear and get his staff to the plane while leaving us to hoof it as best we could. Again, if everyone I loved wasn't in

Washington, I would have wished him luck and pointed him in the general direction. He kept eye contact for another ten seconds, hoping I would yield my position and tell him "fine." He was in for a surprise if he thought that was going to happen. I'd already lost one good person on this fuck-fest of a mission; I would not needlessly endanger anyone else.

"You've got two minutes or I'm taking the van with all your work and leaving. I'm sure the scientists at Etna will be able to reverse engineer it." Then I turned and walked out of the room. "Kirby, Stenzel, keep an eye on the van," I said quietly over my microphone.

"What are we watching out for sir?" Stenzel asked.

"Rogue scientists."

I heard her snort, but when I didn't add anything else, she must have realized I was serious. I found BT on the second floor; he was looking out the window at the city and the ocean beyond.

"You think at some point this will all be over?" he asked.

I didn't have the heart to tell him I didn't think so.

"Feel free to lie," he said when I came up beside him and was looking out, stoically. The ocean was sparkling from the morning sun; the peace and tranquility it offered seemed promising.

"Even with my prompting, you've got nothing to say?"

"Right now, man, I just want to get home. I'm thinking about what I'm going to say to Karen and how I don't want to have to repeat that speech to anyone else."

Uncharacteristically, BT reached out and put a massive arm around my shoulder.

"Nothing you could have done, Talbot. If it wasn't him, it would have been someone else's family you'd be notifying."

I pressed my head against the glass, pondering whether the life I had traded for this one was worth it. BT pulled tight to hug me.

"You at least going to buy me a granola bar?"

"Fuck you, Talbot." He let me go.

"And thank you."

"Any time, man. We're in this together."

We went downstairs and sure as shit, I spotted Doc Jeremy spying the van and the two guards I had posted, he had that look of someone that was wondering if he could get away clean. As I brushed by him, I spoke into his ear, "I would hunt you down to the ends of the earth."

He jumped from being startled. "You don't understand what we're leaving here."

"No, maybe I don't, but I don't think you understand what we sacrificed to get here. Let's go! Everyone get in the van—we're leaving!"

"We're not done!" Jeremy looked panicked.

"I don't care. That plane will leave whether you're on it or not; makes no difference to me. And since we've got all our cards on the table, if you don't get in that van, I'm going to toss all of this research before we get to the airport and say we were attacked and it burned up in a massive fire. Sure, I'm going to be the one that starts the fire, but the end result is the same."

"You can't!" He looked like I told him I was going to make a pile of babies and puppies and douse it with gasoline, he was that flabbergasted. Not sure if that's the right word in this scenario, but it fit at the time.

"I can and I will. Bennington is all hot and heavy to get this weapon; personally, I think it's a massive mistake and should be permanently shelved. We've already witnessed the zombies mutating at an unheard of pace, and now you want to introduce a whole new viral agent. Did you ever stop to wonder if they might incorporate this into their genetic code and use it for their own purposes?"

"That would be impossible." He said the words, but not with complete conviction. He knew something. He also knew if he didn't deliver, he was stuck here. Sure, they were safe, but their supplies were dwindling quickly. It wasn't much of a stretch to think they would fudge some of their trials to make the results more favorable. Wouldn't take much to have Bennington foaming at the mouth. But the commander was smarter than that, *wasn't he?* Surely he would know that by putting out the kind of ultimatum that he had, people would do just about anything to get in his good graces.

"What's the fatality rate?" I asked, trying to catch him off-guard.

He deferred. "It's all in the paperwork."

"Yes, the very impressive stack of paperwork that a camp under duress isn't going to spend an inordinate amount of time studying. I'm asking you, though; what's the fatality rate?"

"Nearly one hundred percent."

He said "nearly" so softly I had to ask him to repeat it.

"Nearly equates to what?"

"A number so small as to be statistically insignificant."

"Listen, Kirby's dick is so small as to be statistically insignificant."

"Hey!" Kirby shouted out, Corporal Rose smacked his shoulder in jest.

"I still want the number." I had moved in closer to the doctor.

"Ninety-nine point four percent."

"Like Ivory soap?" BT asked.

I looked over at him and scowled. He shrugged.

"So, one zombie out of every two hundred or so survives? What happens to the one that makes it?"

Jeremy, all of a sudden, looked like he had itchy skin syndrome, if such a thing exists. He wouldn't even look at me. "It's something we need to work on."

"Winters, ring me up Bennington!" I shouted over the doc's shoulder.

"We're almost out of food!" Jeremy grabbed my arm.

"I strongly suggest not touching me again," I told him as I pulled my arm free.

"Don't mind him," BT told the doc. "He's got a thing about germs."

Within a minute I was once again talking to Bennington.

"Haven't left yet?" was the first thing out of his mouth.

"They're looking for a place to put the sink right now."

"What do you want, Talbot? I've got other things going on and while I generally like talking to you, you're not my priority today."

"Sir, I'm telling you something is wrong here. They're only telling you what you want to hear in regard to this weapon."

"Do you have that little faith in me?"

"No, sir, I don't. I mean, sure I do." Partial lie; I thought it was better to make that one so we could continue the conversation.

"I know more about the weapon than they think I do. We hacked into their computers months ago. I know it has over a ninety-nine percent kill rate; with those kinds of numbers I think we can deal with the ones that fall through the cracks, don't you?"

"Sir, the ones that 'fall through the cracks,' as you say, they're not the same. You can scoff if you want, but what if we are making genius zombies? Ones capable of using tools, of manipulating machinery? Maybe gain access to a nuclear silo?"

"Starting to reach, aren't you?"

"I don't know. Am I?"

"We'll do more testing when they get here. I can't promise, Talbot, because of the pressures this camp is under, but I will do my best to make sure it is as reasonably safe as it can be. That enough?"

I was abundantly aware that Bennington had changed his tactics to dealing with me. Maybe he knew that merely ordering me to do it wouldn't be enough, that I might say *fuck it*, just to spite myself. I was still sitting on the fence with the whole thing, but in the end, none of it mattered. If they'd hacked the computers, they already had all the information they would need. It seemed the question was much more difficult.

"Why are we here, sir?" I asked.

He was silent; he'd seen that I had figured the puzzle out.

"You knew about Dewey; you wanted to see him in action. Wow…that's it. You going to deny it?"

"Would you believe me if I did?"

"I lost one of my men for a mission that didn't need to be performed?"

"We lose people all the time, and yes, it was imperative that you went. We needed to gauge the strength of the survivors. We did not, however, believe them to be so advanced. So, yes. We knew there were side-effects, just not to what degree."

"You fucker!" I raged. "You think you could have maybe given me a heads up before you dropped us into this shithole? Would that have been too much?"

"We didn't strand your team deliberately, Talbot. The mission shouldn't have been so…complicated."

"I'll be back soon, colonel. We'll continue this discussion, and I'm going to…" And that's when I was lifted clean off my feet.

"Hello, sir," BT grunted as he hefted me away. He made a sawing motion across his throat to have Winters cut the feed. "I'd ask you if you lost your mind but that's an established point." BT set me down roughly.

"You heard him, didn't you? He popped us in here knowing full-well what we were in for!" I was pacing, too angry to sit still.

"Maybe not full-well."

"Don't temper my anger, BT."

"Definitely not trying to do that. Just so you know, he's

doing what commanders have been doing since people began fighting people. He was probing the enemy to learn their strength and weaknesses."

"You seem pretty alright with this, considering we're the low men on the totem pole here. Fuck—I'm not even sure we rate being on it! We're more like the part that is buried in the shitty dirt that supports the rest of the pole. I mean, it's something you come to grips with, being expendable, I mean, but you figure that your leader, for the most part, has your best interests at heart, that he would rather see you succeed than fail. That's not the case here! Yeah, we were a tool for Bennington, but he didn't care if we came back broken or…at all, really. Sort of like a cruel benevolence."

"What's that even mean?"

"He comes across as giving a shit when, in reality, he is just giving you shit."

"Mike, think this through. He had to believe we were going to make it, right? Just because he had all the data doesn't mean his people at Etna would be able to work through the notes and processes these guys have done. It would have taken them months, years, even, to get to the same place as these people here. He knows we don't have that kind of time. So yeah, maybe he had an inkling all wasn't right here. So what's he do? He sends the unit with the best chance of success, that can adapt and deal with whatever they find, and still get the job done."

"Fuck you, BT. Stop reasoning for him and stroking my ego at the same time. That's underhanded, even for you."

"Is it working?"

"A little bit…probably a whole lot better if we hadn't lost Halsey."

"Yeah, I'm going to miss the kid too. I know you know this, Mike, but you're going to have to come to terms with the fact that he's not going to be the last one we lose."

"I hate this shit, BT. We should be having barbecues in

your backyard, eating great food, drinking beer…and I'd be telling you about all the Yeti sightings in the general area."

"Yetis? Why yetis? Can't we discuss Australian rules football?"

"Had a weird dream once about them; you were in it. There was a Speedo involved."

"Who had the Speedo on?"

"Not me."

"Why was I playing Australian rules football in a Speedo?"

"Not that crazy thing you call a sport…the dream was about Yetis. It's something I'll never be able to forget. And back to the other thing, the mere fact that they have to distinguish their football by throwing the word 'rules' in there just means it is going to be some seriously skewed version of the way football should be played. They probably have to factor in that they need to avoid deadly animals on the playing surface; that whole country terrifies me. I bet even the puppies there are highly venomous."

"Can we get out of here now? And promise me one thing, Talbot." He stopped my forward progress. "I don't want to hear about the Speedo incident again."

"Was it real?" Not sure why I asked.

"What color was it?"

"Gold. Bright gold like the color of shorts a boxer might wear into the ring or something more up your alley *Rocky* from *Rocky Horror Picture Show*."

"Thanks for the visual. It's possible we had the same dream; it doesn't make much sense though. I was with Linda, and we didn't know each other then. But in the dream, we'd known each other for years. Fuck it…I don't know, and mostly I don't want to."

We were back in the underground garage. Doc Jeremy and his group had piled into one of the two vans.

"Out." The look he gave me was pure panic. "No, I don't mean it like that. I need you to split up the talent here. Two vans. If something happens to one of them, I need to make sure some of your people make it because before you deliver this weapon to the masses, you are going to make sure it's a hundred percent effective or you're going to sabotage it completely so it never sees the light of day. I don't care which, but I need some of you alive to make that happen."

After a few minutes, he had what he thought was a fair distribution of talent and knowledge. I did the same. I took Gary, Winters, Corporal Rose, PFCs Kirby, Grimm, and Springer. BT was in charge of the other van and only took three with him due to the reduced space from all the files. It was a small unit, but considering it was BT, Tommy, Corporal Stenzel and Private Harmon, I figured he'd be fine. We did one final check of the perimeter of the building before rolling up the steel garage door. Not a zombie in sight. I was more than expecting them to start pouring out of doors and around street corners the moment we got on the road; that it didn't happen only began to make my paranoia meter peg out. Now I figured that Dewey knew we had the scientists, and that the best thing he could do would be to allow us to go so that more of his kind could be created. How far out of the realm of possibilities was I? Tough to say. That I'd even thought it lent the notion credence in my mind.

"Sir, getting a relayed message from Etna," Winters started. It was good to know that comm was back up. "We're on live sat; Etna says we should take the next left and lay low at an amusement park there for a few. We've got a horde of speeders about to pass over our path."

"They on an intercept course?" I asked.

"Doesn't appear that way, sir. A herd of deer is being chased."

"Next left, Corporal."

"It's a one way, sir."

"You're kidding, right? We'll be all right. I promise not to deduct any points off your driver's license."

"Good thing, Lieutenant, because I never got one. Failed my first test. Was planning on going back at some point and then this happened."

It was sobering to hear that from her, heartbreaking, really. Not so much the license, but how many things she and future generations would never do. Prom, Friday Night Lights, either playing football or rooting from the stands or even making out under the stands. As I'd gotten older, I thought that as a country, we were getting soft. We coddled our children, attempting to protect them from every possible harm out there. Talk about an exercise in futility. That was something that couldn't possibly be done, and in the end, we were doing them more harm than good. By attempting to shield them from the cruel world, we left them ill-prepared to deal with it. I'm as guilty as the next person of this, but I would never have wanted things to turn out the way they had just to toughen up our youth. Yeah, I fantasized about a zombie apocalypse, but the reality of it...? Well, it just plain blows thick, chunky, chewed-up phlegm balls.

We pulled in to the Victorian Gardens Amusement Park. First thing I saw was the Ferris Wheel. Looked in pretty good shape; as long as the thing didn't light up like a Christmas tree, I'd see if Winters could get it up and running. I convinced myself it would be a good way to survey the city. Then the thought of being trapped on the highly exposed ride changed my mind with a quickness.

"All right, let's set up a perimeter, check out the buildings close by," I said as I exited the vehicle. I headed over to the Ferris wheel and sat in the bottom-most car as we waited for the zombies to run on by. Gary stiffly walked over to join me.

"I've got road rash where no one should have road rash." He was looking at the seat next to me but decided against it.

"Other than that, how are you doing?"

"It's the only thing I can think of, so, I guess by default everything else is fine."

"One way to look at it, I suppose."

I tilted my head back and was looking up into the sky; the car rocked gently back and forth. It's possible I even dozed off. It was a half hour later when Harmon called out to me. I awoke with a start, my rifle at the ready—a learned response I doubt was ever going to be forgotten.

"Sir—you're going to want to see this." She was coming closer, holding a notebook out to me.

I wiped my eyes and took the proffered object. "Winters, anything?"

"Got word the enemy's got the deer surrounded—haven't moved too much farther from where they were.

"Great. See if there's a way around. What is this?"

"I think it's a…sort of like a last will and testament to a couple, I found it over there, it was stuck to a zombie." She pointed to a food stand.

"We talking bars of gold or something?" Not that gold meant all that much, but it was still shiny and fun to look at.

"You might think it's even better, sir."

My interest was piqued. I started reading. What follows is an account of Laura and Marcus's final moments.

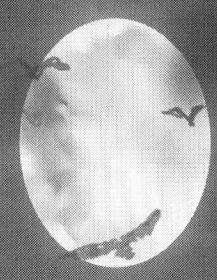

7

LAURA'S STORY

My name is Laura Malvern and this is the story of those first horrible days of when the zombies attacked. Why am I writing this? I honestly don't know. It seems like these last few precious hours I have left to me should be spent praying or, at least, recounting the better times in my life, not these end times that have seen nothing but death and blackness. It's just so much. I want those that come after me to know what we've gone through and I hope there's something better for them. My husband Marcus and I had been married for twelve years–as of three days ago. That was why we came out to Victorian Gardens. Sounded like a corny idea for an anniversary destination, but neither of us wanted to be too far from our home on Long Island. We were, are, I guess–oh please don't be *were* because that would mean they were gone, and I don't think I can handle that. Sorry, let me back up. At the beginning of our marriage, we rescued two English Bulldogs who, at the time, we mistakenly believed were spayed and neutered siblings. It seemed that neither of those things were true.

When that first litter arrived, we had a small apartment in Brooklyn, and with the addition of five new housemates, it quickly got even smaller. This was when we discovered our love for those animals; we did all we could to ensure they found the best homes possible. In the process, we made enough money to put a down payment on a property on Long Island. We learned everything we could about breeding dogs with compassion, to make sure that health and temperament were at the forefront. We attended classes, seminars, talked to AKC people, whatever it took. Finally, I quit my job and dove into the business of making families whole with the addition of a cherished fur-baby. It has been a wondrously fulfilling and satisfying career, but it's come with its fair share of heartache. You see, I wasn't the best person for this job; I became entirely too attached to every puppy that came into our home.

I vetted every person that showed an interest; I sat down personally with them and interviewed every applicant myself. More than once I'd had to turn a person away because I had a suspicious feeling about them or because they didn't answer a question correctly. You have no idea how mad a person can get when you tell them they can't have something, especially when they've traveled across three states to get it. It didn't matter. The money was always going to be secondary to ensuring that each of my puppies found the best home that they could. As our anniversary rolled around, Marcus wanted to get me out of the house. I didn't often leave when we had a fresh litter, but the two pups we had remaining were twelve weeks old, and my niece, Danielle, said she would watch over them—something she absolutely loved to do. Now I carry the pain of having to worry about what has happened to all of them.

I love Marcus more than any other person I have ever known, but of all the people you'd say were ready for some apocalyptic event, you could not travel any farther down the spectrum of unprepared than him. Oh, I guess that's not fair. Maybe some infirm people in the hospital might be worse off, but other than that...yeah. Like, we had this horrible ice storm a few winters back, trees cracked and broke taking down power lines all over our community. I thought Marcus was going to lose his mind–not because we were without power and the cold was beginning to seep into the house–but rather because all of the Dunkin' Donuts were closed! He drove around half the state for the better part of eight hours looking for a coffee shop, bless his heart. The extent of my husband's talent for surviving the apocalypse was to look for open restaurants! And now he's gone. In the end, he died for me, and what better way of expressing one's love is there than that?

I wish we had stayed home, but I blame the show *Carnival Eats* for forcing our hand. I mean, who doesn't want to try a deep fat fried cinnamon roll? Or even better yet, a tempura-covered cheeseburger? The danger of watching food shows in the middle of the night typically only involves gaining a few unnecessary pounds, it doesn't usually mean the untimely death of your spouse. But at least I will be close on his heels. Hadn't made it a quarter of the way down the midway on our quest for the mythical Fireball Deluxe Chili Weiner when I was stopped in my tracks by a fried red velvet funnel cake, replete with cream cheese frosting. Who could look away from that? I told Marcus our treadmill was going to get an extra work-out when we got home. He asked what I was going to do with all the clean laundry already hanging on it!

"Let me at least pretend," I told him.

"We gonna split that?" His mouth was watering as he looked upon the frosted slice of heaven the vendor was handing over.

"I'm sure they have more," I told him greedily. I shouldered him out of the way as he dipped a finger into the gooey goodness.

"Ooh, that's good." He licked his finger. "Another, please!" he ordered up at the truck.

"You still planning on riding some things?" I asked him.

"Of course." His muffled answer came around a mouthful of cake.

"You know what fried foods do to your stomach–especially if you're going to go and tilt-a-whirl it all around."

"I'll be fine." He pulled out a bottle of antacid.

"Look at you, thinking ahead!"

"Sick of looking inside trash barrels while I pay for my stupidity."

"There's hope for you yet," I told him.

"Oh, oh," he said as he threw his used plate away.

"What?! You haven't even ridden anything yet."

He was pointing to a small, red-awninged food booth. I read the sign. "Crazy Larry's World-Famous Tempura Cheeseburgers." I was full from the funnel cake, but what is a carnival for if not over-indulgence in every sense of the word? Come on, they fry Twinkies, for Heaven's sake! I'm embarrassed to say it, but I moaned more during the eating of that cheeseburger than…forget it. Even at the end, I will hold on to my modesty.

After the exquisite experience of food porn we had just consumed, we stood, thinking that maybe getting off the midway would be the right thing to do. The fried Snickers kept calling my name, but through the layer of grease I was coating it with, my stomach thought it might be for the best if we took a break. And I knew Marcus was in even rougher shape as he munched down on three antacids quicker than he had eaten his French fries. I was pretty surprised when, ten minutes later, we found ourselves in line for the Octopus. Not sure if you're familiar with this one? It has eight arms, and at the end of each arm is a car that seats up to three people. The ride spins in a circle while each arm rises and falls, and at the same time, your car itself spins. It would be an exhilarating few minutes, but afterwards, I was thinking our visit would likely be cut short as Marcus raced for the bathrooms. That would still give me plenty of time to grab some of the food we hadn't had a chance to try yet and bring it home. It's never as good as when it's hot and fresh, but we'd make do. And screw the laundry covered treadmill! Anyway, the belt was probably frozen from disuse.

"Are you sure about this?" I asked as we inched closer. He was holding his stomach and quietly belching off to the side.

"Oh yeah, I'm good. Can't come to the carnival and not ride something."

We could, I thought, but I kept it to myself. The carnie had no sooner shut the small door to our car when we heard screams from further down the boardwalk. At the time, I thought nothing of it. I figured it was from some overly frightened riders on the slingshot. I don't care how much greased food Marcus got for me, he was never going to butter me up enough to ride that thing! Heard it felt like being launched into space without a seatbelt or a viable means to ensure a safe landing. No thank you.

As the ride started, there was this intense feeling of acceleration and then the dizzying effects of the cart spinning randomly on an ever-changing axis. Add to that the near nauseating effect of rising and falling. For the first minute and a half, I was having a great time, but as we neared the two-minute mark and presumably the end of the ride, I was more than ready to call it quits. I'm sure I could have gone another five without too many problems; Marcus was a whole other matter. He was fumbling with the antacid bottle even as he struggled against the forces applied by the moving machinery. We were hitting the three-minute mark and the ride wasn't slowing down. The carnie in charge was looking off the way the screams had come. It was looking more and more like something serious may have happened. Maybe a ride failed and someone was tossed off. My mood was souring as rapidly as my husband's stomach.

"Get us off of here!" I yelled, though my voice was pulled away by the rushing wind and the yells and hollers of the riders on the other arms. The carnie had one arm on the lever that would end the forced vertigo, but his attention was completely on the broad avenue that led straight to the rides. I tried my best to see what he was watching, but the spin of the ride made concentrating on any one point a near impossibility. As far as I could tell, it was just a bunch of people heading this way, fairly quickly. Then I had a new set of worries; maybe people were running our way because some idiot with a gun and an agenda had opened fire, destroying multiple lives of those that just wanted to enjoy an uncannily warm day in December.

People were in full-on retreat mode, and still the fucking carnie would not stop the ride. Marcus had long ago evacuated the wondrous food we had so recently eaten, though I'm sure he would have told you it wasn't so good the second time around. He had the good graces to semi-stand up and send the bile out the back of the cart, although the cries of protest from behind us let me know that his act of kindness for me did not go unpunished for some other poor person. And still, the damned carnie did not shut the ride down! Even as people streamed past screaming, he stood there, rigid and simultaneously slack-jawed. I'm not normally so judgmental, but this was an extreme circumstance. I truly think the man was too dense to do more than he already was, as if to process what was happening *and* shut off the damn ride was just too much for him to handle. He stood there. Even as what came running after the fleeing people came, his hand still held the control arm as the first of the zombies bit into him.

All he had to do was fall over backward and we would have mercifully been able to come to a controlled stop. Maybe we could have got out of there before the rest of the horde caught up. Maybe. But no. Calvin the Confused Carnie fell over to the front with three zombies tearing pieces of him away. Instead of stopping, we kept spinning and dipping, as fast as the ride had been designed for…and certainly given its age, much faster than was safe.

"What is going on?" Marcus was green as he burped his question out. I'd always thought it was just an expression, but he really did look the color of split-pea soup. And I've never really liked split-pea soup. At the time, I didn't have any idea of what was going on. All I knew was that people were running from other people. I thought maybe it was a demonstration turned violent, then when I watched some taking bites of others, I thought it might be that weird drug that so many people in Florida seemed to enjoy. I think they called it flakka? Really, though, I don't understand the appeal of taking something that makes you look like a zombie and makes you want to eat people. So that's what I thought. It was a drug-induced craze making people appear to be zombies. I never thought for a second they were actual zombies. It didn't matter much, though. I just knew that Marcus and myself were in danger, but surely the authorities would be coming soon and take care of this mess. I mean, that's what they're supposed to do, right? We just needed to wait–to ride this out, literally. I don't seem to recall ever hearing of anyone dying from staying on a ride too long.

The druggies were everywhere, dragging people down, ripping their faces off, tearing chunks of flesh free with nothing more than their mouths, puddles of blood quickly became pools–and heading straight to a lake's worth. I don't watch horror movies for a reason but right now I was living one and no matter how hard I tried I could not change the channel. Marcus was on his third or fourth sick up, the poor man he kept splashing had passed out either from the shock of what was happening or the disgust of having to marinate in my husband's stomach bile. Either way there was a jealous part of me that wished I could join him–not in being covered in throw up–just the passed-out part. If I didn't have to infect one more memory with what I was witnessing I could live happily ever after. I hope.

"What's going on?" Marcus asked. I think he was too lost in his misery to really register the awfulness happening around us. Or he was looking through the world with those rose-colored glasses he donned so often. Little did either of us know how much he was going to wish he had those spectacles on and real soon.

"Help is coming!" I could hear the wail of sirens over the cries of pain, anguish, and fright all around us. Usually I would not feel comfort in the explosive sound of shots being fired, but in this case, the lunatics needed to be stopped at all costs. There can be no rehabilitation once you start dining on other humans, that must tear right through that delicate webbing within our minds, making them forever broken. The many shots were coming closer, but they were being drowned out by helicopters now. At first, it was the news choppers eager to soak in the blood of the story and feed it to those watching at home. Then it looked like geese were flying south for the winter as planes both big and fancy private ones were streaming past. What did they know, I wonder? Then finally the heavy percussion of military helicopters thundered across the sky overhead.

They were showering a torrential pouring of bullets into the crowds of drug users. What was scary was when I realized they weren't even trying to discriminate between victim and perpetrator. The wholesale slaughter was on. I couldn't imagine what had happened so quickly that even the local authorities could not contain it and the military had to be called in to deal with it in such a brutal manner. As sickened as I was by what the military were doing, I was bereft when they departed.

"What about us?" I screamed as that infernal ride kept twirling around. That was when I realized that even the police sirens and their firearms had been silenced or moved away.

Had they been overrun? Or was it somehow incredibly worse elsewhere?

"They're coming!" someone on the car ahead of us shouted out, her hand was pointing but we were twirling so I don't know from what direction help was arriving. It turned out not to matter. It would have been difficult to miss the mass of them, hundreds, maybe thousands. Even in my over-twirled mind, I knew then this wasn't some drug frenzy. There were women and children interspersed with the men in equal numbers, blue collar, white collar, every race that I could tell. With the government's rapid response, all I could figure was something had leaked from a facility somewhere. I'd read enough Stephen King to know something like that was possible. Now my fear was what if Marcus thought I looked tasty? Then I was even more afraid it would be the other way around, or both, as soon as the poisonous gas made it to us.

"Please don't eat me," I begged my husband.

"If we ever get off this thing, I don't think I'll ever eat again." Impossibly, he let go of more.

We'd been on the ride for twenty minutes with no end in sight. I now knew no help was coming. How long could one ride a ride before medical issues arose? I figured it was far more likely that some of the bolts and connectors would give way long before that became a concern. I was going through the odds of surviving our car coming unhinged, flinging us off into the boardwalk like a leftover pizza crust. The fiberglass housing around us would not afford much protection upon impact. Would we be incapacitated as those fiends began to eat us? It would be better to land skull first and end it quickly than to be just another tasty snack at the park.

"We need to get off of this thing!" Marcus was trying to lift the safety bar from our laps.

"Are you insane!" I snapped. As much as I wanted to get off, I didn't think my soft, middle-aged body was going to take the subsequent flight and crash landing all that well.

"We can't stay here!" he bemoaned.

"Don't let your stomach do the talking." I didn't want to be mean, I was just so frightened I couldn't even think clearly, much less civilly.

"It's not only the acid stirring up my ulcers, Laura. Look at the crazies pressing up against the safety fence."

And I did. There were so many of them the metal brace poles were pushed to an unnatural forty-five-degree angle.

"Once they get through there we'll be in even more trouble."

All of a sudden this seemed like exactly the place where I wanted to be. "They…they can't get us here," I told him triumphantly.

"Are you kidding me? This ride dips to three feet off the ground! Every time we go around, we'll be ripe for the picking."

"Marcus, you know I hate when you're right!" I screamed.

"If we time it right, we can shoot for a landing on the exit platform. They're not up there yet and we won't fall as far. Gonna be tough, though…I'm thinking we're moving at around thirty miles an hour."

Just then there was a sharp, pierced scream from the couple directly across from us. The drug-fueled crazies had broken through and their car missed the oncoming rush by inches. Then, as if it couldn't get worse, it did. We were thrown rib-bruisingly hard into the safety bar just as another one of the cars sent a person flying into the air. His broken body landed some twenty feet away right on a fence that protected the Zipper. I had to keep adjusting my field of vision to watch him as he fell off the fence and somehow miraculously kept moving, albeit at a crawl this time.

"PCP? Is that what they're all on?" My mind was tenuously holding on to a reality I wished I could justify.

Another impact! My world turned black as the back of my head slammed hard into the all-too-thin cushion behind me, then I snapped back to the light. The hits kept coming as the cars dipped down into the pooling mass of fucked-up humanity, like a giant bobbing for apples we were sending them hurtling away. I had a fleeting moment where I thought this might be the solution we needed; maybe we were the squeegee to the bug-gutted windshield of the world, wiping these pests free from our area. The twenty-five-year-old ride had other thoughts. The car that had made the first hit had begun to splinter, the younger couple on board was nearly wrapped around the bar in the grimmest of hopes that this would somehow save them.

The cotter pin, or whatever was holding them in place, finally sheered in half and the car went spinning wildly off into the air! Their screams were somehow louder than the cacophony around us. The car itself shattered into thousands of fiercely glittering neon green pieces. The woman was still alive as she had landed on the man she was with. The grotesque bulging of his neck was the only evidence I needed to know that he would never stir again.

"Help me…." The woman had lifted her head; she couldn't have said those words louder than a whisper but I heard her as clearly as if she had said them directly into my ear. She said it again, this time louder.

"Shut up!" I yelled, not because I didn't want to look at her and think that this could possibly be my fate…okay, so maybe it was a little bit of that, but it was more because the crazies hadn't noticed her yet. If she just shut up there was a chance she could make it.

"Help us!" she screamed as she finally got enough wits about her to look at the man she had landed on. She was slowly moving, attempting to put as much distance from him as possible.

"He's dead! He needs help!"

"Be quiet!" I warned her. She paid me no heed.

"I can't feel my legs! Help me!" She was pulling herself

arm over arm away from the crash site. It was too late. I watched from my spinning perch as three crazies, all female, moved to intercept her slow retreat. One of the them got down on hands and knees and began to crawl after the injured woman–almost in a mocking gesture. Another had stepped on the woman's legs, halting her progress, while the third just fell over like she had tripped. Her face smacked off the back of the woman's head, driving the poor thing into the ground, teeth-first. There was muffled sobbing that was quickly replaced by the high-pitched keening of someone getting eaten alive.

"My God! What is happening?!" It could have been Marcus that shouted that, though I feel like I might have as well. We didn't have time to view the macabre event, as the attackers shook pieces of meat from their victim, but it is singularly an event that will never leave me, although, right now it doesn't look like it's going to be that much longer. That might be for the best.

The ride was still smacking into people, and Marcus and I were covered in the gore of those we'd crushed. Miraculously, our car was holding together reasonably well. The same could not be said for the one behind us. It was still attached, but only the metal frame remained and the things were able to reach in as the car dipped low. It was worse than flying away. Hair was caught and ripped out, their clothes were becoming tattered, they were scraped up and scratched from head to toe. The man had checked out long ago, but the black, warrior woman he was with kept fighting savagely against the tide of ferocious zombies, shaking off each blow she suffered. I thought, *if we make it off of here, I am going to make sure we follow her.*

The woman had been standing, making sure her punches and swinging elbows caused as much damage as possible to the crazies. As her car once again dipped down and struck another pile of the zombies, she was sent soaring. For the merest of moments, she did indeed look like a superhero as she flew. Her ending was quick and savage. The ride was falling apart more and more with each revolution. The center housing sounded like rocks in a dryer, and we were starting to wobble violently from the uneven weight distribution on the arms. We were striking the ground hard now with each low swoop. There were three cars left, all in various states of disrepair. The screaming, for the most part, had stopped. What was the point? Nobody was coming to help. Resignation was reigning supreme, all except for Marcus.

"We're going to make it, Laura," he assured me. I wanted to believe him–I needed to believe him. The grinding sound grew louder and our warble more pronounced. The only decent thing about the ride breaking was that we were slowing down. The center column began to smoke; a thick, black discharge escaped from it. The toxic smell of burning rubber and plastic pervaded, even over the stench of blood and vomit. Licks of fire began to escape the housing and climb up the center. Of the three cars still intact, we were left with the most advantageous position, our arm was as high as it could go. The second was just at outstretched arms' reach, and the third, well, they were dragged free from the wreckage and inhumanely butchered piece by piece. The fire was burning intensely now, to the point where we could begin to feel the heat.

"Any ideas?" the scared man in the car further behind us asked. I turned; he was with a teenage girl and a boy a few years younger, I assumed they were his children. Both were hiding under his arms as he hugged them tightly.

"Live." Marcus moved the lap bar and stood on shaky legs.

I wanted to yell at my husband for saying that so flippantly, it was like telling a starving person to just eat. It wasn't like they were deliberately foregoing food. Then I realized he didn't mean it in a dismissive way; he was being serious, like he was actively thinking about how to get us out of this situation. The flames had consumed the entire middle structure. All things considered, I would rather go by smoke inhalation, but the prevailing breeze was not going to allow that to happen. Now the choice appeared to be roasting alive or being eaten alive. I would think those two scenarios warred for top position on nearly every human's worst way to go list.

"What are you doing?" I asked him, grabbing on to the waistline of his pants.

"I don't see any of them in the water. If we make it to the ocean..." He trailed off.

"Gotta be three hundred yards from here." The man below us was looking now.

"Marcus," my husband said.

"Rollie. This is my niece, Denise, and my son, Derek." Neither of the kids moved when he said their names.

"I don't see any other way. We can run from booth to booth, hiding in or behind them until we get to the water."

"It's December, Marcus. I know it's unseasonably warm out here, but that water is going to be frigid," I said.

"Hypothermia is the least of our problems," he answered.

I liked this "take charge" version of my husband; it was not what I was expecting after the way he'd acted during the blizzard. He'd seemed so out of his element just with the loss of coffee. Maybe there was some hope. Smoke was billowing from our ride. As it drifted away it joined with other large plumes from things burning all along the boardwalk and further into the city, creating an abnormally thick and caustic fog. Whatever had happened was widespread and sudden. There were still guns firing and explosions from what we figured was military ordnance, but it was all far away and moving farther.

"We still have the problem of getting out of here," Rollie said.

Denise squealed as multiple hands slapped up against the bottom of their car.

"Can't we wait them out?" I asked just as the car suddenly dipped a few inches.

"The only thing holding us up in the air is a rubber hose filled with hydraulic fluid. The moment that burns up…" Marcus didn't finish the sentence; he didn't need to.

"They're moving away from the fire!" Rollie shouted excitedly. It was true, a few of the zombies had caught fire and were attempting to get away from themselves, lighting the others as they did so.

"This might work," I said in hushed tones to Marcus. He had a firm set to his jaw. "What's the matter?"

"We're sinking," he replied. He was right. I was watching as Rollie's car slowly dipped down. The hands that were once having a hard time scraping against the bottom were now reaching in and trying to tear at anything they could get ahold of. A ribbon of fire ejected from the side of the center column. Didn't need Marcus to tell me that was the last of the hydraulics causing that. It was true the zombies were leaving our immediate area and quickly, but was it going to be quick enough?

"Denise, Derek, we have to make a run for it!" Rollie shouted, trying to get the kids up and ready. Derek looked around wildly, but Denise was having none of it. Pulling away from him, she tried her best to hide in the footrest portion of the car. He was straining as he pulled up on her hoodie.

"Leave me alone!" she wailed.

"I can't leave you here!"

"No!" She was like a wild cat about to be dipped into a flea bath, she was all teeth and fingernails. She clawed at him wildly, drawing blood from the side of his face as she dug deep.

"Dad!" Derek screamed, he was very much in danger of being dragged out. Rollie turned away from his niece and to the zombie tearing at his son's clothes. He kicked and punched at anything and everything that came within range. Once he'd created a small opening, he picked up his son and placed him on his shoulders.

"Hold on tight!" he needlessly told the boy. "Denise, we're running for it. It's now or never." He reached down and grabbed a fistful of her hair; her eyes had a feral quality to them as she reluctantly stood. "Run or die," he told her just as the car touched down on the ground. He stepped out.

"Don't leave me here!" she begged.

"Run!" I screamed at her. She looked over, that seemed to snap her free from whatever leg-lock she had. She got out. The trio was running, moving around pockets of the undead, barely avoiding their outstretched arms. Between the fire and the zombies being drawn to the moving meal, we had a relatively open avenue of escape.

"You ready?" Marcus asked me.

I looked at the zombies, the fleeing family, and then back to him. I didn't know what to say. I wasn't out of shape, exactly. I didn't use the courtesy electric cars at the shopping centers, but really, when was the last time I had run? Truly run for my life? The answer was easy, it was *never*. I was athletic in high school, ran track, and then in college I had stayed active, but then I'd met and fallen in love with Marcus. We got married and pursued our careers and then when life offered me the opportunity to breed dogs I'd gladly jumped at the idea. The puppies had always kept me on my toes, and there were more than a few times where I'd had to make a dash for them to prevent them from going somewhere or chewing something they weren't supposed to. But a full-on sprint for who knows how long? Was I up for it?

I gave him a "Yes," but it was weak and did not carry much confidence behind it. We had two zombies immediately in our way, after that we had a decent path as they ambled along.

"We're heading for the Pigs in a Blanket booth first. We'll catch our breath there and figure out our next move."

I wanted to bless Marcus's heart. The booth was a hundred yards away; he could run that in his sleep and not be affected. He played racquetball with his buddies, two, sometimes three times a week; he was in better shape now than when I had met him. I smiled; Marcus had been a gamer back then who rarely left his apartment except for work, but that had all changed. Suffice it to say, this stop for *us* to catch our wind was really for *me*.

I gave him a quick kiss. "Just in case I can't later."

"Don't even think it. We have puppies we need to get back to."

We didn't wait for the car to hit the ground. We jumped when we were a foot away. Marcus stiff-armed the closest zombies and dipped low to shoulder the next one and then we were running. I don't remember moving that much; I was terrified and Marcus was half dragging me. By the time we made it to the booth, I was sucking for air and my stomach wanted to heave up everything I had ever eaten in my entire life.

"How are you doing?" Marcus wasn't looking at me, but rather around the corner to where we were headed next. I couldn't catch my breath enough to answer. He turned to look. "Listen, Laura-Loo," he used his pet name for me. "We have a couple more sprints ahead of us. Going to need you to dig deep. The next one is just a little bit longer than this, okay?"

I nodded but I was ill just thinking on it. "Couple secs." I held up my hand.

"Nope…now." Then he was dragging me. A hand slapped by my face and smacked into the booth. I looked over my shoulder to see a bevy of zombies take up right where we had been. We were halfway to the Southern Fried Steak booth when I felt my hamstring seize up. I'd run enough laps around a track to know what was coming next.

"Cha…charley horse!" I was hopping on my good leg.

"Gotta keep going!" Marcus said and I had to. The zombies nearby had seen our less than stellar escape attempt and were now moving toward us with intent. Marcus had slowed as much as he dared and I thanked him for that. If we made it out of this, I was going to finally go with him when he invited me to play at the club. He always asked; I always politely declined, citing too much to do at home. Not anymore.

"Catch your breath quick, Loo, we don't have a bunch of time. One last push! We're heading that way." He pointed to the beach and the surf beyond.

"I...I can't." I was disgusted with myself before my words could even fill his ears.

"Don't give me that crap! I'm not going home to take care of all those dogs by myself. You've got five seconds, then we go."

He gave me the deadline, but had no sooner said it when he was once again yanking on my hand. I was flat out crying halfway across the beach, my left leg had locked up, and I was afraid to bend it, worried that the muscle would contract and pull it into a shape I would not be able to unravel from.

"I hate you right now!" Half of that was for the leg betraying me and the other half for my husband dragging me hurriedly along like old luggage through an airport terminal as he fought to make a flight.

"Better hold on to that thought...wait until I bring you into the water," he replied.

The zombies weren't hot on our heels, but they were close. Stopping wasn't an option.

"These are brand new shoes!" I protested as Marcus was the first in.

"We'll get you another pair! Come on!" I ripped my hand free; he'd gone another couple of steps before turning to look at me. "Laura?" He had a bewildered look on his face as I shook my head.

"This can't be happening," I said once or fifty times–hard to tell when you feel like you might be losing your mind. Marcus splashed through the few inches of water he was in and reached out to grab me; I quickly pulled my arm away and backed up.

"Laura, forget the shoes."

"It's not about the shoes!" I screamed. He came onto the shore and tenderly placed his arm around my shoulders. "We just watched people get eaten, Marcus."

"I know, I know." We were looking out over the water, I felt him shift so he could peer behind us. "It's a terrible thing and I'm going to have nightmares about it for maybe the rest of my life, but I'd like that to be another forty or fifty years." He did not force me into the water, but I could feel an involuntary squeeze on my arm as he saw what was coming. When he realized I was taking much too long, he hit me with the hardest and lowest blow he could. "If we stay here, who is going to take care of the dogs?"

"I should have married Jerry Brockenstein."

"What? That guy who owned the bakery over on Seventh? He died four years ago."

"Exactly," I answered as we walked into the surf. The icy water entered my new shoes like they were leather daiquiri glasses. I had not been expecting it to be quite so bracing.

"Gotta go further." He was still looking over his shoulder.

"How close are they?" I was wincing as the water clawed up my calves.

"Just keep concentrating on moving forward."

"Deeper? Really?" I was genuinely mad at myself for sounding so pathetic. The water had soaked through the material around my legs, making it cling like original Saran Wrap–not that stuff they have now that barely even sticks to itself. "Oh, sure, it was difficult to use," I said aloud through chattering teeth. "I mean, it practically stuck to air! It was n... nearly impossible to s...seal a container! By the time you ripped it off the roll and br…brought it to the bowl, it was already hope…hopelessly bound to itself!"

"Keep moving!" Marcus shouted.

"B…but that's no longer the case! N…now you gotta…I find myself using rubber b…bands to hold it in place! I'm not even…sure why I even continue to buy the product! It's almost like…as if I can't believe how b…bad it is and I'm stuck! I'm stuck, Marcus! I can't move past my old memory of it…of how good it used to be! Maybe…maybe this is why some of my friends stay with their asshole husbands. They remember the…the man he used to be and not the one that fucked his b…bitch secretary."

I just kept chattering on, thinking about anything except the stabbing cold of the arctic daggers. Thankfully, the bottom half of my legs were numb, though that didn't help my privates as they journeyed into the icy hell. When I looked to Marcus, his lips were that pretty blue color of my favorite popsicles.

"You all right?" he asked.

"This is where not playing racquetball works to my advantage," I told him. He looked confused. "Extra layer of fat." I laughed shakily, though I was feeling anything but mirthful. It did get a smile out of him, which made it worthwhile. "They still following us?"

He nodded, I think afraid to speak for fear that his shivering might travel up to a chattering of his teeth and he would start to break them from the force of the toothy collisions.

"How much d…deeper?"

"I…I think chest level should do it. They're…they're losing their footing. Doesn't look like they have much in the way of co…coordination. Won't…won't be able to swim." He had to gulp to get those last words out.

"Thank you," I told him. I took his face in my hand and turned it so he was looking at me.

"For what?"

"For getting me out of there. I don't think I could have done it on my own." Now it was my turn to help. He looked way more miserable than I had ever seen him, except for maybe two years ago when he caught the flu. You would have thought it was the Ebola virus by the way he was carrying on. We got through that, we'd get through this. "Come on." Now it was me grabbing his arm and yanking him along. Marcus was right; once the zombies began to float, they were at the mercy of the current. It wasn't a rip-tide, unfortunately; they weren't quickly whipped out into deep water to bob around like discarded pop bottles, but they were moving away from us, and that was just fine with me. We were walking parallel to the beach; zombies kept pouring into the ocean as we walked. They were not learning the lesson that we could not be caught this way. The downside was that we would not be able to stay in the water for all that much longer. Soon we would need to leave its chilly but safe embrace. Marcus was beginning to walk with a wooden gait.

"Muscles aren't…working right." His face was beginning to take on the same hue as his lips.

"There's a pier up ahead. Maybe we can lose them there." He trudged after me. Now I was frightened, but not for me anymore. Marcus was slowing down and while the pier was a good idea, even from here, I could see those things shuffling along up top. It would not be an escape route we could use. We made it underneath, the waves lapped lazily up against the wooden supports we hid behind, but each one crept up a little higher on our bodies as the tide rolled in. We were effectively protected from the zombies, but as of yet had no clear way to escape the sea.

"You remember that ta..time I met your parents?" Marcus had his eyes closed and was leaning his head back against a column.

"How could I not? I knew right there that I was going to marry you."

"What?" He pulled his head up and was looking at me.

"They hated you so much I knew it was the best way to get back at them."

"That's a strange way to fall in love with someone," he replied.

"I think my father disliked you so much because you were so much like him."

"I really didn't think this day could get much weirder. So, to be clear, you married me because I reminded you of your father?"

"Only in the best way. My dad was a good, loving father and husband. Worked hard his entire life to provide for us all. Why wouldn't I want all of that in my man?"

Even as cold as he was, Marcus's chest puffed out in pride. "Did you know he offered me three grand to never see you again?"

"What?" My eyes grew wide. "You never said anything." I wanted to shout, but was cautious of any eavesdroppers.

"I was holding out for four grand. We got as high as thirty-five hundred before you came out to see what was taking so long on the grill."

"I remember…you looked so angry."

"I was so close! I was going to buy Jimmy DiCarlo's Mustang if I got that money. Of course, I was mad."

"I saved you, then. If you remember correctly, his engine blew two months later; turned out the transmission was also filled with sawdust to keep it from slipping on test drives."

"Right, right." His teeth were chattering hard now. I hugged him tightly, not sure if it helped; all it did was press our wet clothing against our skin.

"We're going to get out of here." I moved some of the wet hair from his face. "You believe me?" I asked when he didn't reply.

"I wish I had that car right now. I'd drive us out of here. Or at least turn the heat on."

"It's going to be dark soon."

"Bet…better be soon," he struggled to get out.

We kept moving from column to column to keep up with the water; that meant the shore continually moved away from us as if it wanted to keep us trapped. We could hear them above us, walking around, not doing anything. Occasionally one would fall over the railing and into the water; more than once we had been spotted, but the sea was a friend to no one.

"Good thing they can't yell," Marcus said as we watched an old man in fishing gear go bobbing along much like his tackle.

"What do you think?" I asked just as it became difficult to see.

"I think I feel like my legs have completely frozen and I'm going to look like the human equivalent of a popsicle with the stick shoved up my…"

"Marcus."

"Fine, I'll be fine."

We moved slowly. I'd hoped for relief from the frigid waters, but now that we were finally climbing out, we were now exposed to a strong salty breeze and dipping nighttime temperatures.

"Ah…." Marcus placed a hand in front of his mouth as he fell in the shallows, his muscles had contracted to the point where he could not stand. I could see shadowy figures on the beach, but as of yet, none were looking our way. The city was mostly dark, though there were a few spots still lit up, and even more was on fire. Sirens had long ago stopped as had most of the gunfire. Helicopters flew overhead at regular intervals; I imagined they were still evacuating those lucky few that happened to have the ways and means.

"Where is the military?" I asked, helping Marcus to unfurl his muscles.

"Question for another day. We need to find some shelter, get warm and dry." He stood on wobbly legs.

"I think the beach ahead is open; can you do it?" I asked.

"If I can't, will you go on without me?"

"Not a chance," I told him.

"Then yes, I can."

The zombies moved with a shuffling gait that looked painful and awkward but they were still making better time than us. Marcus was trying his best, God love him, but he was dragging his left leg, leaving a runnel in the sand. We hadn't been noticed, but they were all over the place, just moving along. It was difficult to discern what they were up to, if anything. Maybe they were just trying to go on with a semblance of their past life, or hoping to eventually run into some food. We were halfway up the beach when a little boy no older than six spotted us. I'd been looking at adult height, never expecting, or more likely hoping that children hadn't been sucked down into this nightmare as well. I had put my knee into the back of his head; sent him sprawling face first into the sand. Instead of crying and running to his mother, he pushed up and got back up on his feet.

What was ominous was how silent he was doing it all. I thought at first, he had a knife in his outstretched hand, but it turned out to be a plastic shovel. He hissed and advanced. I looked in horror at that little mouth filled with gritty sand and the murderous intent in his eyes. The hunger that compelled him forward. Marcus was missing the entire scene, too locked up in his misery as he desperately tried to get his shivering muscles to fire right.

"We've been seen."

"Shit." He looked over at his shoulder at the young child who was gaining on us. He turned to face the threat and fell over his own feet when his left leg would not pivot and he got them tangled.

It seemed absurd that we should be in danger of death by a six-year-old, but that was exactly what was going on. We didn't know it then, but just one bite would have been the end.

Marcus was kicking out with his right leg, missing most times, but connecting on more than one occasion. The boy would fall back into the sand noiselessly, get back up, and resume the deadly dance. I was caught in indecision for a moment, whether to help my husband to stand, or to drag the boy further away. Marcus kicked out with his left leg, it was a weak thrust and the boy was able to wrap his arms around his calf. His mouth immediately bit down onto the top of Marcus's sneaker.

"Ow, you little shit!" Marcus kicked out with his right leg and connected hard, sending the boy angrily spinning away. But it was too late; he'd been heard. It was dark, but not so dark we couldn't see the nearby zombies beginning to converge.

"You alright?" I asked as I helped him up as best I could.

"He bit me."

"Did he break the skin?" Whenever a bite broke skin it was cause for concern; I didn't know at the time just how much.

"Maybe." He was bending over to look.

"We have to go." I pulled on his arm.

"Laura, I'm hurting, here."

"I know, but we don't have time to think about it." We had twenty feet on the closest of them—except for the tenacious boy who would not quit. He was back up and raring to go. "Didn't your mama feed you?" I pushed on his shoulder, snatching my hand back just as he turned to bite where my fingers had been.

By the time we made it off the sand, Marcus was walking with a more natural gait, though he had a slight limp from where the boy had bit. There was a hotel up the street; the lights were on but they had not attracted the type of company we wanted to keep. Every once in a while we could see and hear muzzle flashes and bullets coming from broken-out windows higher up. All in all, it was a place we wanted to avoid. The only good thing about it was that the light and sound were bringing in all the zombies from the area. The bad thing was we needed to cross the street but there was a slow parade going by. Where we were, we were mostly hidden in the embankment; it offered shelter from those looking for a meal, but not from the elements. The wind had picked up and the temperature was dropping. If I remember correctly, that morning my weather app had called for a fifty percent chance of rain, but given the current set of circumstances, it was most likely up to eighty or ninety percent by now. As if cued by my sour thoughts, I felt a large drop hit me square on the forehead.

"I wonder if we should have just stayed in tonight," Marcus said. I looked over to him; he was smiling.

"This is somehow funny to you?"

"Absurd, actually." He kept on smiling, but then hid his face as he stifled a sneeze. My eyes grew wide. A group of teenagers were walking by; I was watching to see if any of them would react to the noise. I liked it so much better when they had their noses tattooed to their cell phones and only acted like zombies.

"Look who's back." He was pointing behind us.

"Shhh." I motioned with my hand, all of my attention on the group. When the immediate danger passed, I turned to look. "Wow, you must really taste good."

"It's the Nikes." He held up his trainer; the front looked darker than the rest.

"Street's clear enough. Let's go."

"We trying for the car?" he asked.

"Maybe tomorrow. Tonight, we just need to get inside somewhere."

"You think the dogs are all right?"

"As long as Danielle doesn't open the door, nothing is getting to them through the fence in the backyard. I'm glad you convinced me to spend the money for the extra security."

"Bulldogs, Laura. Can't be too careful. You know how many people would try to steal them?"

"Personally, I think you watch too many crime shows."

Marcus *pahed* me as we moved as quickly as we could across. "A guy on 28th killed a man for thirty bucks and his shoes; what do you think he would have done for a bulldog?"

"We already have the fence. You don't have to keep arguing the point."

"I just hope they're safe," Marcus said.

"Me too, honey." Once across, there was a large apartment building. We checked it out for a long time and didn't see any movement. "Got an idea," I said as we began to move again. We circled to the far side of the building and went down a short flight of concrete stairs. "Thank you, God," I said as I twisted the unlocked knob to the apartment building's laundry room.

"I knew I married you for a reason," Marcus said, peeling off his clothes as we walked in, not even bothering to check our surroundings. "Brilliant," he muttered.

"What are you doing?" I wanted to punch him.

"We're in a laundry room...I'm gonna get some clothes. What do you think I'm doing?"

"Oh right." I hadn't even meant it to be that fortuitous, but I'd take the credit.

"This is heavenly!" Marcus tossed me a towel that was still warm from the dryer. Fifteen minutes later we had found enough clothes to wear to keep an orphanage warm through the upcoming winter. The only thing we couldn't change out were our shoes, and I wasn't about to announce our location by having them tumble around in a dryer, though, judging by the lighting, it looked like the power was off anyway. We had pulled out most of the clean clothes and made an impromptu bed; it was a good long while before Marcus came out of the cocoon of clothing he had made for himself.

"I was in a bit of trouble there, Loo. I want to say thank you for helping me."

"Totally selfish reasons…you pick up most of the puppy poo," I told him as I gave him a light kiss. "Are we going to get back there? I can't think of much worse than something bad happening to those magnificent little beasts."

"We'll get there. We'll get a fresh start in the morning; hopefully by then whatever is going on will be over."

I wanted to believe him and I almost did, right up until there was a soft thud at the door. I would have ignored it, if it hadn't happened again. We had set up our camp on the far side of the laundry room, a bank of machines between us and the door. Marcus got up to check what was going on.

"What are you doing?"

"Seeing if someone needs our help."

We'd locked the door; if I had my way we would have put a machine in front of it as well, but Marcus was concerned we might need to leave in a hurry or that someone might need to get in quickly.

He'd walked half-way across the room before he stopped. "Jesus Christ," he said; tough to tell if it was in reverence or as a swear.

"What?" I was nervous to look.

"That kid is here." He didn't need to elaborate; I knew exactly who he was referring to. "He's like a bloodhound! I hate to say it, hell I hate even to think it, but I feel like we should have killed him when we had the chance."

"I don't know what chance you're referring to Marcus. Do you mean when he was trying to gnaw through your shoe? Or when you were scrabbling in the sand to get away?"

"Smart ass."

"And we can't just go around killing people, especially kids. What if we find out he's just got some weird sickness that passes in twenty-four hours?"

"Pretty sure this isn't a food poisoning problem from the fair."

"You don't know that! Could be tainted churros."

"Loo, the kid tried to eat me."

I wanted to forget this day had ever happened, pretend that everything that was going on was some elaborate hoax. Maybe a demonstration of sorts or a military training exercise. But it would be impossible to forget those people that had been pulled apart and eaten or the ones destroyed by the Octopus ride.

"So what are you going to do? You can't let him in."

"No, I suppose you're right. Maybe he'll leave."

I don't think either of us believed that. It was a great many minutes before Marcus rejoined me on our bed. We did not get much sleep that night as the child repeatedly banged his head into the door. I was glad that on my third walk around the room I stumbled upon Jenny Addison's notebook, replete with a rainbow and unicorn cover. I decided while Marcus slept that I was going to write down everything that had happened today. Maybe it was because it would make the events more concrete, I could stop wandering around like I was in a dream, a surreal dream. But more importantly, I'm not all that confident we're going to get home. I hope it's just the night that is making my spirits so bleak, that when the sun rises so will my hopes. But right now, I feel like I am writing my last words. If that's the case, I want to leave a record of who we were/are. That, and I need for anyone that sees this to please, PLEASE go to my house at 436 Crescent Street, Long Island, and check on my dogs. We have three adult English Bulldogs and six puppies from two different litters. Please! They don't deserve this. I'm going to sleep now, hopefully all this worry and panic will have been for naught. God Bless America.

8

THE DEMISE

"Geez, hon…I was going to cuddle with you, but you're like eleven hundred degrees." Laura reached around and touched her husband's forehead. Her hand was wet with sweat when she pulled it away. "Fever must be from the cold water."

Marcus grunted a reply.

Laura fell back to sleep, hoping he would be better in the morning. When she awoke, a thick ribbon of bright sunlight was streaming through the sidelight window.

"Better," she said as she sat up and stretched. She reached over to shake her husband awake. "How are you feeling?" He was slow to turn; when he did, she screamed. His face was blue, mottled with lines of red and purple. His eyes were clouded over and opaque. The thumping at the door, which had continued through the entire night, increased as the boy sensed that his prize was now in danger of being claimed by another.

"Marcus…?" Laura asked, simultaneously wanting to help him and get away. An alien sound gurgled forth from his throat and open mouth. Marcus sat up, his eyes never leaving his wife's. If he had not gotten tangled by the small mountain of sweaters wrapped around his legs, he would have grabbed hold of her long before she could get her feet underneath her.

"Stop!" she pleaded as she headed for the door, thankful that she had heeded her husband's advice and not barricaded it. She still had the child to think of, but between the two dangers she was exposed to, she'd take her chance with the smaller. "Come on, come on!" She fumbled with the lock, never daring to take her gaze off her husband. When she opened the door, she realized the boy had brought his entire extended family with him to the party. She tried to shut and latch the door again. It was all in vain as her head was wrenched violently back. Blood plumed from the rend in her flesh. The boy zombie and his father came to join in the feast, when they were done they headed out to the boardwalk in search of another meal.

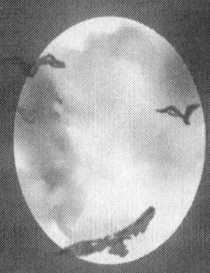

9

MIKE JOURNAL ENTRY 7

"Holy shit." At some point while reading, I had gotten up and started walking around the destroyed Octopus ride. When I finished, I'd already made up my mind.

"No!" BT roared when I told him what I wanted to do.

I ignored him as I asked Winters how far the address in the journal was from where we were.

"Mike, I understand they're bulldogs and for whatever reason, you have an affinity for the slobbering fools. But it's a zombie apocalypse and even if they escaped the first barrage, what makes you think they could survive out in the wild? I love Henry; I do. He's a wonderful dog, and yeah, he sounds an alarm once in awhile, but do you think he's capable of going out on a hunt? Of dragging down food? He gets tired heading to the kitchen. I've seen him fall asleep mid-migration. If a rabbit doesn't willingly walk into his jaws, he isn't going to catch it." BT was not going to let it go. Thing was, neither was I.

"This is a sign," I said as I shook the notebook in his face.

"You're the last person that needs another portent to how crazy you are."

"Ten miles," Winters said, looking up from his map. "And

it avoids the zombie horde. There's a way we could go, swing us right around; this address is on the way."

BT shot him a glance that made the other man begin intensely studying what was in his hands.

"You heard him. It does not distract from what we already have to do."

If BT's body had been supplied with gaskets, they would have blown.

"Five minutes! Five minutes to check the house out. That's it." BT turned and was heading back to his van.

"Mount up, people! We're heading out."

"Zombies have cleared out?" Stenzel asked.

"Detour. We're going around," I told her. She knew something was up by the way BT was storming around, but left it at that.

Winters turned off his radio. "Sir, it's not technically on our way; it will work to get us around the zombies, but it's going to add forty-five minutes to our timeline. That's without meeting any problems."

"Will we still make the departure time?"

"*Just*, and that's if you take the Gunney's five-minute search to heart."

"Thank you for your discretion."

"About that promotion."

"Ah. An ulterior motive. We'll talk when we get back."

"Fair enough, sir."

We made good time; in a half an hour we were standing at the top of a cul-de-sac. The house was a beautiful ranch style in a suburb I don't think I could have even afforded the taxes on. The neighborhood was quiet; it hadn't always been that way, though, as the shell casings, blood stains, and carcasses would attest to. But right now, yeah, it was eerily quiet.

"Make this quick. Someone around here sees a black man they're likely to call the cops." BT was looking around, he had his mean face on.

"I'd call if I saw you; you're a terrifying man."

"Good," he replied to me.

"Better get moving, sir." Winters was looking at his watch.

I looked to the journal, making sure I had the right address. I was nervous, like butterflies before a first date nervous. And afraid, too; afraid of what I might find in there. Humans, zombies...those were one thing, but something about seeing a dog injured or killed just shredded my heart. That's a weird feeling...now that I'm thinking about it. What's that say about me if I'm more concerned about the fate of a dog? Well, that's not entirely true; if we're talking family and friends it's very comparable, but the populace in general? Wait, did I say it was *comparable* to the loss of a friend? Maybe I'll just let that thought lie dormant; some things are better left without voice.

"Why am I here?" I asked myself as I placed my hand on the doorknob. The idea that any dog would be all right alone for all this time, never mind the new set of predators, was ludicrous, especially this particular breed. And now, even if they were doing well, what were the odds that they would want anything to do with me? They were puppies no longer and had not had human influence in a good long while; if they were alive, it was very likely they were feral. Seemed strange to picture an English Bulldog as feral, like, it would take too much energy to be ferocious, but I suppose it could happen. The door was unlocked. I didn't take that as a good sign, though if it was locked, I'm not sure that position would have changed. I took one step across the threshold and the feeling of dread increased, the smell was not a pleasant one.

The house was destroyed, but not in the zombie invasion type of way. Hope surged as I looked upon them; furniture destroyed by chewing, carpet well and truly soiled. There had been untended puppies here, no doubt about that. Now the question was, were they still here, and if so, would they be happy to see me or angered I had invaded their space?

"Hello?" I asked shakily. No response. I walked through the narrow foyer and took a right; there was a small area in the living room sectioned off with plastic panels. This must have been where the puppies were kept. I gulped before I looked in, fearful for what I would find. I almost laughed, so thankful was I when it was merely overturned bowls, ripped up toys, and very old excrement. The gate that was supposed to keep them penned-in had been chewed clean through, a decent puppy-sized hole at the bottom.

"Well, they got out," I said the words aloud, mostly as a way to alleviate the quiet. If the rest of the house was a whirlwind of destruction, the kitchen was the epicenter. Cabinet doors had been ripped free in an attempt to get at the food inside, even the ones high up, which given the average height of a bulldog, was a mystery to me as to how it had been done. The table and chairs were on their sides, the fridge door had been pulled open, Tupperware containers ripped through, and a semi-solid, thick crust of spilled and dried condiments coated a fair portion of the floor. At least I hoped the brownish colored detritus was old mustard and ketchup.

Once through the kitchen, I looked to the left where there was a series of kennels, seven in total. Six were empty. My heart jumped up into my throat where it was firmly lodged as I looked upon a large lump. It was covered by a dog bed, but it would be hard to ignore what the shape underneath was.

"Poor pup," was all I could manage to say with my heart pressed against my vocal cords. The timer in my head was quickly running out and as of yet, I'd not discovered anything to make me think this wasn't a waste of time in addition to something that I would not soon forget—pretty much the definition of a double whammy. I was turning to find my way out when I caught sight of something outside in the backyard. I was looking at the white rump of a bulldog staring at a fence. It was stock still, so much so I mistakenly thought it might be a statue. From this distance, I couldn't be sure. I found the

French doors that led out; the tenants here had been as kind to the doors as they had been to every other impediment placed in their way. Meaning that the paint had been completely gnawed away three feet up and one door was hanging askew.

"Pup...?" I said cautiously as I went through. Nothing. Didn't even turn its head to ignore me further, a common trait among bulldogs. "Puppers!" I said a bit louder, not wanting to startle it if it was real. The dog kept staring at the fence. "What's wrong with you, girl?" I noticed she did not have any tackle gear. I was afraid she was sick—or worse. "Pretty girl." I was halfway across the modest yard and still nothing. I finally saw her lift her head as if she smelled something. Her large head was swiveling my way just as I heard a grumble, sounded much like I figure a train barreling down on your location might.

"Oh, oh," was all I could manage to say as a fawn-colored bulldog came bursting through the fence to the side of me. The pickets swung out to allow her in and then fell back into place. I didn't have much time to think about it as she bounded toward me—and not in a friendly way. If I had to take a guess, I'd say this was their home and they'd found a way to leave and hunt for food and come back for safety. The fawn-colored dog slammed into my right leg and knee, dropping me to the ground. We were now face to face and, all things being equal, it was terrifying. Her lips were pulled back, she was growling, drool and saliva flowed from her teeth and hung from her jaws. Her excessively large mouth was inches from mine. She was growling deep in her throat and let go two savage barks, spraying me in a thick mist of spit. At any point over the next thirty seconds, she could have stripped my face clean of meat and I couldn't have done much about it. I knew instinctively that to reach for my gun would end painfully for me.

By this time, the white one had got into the fray. She had circled in behind me and was sniffing at my neck. Pulled apart by two bulldogs was not how I envisioned me leaving this plane of existence.

"Fuck, Talbot! You could get in trouble locked inside a padded room." BT was framed in the French doors, his rifle raised.

"Don't fire!" I had my palms facing outward and was showing them to the dogs, letting them know I had nothing in them. The fawn-colored one let out another bark as she reacted to BT's words; I noted she adjusted her angle so I was in between her and him. Again, the white one did not react, though she did take a cue from the fawn-colored one and turned when she saw BT. Then she began to bark as well.

"Mike." BT didn't know what to do. Neither did I.

"Not unless they start biting."

"You want to take it that far?" He took a step towards us; the fawn-colored one moved closer to me, her whiskers rubbing against my face.

"I'm a friend; I won't hurt you." I was speaking as soothingly as I could, can't say I felt like I was defusing the situation. "Gonna get something for you." Like diffusing a ticking bomb, I slowly moved my hand down to my pocket. As I reached in, powerful jaws wrapped around my neck. As of yet, she was not applying pressure, but clearly, if I pulled out something she didn't like, I was going to be in some serious trouble before BT could extract me from it. I grabbed a granola bar. The fawn didn't let go. I moved my hand to the side of her face so she could see it. "Food," I said with some difficulty, as she was getting nervous. I moved my other hand to grab the wrapper; she liked that even less. It wasn't until I ripped the food package open and she got a whiff that her attention was diverted. "Food, I have food."

"You better hope they're vegan."

"Haven't met a bullie yet didn't like a good granola bar." And luckily, this was no exception. She let go of my neck and grabbed that bar lightning-quick. I expected her to inhale it whole and then go immediately back to not trusting me. Instead, she did something I'd been completely unprepared for. She nudged her partner in crime and showed her the bar, which the white one gladly took half of. They did eat quickly, but did not go back to attack posture. They settled a few feet away, watching us warily.

"Now what, Cesar?"

"I'm far from a dog whisperer. Put your rifle down."

"You see the maws on them?"

"Then go back in."

"My momma, bless her heart, said I should make some white friends because they'd be more likely to get out of any kind of jam with the police. I'm going out on a limb here, but I'm guessing she never came across anyone like you."

"BT."

"Yeah, yeah. Asshole." He shook his head, but he put his rifle down.

The fawn-colored one started sniffing around me.

"You got any more bars?" I asked.

"I'm hungry too you know."

"Give me the fucking thing."

"It's so far past hate I don't even know what to think about you." He was fishing through his pockets.

"Slow, man," I said as the two dogs began to give warning rumbles deep in their chests.

BT tossed five bars my way.

"How many of these do you have?"

"You know how much fuel it takes to run this body?"

Couldn't argue with him there. I scooped them up and unwrapped them quickly, I had one in each hand and my arms were extended to each dog. The fawn-colored one took hers first; the white one waited to see what the other did before she followed suit. BT dropped a magazine, the fawn-colored one jumped back, dropping the bar; the white one did not react. It dawned on me then that she might be deaf. I whistled, the fawn's ears perked up, the white one was busy scarfing down her treat.

"You watching out for this one?" I asked soothingly. I had picked the bar back up and was holding it out. I could see in her eyes she was hungry, not starving, but definitely skirting the edge of the gut-twisting sensation. She looked over to BT then back to me before taking it.

"Sir," Winters came over my comm, "we have got to go."

"I can't leave them here." Not sure if I said it to him, BT, God, or myself; most likely all four.

I stood slowly, the fawn one backed up.

"You two want to come with me?" Nothing from either, until I showed them the other three bars. Had their interest then. "Hey, behemoth. Back up. We're coming your way."

"Loathe, yeah, I think loathe begins to touch on it. That's like an all-encompassing kind of dislike. Hate is something said in the heat of the moment; it dissipates quickly. But loathe…well, you can marinate a person in that word."

"Just get your ass out of the way. You can feel however you want about me once we are heading back home."

"Loathe, though, it just doesn't have enough *oomph*…needs something more immediate." He was looking up and off to the side. "Wish I had a thesaurus…wait, *abhor*. That's the ticket!" He shouted loud enough that the fawn dog began to bark again. "Detest? That's a good one, too." He at least moved aside from the doorway.

"Dogs…come on…running out of time."

"Give them some names, maybe that will help." He poked his head back through. Tough to say if he was giving me a hard time or was trying to be helpful.

"Give them names? I can't just think up something on the fly like that."

"What the hell are you talking about? You are constantly thinking up things on the fly."

"Yeah, but this is important."

He froze up for a moment like his internal operating system seized. "I'm sticking with abhor. You realize that the vast majority of your 'on the fly' shit involves our lives, right? And now you don't want to name the dogs quickly because it's too important? What the fuck is wrong with you? Like, seriously, man. I'd love to know."

"Fine, asshole, I'll call the fawn one Holly and the white one Chloe. Happy now?"

"Ecstatic. Can we go?"

"Holly, girl." Her ears perked up. It was doubtful I had nailed her actual name, but it was likely it had been two syllables, and the way I delivered it was in a universal dog language. She knew I was talking to her. "Holly." She cocked her head to the side, her aggressive stance lessened. "I know Chloe takes her cues from you and we really need to establish a little trust in the next thirty seconds."

"Just grab her."

"You see that mouth?"

"What do I care? It'll be you she's biting."

"Loathe works both ways."

"Moved on to abhor; keep up."

"Holly." I held up another bar. It was Chloe who came closer.

"Sir." It was Winters again.

"I know, I know, we need to go."

"Well, yes, but now we have real incentive to get gone."

"Zombies, it's always zombies. How many?"

"Many and moving quickly," he responded.

"Mike." BT was serious now. "I like dogs too, but…"

He left it there. We could not risk the mission, or more importantly, any of our people. I had all of my attention focused on Holly and was not prepared for the emotional grip I felt when Chloe came up to me, her stubby tail wagging, tongue hanging out as she gazed at the proffered treat.

"You going to be my in?" I got down on a knee; Holly

backed up thinking this was some kind of trap. Chloe inched closer; I pulled my arm in. As she moved to grab the granola, I reached out and wrapped my arms around her. If I was going to get savagely ripped into, this would be the time. Luckily, she was all bulldog and was too busy eating to give much of a care that I was carrying her. I was running for our van, hoping beyond hope that Holly would follow, not willing to let her charge be kidnapped. I was right, though it wasn't happening quite as well as I had planned. There's that word again, *planned*. Let's all agree I use that word liberally, as opposed to literally.

Holly was following, that was a fact, but in an attempt to halt my forward progress. She was pawing at my ankles and nipping at my calves–not enough to break skin, but enough to let me know she was not on board with whatever the hell I was doing with her sister. Her tune changed the moment we made it through the house and were now out on the main street. I looked down and over my shoulder when she stopped biting me. Her nose was going and she was smelling what she'd not seen yet: zombies. She looked up at me, I swear I could see the decisions warring in her head, bite me and make me drop Chloe so they could retreat to safety, or trust the human who had shown them a small kindness in the form of food. All of a sudden, we were best buds as she came up beside me. She saw the people waving us forward. I noted she did not bark; alerting the enemy was never a good thing and it was a lesson she had learned well.

Not gonna lie, I stood in amazement when she hopped in without prompting, though, in hindsight, I knew she was a survivor. She'd done the math. So far we'd shown nothing but kindness, meanwhile, the zombies they were an enemy she knew. We were speeding away without a shot fired. Chloe licked my face twice and then lay her head down in my lap; she was fast asleep. Holly was guarded and kept as much distance as she could in the confines of the van, but even she could not resist the pull of sleep. She was of the: "if you can't beat them, join them" ilk. She pushed BT over so she could lie against my thigh.

"Happy now?" BT asked.

"You have no idea." Pretty sure I was beaming like a proud papa.

"Lieutenant Talbot, this is Major Eastman. Can we get a progress report?"

I looked over to Winters; he held up nine fingers.

"Twenty minutes," I replied.

Got confused stares from BT and Winters. I held up a finger.

"You have ten," he said curtly.

"I'll see what we can do."

"You know how Northerners always thought Southerners were slow and not very smart because of the way they spoke?" BT was leading his question, all I could do was reply with a "Yeah?" "Well, that's how I feel when I look at your face. You seem like the type of person that would be stupid and uneducated, but then without warning, you go and do a smart thing. It's very disconcerting."

It got the rest of the people in the van smiling, and I was fine with taking a small barb if it was all in the name of morale.

"Love you, buddy," he mouthed.

I flipped him off.

We showed up to the airfield eight minutes later; one of the planes was already running, and I could see five men working on our ride home. I'd no sooner stepped out of the van when a major I didn't know walked over to me.

"Nice of you to finally show up, Lieutenant."

"Don't," BT said so softly his throat mic barely picked it up.

I was stewing, but I walked past the major and over to Eastman.

"I'm talking to you, Lieutenant Talbot!" The major turned as I passed.

"Sorry, I'm pretty busy right now. Will it be a problem if I ignore you later?" I asked.

"Shit." BT buried his face in his hand.

My squad wisely began to shuffle the scientists, their work, and the dogs to their respective flights. Holly wasn't keen on all the noise the other plane was making, but she was hard-pressed to resist the MRE Harmon was flashing under her nose. Chloe could barely contain herself at the prospect of the packaged meal. Her butt was wiggling double time as she attempted to coordinate the movements between walking and wagging.

"Come on, girl," she urged, wanting to get away from what was certainly going to be a scene ending with the major dead and me a fugitive from justice.

"You do realize that you're talking to a major and you will show me the respect due that rank."

"Mike, no." BT had stepped in front of me as I turned.

"I've got this. Relax…you worry too much." I placed a hand on his chest as I walked around him.

"One of us has to."

"Go on with yourself Major Randing, I'm listening. I realize it must have been extremely stressful as you flew thirty-five-thousand feet over the muck, death and destruction that us lowly infantrymen have to mire through."

"Why you little fucking piece of shit. I'm going to take that puny bar of yours and have it shoved up your ass."

"Ah, that's the thing, Major; you're going to have someone else do it. How about you give it a try? Or is getting your hands dirty beneath you? Why risk anything when you can get some other pleeb to do it? Maybe shut the fuck up about it or give it a go."

The major took a step but advanced no further. "Those animals are not authorized to get on that plane!" He was pointing to Harmon, who was ushering Gary and the pups aboard. "I will not allow it."

"While your little pasty ass was riding up in the clouds, I lost one of my soldiers today. Watched him torn apart, actually, and the kicker was that the mission I lost him on really didn't even need to happen. So I lost a kid today for nothing. Those *animals*, as you called them, besides not losing any more of my people, are the best thing this shitfest has had to offer, and they're coming home with me."

"Are you disobeying a direct order?"

"What was the order? So much sewage was seeping out of your mouth it was difficult to discern the chunks of crap from the words."

"If I didn't want you to stand trial for a court-martial so damned bad, I would be ordering that you be banned from that flight, but as it is, those unauthorized animals will not be getting on that plane."

"Good luck with that. You should get going; the scientists are on your plane. I'd hate for you to have to breathe ground air for any longer than needed." I was walking away.

Major Randing went over to where Eastman and the others were working on the tail end of the plane. I was hanging out by the nose, knowing full-well this was far from over. I'd started a pissing contest with a dickless man and he was going to go to great lengths to prove just how far he could reach without one. Should be interesting.

Hadn't seen the SEALs since we'd come back; I knew something was up when they began to file off of Randing's plane. I nodded to BT.

"What are they doing?" He asked.

"Squad, look alive." They all looked over to me; wasn't hard to figure out what was going on. Randing was pissed off that I wasn't following his orders and was going to attempt to use some muscle to get his way. I had no desire to go up against the special forces unit, but I would. Randing pulled the captain to the side and was telling him something. The captain never took his eyes off of me. When they were done, he nodded to his men, who followed him over to where BT and I were standing.

"The major says you have disobeyed a direct order."

"And?" I asked.

"Just checking. This is what's going to happen; we're going to keep talking and you're going to tell me to go fuck myself or something equally as witty–something a Marine would be able to come up with on the fly. Then I'm going to go back into that plane. Fair enough?"

"Why?"

"Mostly because Randing isn't my type of officer, and I much prefer dogs."

"And me?" I asked.

"Really, man? You need validation from a squid?" BT wanted to know.

"As far as crayon eaters go, you and your squad aren't half bad. Okay–lay into me a little bit; we were right in the middle of a great game of spades; got a bottle of twelve-year-old Scotch riding on the outcome."

"Thank you, Captain…?"

"Smoltz." He shook my hand.

"Get the fuck out of here you puddle pirate!" I yelled at him.

He looked confused. "Puddle pirate?" he mouthed.

I shrugged. He shook his head as he turned and went back to the major. I could hear him say he tried.

"That's it? That's all you're going to do?" Randing was turning red.

"Sir, I'm not getting into a firefight over a couple of dogs. Best to just let them on." With that, he and his unit went back onto Randing's plane.

"Fuck, I wish I had a cigarette," I said.

"He's going to try and hang you upside down." BT said as

he watched the whole exchange with disbelief. "On a side note, it looks like the squad and the dogs are growing fond of each other. Here."

"Menthol? Really?"

"You're probably the same person that scoffs at the water in an oasis because it's not Perrier."

I smoked the thing; it tasted much like I figured the front end of a Corvette did. Fiberglass. I mean it tasted like fiberglass, if that wasn't clear enough. I was three puffs in when I got Eastman's call to come and talk to him. I hated the cigarette and was still pissed off I had to discard it before I was finished. I thought for a moment that this might be what it felt like to be a woman; I quickly vowed to keep that thought completely to myself.

"Yes, sir," I said as if I had no problem with authority.

"Follow me." We walked far enough away from Randing that he could not hear.

"Major Randing has ordered me to get the dogs off the plane."

"You're both majors; how does he pull rank?"

"He was commissioned a year earlier than I was."

"Are you fucking kidding me? Just because he's been a dickhead longer shouldn't make him the boss of you."

"Are you saying I'm a dickhead?"

"Well, less of one, sir. Wasn't how I meant it."

"Listen, I knew Randing long before any of this shit ever happened. He was a hard-ass then and it's only gotten worse. Do yourself a favor get the dogs off the plane, apologize, kowtow a little, and let's get out of here."

"With all due respect…"

"Let me stop you there because you're about to give a great long litany of not-so-good things to say, and 'with all due respect' is not a get out of jail free card, Lieutenant."

"Noted. The dogs stay, I'm staying."

"Lieutenant, don't be obstinate. They're dogs; you have family back in Etna, and a dog, if I'm not mistaken."

"No offense, Major, but I've seen your flying. I'd rather take my chances in that van, probably beat you back and in one piece."

Eastman looked at me for a moment. "You're serious, aren't you." It was a questioning statement but had no up lilt at the end. "I could order you."

"You could, sir."

"And if I told your squad to force you on there?"

"How do you think that would go down?" It was my turn to ask a question.

"I have no desire to see what a mutiny looks like." Eastman sighed. "So what do you suggest I do?"

"I would never presume to tell a major what to do."

"You are so full of shit, Talbot. I read your file before I took you out here. I do it with every squad leader."

"And?"

"And I know you were a troubled corporal, saw a lot of action and performed your duties admirably, although, I saw numerous instances where you had issues with authority."

"And I stand by my actions. If I remember correctly, the Marine Corps doesn't want automatons, but rather thinking soldiers so that, God forbid, if anything happens to command, we could still function."

"You punched a supply sergeant. I'm having a hard time seeing how losing a commander in a firefight applies to knocking out rear echelon personnel."

"Staff Sergeant Jonders? Putz."

"You want to elaborate?"

"I hate reliving this shit, but it was Kamdesh…that's in Afghanistan."

"I know where Kamdesh is; I was there."

"After?"

"During."

"Fair enough. Then you know the clusterfuck that it was. We were assigned to protect the contractors there and the narrow roadway they were working on. Intel, as always, was spot on. That's sarcasm...sometimes people don't get it."

"Again, I was there, Lieutenant."

"We were told there wasn't an enemy within fifty miles of our location. We got ambushed, lost three men–two of whom I counted as friends, within the first couple of rocket attacks. Our LT took a rocket to the chest; I don't know if I've ever seen someone cease to exist so violently and quickly. We were pinned down as they rained everything they had from the high ground. It was the flyboys that saved our ass."

"You're welcome."

I nodded. "In the ensuing firefight, I lost my helmet at some point and I'd used my flack jacket to...put out Lance Corporal Hennessy. See, a truck had been blown up and shrapnel from the gas tank had doused him. He was screaming and running around; I tackled him and did my best to smother the flames. He lived, but was burned on over seventy percent of his body. That was the point I thought I might become a vegetarian. I didn't realize that a cooking human could smell like that." Even now as I related this story, I had to work hard to quell the gorge threatening to rise within me.

"How does this relate to Jonders?"

"When I got back, and after a stiff bottle of something that was supposed to be whiskey, I went to requisition new gear. Jonders wanted to charge me for the lost gear. I snapped; I don't even remember what happened other than I jumped the counter and laid into him like he had ordered the rocket attack. So it wasn't the fact that he outranked me; it was more because he was a callous asshole. Like I'd lost my flack jacket just to piss him off, and not to try to save a burning man that smelled suspiciously like a Saturday barbecue. So yeah, I punched him, and I'd do it again in a heartbeat."

"There are other instances."

"How many stories you want to hear? Not once did I haul off and do something that wasn't justified, at least, in my mind. I know I'm not cut out to be a soldier; unfortunately, it would seem I'm not cut out to do much of anything else either, but you know what I've found out? I'm good at it. I'm good at killing and even better at not dying, and I completely agree with the old adage about not dying for my country–but letting the other bastard do it for his."

"Fuck, Talbot, you go against almost everything I believe in, regarding my Corps, and still I want to root for you."

"Weird, right? Damn near the same thing my wife says every day."

Eastman laughed at that. "I'll get your dogs home, but you're going to have fallout when you get back. Not much I can do about that."

"Don't worry, Bennington owes me one."

"What do you have on him? Forget it, the less I know, the better. I'll get Randing out of here. You watch our perimeter; we should be ready to go in four or five hours."

"There's more, Major." He was listening. "We ended up in a church for a while. There are people there; I promised them I would do my best to get them to Etna."

"What do you want me to do, Lieutenant? I can't give you the authorization to get those people. Colonel Bennington will have my ass."

"Would you turn your back if I did it? Already got my ass all slung up and ready for a good paddling."

"Shit." He turned away to think on it. "How many?"

"Thirty-eight. Women and kids, too."

"You know the deal at Etna. They all going to be able to contribute?"

"Doubtful."

"They know this?"

"They do. They're stuck in that place and they're running

out of food. At the worst, they would have someplace new to hole up."

"How long to retrieve?"

"Couple of hours without any problems."

"And what are the odds of there not being any problems?" he asked. Fair enough question.

"You really want an answer?"

"When the plane is repaired, Lieutenant, I have to go whether you've returned or not."

"You won't, but thanks for the heads up."

He was shaking his head. The desire to flip Randing off was a physical need, so much so that I figured it best to go in and check on the dogs. Harmon had fashioned some water bowls out of MRE wrappers and duct tape; they'd slobbered all over the place and were now looking for a place to nap. Holly barked at me, Chloe came over without any prompting from me. She licked my hand; I choose to believe it was in thanks. I got down on my haunches and petted her head; I was looking over at Holly, who barked again.

"You already forget who I am?" She let her head dip before hesitantly coming closer. She tried to remain standoffish, but there is only so much butt patting a girl can take before she caves. I was winning her over one scratch at a time. "You're a good girl, aren't you?" I asked as we were face to face.

"Huddle time," I told my squad, wanted them all within earshot.

"This about the church folk?" Winters asked.

"It is. I promised those people I would try and get them out, and I hate not fulfilling that. The problem is, we do not have Eastman's blessing. Anyone goes out there with me can count on being in some hot water upon our return to Etna."

"You know we're with you, Lieutenant," Stenzel said.

"I know that, and thank you. I need to leave some people behind to watch Eastman's back."

"I'm a private, sir…can't bust me any lower," Harmon said, smiling.

"I'm only taking Tommy; space is going to be at a premium." BT was pissed, like I wasn't taking him to Disney World as opposed to back into a hostile situation. As Tommy and I headed to the van, Randing was getting on his plane. I gave him a weak wave, which he ignored completely. BT walked with us; pretty sure he was going to attempt to force his way into the mission.

"Do you think he should call a doctor?" I asked BT as I got into the van.

"Who?"

"Randing."

"Why? No…you're about to give me some half-assed joke you think is hilarious and I might have found funny in the fourth grade. Screw it. Let it out–not like you're going to hold it in any way. Never met anyone with less self-control."

"Not gonna do it now. You ruined the mood. If I'd had the opportunity to let it flow naturally, it would have slain."

"Oh, whatever, so now you're not going to tell me? You are such an asshole! I'm not going to beg for one of your lame jokes. We're talking Talbot, so it has to be something gastric related, although, that word seems a little above his vocabulary." BT was talking softly, attempting to reason out what I was going to say. "Smelly farts?" BT asked, looking up hopefully.

"Gunney, I hardly think that's appropriate military decorum, especially when it concerns senior officers," I said. I've yet to understand my fascination with giving the mountain of a man a hard time; I would imagine those that lived in the shadow of Vesuvius did all in their powers to appease the volcano gods, not provoke them. Then I completed the thought–what good had it done them? In the end, they'd been blown away or covered in ash and lava. Might as well have fun while you're going down. "We'll be right back." I was trying to appease him. He didn't believe me; easy enough, especially since I didn't believe me.

"You know I don't like not being able to watch your back."

"I know that, man, I do. Tommy, lets go." We pulled out of the airport and onto the highway.

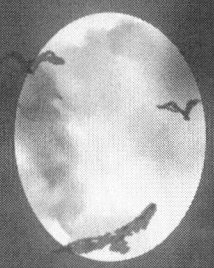

10

MIKE JOURNAL ENTRY 8

"They're already on the road," Tommy said not more than five miles from where we'd left.

"What? Who?"

"Jason, his son, and the others."

"How many 'others' and how do you know this?"

"Lyle is open." He didn't explain further; I guess he meant his mind. "It wasn't purely luck that he was on the roadway."

"What…you just reached out and touched him? Like AT&T?"

Tommy looked befuddled.

"Don't give me that crap. Of all the people I can't 'date' myself with, it's you. You know what I'm talking about."

"Yes; I've been alive for a great many years. It doesn't mean I spent a bunch of them in front of the television."

"Are you going all elitist on me?"

"I loved *Bonanza*."

"There's a lot not making sense right now. *Bonanza*?" I asked, halting my other thought.

"Hoss was my hero."

"Okay, back to it. Jason didn't look like he'd leave if the

building was on fire. Why now, and how do they know where they're going?"

"Lyle convinced him to come, and I gave them directions before we headed out."

"This is all a little too coincidental. Too easy."

"You can catch a break every once in a while, Mr. T; not everything needs to be a deadly quest."

"You say that but it seems for every easy thing handed to us, we have to pay double for it on the back end."

Tommy smiled and let the back of his seat recline.

"How long?" I hated waiting–drove me nuts, as a matter of fact. Too much time to get myself in trouble.

"Fifteen minutes." He placed his hands behind his head; I stepped out of the van to look around. Tommy seemed at ease; I wasn't getting that kind of vibe, I was at an agitated unease. I slowly did a complete turn, looking in every nook and cranny I could. I saw nothing, but that didn't quell my whipped up innards. No matter what the kid said, something was up. No, I couldn't just "catch a break."

"BT, can you hear me?" I'd grabbed the walkie out of the van.

"You cannot already be in trouble," he replied.

"We're good...going to be back sooner than expected. Apparently, they're coming to meet us."

He wisely didn't ask how over an open channel. "See you soon, out."

On cue, I saw a bus coming. Couldn't hear it.

"Electric," Tommy said. He had soundlessly exited the van and was looking as well. He waved as they got closer.

The bus slowed down; Lyle was hanging out a window and yelling enthusiastically. Jason was driving; didn't seem quite so happy. In fact, it looked like he'd somehow bitten down on an overly sour lemon. The bus had no sooner stopped when a man in a blue flannel shirt stepped off. I remembered seeing him at the church; he was one of the ones holding a gun on us, but he'd not said anything then. Apparently, he wanted to now.

"James M. Lemon," he said as he extended his hand. "The M is for Motherfucker."

"Okay. Nice beard," was all I could think to say.

"You getting us out of here?"

"That's the idea. Everyone with you?"

"Fourteen. The others wouldn't leave."

I looked over to Jason, who had not left the confines of the bus and would not allow his son to do so either.

"Fourteen it is." The other twenty-four had sealed their fate. I could not help those that did not want it.

James followed me back to the van. "Don't you want to ride on the bus?" I asked as he hopped in.

"I figured you'd prefer my company, let's go."

"You heard the man, Tommy."

Relief covers what I felt as we drove back onto the tarmac. That lasted for all of ten minutes.

"Lieutenant, we have a situation." It was Winters. I hoped briefly it was just Randing heading into round two. We turned as Randing was firing up his engines in preparation for take-off. So it wasn't him. Didn't need to be Sherlock Holmes to figure out where this was going or to explain what I had been feeling while we were on the highway. I knew it was Randing's mission to get those scientists out of here, but right now it felt like he was abandoning us in our time of need. Prick couldn't wait to see if we got our ride fixed, and he sure as hell didn't care if we made it out of the battle that was coming. They were on the runway to our left, and I sincerely hoped he saw my finger as he taxied. "How are you going to explain that at your court-martial?" BT asked.

"He makes me wish I had more middle fingers. Let's see what Winters wants." He was a hundred yards in front of our plane, looking through his optics across the airfield. The question now was: how many and how long did we have?

Winters handed over a small pair of binoculars. "They're at the far side, and they're moving. I think they've found a way in, but I'm not sure where."

I was watching the line of them. They looked like ants following a chemical trail to a picnic. They were heading to the small concourse building. Once they found a way out of that building, they were going to be immediately to our right.

"Winters, get the rest of the squad up here. We're going to need to watch those exits. I was pointing to a half dozen doors. Major Eastman…?"

"Little busy." I could hear him straining; guarantee it was the last bolt on whatever they were trying to remove.

"Going to need a revised number on repairs."

"I'm not Scottie, Talbot. I said four or five hours and I meant it."

"What is it with you military guys and the nerd references?" BT asked.

"Funny that you know what he meant."

"I also know Barry Manilow songs; doesn't mean I'm singing them out loud to people."

"*Mandy*?"

"Well, yeah, of course…I mean, that's a classic."

"*Copacabana*?"

"How does anyone make it through a summer without that one?"

"*I write the songs*?"

"Don't fuck with classic love songs." With that, he turned away.

At some point, Winters had taken the glasses back. "I see them." He was pointing to the building. Didn't need the magnification to see the line of them moving through the airport and with a quickness.

"Major, far be it for me to tell you how to do your work, but you might want to shoot for 'good enough' on the repairs."

"Good enough? You want duct tape on your ride home across the entire US? How bad?" he asked when he realized why I was bothering him again.

"Couple hundred so far, more on the way."

"You there, Sergeant!" I heard him yelling.

"Yes, Major." It was Tommy.

"There's an M2 in the back of the plane. Looks like you're going to need it."

"He has a .50 caliber machine gun in the back of the plane and we're just finding out about it now?" BT asked me.

"Damn thing is close to ninety pounds without ammunition…you want to run around with that thing?" I was moving quickly to the plane. We needed to set up a defense and in the middle was going to be that machine of war. Tommy let Kirby help him carry it, but I knew the boy could hold it by the barrel with his arm fully extended if he wanted to.

Harmon and Grimm were waddle-walking a large ammunition can; Corporals Rose and Stenzel were right behind them, carrying another.

"This ought to be fun." I honestly wasn't sure if I was being serious or sarcastic. On one hand, firing a machine gun is just fun–it is–I don't know specifically why. It would be much better if we were blowing up bottles of soda, an old car, maybe even a washing machine. Instead, we had bloodthirsty zombies. The fifty cal was not going to be kind to them. Tommy and Harmon were working quickly to get the weapon set up. As of yet, no zombies had broken through.

"Gunney, get everyone deployed. Stenzel, get the civvies in the plane."

"Harmon, you're with me." I was heading back to the plane.

She looked at me like I doubted her abilities. The rest of the squad was staring at me.

"I need you to help me find a way to secure the dogs,

make them as comfortable as possible before we start firing. I don't want them making a run for it."

"Sir, I need to be with the unit," she said as we moved.

"And you will be. I just need your help while I move stuff around, make them a secure dog house, see if I can get them corralled. How you doing?" I asked as we made it on to the plane. I was happy to note both dogs were sleeping, curled up with my brother, as a matter of fact, although that was going to change for Holly real soon.

"Good to go, sir."

"Don't need the standard 'oh rah' line, Private."

"Better, sir."

"Good." Holly was curled up on Gary's feet and Chloe's ass was planted firmly on his face. "Wish I could join them, except for the ass part. She lets anything go my brother is likely to be asphyxiated." We disturbed them all as we flipped the wooden crate over that the machine gun had come in. I was happy that they both came over to investigate this new development as opposed to shying away. Threw a couple of blankets in there with some granola bars. I got down and petted them, reveling in the fact that both massive heads were in my lap. Then the action began. Holly's ears perked up as small-arms fire began to chatter. I stood. "You watch out for your sister, okay?" The plane did a good job of muffling the sound, but nothing short of a concrete bunker was going to keep out the deafening reverberation of the fifty cal when it began to sing. Harmon was itching to get out and was by the door waiting.

"How's it going out there?" Gary asked. Instead of looking better, he looked worse, drawn, worn out. Good guess he was fighting an infection of some sort.

"Could be better. I wish we were in the air."

"You need me?"

"No. Try to get some rest but keep your rifle close; there's a chance you're going to need it."

"You realize that what you said is not at all conducive to getting some rest."

"Do the best you can." With that, he rolled away. I noted that the back of his shirt was soaked with sweat.

"Go," I told Harmon, who'd seen what I had. "I'm going to close the door when I leave." She was out quickly.

"Lyle." The boy was watching me, as was his father. "These dogs are going to need you; can you stay with them and make them feel better?"

"Of course." He smiled with relief, and pride, I think.

"I'll be back. Be good," I told the dogs. "We got a bunch of people and animals that are going to be thrilled to meet you. Maybe not Patches…she's a tough nut to crack. But all the rest for sure. And just so I can get it out of the way now, I apologize for Ben-Ben; I think he might have been dropped on his head a few times as a puppy."

"Mike, you know we all can hear you, right?" This was BT.

"This is a private moment; avert your ears." I gave each one a small kiss on the head before following Harmon out. Out of the obvious six exits, the zombies had picked the farthest one down the concourse. Didn't make much sense; they were usually all about the shortest route between them and their meal. I was hustling to make it to the squad.

"Winters, Stenzel, find out where else they breached." This had Dewey written all over it. Especially since only seven zombies had come through the door. We could see hundreds through the windows, and instead of looking toward the doorways out, they were watching us. *Unsettling* comes to mind; they were pressed up against the glass, just looking.

"What are they doing, sir?" Kirby asked.

It was a hell of a good question for which I had no answer.

"BT, light up that building."

"Finally, you say something worth listening to." He pulled back on the charging handle; Tommy gave him the thumbs up regarding the ammo, and away we went. He peppered the living shit out of the brick building. At first he was shooting low, then I remembered it was a fifty cal; he was doing horrific damage. I could see zombies falling over as their legs were quite literally cut off from beneath them. He adjusted the angle up and tore through the windows and the multitude of zombies within. Fifty cals weren't designed with humans in mind, according to the Geneva Convention. But I'd yet to see a warrior pull up a document in the midst of a full-scale battle. You use the tools at hand when it comes down to preserving your life, regardless of what the fucking rules say. Once "Thou Shalt Not Kill" is broken, doesn't make much sense to say there are still rules.

Rows of the fuckers were being hewn down as midsections exploded, lending credence to the term "chest cavity." Heads dissolved under the assault; one moment there was a body capper, the next just a fine mist as it became an aerosol spray. The heavy gun drowned out all noise. The rest of us were standing there watching the weapon do its damage, and I, for one, was thrilled at the level of destruction it was imposing upon them. If they were human, there would be a part of me that felt pity, but the zombies? Yeah, fuck them.

BT was screaming something, his powerful arms absorbing the recoil of the heavy gun as he fired. "Get some!" he let out just as the last of the rounds came up and through the rifle. "I have got to get me one of these!" He turned to help Tommy load up the new box.

"Hold up, BT, I don't want to use everything in the first five minutes. Grimm and Springer, go check out the far side. Stenzel, Kirby, south." I pointed where I wanted them to go because, I thought it was south, but only because of the way we were oriented. "Winters, Harmon." I pointed.

"On it," they replied.

We had eyes on all avenues of approach. My asshat of a stomach told me I was missing something. I felt like a zombie was outsmarting me; in fact, I was fairly certain about it. How bad was that going to look if the brainless ones pulled an end around? Maybe that would save me, you know, once they realized there was nothing to eat here. Yeah, I know it's been done; didn't stop it from going through my head.

"Dewey, what the fuck are you up to?" I was looking around. The zombies that had survived the barbaric slaughtering in the airport were once again at the windows now that there was no glass, hardly any framing, and even the structure itself had suffered a lot of damage.

"You might be wrong, Talbot. I think the zombies are getting stupider." BT had a grin on his face as he fingered the butterfly trigger.

"You think so? Because right now, where is all our attention directed?" I responded. He didn't like that answer.

As if to drive the point home even further, all of my scout teams reported in saying they had spotted zombies. We were in the open of, basically, a giant field. Sure, an airfield, but a field nonetheless–it was an indefensible position.

"Sir, they're running." Stenzel sounded concerned.

"Eastman."

"I heard. Nothing I can do about it."

"Pull back! Everyone pull back to the plane." That got a reaction from the zombies we were watching, like they had been waiting for this very moment. They began to flood out of all six exit doors. BT looked over. I nodded. If we didn't try to hold them back now, it would be a footrace to the plane.

BT looked grim and determined as he fired. Tommy didn't know whether to watch and make sure the clipped-together rounds fed through smoothly, or fire his own weapon.

"I've got this!" BT had to roar to be heard.

"I'm here now!" James M. Lemon shouted; he was holding a revolver like his gun was the key to getting us out of here.

So there we were, the four of us, doing our best to stem

the tide. Unfortunately, it was high tide and we were using a tiny plastic pail to keep the water away from the sand castle we'd spent all day building. Unlike BT's first barrage, he was keeping it to much more controlled bursts; by himself, he was keeping three of the exit points free from the enemy. It was up to Tommy, James and myself to work on the other three.

"So many," I breathed out. I was torn between emptying magazines at an unsustainable rate or measuring my shots for maximum effectiveness. I am a good shot; I qualified as an expert on numerous occasions when I was younger, in the Corps, and even at my most recent range qualification. What I wasn't, was *fast*. I measured my shots. I generally applied slow, even pressure as I sighted-in the rifle; expelling a bullet would almost come as a surprise. Then I would acquire another target and do the same routine. Effective, yes; deadly, even, more so, perhaps, just not *rapid*. There were a few in my squad that made me look like a geriatric ex-acrobat attempting to do standing somersaults. Stenzel, I was convinced was a descendant of Annie Oakley. She could shoot bullseyes at a rate of three to my one. The point I'm making is we weren't going to be able to hold this position much longer, no matter how many bodies we piled up on that tarmac.

"Getting low!" BT's rounds were cutting zombies in two, crippled, broken, bodies flopped around on the ground like beached fish. This one would get cataloged with the rest of the disturbing imagery I now carried around with me. When the teeth-rattling percussions finally subsided, I told BT to make a run for it.

"I've still got rounds." He meant for his other rifle.

"Can't afford to lose the M2. There are more cases of ammo on the plane. Get back and set up. We'll cover you."

He looked to the zombies beginning to swarm, nodded at me, and picked up the weapon and the tripod like it was a toy gun and not a hundred plus pounds of deadly metal. BT hadn't made it more than twenty-five yards before I called it a rout. We couldn't hold them back.

"Gotta go!" I yelled at Tommy and James.

"Gary! Need you to drag a fifty cal box out!"

"Got it," he replied, but by the tone of his voice, I was having serious reservations he would be able to perform the task. Rifle fire came from every direction. The attack appeared coordinated.

"Lieutenant, you need to stall them," Eastman warned.

"I'd take them out for drinks, Major, but they don't seem the type or more importantly my type," I huffed as Tommy and I ran.

I could see Gary dragging the box off the plane just as BT stashed the tripod under a wing. He went and manhandled the box and had made it back to the machine gun as Tommy and I pulled up.

I was going to yell at a swaying Gary to get back on the plane, but this was an all hands on deck call. We stopped them here or we didn't. Sure, we could seek refuge on the plane, but what good was that going to do? We couldn't take off and if we could have, we'd face another problem. Even if Eastman somehow pulled a miracle out of his ass, I'm pretty sure he would balk at the thought of trying to take off with an army of the undead parked in front of his plane. The rest of the squad was making it back, some with zombies following close on their heels, others with a much larger cushion. Again, didn't matter much.

"Talbot! Are you going to be able to hold them back?" Eastman was peering around the tail of the plane so he could see me directly, and especially to better spot any signs of bullshittery on my part.

We had plenty of rounds, thanks to the plane. What we lacked were the number of people to shoot said rounds and a proper defensive position.

"I can't promise anything past ten minutes." Even that I

felt was pushing it by four or five minutes. Without any direction from me, we had roughly spread out evenly around the plane, including Gary, who had flushed cheeks and drawn eyes. The situation was so serious, even his ridiculously colored wardrobe could not elicit a smile from me.

"How long are we holding?" BT asked.

What was the right answer? If we were overrun, we were dead. If we were forced into the plane, we were dead–only at a later point. No, the play was to hold out as long as possible and get on the plane. We had long-range communications now; the bigger question was would Bennington spare any resources to get us back? I felt fairly confident he would. Not so much me and my crew–he'd already written us off–but trained pilots? He couldn't leave them by the side of the road. Rounding out the second spot would be the recovery of the plane, and thirdly, if it was possible and didn't endanger any other personnel or equipment, we'd be allowed on.

"They get within twenty yards, give a shout out and we collapse into the plane. Drag the major and his crew with you if need be."

Our side began the festivities first, the rest followed quickly enough. BT and the M2 were doing exactly what they were designed for. My shots would be superfluous at this point; I figured it was as good a time as any to grab what ended up being the last box of 50 cal ammo. BT spared a glance at me.

He yelled, "Where the fuck are you going?"

"Donuts!"

He turned back to the business at hand. Ask a crazy person a question, you're bound to get a crazy answer; as far as I can tell, it was his fault. Got on the plane; Holly was standing next to Chloe. Her legs were shaking; the plane was vibrating from the percussions outside, and this had awakened Chloe. She was looking around, and looked scared herself, as she was taking cues from the other. Lyle was doing his best not to show how afraid he was.

"I hope I did the right thing taking you with me...looked like you two had it all figured out." Both pups were okay with my quick approach; Holly shied away slightly but still let me stroke her side. Chloe licked my hand. "I'll get you two to safety; I promise." I grabbed the box and headed back out.

"Michael?" Jason asked worriedly.

I gave him a thumbs up, which was worlds better than dragging it across my throat.

"Where the fuck are the donuts?" BT asked when I started prepping the ammunition.

"Huh?" I had forgotten entirely about my less than witty quip.

"Just like you to go and eat all the motherfucking donuts!"

He seemed to be getting pissed off about the imaginary fried dough. He was more than three quarters through his stash and was keeping our side at bay all by himself–couldn't say the same about everywhere else. The ten minutes I'd promised was in severe jeopardy.

"Can't stop them, sir!" Winters shouted, partly to be heard, but a fair portion was fright. There was a complete three-sixty of zombies barreling down on us. Hundreds, bordering on thousands, of zombies were fixated on this one little spot and we were at the epicenter.

"Eastman, inside now!"

"Need more...time." He was breathless.

"Grimm, Harmon, get them inside now! Don't care if you have to shoot them and drag their bodies!"

There was shouting as a couple of privates ordered some officers around; I didn't have time to interject.

"Rose, help the gunney with the M2 and the ammo! Tommy, Winters, stay with me by the door. Everyone else get your asses on that plane now!" I could feel minuscule tears ripping through my vocal cords as I made sure, even without the headsets, that I could not be ignored.

Eastman glowered at me as Harmon roughly shoved him

up the steps. "Yeah, sorry I saved your ass" was going to be my argument when he laid into me. I imagined an aerial view of this would be even more frightening. I tapped Winters on the shoulder and thrust with my chin that he needed to go. Tommy was next. Stenzel was at the top, giving us a few extra seconds as she picked off the closest ones. A hand swept past my face as I ran into Tommy. He was pointing at James Motherfucking Lemon, who had not heeded my order.

"I've got this!" He was smiling broadly as he loaded rounds into his pistol.

"You are absolutely shitting me," I said as I was going to go back down the steps. Tommy held me fast and shook his head. James barely got his hand up in time as the first of the zombies descended upon him. I'm not sure what he considered fun in the normal world; maybe parachute-less free falling or telling a card-carrying feminist to fetch him a beer? Both were equally dangerous in my book.

He was grinning from ear to ear, his white teeth shining between his heavy beard and mustache. "Fuck!" He shot. "You!" He fired again. He repeated this small mantra four more times until he was out of bullets. He never screamed out once as those zombies tore into him. He turned his head to look at us, then let it fall back so he was looking up into the sky. "Finally!" he yelled as he was buried in a pile of zombies. He had indeed given us the time we needed to get aboard, but at an awful price. Though, he had seemed more than willing to pay it.

We pulled the stairs up, all of us looking around at each other. I, for one, was breathing heavy. I looked up to the cockpit. Eastman was in his seat, hitting buttons and getting the plane ready to go.

"Get everything secured," I said to no one in particular. "We good to go?" I asked as I went up to the pilot.

"Not even close," he responded.

"Um."

"Relax. I'm not putting her up in the air, but we need to move. Enough of those zombies crowd around into the landing gear and it won't matter what I do to the tail; we'll never leave here."

Major Jackson was speaking into the radio set. "Etna this is Raven. We are down and surrounded, need an extraction. Please advise."

Nothing. If Etna was adhering to radio silence, they were doing an admirable job.

"Comm down again?" I asked.

"Got a feeling, Lieutenant, we have received all the help we're going to get."

"That's bullshit. I know my kind are a dime a dozen, but you guys, the civilians…"

"You should check on your people," Eastman said, dismissing me without ordering me.

He motioned for Major Jackson to shut the door from the cockpit to the transport area.

"What's going on?" BT had taken off his headgear, as had I. "We taking off?"

I shook my head and was about to bring him farther back in the plane where we could talk without others hearing; that was right up until Tommy spoke.

"Bulkers!" he warned.

"They're trying to climb on the wings." Stenzel was traversing the plane, looking out both sides.

I ran up to the front and banged on the door. "Major, fuck your pre-check! Get this thing moving!"

He was aware of some of what was going on as the engines wound up. It got loud enough inside that having a normal conversation was out of the question. We were pulling away; the plane was bouncing as we ran into zombies not willing or able to get out of the way. I thought for a moment that this could be a game we won. Drive far enough away down the runway, the major could set up shop, do some repairs; we'd hold them off for a little bit, then repeat the whole process. Then the realization hit me: yeah, with an unlimited supply of fuel we sure could do just that. I had to think that while we were out on our mission, the first thing the major had done was top-off the bird, if fuel was available and hadn't gummed up. Had no clue if airplane fuel gummed up like the ethanol crap we used to put into our cars, but I didn't see why not. Worst case scenario would be we needed to be airborne to get one of those ass-clenching refuelings where the planes flew close enough to smell each other's exhaust in greeting. We were picking up speed. By now I was thinking we had left the zombies behind.

"Got some clingers." Stenzel was riveted to her window. I went over to look. Three zombies had not only somehow found a way onto the wing, they were hanging on for dear life as we rumbled down the runway. "They going to mess up the flying?" She didn't look up at me; something about those three zombies had her attention rapt.

"Not flying." That got her to break the locked gaze.

"Huh? We're going pretty fast not to be about to. He's not planning on banging a turn going this fast, is he?"

"Hadn't even thought about that."

"He'll drop the wing right on to the pavement and whatever fuel he has in there will light up like a roman candle and sir, I love the 4th of July just as much as the next person, but I've never in my life wanted to be inside a firework."

"You sure we can't make that turn?"

"There should be limiters in the gearbox that prohibit the major from doing it, but I'm not sure what he's got in mind. We're still accelerating and this runway is only two miles long. If we're not taking off, what's the alternative?"

"There a fence on the far side of the runway?"

"You think he's planning on going through it? This isn't a four-wheel drive vehicle! He can't go plowing through fields."

"Give me your headset." She did so quickly.

"Major."

"Little busy here," he answered curtly.

"Looking for some direction. Do we need to brace for impact?"

"It's going to get bumpy. Grab a seat and get buckled in."

"Shit. Everyone in your seats! Buckles on!" I was moving quickly through the cabin.

Yeah, there were a lot of worried stares, but when you're in a moving plane and someone tells you to get your seatbelt on you tend to do as your told and ask questions later–provided there is a later. The engines began to throttle down; I felt a modicum of relief, right until I felt us turning.

"Umm."

"I've got this, Talbot. You just worry about your squad and the civilians," Eastman said.

"What the fuck is going on?" BT asked. He was strapped in tight and holding on to the seat.

"I think he's going kamikaze."

"Kamikaze means to self-sacrifice," Eastman clarified. "The only ones doing the dying will be them."

I got it. He was going to drive into the horde; I was worried about what kind of punishment the plane could take. Would it fold in on itself like Tracy's Jeep did, seemingly a decade ago? I mean, this thing was only a flying aluminum tube. Sure, it had twenty, six-foot props revolving at rpms I couldn't even imagine, but still, they weren't immune to damage. I turned over my shoulder as we came broadside to the zombies still pursuing and then they were out of sight as we were heading back down the runway.

"This is your fault." BT let go of his seat long enough to point at me.

"I'm sitting next to you; how is this my fault?"

"It's that cloud of crazy that you live in! Anybody walks through that haze of insanity, they pick it up. You transfer it like some psychoactive Typhoid Mary!"

Eastman thrummed up the engines again; we could hear the props straining as he sent more juice to them. Sounded like a blender on high. At first, there was nothing, then we began to shudder and there were loud knocks. Going back to the blender analogy, it was like a few large bananas had been dropped in, followed by a whole chicken. All sounded relatively normal until jets of bone, blood, hair and clothes flew past our windows in the gale force winds caused by the wash of the props. Then the sound took a turn for the worse as if an entire avocado, pit and all, had been mistakenly dropped in the macabre mixture. There was a distinctive whomping sound as Eastman continued his crusade. Us getting out of this particular jam was looking more and more dour, and even if we did, we now had the unenviable task of doing it over the highways and byways.

"I wouldn't do this," I told BT, and I meant it.

"Bullshit. I could see you standing on top of the plane, holding on to a rope like a wing walker. Probably be whooping it up, swirling your cowboy hat in the air like a rodeo rider."

"None of that even makes sense; I've never owned a cowboy hat."

"That's what I'm saying. The only part you balked at was the Western wear."

Eastman was cutting swaths through the zombies, who had finally figured out that facing the behemoth machine head-on might not be the best strategy. They were trying to get away. The ones on the outer edges were somewhat successful, but the ones packed in tight, dozens heading towards hundreds of them, were being pureed all the way down to their thighs. It had happened so fast for many of them that their legs were still standing, though their bodies had long ago been reduced to shredded goo.

Before I'd ever left my twenties, I had seen so many things I never thought I would. Figured I was desensitized to some of the worst things imaginable. When the zombie apocalypse started, I added on to that pile, in fact, I nearly replaced it. Early in, I absolutely knew without a doubt I'd borne witness to every horrific thing imaginable. But as I stared out at the tarmac, now covered with ribbons of meat, miles of intestines, lakes of blood and baskets of bones, I knew how fundamentally wrong I'd been. There was always going to be room for more in that crowded space, as if the walls would ever expand to accommodate the horrors.

11

MIKE JOURNAL ENTRY 9

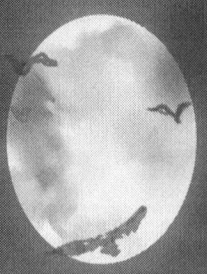

EASTMAN WAS TURNING the plane when we all saw the first signs of something amiss. I know, I know, everything about this was amiss; this was amisser, and I don't give two shits if that's a word or not, and, anyway, it is now because it exists in this journal. Smoke; thick, black smoke was pouring from one of the engines on the far side of the plane. I'd like to think that some of the zombies had begun to combust, but that was too much to ask for. I knew the four-prop plane could fly with three working engines; how far was the major going to push it? The plane was vibrating even more than it should have been, given the circumstances. Like maybe the engine that was smoking had thrown its bearings and the prop was turning unevenly. I didn't know much about planes other than I was happy when they landed and I got off the fucking thing. But if the prop was jacked and not running true, could it wobble off and fly into the plane? It would cut through the shell like a fillet knife through a fresh fish. I'd do the hot knife through butter analogy but that one has been overplayed. There were nervous stares from my entire squad. BT was still glaring at me.

The zombies had dispersed, not completely, but they were

keeping a respectable distance away, Eastman didn't chase them or turn the engines down. I was waiting for the order to cover them while they raced out to work on the tail. It didn't come. He must have been shutting down the bad engine, or it was seizing up, because the bounce in my eyes was subsiding. Then all of the engines began to slow. The door to the cockpit opened.

"The major wants to see you." Major Jackson pointed at me.

I unbuckled and headed that way; I felt like I was being called into the principal's office. Not sure why I always felt guilty about something, but there it is. The Catholic runs deep in me, and let's be honest, I've usually done something worthy of a berating. Chloe and Holly followed; I was happy for the company.

"Could you shut that," Eastman asked as the three of us stepped in. He took a look at the dogs before talking. I missed the first few sentences as I was busy staring out a windshield that had been covered in zombie gore. The windshield wipers were doing their best to push the material to the side and off, but were failing miserably. The blades of the props were dripping blood to match that of a Kosher slaughterhouse's instrument of choice. The nose of the plane was a deep crimson color, so much so, that the tiny spots of shiny metal that shone through looked out of place like diamonds in the mud.

"Lieutenant," he said loudly to snap my attention to him.

"Yup, I'm here," I told him, though I'd yet to look his way.

"Look over there." He was pointing to the engine that was still smoking; thick wisps roiled off of it. At first I thought it was a trick of the eye, then I saw the tentative licks of flame.

"Shit. Now what?"

"I'm going to get the plane moving again, but I'll be dumping the fuel, otherwise we're just a rolling bomb. There's a freeway past that greenbelt up ahead; I'm going to drive as far as this old bird lets me."

"Any guess on how far that might be from them?"

"Could be two miles or as many as five; after that there's an overpass we won't fit through. I wanted to ask you if you would prefer the distance or my attempt to kill more of them."

"Get this thing moving. You kill another ten or hundred doesn't matter; they're like Fritos."

"Fritos?" he asked.

"Yeah, they'll make more."

He could only shake his head. Not sure how thrilled he was that his survival was now so tightly intertwined with mine.

"Get us the distance so we can make our next move."

"Buckle up again–not sure how friendly the terrain in that greenbelt is going to be." He reached back and petted Chloe's head; she licked his hand. Holly nudged the other on the hindquarters as I was leaving to let her know they needed to go.

"Go lay down, you two." I pointed to their makeshift bed as I sat back down, they decided instead to crawl under mine and BT's seats.

"What's going on?" BT asked as the engines throttled up.

"I'm not telling you shit. You'll just blame me for it again."

"Tell me or I'll start going into great detail about this role-playing thing your sister and I do."

"Don't you fucking dare."

"She likes to dress…"

"Fine! We're on fire. Happy? Eastman is going to dump all the fuel while trying to get us on the freeway where we will once again be hoofing it in an attempt to get away from Dewey."

BT's head sagged.

I was worried for him, but even more so for the dogs. Yeah, they were survivors, they'd proven that point. But fast, fleet of foot, and tons of stamina were all things they did not possess. They'd relied on smarts. Tommy could carry them for days, but was it right of me to ask him? I looked over to the boy, who gave me a thumbs-up like he knew what I was thinking. Not sure how they would react to it, as they were still getting used to being around people again, but one thing at a time. We were moving down the runway, although this time, a lot slower.

I was thinking the fence wasn't going to be much more of an impediment than what I was used to seeing in shows and movies; cars generally blew through those like they were made from wet, used toilet paper. Not sure why I went down that road; maybe because most of the events of the day were shitty. Should have known Hollywood got it wrong, given how many other things they had taken liberty with. My head swung back and forth violently as we crashed through. The grating sound and the jarring collision made for some very disorienting moments.

The plane rattled like an angry baby, infused with steroid laced milk and shaking the hell out of its toy. Does that even make sense? I felt like we were in said rattle. I was thankful the dogs had decided to stay with us; the equipment and boxes in the back were smashing against everything around them. Cases of bullets blew open spewing rounds all around the floor. This was another strike against us, as we were going to have to spend some time picking up as many of those as we could before we made a go at getting away. One of the larger crates shattered; wood splintered and intermingled with the rest of the debris. The front of the plane hopped up as we either hit a large divot or finally went up and over the section of fence we were taking for a ride. As if the butterfly riot in my stomach wasn't enough, I bit down hard on my tongue when the ass end slammed into the ground and forced the front end back to the earth in a concussion-inducing seesaw impact.

A crinkle in the aluminum appeared in an arc near the cockpit from floor to ceiling, and, I would imagine, completely around the underbelly. Safe to say this bird's wings had been clipped. If this thing ever went airborne again it would crack open like a rotten egg. I'd had my fair share of turbulent flights through the years, but I was going to demand my money back at the end of this ride. If this had been a commercial flight, we would have been pelted by luggage popping out of the overhead bins, and orange cups with bags that didn't inflate would be dangling in front of our faces. If I had to use the dirty-ass seat that a thousand people had flatulated in as a flotation device, it was safe to say I was going to be ornery. We were hopping around—nothing overly worse than what we had been going through—right up until we hit what must have been a deep culvert. When the front end of the plane hit, it had bent up the props, blew out the glass in the cockpit, and most likely gave me four herniated discs in my back. It was so bad I barely even noticed when the tail of the plane followed.

The worst of it was over as Eastman got onto the road, but even then, it was not a smooth ride; sort of like my Jeep on a barely maintained trail. Rough, but not gut wrenching. Eastman had done enough damage; he was not going to get his security deposit back. I could only hope he took out the supplemental insurance the rental agency offered.

"What do you think the deductible on something like this is?" I asked BT as I tried to regain my bearing.

He didn't even bother to answer. I wasn't sure I could stand, as I began to unbuckle. "Harmon, Springer, Grimm, Kirby…get on that brass. I want as much of it picked up as quickly as possible." I felt like I'd done an adequate job of not swaying too much. "Winters, help Tommy rig up some carrying harnesses for the dogs."

BT pulled me down by the shoulder to whisper into my ear. "That's not going to look too suspicious? Him carting around a hundred and twenty pounds of dog like it's a Pop-Tart box?"

"It's you or him."

"I think he'll wear it nice."

"Figured you might say that."

"Rose, Stenzel, start packing magazines. BT, you want to help Gary?"

"Might want to think about rigging a carrying harness for him," BT replied. My brother was awake, but calling him entirely aware and alert would have been a stretch. He was sick; not zombie virus sick, but he was fighting off an infection and it was going to get worse before it got better. We've all at some point in our lives dragged our asses out of bed and gone to work feeling under the weather, but very rarely did that job you secretly couldn't stand involve life or death struggles. Sitting up in bed to change the channel from Dr. Phil to Jeopardy was usually about the most intensive thing I wanted to do when my throat was on fire. Running from zombies wasn't really an option; I felt bad for him, but it was what it was. Couldn't do anything about it.

"Lieutenant."

"No. Every time you call me up there it's shitty news, and I'm all shittied out for the day. In fact, I'm probably not going to have any room for shit tomorrow, either."

Stenzel looked up from her loading duties, unbelieving in the fact that I'd said that to a major. The astonishment was her fault; she'd been around me long enough to know how this goes.

"Lieutenant." The major seemed more mildly annoyed than perturbed.

"Yes, sir." I reluctantly went up. Eastman was busy putting on his duty belt holster and his 1911. "I take it we're abandoning ship?"

He didn't look up while he was getting ready. "Everyone doing all right back there?"

"As good as they can be after going through the spin cycle."

"Randing's coming back." Now he looked up to gauge my response. "Now before you say anything about his character, I want you to know that he is disobeying a direct order to do so."

"Bennington told him not to, and he is anyway?"

"Not quite like that, but he was told to return to base immediately once he had the scientists aboard."

"I know that tactic; better to ask for forgiveness than permission."

"Exactly. I don't think any amount of pleading is going to forestall the punishment he's going to receive."

"He coming back for me?"

"I'm sure that's it." Eastman was being sarcastic.

"He needs the runway," I said as I began to piece out where this conversation was going. "He needs the runway clear of zombies. Should draw most of them out here with your little off-roading adventure. We'll circle and wait." I was anticipating a response from Eastman. When it wasn't forthcoming, I was confused. "What aren't you telling me?"

"There's a crate in the back needs to come with us."

"What is it?"

"That's a need to know, Lieutenant."

"You're going to pull rank right now? Pretty sure I need to know how big it is, how much it weighs, and if it's dangerous or not, considering it's my people that are going to be transporting it."

"My people," Eastman said.

"Every time I feel like we go over a hurdle together you do dumb shit like that. Go back there right now, Major, and give them an order. See if they look over to me for approval before doing it. Then you can go and threaten their careers and freedom. See if that tact works. Or we could just work together and get shit done."

"It's a nuclear device."

"Fuck you," I blurted out, didn't even mean to.

"This is why I didn't want to tell you."

"Well no shit. How much danger were we in after your little paint shaker experiment?"

"As long as it didn't break free from its straps, we should be fine. If not, I don't think you would have even noticed."

"Comforting, Major. Can't tell you how much fun it is for me, knowing that thing is aboard. And why?"

"Treading again on need to know."

"Eastman."

"Major."

"Major." I acquiesced. "What does Bennington want with a nuke? Can't deploy it on the zombies; wherever they are, there are people too."

"I'm not at liberty to discuss what the Colonel wants with it."

"The SEALs." The light dawned in my head. "I was wondering why they were here. I figured they were a back-up plan if we didn't make it. That was the primary mission, wasn't it? The scientists were just a little gravy on top of the meat and potatoes."

"Colonel Bennington ordered me to retrieve the weapon and that's what I did."

"Just because you were ordered doesn't mean you had to follow through."

He paused. "I have family on that base, just like you."

"You realize where we rank in all of this, right? He wanted to make sure those scientists got back safe and sound, so he left us behind to bring back the bomb."

"Talbot."

"Lieutenant."

He didn't bother adding that part when he replied. "We're in the military. Our entire life consists of doing things we don't like on someone else's orders."

"That is a pathetic excuse."

"We're not all like you. We can't simply do what we want and get away with it."

"Does Randing know what he's coming back for?"

"No."

"I'm sure he's going to be thrilled."

"Sir." It was Sergeant Winters.

I turned back. "Are you ever going to address me and it not be zombies?"

He shrugged.

"How we doing on bullets?" I asked.

"Locked and loaded," Stenzel informed me. "If Grimm would stop eating for a minute or two might have all the ones up off the floor, too.

"All this running around is making me hungry," he called out.

"How heavy is it?" I sighed. I had serious misgivings about taking the thing, not only the danger it put us in right now, but the long-term consequences.

"Around three hundred pounds…with the case it would be approaching four hundred."

"I don't want to be a stick in the mud, but without a vehicle, how do you think we're going to heft this thing around an active battlefield?"

He didn't respond.

"Great. You make the shitty orders and I'm just supposed to magically find a way to grant your wish. Want me to do a little jig for you as well?"

"Good god no." BT had come up to see what the problem was. "I've seen you dance. You look like you're trying to stomp out a brush fire, even have the arms flailing about in no particular rhythm." He let it go, stopping in mid-windmill, when he realized I was not sharing in his amusement, though he did my unique lack of grace on the dance floor justice. "Spill it, because that was comedic gold; nailed the visuals, too."

"Major?" I deferred.

"Is this going to get us out of here quicker?"

"Beats me," I told him.

"Fine." He turned his attention to BT. "Gunney, there's a thermonuclear device in the back that we need to get back to the runway."

"Fuck you."

"That's what I said!"

"Mike, what are we supposed to do?" He looked to me, completely ignoring the major.

"I'm going to throw this in there, because it might affect your decision making," Eastman said.

"*If* he had decision-making skills, you mean. Sorry," BT added at the end when he realized I wasn't liking any part of this. "It's difficult when they are set up so beautifully. It's like walking in a room with dominos all lined up and no one there to tell you not to touch them. I mean really, how can you not set that in motion?"

"Done?" I asked.

"For now." At least he was truthful.

"We don't bring that thing back, we'll all be packing our bags."

"Fuck." I was looking out the cockpit, hat in one hand, the other I was running through my hair. My family was starting to get into the routine of a more normal existence. The road was nowhere anybody should be. Bennington had many faults, like any of us, but he had that installation buttoned up tight. "What if we tell him it was ruined in our escape attempt? Leaking radiation, maybe." I had turned back around to gauge Eastman's reaction.

"He'll know we're bullshitting him."

"Yeah, he will," BT piped in. "Guy has cop instincts."

"Lieutenant, I'm sure whatever you're doing up there is important, but, well, you know…zombies," Winters yelled up.

"All right people–we're gearing up. We're out in three minutes," I said, going to the back.

"And the crate?" Eastman asked.

"I don't see the Hulk anywhere around here, Major. Right now our objective is to get away from the zombies and to keep them from congregating here. We'll get some transportation and swing back by."

"I will absolutely not leave that untended!"

"Perfect. You hold down the fort and we'll swing by and pick you up."

"You insolent piece of…"

"Careful, Major," BT said, stepping up. The rest of my squad's attention was now rapt on what was happening, though they were doing their best to pretend not to notice.

"Two and a half minutes, people." I was in the crew area.

BT stared the Major down before joining me. It was a good bet when we got back we were both going to be made Private, and we'd be cleaning out overused latrines with our own toothbrushes for a very long time. The major and his crew were in a small huddle, I'm sure discussing how they were going to deal with the mutiny. There was a chance, albeit a small one, that they might draw down on us. It would be a bad move on their part, but one I needed to be prepared for. I made hand signals for everyone to change their channels to a private one before I spoke.

"We've got a situation here; I'm not prepared to go into details at the moment, but the major and his crew might try something. If they do, I want them disarmed quickly and hopefully free from injury, but you are authorized for deadly force if it becomes necessary." Yeah, you can bet that got a bunch of looks around. BT wasn't a fan of that. What the major wanted us to do was within his rights to order, so this would be construed as a major offense, one that could land me and some of my team in front of a firing squad.

"You sure about this?" BT covered his mic.

"No," I answered him as honestly as I could. "BT, we try

and drag that fucking bomb past a thousand zombies what do you think is going to happen to us?"

I managed a brief smile as I looked over at Tommy; he had one bullie on his back and one in front. They all looked pretty content with their lot in life. Never met one of those dogs that would forgo a good ride as opposed to walking. I let out a sigh when Eastman said he was coming with us.

As I exited the plane, there was a conga line of zombies just hitting the greenway. I got everyone to the front of the plane and out of sight of our pursuers. If we moved quickly enough, we could make it to and up the overpass, roughly a quarter of a mile away, without them ever seeing us. What they did once they got to the last place they saw us was anybody's guess. Normally they'd just kind of shuffle around in the general area until they caught wind of new prey. I had a strong feeling that Dewey would send his lackeys to check out that overpass.

We were making good time, even with the civilians. Tommy was making a show of the dogs being heavy, but the slow link in our procession was Gary. BT and I were dragging him at a decent clip. Stenzel was leading the way and Winters was watching our collective asses.

Within five minutes we had climbed the embankment and got to the far side of the road and out of view. Winters was lying down on the road, keeping us informed. We took a left, heading to a gas station and fast food joint a quarter of a mile away. We'd regroup there and then head back to the airport where I could drop off the major and most of my squad, including my brother and the church people.

"Sir, the zombies didn't stop at the plane," Winters informed me. I'd left PFC Grimm with him to watch his back while he was lying prostrate on the roadway. "I don't know how they could have seen us, but they're heading straight this way."

"We're just going to have to footrace them back. Withdraw and meet us at the Exxon."

"On it."

Winters and Grimm were with us in under five minutes. I would have loved to spell them a breather, but we were under some serious constraints. Randing was heading back and we still needed to get the bomb. We got underway the moment they stepped into the lot.

"What about one of those ramp trucks?" BT asked while we were running.

I was on a different track. "Where the hell did they even get the nuke from?"

"Does it matter at this point?"

"Sort of. Do they just leave those things hanging around like those green mailboxes where mailmen can grab a raincoat if they need one?"

"You realize that those two things have nothing to do with each other, right?"

"I'm serious man! Where the fuck did they get a nuke? Are there silos around here?"

"I was under the impression they had all shut down. I guess not."

"That's the best you got? You guess not?"

"You're obsessing about the wrong thing," he said, wanting me to close the book on the subject.

"Don't you think I know that? I just don't know what else to go on about. It's a fucking nuke."

Stenzel halted us as she got to the edge of some brush that led to a greenway, a fence, and then the airport. "Sir, looks clear."

"Too clear?" I asked over the headset.

"*Too clear?* Keep going on with your paranoid self." BT was getting ready to break for the front and out.

"Hold on there. Let's go over a few things," I said.

"What?" he fairly growled.

"Winters, how many zombies were tailing us to the overpass?"

"Ballpark…I'd say a little over a hundred."

"Tommy, how many zombies do you think were on the tarmac?"

"Had to be eight hundred, possibly a thousand."

"Major Eastman, how many zombies would you guess you blended into oblivion?"

"Wasn't planning on counting them, but if pressed for a number…two hundred, give or take?"

"Now BT, I'm going to be completely honest with you. In high school, I smoked a lot of pot, like, to the point where I single-handedly bought a Taco Bell, and I was never really good at the maths. Pretty much made sure I had a hall pass for my entire senior year, but even taking the minimums and the maximums into account, there are roughly five hundred zombies still in the general area."

"Movement in the concourse," Stenzel said.

"They're hiding," BT said through gritted teeth, looked like he was about ready to grind them down.

"How are we going to clear them out before Major Randing gets here?" Eastman asked.

"Not going to be able to. BT and I will draw a few off as we grab a ramp truck and go retrieve the package."

"You volunteering me now?"

"You're the strongest here by a factor of three or four. Yeah, I'm volunteering you to help me move a stupid-heavy box." I'd learned I could get BT to do damn near anything if I made him look like Superman first. Who among us doesn't like a good ego stroke? Plus, no part of what I'd said wasn't true.

"Don't think I don't know you think you're manipulating me."

"Let's get this done." I smacked his chest. "How much time do we have, Major?"

"Randing can circle for half an hour; after that he either lands or flies off before he gets into fuel issues."

"And if we can't get a truck started?" I was now up front with Stenzel, looking at a row of the belt trucks. Eastman's lack of a response was a response in its own right.

"As long as they're using ethanol-free gas we might be alright."

"We'd better hope they were using it or the fuel lines are going to be gummed up." BT tapped my shoulder and we got moving.

We pulled ourselves up and over the ten-foot fence, and as soon as our feet touched the runway Stenzel warned us that she thought the zombies in the concourse had seen us.

"They holding up a welcome home sign?" I quipped.

"Worse. They're pointing," she responded.

"Ruined my joke, Corporal."

"Sorry, sir…it wasn't that funny anyway."

BT snorted at that. "You could order her to laugh."

"Kiss my ass. Let's run; no reason to be stealthy now."

"We should have circled further," BT said, far too late. We had a thousand yards or more to get to the trucks which were inconveniently parked right next to the terminal.

"No time for that."

"And if we die now?"

"Then we probably should have circled further," I told him.

"Eat a dick."

I think it was Stenzel who laughed, though it could have been anyone on the party line.

We were halfway there when the zombies exited the building. We had a sliver of good luck when the door nearest the trucks must have been chained or inaccessible. Still was going to be extremely close. These might be Dewey's zombies, but they weren't Dewey. Instead of figuring out where we were going and attempting to cut us off, they were all about hitting us in our current position. Eventually, we would be running for the exact same spot, but for right now, they were trying to get to us and that played in our favor.

We were about a hundred yards from the trucks when BT came up with this little gem: "What about the keys?"

Such a fundamental piece of the pie, and yet we'd overlooked it. One of those "trees for the forest" types of miscalculations. This was like trying to make an apple pie without apples. Sure, it was something my sister would have a go at, but it would fail miserably, a lot like this whole venture, should there not be keys. Had about a three-second window where we could abort the entire thing and veer off, head to the far side where we should have come in on in the first place. Go over the fence and circle back around to be with the squad. The two other scenarios were, we get into the truck, there are keys and it magically starts, we continue the mission. Or, two, we barricade ourselves in the non-moving vehicle surrounded by hundreds of zombies while Randing hot-lands, grabs up my squad, and departs for home. I gave option one a solid ten percent chance of success, so which way do you think we went?

"What if the door is locked?"

"Stop asking questions!"

"That's your solution? Stop asking questions?" He would have rebuked me a second time, but oxygen was at a premium at the moment. I was hoping there was no reason to lock up one of these trucks; I mean, what fucking chop-shop worth its weight in criminals is parting out a belt truck? We were going to beat the zees to the truck, but by inches; once I touched that handle the decision was made. I took note as I got closer that there was, indeed, a slot for a key below the handle. I spurred myself on. I took the side closest to the zombies; it happened to also be the driver's side. BT rocked the entire vehicle as he used it to slow himself down. He was halfway around as I gripped the handle. I pushed in the button, expecting to feel the locking mechanism release; instead I was met with the very anti-climactic feeling of it pushing in without resistance, meaning it was locked.

The truck rocked as I frantically worked at opening a door that was dead set against it. My options were limited and very time constrained: bust out the window or start shooting zombies.

"Get in here!" It was BT. I spared a glance; he was sitting in the passenger seat, I would imagine trying to figure out what the fuck I was doing.

"Locked!" I shouted over my shoulder. BT, in his haste to get the door open, nearly pushed me into the approaching horde, whom I was now busy attempting to slow down. I shot two zombies without even having to aim, hitting the first low in the neck and sending it spiraling off to the side as it attempted to hold its head up. The other I stopped dead in its tracks, the bullet making a neat circle under its right eye. That was when I was so rudely pushed forward.

"Get in!"

The command needed to be verbalized as much as a young child heading down the stairs on Christmas Day needs to be told to open his presents. Or a starving person told to eat Thanksgiving dinner. Or a foot fetishist needs to be asked if he would care to lick toes at a sandal convention. I don't know if those actually exist, but if they did, there would be some very happy, albeit strange, people.

I dove in, making sure to lock the door quickly. BT was dangling the keys in front of me; he nearly dropped them as the first of the zombies slammed up against the side of the truck. I snatched them and put them in the ignition just as the window behind me exploded inward. I noted a zombie with what looked like a gargoyle statue in his hand, straight from some Gothic cathedral. Not sure where he got it, but he was wielding it effectively, slamming it into the side of the truck as he tried to make his way closer to my window. Fortunately, because of the press of zombies, Quasimodo was having a difficult time getting in there.

"Start the truck, Mike." BT's voice wasn't hysterical or even raised, but his tone left no doubt what he wanted me to do and when. I turned the ignition. I got the same response I got from my wife if I gently touched her shoulder at three in the morning after I had spent a night of heavy drinking with my buddies and I was feeling a little randy. Nothing, that is. I got absolutely nothing.

Quasimodo had his gargoyle raised and was inching his way closer. From behind, a few zombies were trying to reach up and grab some part of me; again, the only thing saving me was that there were so many they could not reach in unencumbered. My seat was being pushed and pulled as they clutched at whatever they could.

"Not gonna say it again," BT warned. Not sure what the fuck he was going to do about it. If the truck didn't start, beating me into a pulp wasn't going to help the matter. Might make him feel better, but that'd be about it. You'd think that by this stage in the z-poc, I'd know about glow plugs and their need to warm up before you can turn the engine over; maybe that tidbit would also help me with the wife. Just some shit goes right out the window when you're up against it. There were zombies on the hood, and some were crawling up the belt in the back. We were pressed in from all sides, and the creepy part—yeah because that wasn't ramped up enough—as near as I could tell, they were all staring at us. Yes, they were moving and trying to get in, but continuously through it all, their eyes never left ours. Whatever was flowing through Dewey's brain, he was sharing. Quasi was close; I kept alternating between him, his raised arm, and the glow plug light. When it finally turned a bright yellow, I turned the key. There was a dreadful beat of my heart where again, nothing happened. Then, through the plume of a thick, lung-choking cloud of smoke, the engine chugged and turned over.

"Motherfucker," I said as I put the truck in reverse. Quasi's statue-clad hand smashed my side view mirror into oblivion. The truck was moving slowly; not sure if it knew another speed, considering what it did for a living. That, and the zombie bodies to the rear were taking away any momentum I could muster as I slammed the accelerator to the floor. The truck took off like a turtle high on crack. Same ponderous gait but with jerky movements.

"Any chance you could move a little faster?" BT was pressed against his seat staring down two zombies holding on to the lip in the hood, their faces comically smooshed into the windshield as they clung fast. The truck jostled and kicked before finally breaking free.

"Be aware, LT, you have seven stowaways on board with you."

I thanked Winters for the information. The truck had a governor on it, maxed out at twenty-one and a half miles per hour. Couldn't shake a sleepy toddler at full bore. Poor analogy; why I'd imagine a baby hanging on to a moving car I don't know, and why I'd curse my inability to throw him off? Got no reasonable answer for that either. Although, a baby apocalypse would be terrifying in its own right. Just think of the biological warfare they could wage. There you are, a bunch of macho men sitting around a campfire discussing your conquests, when all of a sudden there is a barrage of incoming projectiles, fully-loaded diarrhea-laden diapers. The carnage would be incomprehensible.

"The exit is that way." BT was pointing to his left; I wasn't sure how he could see anything with the zombies planted in his face. "Get through the gate, then stop." He was right, we needed to deal with our clingers before we got back to the plane.

It was the sun that saved my life, or rather the direction I found myself facing. Let me clarify. The sun was casting the shadow of the zombie standing on top of the belt directly over my head, where I could see it as I stopped the truck.

"Stop!" I shouted to BT just as he reached for the door handle. "Watch this." I opened my door about a foot then pulled it shut quickly. Nothing happened.

"What?" BT asked, confused.

"Hold on." This time I opened the door a little wider and actually moved my left leg out. That got the zee to move. It was a lot closer than I'd thought it was as it jumped down trying to grab me. I pulled my leg in.

"Damn! How'd you know?" he asked.

"It's my attenuation to the enemy, my ability to put myself in the minds of those trying to do me harm."

"Just answer the question."

"Shadow."

"Thought so."

I pulled up a couple hundred yards to get some distance from my potential waylayer.

"You ready?" I asked as I put the truck in park.

"Yeah, if only to kill these two fuckers." The zombies on the windshield had created enough drool that it had at first pooled on the windshield wiper and then flowed over. BT darted out, daring anyone from above to jump on him. He moved quickly to the front end of the hood before either of the zombies could react. He grabbed the closest one by its boot-clad feet. I thought he was going to merely pull it straight down; should have known that wasn't going to happen, just because of who BT is and the strength he possesses. He whipped that zombie into a position where it was standing straight up before he brought it down violently. Its head crashed into the pavement with enough force to crack it wide open, the fissure big enough its brains poured out and began to flow down the crown in the road.

I wanted to comment on the grossness of it, but we still had six others to deal with. The other zombie, having witnessed what happened to its friend, was doing its best to make sure that the same fate didn't befall him and was scrambling farther up the hood to get into attack position. BT had turned and was waiting for the zombie to launch. I fired two quick shots, the second one doing the deed, blowing its brains off to the far side of the road. It immediately collapsed on the hood, severely denting it; I hoped not enough to interfere with the fan.

Two of the zombies that were riding on the back found their way down while the other two were coming closer from above. Plus, we had a speeder running down the road toward us. I was backing away from the truck, realizing that this could go south quickly.

"Need a little help here!" I told BT when I realized that they all seemed focused on me. "Up top!"

It's a hard thing to implicitly trust that someone is going to have your back. BT was easily one of my most trusted friends, and I know without a shadow of a doubt he would lay his life down for mine, as I would for him. It wasn't that I doubted he would help; it was that I had fears he wouldn't be able to kill them before they got to me. He fired a few shots, as did I. I was parallel to the truck and had just killed the zombie closest to me before I was hit from the side. The impact was jarring, and I was immediately sent to the turf. My right shoulder took the brunt of the force then, to a lesser extent, my head as it whiplashed down. Luckily, there's not much housed there to suffer any damage.

The zombie took one lackluster snap at my ear before it was called into the great beyond or below or wherever plagues go to die. I was happy he'd killed whatever virus had kept him animated, but there were still three zombies in play and I was in no position to do anything about it. I felt a rough hand on my collar as BT was pulling me up with one hand and firing with the other. I was scurrying backward, doing my best to assist him, realizing that until I got my feet under me, he wasn't going to aim properly. I wanted to shout at him to leave me and shoot the fucking zombies, but things were happening so fast, and by the time I got all of that out it'd be over, one way or the other.

He was Ramboing rounds, shooting from the hip, to clarify. He yanked me sideways; I was pinwheeling backwards, doing my best to not fall over again. He finally, and thankfully, brought his rifle up to his shoulder and fired into a zombie that was close enough to me that I could have figured out if he was happy to see me; he fell to the side, a gaping hole where his temple had been. I got myself under control and returned the favor to BT, who was so fixated on my well-being he completely missed the one about to run into his blindside like a ball-hungry linebacker to a defenseless quarterback.

I had a crappy angle and still took the shot; if I had one of those super slow-motion cameras, I could have watched the bullet travel past BT's chest close enough to ripple his uniform before colliding into the zombie's shoulder. I had a bit of luck as the bullet must have careened off its clavicle, came back up the side of its neck, and blew a hole in its skull. Sometimes the 5.56 round got a bad rap for not being lethal enough, but in this instance, it worked much better than the heavier 7.62, which would have just gone deeper where it initially struck and thus, not killed it. We took care of the last one together. The adage, "friends that kill together stay together," crossed my mind. Wasn't much left of its head by the time it took its final convulsion.

"That was close," BT said as the smoke from our bullets dissipated. We spent a few seconds catching our breaths. I heard the rumble of a plane high overhead.

"Randing. We have to go."

"How about a 'thank you?'" BT asked as he got back in.

"You're welcome."

"You too."

I pulled up to the destroyed plane then backed the truck

up to the rear cargo door for easier offloading. The aircraft did not have power, and we had to spend a few moments manually opening the hatch. The bomb, unlike most of the other stuff in the plane, was still latched down.

"What the actual fuck, Mike?" BT asked as we worked to get the straps loose.

"If I knew anything about bombs, I would sabotage this thing," I said as I kept moving.

"Talbot's hands in a nuke. Yeah, best not to think on it."

I flipped a bird over the top of the box. When it was loose, it began to move toward the back of its own volition.

"You hold it and I'll get the belt going," I told BT.

"Perfect. I'll stand here and hold the thermonuclear device in place. Sounds like a wonderful idea."

As I got out of the plane, I did a quick scan of the area. I almost missed the lone zombie standing on the overpass looking at me. He was so still, I wondered if it was the mannequin that had plagued Will Smith in, *I am Legend;* it was just as freaky. Then it moved. The thought lingered a moment; I knew that the director of the film, in a bid to make that scene more intense, had made the mannequin move. But instead of a quick, cinematic head twist, my zombie started running toward the embankment.

"Shit." I quickly went to the truck. What I figured was going to be a quick on-off switch ended up being three levers, none of them marked. The truck shook as the belt rumbled to life.

"Wrong way!" I heard BT yell.

I wanted to tell him to keep his eye on the very large bomb and not worry about what I was doing. There was grinding and crunching as I switched the direction of the belt; I think I was supposed to stop it completely, before changing its direction.

"Got it. Back up a little more!" he yelled.

With BT's help, I got the truck close enough that the belt

was less than an inch from skimming the floor of the plane. Once again, if I'd thought this through I would have realized the problem we were about to encounter. In all fairness, BT should have picked up on it as well.

"Zombie coming," I told BT as we lined the box up.

"One?" he grunted.

"So far…but I doubt it. You ready to get a corner up?"

"Let's do it."

We'd no sooner dropped that box on the belt than the weight of it pushed the belt to the floor. The screeching and smell of burning rubber was intoxicating, and not in a good way. It had slowed to the point where it wouldn't even move the bomb.

"Lift it!" BT bellowed.

I helped him heft it.

"The truck, the truck! I've got this!"

One lever was for reverse, one for forward. The other had to be to raise and lower, I reasoned. Had a fifty-fifty shot of raising the belt…yup, I dug that fucker deeper into the plane. BT was cursing up a storm as I quickly pushed the stick forward.

"Far enough!" There was a *thud* as he dropped the box back down. I was about to go and help him, when I saw a half dozen zombies closing quickly.

"Box is yours!"

"It's not on right! It's going to fall!"

"You better make sure it doesn't." If he wanted to yell back, it was going to have to be after I fired some kill shots. Took out three before the others halted their progress and headed for the side of the road. I knew they were waiting for back-up; it was my sincerest hope we would be long gone before any could arrive.

"Mike!" BT was following the box as best he could, holding up the half that was doing its best to inch over and off the belt; the big problem was going to be when it went higher up, past his outstretched hands, and either fell to the side or somehow miraculously kept going until it dropped straight down on the hood, completing the job the zombie had attempted earlier. A lot of things were on the brink right now, and each of them lethal in their own way. Maybe the bomb went off when it fell, or maybe it made the truck into a paperweight, or the fucking zombies got us. If we had to make a run for it, it was safe to say we were going to miss our ride.

I streaked past BT; I may or may not have got a "What the fuck?" Hopped into the cab and shut down the belt. In what felt like two heartbeats, I was back outside. BT was on his very tiptoes, outstretched arms and extended fingertips straining to keep the package aloft. There wasn't going to be anything I could do from the ground. I hopped onto the ramp and grabbed an edge of the box; I was pulling for all I was worth. Hardly felt like it was moving. In contrast, the zombies were flying toward us.

"BT, you're going to need to defend us."

"Hold the damn thing."

I had to jump on an edge and put my entire body weight on it as BT let go. I was expecting to hear shots soon, instead, he got on the ramp and was striding up. The rocking of the entire truck was definitely accentuating the whole teeter-totter effect I was trying to prevent. This was one of those cases where if a pair of mating dragonflies landed on the other side of the crate, it would be enough to tip the scales. My end lifted an inch; this was it. We were both going for a short ride followed by an explosive conclusion. BT must have seen this because he lowered his shoulder down and drove it into the side of the box closest to him. Managed to get the whole thing on the ramp while sending me off to the dirt.

My shoulder hit first, then my back; felt most of the life-giving oxygen head out to parts unknown. It wasn't that crippling "can't breathe!" feeling, but he certainly wasn't getting a Christmas card from me this year.

"You all right?" BT's face swam into focus above me.

"Dandy." I stood with as much alacrity as was possible. The zombies had reached the back of the truck. I was getting into position to fire.

"Just drive! Get us out of here!"

Can't say I was thrilled with BT being exposed up there like he was, but he had a point. Staying and fighting was a rapidly losing proposal as more zombies were closing in. I got back in the cab, careful to not take off too quickly–not that that was really an issue, given the gearing of the truck. Through the windshield, I could see Randing making his final approach.

"Package in hand…how's it looking?" I asked.

"Sir, this is Winters. Runway is awash with zombies. Major Randing is taking the only clear avenue and he told Major Eastman he's only stopping long enough to pick us up. You've got maybe five minutes."

"Roger that." I looked to my speedometer which, for some reason, went to eighty. We were hovering at a blistering nineteen. In my rearview mirrors I could see zombies climbing the ramp and half the population of Rhode Island following.

"BT–you need help?"

"Naw…I'm cool, surfing on a moving ramp truck, giant bomb next to me, and a half dozen of my closest friends coming to visit. Everything's fine."

"Well, when you say it like that."

"Just keep moving. They're picking their way slowly."

"Winters, have the squad ready. We're bringing our own company."

"Got it, sir."

Saw the puffs of burnt rubber float up into the air as Randing put his plane down. We had just made it back through the gate. Randing was like that one final hottest game system left at a department store on Black Friday. The convergence was underway.

"This is Major Randing. I am going to attempt to pull as many to the far side of the airfield as possible; we will do the pick-up and the on-loading at the opposite side."

I appreciated what he was doing as it afforded BT and myself an extra minute or two, but I wasn't sure what he was thinking. There was a good chance zombies were going to be flooded on the runway. I'd let the flyboy worry about it; my plate was overflowing with a whole bunch of inedibles; looked like a buffet of kale, Brussels sprouts, and cherry glazed ham. Oh, and that weird shit the health freaks keep trying to pass off as tasty: pureed cauliflower that was supposed to be like mashed potatoes. What kind of abomination is that? No matter what you believe about capital punishment, the inventor of that cuisine needs to go. If left to his/her own devices, who knows what they could come up with. Beet fries perhaps? Chocolate covered liver? Maple glazed ham? People like that need to be stopped at all costs. BT began to fire his rifle; the zombies must have moved closer. I couldn't spare a glance to see how he was doing as I was now entering the minefield of zombies.

"BT! You need to hold on; going to start evasive driving!"

"They're close." Another shot.

I was doing my best to make the turns as sweeping as possible, clipped a zombie in the hip; I could hear the crunching of her pelvis as the bumper cracked into her. The jolt was far from jarring, but it was enough to have BT swear at me. There wasn't anything I could do except to keep driving. I swerved again; I was doing my best to miss them but they seemed determined to make a claim against my insurance. The latest victim was not going to enjoy any payout; as I hit her side she spun down and in front of the truck where I proceeded to go straight over her skull, shooting out the contents like a stomped-on ketchup packet. Had enough experience with those to know.

The zombies were tightening their vice, moving in so close

that it didn't make sense to try and avoid them. The truck had a steel bumper on it; I guess it was time to see if the welder who had put it on was worth their union wages. At twenty miles per hour, I wasn't getting the explosive hits with the guts pouring up and over the hood; it was more of an ushering to get the fuck out of the way. Kind of like what the cops do at the end of Mardi Gras; assemble en masse at the end of a street on horseback and just push the drunks out of the way.

And much like those revelers, the zombies weren't too pleased about it, either. Those that weren't beating on the truck were finding a way to hold on for a ride. Felt very much like I was wheeling a banana cart into a monkey house, or more aptly, like a modern-day virus injecting into a decent operating system. Randing was turning the plane around; it was going to be a race to the finish line. I heard BT yell out in surprise–I was fully expecting to see his body rolling away from me and had hit the brakes so I could help him.

"Why the fuck are you stopping?" he yelled.

"Why the fuck are you yelling? Thought you were about to fall off!"

"Readjusting the box!"

"How you doing up there?"

"Just hurry up, Mike."

Whenever BT used my first name, I knew it was serious. The collision of so many bodies was slowing our progress, Randing looked like he was speeding up, and considering what was happening, I couldn't blame him. Eastman, his crew and my squad looked in danger of being cut off from all avenues of escape. If Randing didn't get to them soon, they would have no choice but to make a run for it. Randing would take off, and then it would just be myself and BT in the midst of all the zombies, armed, of course, with a nuclear warhead. At that point, I'd want to pull the pin. Pretty sure they don't work like a hand grenade, but it sounded good. There were some more shots from up above; I could see in my one, good side-view mirror zombies falling off and tumbling into the throngs of others. My heart skipped a beat every time I witnessed this, not because of the zombies, but at any moment I expected it to be the oversized BT doing the falling.

I was so tense, I would have been hard-pressed to slide a pencil out of my ass. Wait…that's really weird; what the fuck was the pencil doing there in the first place? Maybe I should have just said my cheeks were clenched tight. If I ever edit this, I'll take out that other sentence. I was frustrated; I just wanted to shout at the zombies to get the fuck out of the way. We were in range of getting some assistance from my squad, but they were having their own problems. Randing was grinding down the occasional stray zombie that ventured into his path. If I thought it had been gross watching from a seat on the plane, where I could only see the final outcome, witnessing the event firsthand was something I don't think I'll ever be able to scrub from my memory. When I'm old and drooling and don't remember how to operate a television remote, I will still see those bodies turned into watery confetti. It sprayed up and around the props and backwashed some fifty feet before settling to the earth like a macabre snowstorm that might fall in some version of hell.

Randing had, thankfully, gotten to my group. The side door had opened and he was urging them in. I could see them looking our way; I was waving them into the plane.

"Go! I'm ordering it!" I told them.

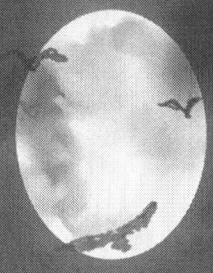

12

MIKE JOURNAL ENTRY 10

THE PLANE TURNED; I figured this was where he went back down the runway and up, leaving us to our own devices. Instead, he turned his ass. We were looking at an open cargo bay and a well set up machine gun nest–even had sandbags. Somebody'd been planning accordingly. From this angle, it looked like it was firing head-on, but he was clearing a path to our right. The heavy rounds and the rate of fire did an adequate job.

"Going to get bumpy," I told BT as I was preparing to get onto our bullet-plowed lane.

"Like it's been smooth so far."

"How many with you?"

"Ten, maybe twelve...not moving. They're holding on, waiting for the ride to stop."

Most of my squad had fanned out around the machine gunner and were firing in lanes, knocking down zombies like bowling pins. I was beginning the process of turning us in a slow arc so I could back the truck up as close to the plane as possible and let the belt take the bomb down.

"BT–you're going to have to guide me in." The passenger-side mirror was still there, just pushed in so far that all I could see was the logo of the transport company that guaranteed to move my luggage with as much care as I would. That's a crock of shit. They toss that stuff around like politicians do promises at election time. Just fling those words helter-skelter to see which ones stick or resonate, I would imagine.

"That's what she said."

"What?" Then I remembered my last words. "Are you kidding me right now?"

"Sorry. You're not the only one that tries, and fails, by the way, to use humor in a terrifying situation."

"What fucking situation am I ever going to be in that necessitates you being there to help guide it in?"

"You are seriously analyzing a 'that's what she said' joke? Just drive to the left…your other left! "Your other, other left!" he yelled out after I figured I had corrected my trajectory.

"How many fucking lefts do you think I have?"

"Don't hit the plane!"

"BT–I can't see the plane!"

On paper, this may come across as a humorous interlude; while it was happening it was anything but. The truck was jostling around as I plowed into zombies and with the herky-jerky movements you tend to make when you are backing up with any speed. Zombies were smacking at the side windows as I went past; on more than one occasion I would watch as a zombie's head blew up under the stress of a high-speed projectile added into the mix.

"Another hundred feet!"

Telling someone "another hundred feet" when they can't see where they're going is like telling a starving person how delicious the hamburger you're eating is. Basically, no help, is what I'm shooting for here. I could hear my squad yelling.

"Winters, guide me in."

"Start slowing down, sir, and go to your left," he responded. After a couple of seconds, he added, "Your other left."

"So help me, I'm going to demote all of you," I hissed.

Stenzel and Grimm came up on my passenger side, Kirby and Rose the other; they were firing.

"Sir, come to a stop." I wasn't going fast, but the suddenness must have been enough to start the bomb rocking because I heard BT's litany of swears.

"The belt," BT said as he began to scrabble down. "Wrong way!" I quickly reversed the direction. Tommy and BT, along with Springer, Harmon, and the SEALs were in position and helped get the box down and onto the ramp of the large plane. Captain Smoltz hooked a winch up to a handle and pulled it the rest of the way in, although the mechanism was on its own pace, some in the squad pushed, getting the process to move as quickly as possible. I was between my shooters and the loaders, gauging when it would be safe to collapse the defense.

"Package is secure!" Captain Smoltz reported. "Get your people in here."

"Fire team! Let's go!" I was waving with my arm. The zombies were fast on our heels. "Start putting the ramp up!" It moved slow enough that the lead zombies would be able to get on it. Heard the props rev up as Randing was getting antsy to move. Hard to fault him that, as we were now completely engulfed in a zombie horde. I had to jump up onto the ramp; Stenzel, Rose, and Kirby made the jump as well. Grimm stepped in a steaming pile of rotting intestine; his lead foot slid out from under him and instead of jumping, he made an awkward slide that partially obscured him from me as I kept rising in the air.

"Fuck," I said. Stenzel turned; she and the rest had been heading down the ramp into the belly of the plane, which had lurched forward. I was looking straight down at PFC Grimm, who was panicked as he was trying to get his legs under himself. Looked like he was on the world's grossest slip and slide. Every time he planted a hand to give himself leverage, it would splay away. I was jumping from a perfectly good plane and into a zombie storm. I was careful to avoid the brunt of the viscera and still almost went for a ride. I reached out to yank Grimm, first out of the quagmire he found himself in, and then up onto his feet. Unidentifiable goo dripped from the majority of his body…the odor was indescribable.

By now the plane was slowly beginning its taxi. Stenzel had halted the door closing and was making it go back down. Even over the sound of the engines, I could hear Randing screaming for the door to shut.

"Let's go, Marine!" I grabbed his shoulder and shoved him toward our ride, which was getting away. Don't know where it came from or what it was anchored to, but a thick rope was tossed out the back.

"Grab it!" BT said.

Liked that idea about as much as I liked the idea of eating the weird cat lady's casserole at the office pot-luck. It always smelled like old tuna fish and looked surprisingly like Fancy Feast. If we lost our footing or got tangled up in it, we would be dragged to an ugly conclusion. But we did it anyway, because there were no other choices. The plane was moving at a clip that would have been difficult to match. Randing was either oblivious to our plight or didn't give a shit. In one fluid motion, I bent over while running and wrapped my right hand around the rope; with my left I grabbed Grimm. We were running full tilt and my squad was pulling on the rope, attempting to draw us in. I was four or five steps from letting go, realizing we were going to come up short. Stenzel must have understood this as well; she dropped that ramp completely to the ground.

I lost sight of her in the resultant showering of sparks. The bits of superheated aluminum burned my skin wherever they made contact, but it was enough to slow the plane down–or make Randing slow it down–same thing. BT was singlehandedly pulling us in like a hooked and prized catfish. Zombies were no more than a few steps behind; no way we were going to make it on without bringing a couple of friends. I could hear yelling through the microphone. One of Randing's crew was attempting to shove Stenzel out of the way to get the door closed.

It was BT to save the day again. "You touch her and I'll toss you out like yesterday's leftovers!" I appreciated the help, but he was talking to an officer; gonna bet that the majority of my squad would be facing the Uniform Code of Military Justice when we got back.

Grimm stumbled, but I had my left arm securely wrapped around his mid-section and a death grip on the rope with my right. We were running, stumbling, and were yanked forward to the edge of the cargo ramp. BT had the rope wrapped around his waist; I could see Rose, Kirby and a few others holding on to his life-line in a desperate tug of war with us on the other end. We were all going to make it or we were all going to be spilled out over the runway like a burst open piñata, the zombies jumping on their prizes like kids on candy.

As my foot hit the lip, I did my best to toss Grimm aboard. BT yanked him by the shoulder and gave him enough thrust I didn't know if he'd stop until he got to the cockpit. He then extended his hand and grabbed mine tight.

"The door!" he yelled to Stenzel, who was doing her best to get it up. Three zombies joined us on that platform as it raised into the air. It was my feverish brother that helped save us from further casualties. He swayed to the back of the plane and drilled one of the zombies in the skull, then put two shots in the shoulder of the second, containing enough momentum to force it tumbling backwards out of the plane where it broke open upon contact with the pavement.

It was the third zombie that was going to be my undoing. I was partially wrapped up in the rope and the zombie was leaning down to get at me. A brown blur passed on my right as a white one flew past on my left. Holly had circled in behind the zombie, dangerously close to the edge of the hatch, and Chloe had driven her head straight into the monster's knee. I heard the crack of its patella as it was pushed backward and fell over Holly, who was in perfect position for what looked like a very practiced routine between the two. That last zombie joined the other two, rolling into unmoving lumps upon the tarmac.

"Fuck me," was all I could manage as I got more securely inside and saw what had happened. Randing had the nose in the air before Stenzel got the door shut.

BT was leaning down, looking at his hands, which were raw after having lost more than a few layers of skin.

"Thanks man," I told him.

He didn't look up. "Welcome."

Grimm was on the floor, his chest heaving. Most of my squad was sitting in the cargo hold, the rope in their laps. Captain Smoltz clapped me on the shoulder before he and his group went to sit down. We were all taking a moment to collect ourselves. Thankful, yes. But saddened, all the same; we had lost one of our own.

"Thank you." I walked down the line and let everyone know how appreciative of their efforts I was. Chloe came over and waited patiently for her turn. Her, I took a few extra moments to thank as I got down on my haunches.

"Everyone up, get in your seats and strapped in," BT said. As he walked past me, he let his hand drag across the top of my head. "Holy shit, Talbot. Can't say it's never interesting." He turned to offer a hand up.

"I'm gonna stay here a minute." Holly had joined me. I wanted to get lost in a little bullie huddle for a few. I knew underneath my cammies, I was trembling; I didn't want anyone on the squad to know how rattled I was.

"When you're ready, Major Randing wants to see you." Eastman had come up. "How are you doing?"

"I'll be fine."

"Damn good job out there. I'll make sure Bennington knows."

Wanted to tell him I didn't give two fucks what he thought–or Bennington, for that matter. Instead, I thanked him. Every once in a while I let discretion take hold, although at that moment, I'm pretty sure I just wanted to be left alone, and I knew if I said something untoward, he'd feel compelled to let me know exactly what he thought; just wasn't worth it.

We had climbed to our cruising altitude, and the flight attendants were getting ready to come down the aisles with our beverage choice and miniature bag of pretzels. I extracted myself from the dogs, who wanted to follow me up. Stenzel intercepted them with some treats from her MRE. Bullies are very loyal, loving dogs, but when you look up breeds that are food motivated, I'm pretty sure they ate their way to the top.

"Sir, you wanted to see me?"

Randing made sure to leave me at the position of attention for a lot longer than was necessary before he pulled off his headphones to look at me.

"I've been in touch with Colonel Bennington."

Again, I wanted to say something about the little bitch tattling or running to momma, but I was beat–both mentally and physically. There was no sense in heading into another battle at this point.

"Told him you got the job completed."

"Thank you, sir."

"I'm not done, and it would behoove you to not interrupt a senior officer when he's speaking."

I slowly clenched and unclenched my hands, considered counting to ten; didn't.

"You get the job done, that's without question, but I believe you are not fit for command. Perhaps a better officer would not have lost Private Hendley."

"Halsey, sir."

"I don't give a good goddamned!" He stood.

"Private Derrick Halsey. Twenty-one years old, born in Stockton, California. His girlfriend is Karen Slackmon; wonderful girl. Makes the most incredible cupcakes you've ever had. He was planning on asking her to marry him when we got back; showed me the ring–little gaudy, but when you can literally choose from any stone you want in a jewelry store, why not? Now I have to tell her that he died in the line of duty."

"Are you listening to anything I have to say?"

"I was just giving you some background information on the man we lost back there so perhaps you would be less inclined to mispronounce his name again."

"If I had my choice, I'd save us all the trouble and have you thrown off this plane!" Not even sure what I'd done to cause his face to turn so red and the veins on his forehead and neck to bulge out. Usually, I can pin it on something, this seemed entirely out of the blue.

Captain Wendley of his crew spoke. "Sir, I don't think this is the time or the place." He was looking back at my squad, who I'm sure were half a tick away from a mutiny at air. Not sure if it had ever happened before, but I wasn't above pioneering it.

"This is my plane, Captain. I'll do whatever I want," he said in no uncertain terms. "Why the hell are you still in my cockpit? Lieutenant, you're dismissed."

I turned and left.

"Get back up here!"

"You just told me to leave."

"You will give me a proper salute!"

"I don't think so." I left and sat back down.

"What are you doing, Talbot?" BT whispered. "Couldn't you just give him the damn salute?"

"Wouldn't have mattered. He's going to try and hang me out to dry. At least I have this to help me sleep at night."

"Oh shit," Winters mumbled as Randing came storming out of the cockpit. His hand was on his sidearm.

I did not pick my head up as he was laying in to me. I just tuned him out. I've had way better than him dress me down, that, and if he did manage to get my feathers any more ruffled, I was going to be compelled to put him on his ass in a most unsavory manner.

"You will stand, Lieutenant!"

I stood slowly. BT tried to grab me so I wouldn't do something impossible to come back from. It was Major Eastman that must have noticed a shift in the cabin.

"Major Randing, you can deal with this back at Etna."

Randing had a crazed look in his eye; he was close to diving off the edge himself. There was something more here; yeah, I'd angered him, but if I had to take a guess or two, I'd say Randing had barely passed his last psych eval, or had entirely lied his way through it. He paused to look at me, to really look me in the eye, before his gaze swept across my people and how close to springing into action they were. He backed away, rational thought seemed to take hold.

"This isn't over." He pointed a finger at me before heading back.

I sat back down instead of flinging a retort. If I provoked him, and he did something stupid that got him injured or killed, that would be on me. The rest of the flight was unremarkable, which was just fine with me. I sat back with my eyes closed; I wanted to sleep. I couldn't get the images of Halsey being ripped apart out of my mind. Not sure if sleep would have allowed me an escape or would have only furthered the trauma as I watched him killed a half dozen more times, each in a progressively worse manner. When we landed, there were twenty MPs waiting for me. I thought it was a bit of overkill.

"What do you want us to do?" BT asked.

"Get the squad home, get the puppies to Tracy; go say hi to my sister and have her make you a warm meal."

"Kiss my ass," he responded to that last part. I smiled before I turned to the MP.

"Lieutenant Talbot," the Master Sergeant was holding a pair of handcuffs, "will these be necessary?"

I handed my weapons to BT. "No," I told him truthfully. Randing was off to the side, a look of smug satisfaction played along the lines of his face. We went one way, my squad another. Ended up in a cell at the MP barracks. They let me get showered and gave me new cammies, even got a hot meal before I settled down onto the real punishment: a cot. About as comfortable as a cement floor, and the added beauty is they always tend to be about a foot short, so even if you find a decent position on one, some part of your body is hanging off, and don't even get me started on the blankets that are made from surplus coconut husks. When you're done sleeping with them, they make for effective sandpaper. It was maybe an hour later when Tracy showed up.

"Got your gift," she said, referring to the dogs. "BT wasn't sure which one was Holly and which one was Chloe."

"Chloe's the all white one."

"I heard about Derrick; how are you doing?" She had grabbed the bars. I leaned my head up against the cold steel; she stroked my forehead.

"Been better." My eyes watered up.

"What's going to happen to you?"

"If Randing has his way, he'll string me up by my balls."

"That won't happen."

I tilted my head to the side, wondering what she knew that I didn't.

"Can't string up what I have in my possession."

"That's pretty funny."

"You're not the only one." She smiled, but it had a sad tinge to it. "What's the worst that can happen?"

"I won't get shot for treason."

"Mike."

"Sorry. Worst...? They boot me out of the Corps and then I lose my value to being here."

"We'll be on the road again." She let her head rest against the bars this time.

I was going to say she and the rest could stay, but that wasn't going to happen. Where I went, so did the rest. "I'm sorry," was all I managed to say.

"We'll figure it out. We always do." We talked for a couple of hours, even managed a kiss or two through the bars. "I'll be back tomorrow. Henry is going to want to see you."

"Looking forward to it," I told her before I reluctantly let go of her hand. Dozed off for a few hours or more; the light of dawn was making its way toward me, but that wasn't what woke me up. It was the smoke.

"I thought you were going to give those up?" I asked, not even having to roll over to know who was there with me.

"Just can't help yourself, can you?" Her raspy voice slid like broken glass across concrete. "I don't have the whole story just yet, but Randing not only wants you out of his Corps, he wants you off the base. Even talked about having you removed from the earth, if my informant can be trusted."

"Why are you here? I can't imagine it's to offer any help."

"Of course not. I'm looking forward to the time where I won't have to look at you anymore."

Now I turned. "What have I ever done to you except call you out on your bullshit? Oh," I said as the light of realization finally dawned on me. "That's it. You don't like being called out. You want to hide in the shadows, strike out when no one is looking before retreating back into the blackness of your soul."

"You're one to talk of souls."

"Nice deflection. Speaking of..."

"I'm not going to say anything, if that's what you're implying. If they tried to hurt you, you would feel the need to defend yourself, and there's no telling what would happen. But if they kick you out? You would go meekly into the night, and I would be rid of you once and for all."

"I'd feel sorry for you, but you like it this way. Living alone, making sure you survive and thrive at all costs. Someday, Vivian, I am going to do a nice dance on your grave."

I sensed I'd somehow gotten under that extra-thick layer of skin she wore. She snuffed out her cigarette. "Good day, Michael."

"See you at the trial."

"Wouldn't miss it."

Had a steady stream of visitors the entire day; Henry and Tracy being the first of them. "Deneaux?" she asked, sweeping her hand past her face, attempting to wave the smoke away.

"Came to gloat."

Henry's stub of a tail was wagging as fast as I'd ever seen it. Though he was pissed that we had a barrier between us, if given the time, I think he would have broken through. Saw the kids, my squad came in, then finally BT and my sister, who was carrying a serving dish.

"Made you something!" she said proudly. "Meat casserole!"

It looked like a chunk of sandstone and smelled like fried rubber. "Thanks, but they won't let me have outside food."

"No worries; the guard said it was fine." BT was smiling.

"Oh, fantastic." I did my best to not have any sarcastic inflection in my words. She passed it through the food slot; I was surprised at the weight of it. Like she had somehow packed extra density into it. After a while, my sister excused herself and it was just BT and myself.

"Hear anything?"

"Been talk about reassigning the squad."

"What about you?"

"Come on, man. Do you even need to ask?"

"I think I do. My sister is pregnant; you'd be a lot smarter to stay here have as normal a life as possible."

"You better pull your head out of your ass, Talbot, and fight this. We've been on three missions since we've been here. You lost a person, and yeah, man, it sucks, sucks bad. But the other squad leaders? They lose two or three every time they go out. The mortality rate is through the roof. You need to get out of here, not only for you, but for your family and your squad. They get stuck in some other shitty platoon and you're signing their death warrants. I admit it's fucked up, but our best chance is you."

"You amaze me, BT. You always know how to kick a guy right in the feels."

"Kiss my ass. You know what I'm talking about."

"Maybe Randing was right; I'm not fit to command people."

"Well no shit. Don't need to be a frigged-up major to know that. That's why I run the show; you're just the figurehead."

"That's what you tell my sister, isn't it?"

We were laughing just as Colonel Bennington came in.

"Colonel." BT got to the position of attention and saluted. I did not salute, though I did acknowledge his presence.

"Could we have a few moments alone, Gunney?"

BT looked to me before I nodded. "Yes, sir. I'll talk to you later." He was pointing to me.

"Do not bring me any more food."

"The more you take, the less I have to eat of it. You can bet your ass I'm bringing more by. Sorry, sir." Then he left.

Bennington pulled up a chair.

"Sir, what are you doing with the nuke?"

"Direct. That's the nice thing about you, Lieutenant. There's no underhandedness. You just put it all out there for everyone to see and damn the torpedoes."

"I take it by your witty non-answer, you're not going to tell me."

It was like I'd never even asked the question when he spoke. "Randing wants you out."

"Shocker. And you?"

"I don't know yet. You have an uncanny ability to get a mission completed."

"I lost a man on a mission that didn't need to happen. The nuke was the primary all along; you had everything you needed from those scientists."

"It doesn't hurt to have the actual men and women that worked on the project to be involved."

"Etna is supposed to be a safe haven and you've made it explicitly more dangerous *and* implicated my squad and me in there as well. That virus is not the answer. If you were smart, you would burn all the research and delete the files."

"You are being short-sighted on this. We have a weapon that makes killing our enemy a near certainty with any shot. A graze to the fingertip will now kill one of them."

"And the one percent that doesn't die? Who becomes, in essence, a super zombie? What about them?"

"Unconfirmed."

"I'm confirming it. I saw it with my own eyes; my squad saw it."

"You're making my answer on your fate that much easier."

"Oh, that's what this is. I keep my mouth shut about the nuke and the faulty bio-weapon, and everything runs hunky dory? What if I don't, sir? Do I mysteriously disappear on a secret mission you sent me on in the middle of the night? My squad won't buy it."

"I'm not sure what kind of conspiracy theory videos you used to lose sleep over late at night, Lieutenant, but I'm not in the habit of making my men disappear. In case your little trip to New York wasn't proof enough, we're getting our collective asses handed to us. The brainiacs over in the think tank give humanity a two-percent chance of survival, and usually, I believe they tend to err on the side of caution; this time, I think they're being optimistic. Maybe because to think otherwise makes it all futile and worthless. The doomsday clock is quite literally on midnight. Right now, the zombies' overwhelming numbers will be our undoing; the math shows it; you've seen it firsthand. So that means at this very moment in history, I have to do whatever I can to make sure the few of us that are still here, stay that way. If there are, indeed, a smart one percent of zombies left after we've unleashed our weapon, then we'll be on equal footing."

I was still locked on the conspiracy theory part. When someone says you aren't in one, that's more than enough reason to believe you are. "Wait, one percent? That's all that's left of people?"

He nodded; there was a grim set to his lips. "Less than that. At best, we believe there are ten million people still alive, and the vast majority of them are individuals or scattered into small groups."

"Ten million?" The number sounded monstrous in regard to any particular city's population, but spread throughout the entire world, it was paltry. Had to be thousands of years B.C. the last time people were so few, and even then, we were on the uptick. Here and now, we were still losing numbers; if the colonel was right, individuals weren't making babies and small groups would not be so inclined to bear children while constantly fighting, hiding or running. "How many zombies?"

He sat down heavily in the chair Tracy had used earlier. "Somewhere just north of two and a half billion."

I whistled; couldn't help it. Somewhere in the back of my head I knew the figures were somewhere along those lines, it only made sense. "How much time do they estimate we have left?"

"Now you're asking the questions you need to, but I'm afraid you're not going to like the answer."

"There's a lot I don't like. What's one more thing?"

He smiled a little before leaning forward in a conspiratorial manner. "What I am about to tell you does not go out of this room."

"I'm in a cell; can't go anywhere anyway."

"Lieutenant."

"Scout's honor."

"They let you in?"

"Didn't even try...all that camping and hiking made me itchy, and knot-tying...don't even get me started on that."

"Three years," he said as a way to shut me up. "If things keep going as they are, we have three years. Sure, there will be people that will live out their normal lifespan, but as a viable population with a significant gene pool, we will hit the teeter point in three years. After that, there will be no bounce-back. So yeah, I'm going to make some extreme decisions and some radical moves, that, hopefully, may walk that number back until such time someone that knows more than me can come up with a better idea, or an outright solution. I don't have all the answers, Talbot. I'm scrambling, just like everyone else. Want to know something?"

"Do I have a choice?"

"Not really; doesn't look like you're going anywhere."

"Then talk away."

"I was all set to retire. Had my papers in, my CO had signed off on them. I was going to spend the rest of my days down in the Bahamas with my wife, collect my military retirement pay, sip those fancy drinks with the umbrellas. I invested my money wisely, made a decent nest egg—enough to live comfortably."

"Do colonels make decent pay, or did you have a side business, like the *A-Team?*"

"Never really liked cigars," he answered, referring to Lieutenant Colonel John "Hannibal" Smith's propensity for them as the leader of said *A-Team*.

"It's my wife with the deep pockets; she's got DuPont blood in her."

She had the type of money where there's so much wealth you don't even think about it. As a person who'd spent the majority of his life going paycheck to paycheck, I couldn't even imagine the relief of burden, having this kind of cash entailed. Never concerned with the next bill, or late charges, or the worst of all–the dreaded "decline" of your payment method as you stand in line at a crowded supermarket. That walk of shame as you leave the store empty handed before the manager can get someone to put all your groceries back. Can't even tell you how shitty that is; especially if you have a kid with you and they start asking why you're leaving the food behind. Was heading down that rabbit hole when Bennington began his narrative again.

"Money is an antiquated notion now. Means nothing. All the money we have couldn't buy our way out of this. My CO, General Cower, he was the first on the base to get that flu shot, wanted to set an example for his men. I would have been right behind him, but my wife and I were coming back from a trip to the Bahamas…we'd been house hunting. Even put a hefty deposit down on a home four times bigger than we'd ever need, even if all the kids and grandkids came to visit at the same time. My whole life I'd lived frugal, Margaret less so, but I could not begrudge her; she'd grown up a certain way and she was used to it. If she wanted another Louis Vuitton handbag, then it wasn't my place to stop her. As for the house, I figured what the hell. Let's enjoy the golden years."

"I'm sorry, sir."

He waved his hand. "What's past is past, although I see my Margaret often looking out the window in the direction she believes the Bahamas to be. Most times it's just a sad look on her face, other times there's a tear or two. Don't have the heart to tell her she's looking the wrong way."

"I'd call that wisdom, sir."

He laughed. "Probably right. So what happens to you, Lieutenant?"

"Well, you keep calling me Lieutenant, so I don't think I have to go too far out on a limb to say you're not quite through with me yet."

"I don't know why I let you get away with half the crap you do or say."

"It's because I make you laugh. That's how I've kept my wife from killing me a dozen times over the years."

He raised his eyebrows in question.

"Yeah, it's probably more than a dozen."

"There's going to be a trial. I've tried to steer Major Randing off this course, but he wants his pound of flesh."

"He's such a prick." I let it out long before I thought to censure myself. "Sorry, sir."

"I'm well aware he can be difficult. Lucky for you, I'll be presiding over the proceedings, and unless he can give me anything else worthy of a court-martial than what he's already presented, you'll be fine. I'm going to have you released tomorrow on your own recognizance; try not to fuck anything up between now and the trial."

"How long are we talking?" I asked as he stood to leave.

His shoulders sagged; he kept his back to me as he spoke. "I've got a feeling if I walked you over to the courtroom now you'd find a way to get into trouble before we got there. Stay close to your wife; she seems to have a good head on her shoulders. If anyone can keep you in line, I would imagine it'd be her."

True to his word, Bennington let me out. Apparently, Randing protested, said I was a flight risk. I mean, I was, but fuck him for saying it. Had a couple of weeks until the trial, which was a good thing and a bad thing. Good because it meant myself and my team wouldn't be going on any missions in the meantime, but bad, because it was always hanging around in the back of my head. Kind of like a dental appointment for a root canal. Nothing quite like waiting for pain.

    First thing I did when I got out was go to Halsey's fiancee's apartment. Obviously, she knew, but I felt that she deserved to hear it from me. She was an understandable mess; she no sooner saw me standing in the doorway that she broke out into uncontrollable crying. I stayed with her for four hours, the vast majority of it with her face buried in my chest as she sobbed. When she had finally cried herself out, I gently eased her head down onto a pillow on the couch, covered her up with a small blanket before getting ready to head out. I looked over to the kitchen table; it was piled high with Halsey's clothes and some of his possessions. I imagined her holding those things in her hands, bringing them up to her nose, trying to find some residual trace of the man she loved in the things he wore or used. I was familiar with the breadth of her grief, but perhaps not the depth of it. Maybe it was selfish of me, but I never wanted to be, either.

    I went home; I wanted to spend the rest of the night hidden deep in a bottle of Vodka I'd been saving for just such an occasion. Chloe, Holly, Henry, Riley, Ben Ben and even Patches, to a degree, had other plans. Spent the majority of the night on the floor. I think Tracy ended up throwing my clothes away. Between the volumes of snot and tears on my chest, and the slobber and fur on the rest of my clothes, they were barely salvageable.

    For once, I did what was requested of me and kept a low profile. I went out once with the squad, and only because we were going to honor Halsey. I talked to the bartender before they started drinking, made sure that my vodka shots were water, slipped him a twenty to make sure there were no mistakes. I thought I was going to get busted halfway through the night when a boisterous BT ended up doing everyone's shot for them; he never even noticed as he powered through them all. I stayed sober; I was worried that Randing might try to set me up, wait until I was drunk and have someone under his command start a fight with me. Never materialized, but I wasn't about to take any chances. Even walked back home, in case I got pulled over and the MP's smelled the liquor that had been sloshed all over me. You know, they say you don't need to drink to have a good time, but if you're going to hang out with people that are drinking, it's best to join them otherwise they're fucking nuts. Basically, they're a bunch of people slowly going insane as they downed poison.

When I got home, it was late. Everyone was already in bed. Everyone except Chloe. It was pretty funny; as a deaf dog, she should have been the easiest to sneak past, but she was very sensitive to changes in air pressure when a door was opened and even more so to the vibrations caused by people walking. She greeted me halfway across the living room. I'd not planned on the intensity, severity, and suddenness of the breakdown that struck, but there I was. Kneeling, face buried in her fur as I silently sobbed. It came in heavy wracking heaves and hitches. As the supposed leader of the family and of my squad, it was my job and duty to appear unflappable. Right now, I was anything but. The accumulated stress and loss was shaving thin my humanity; soon it would be see-through—if it wasn't already.

More than a half dozen times I thought to soak up the puddle of myself and head for bed, but each time, crippling anxiety overwhelmed my diminished defenses and I couldn't make it. It was Chloe, who was soon joined by the rest of the menagerie, that stayed around me. Did they realize the depths of my distress? Or perhaps they liked the novelty of me sleeping with them. I hoped it wasn't going to be difficult to explain to Tracy, come morning. It was the aromatic wafting of coffee and the savory smell of bacon that got our little pile moving. That, and the sun shining in my face

Tracy slid a cup over without saying anything.

"Am I in trouble?" I asked after taking a sip.

"What for?" She turned to look at me.

"I'm thinking you probably think I drank to excess last night and could barely stand, much less make it back to the bedroom."

"Is that what happened?" she asked the question, but somehow she already knew the answer.

"No, but how would you know?"

"Mike."

"Right, I know...you know all."

"I was wondering when you were going to come to that conclusion. Are you going to talk to someone? Scarborough, maybe?"

I was about to protest and ask what would I talk to someone about, but we'd already traveled past that marker in the ground. She took another sip of her coffee; her eyes never left mine.

"Him? He couldn't counsel a teenager to wash their gym shorts. Plus, it was an isolated incident," I protested weakly.

"And the screaming out at night? That an isolated incident as well?"

"What? That's news to me." And it was.

"You professed your undying love for BT."

"What?" I tilted my head. "Makes sense, though."

"Seriously, Mike. You yell out the names of those we've lost, and in a way that sounds like you're trying to save them. It's unnerving...no, it's more than that. It's terrifying. It's not like I sleep peacefully most nights, and to be awakened in that manner—it instantly brings me back to the danger. Like maybe we're being attacked."

"I'm sorry." I let my head sag.

She grabbed my chin roughly and pushed it up. "I don't want you to be sorry. There's nothing to be sorry about. I want you to get help, Mike. This is bigger than you, and it's not something you can outrun, or fight head-on. Not alone, anyway."

"I go to get head counseling and I lose my command. Scarborough reports all of the sessions back to command."

"They'll pull your bar because you went to seek help?"

"They'll put me on a desk."

"Is that the worst thing that could happen?"

"It's not that easy. I keep those men and women under my command alive, Tracy."

"And if what happened last night happens while you're out in the field? What then?"

I looked at her face; there was pain and hurt in my gaze.

"I heard you come home. I was going to see if you wanted me to warm you up some dinner. Mike, you were as pale as a ghost when you crossed the room. When you dropped to one knee, I thought it was on purpose to say hi to the dogs, but that wasn't it. It was like it gave out on you."

She was right, and the fuckery of it is, I can't even finger what the trigger was. If I could avoid that, there was a chance I could soldier on, but if it reached out from my blinded angles to drop me, what defense could I muster?

"After the trial. I can't do it before."

That was the wrong answer. Tracy looked like she was going to bite through the edge of her mug. Her battleship grey eyes prepared to do battle.

"Randing catches wind I'm getting my head shrunk, it won't just be a desk job. He'll drum me straight out. And while I would like to have my fighting days behind me, I'm not cut out for any of the higher skills that are needed here, and you know what that means. How low do you want me to go with this?"

"You bring in how we'll have to take the kids out of their schools and I'll throw this at you." She was referring to her coffee, which I'm sure was still very much hot enough to do some damage.

"It's the truth though, and you know it."

"I'm worried, Mike."

"So am I woman. I figured I had the insanity thing under control, didn't figure I had so much further to go."

"That isn't funny." Although it was the first hint of a smile I'd seen on her lips.

"Why didn't you say anything last night?"

"You know as well as I do that if I'd turned the light on you would have played it out like you stumbled. You would have come to bed, we'd never have mentioned it. Sometimes the best thing you can do is let it out, and besides, you looked like you and your girlfriend were getting close."

"She's a better kisser. Sure, her breath smells like wet meat most of the time, but yeah…"

Tracy smacked me. "You're going to promise me right now, that the moment that farce of a trial is over you're going to get some help."

I was tight-lipped.

"I'll go to Bennington right now, tell him you can barely manage to tie your shoes in the morning."

I wanted to protest, to come out with some worthy argument as to why I didn't need to do that.

"You're flapping your gums like a fish out of water. Mind's working a mile a minute but no words are coming out. That's because there's nothing you can say right now that disproves anything I've said."

"Well that's not fair. Nothing I've said in all the years we've been married has ever disproved you."

"That's true, but this time deflection isn't going to work for you. You get help or I'll get it for you." She was adamant.

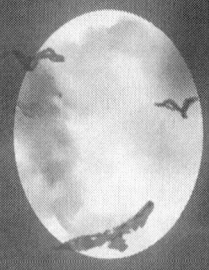

13

MIKE JOURNAL ENTRY 11

THE TRIAL CAME SWIFTLY. Time is a funny thing; as a child, I can clearly remember that Christmas seemed as if it would never come, but just like the end of summer, as an adult, it rushed at you with a speed that defied reality...or was it relativity? The trial split those cross-hairs, sort of. At times, I felt like it was so far away I wasn't going to worry about it, and then in the wink of a faulty sphincter, I was being led into the proceedings by a bevy of MPs. What the fuck they were for, I don't know. If I was going to do something, which I'd thought about a lot, I would have done it when I didn't have an escort. Then I got worried that perhaps Bennington had been screwing with me and wasn't presiding and I was about to get railroaded. Seemed like a lot to go through for one lousy Marine, though. Plus, if that were the case, his safest bet would have been to have kept me locked up. Even with my reasoning, I was happy to see him sitting at the judge's table. The room mirrored what you would expect in a courtroom, though the judge's seat was not raised, and yes, there were seats for a jury, but they were not tiered, nor were they occupied. Only civilians got to have their fates determined by twelve total strangers.

Randing was sitting at the prosecution's desk. He still looked as salty as he had the day we left New York. That is a seriously long time to stay pissed off, can't be good for your system, probably hadn't had a decent shit since then. My council was Captain Alomar, nice enough guy, but he absolutely hated that I would not take any of this seriously. Would go on and on about how we needed to practice my testimony and how I was going to respond to Randing's accusations. I realize I should have listened to him; I just didn't want to be continuously reminded of the event. Would have been like watching movies of dental procedures every day until you got your root canal. Who needs that shit?

My entire squad, my family, and the Civilian Council board that Mrs. Deneaux now headed up, were in attendance. She'd wasted no time garnering what power she could. She was beaming, which I found exceedingly disturbing. What did she know that I didn't? Most likely a lot, but was it pertinent to this case? The prosecution led off with their star witness, Randing, then his entire crew, who, not surprisingly, echoed everything the major had said. Talk about practiced. Next came Eastman and his crew; they were much more favorable to my cause, but not a slam dunk. The prosecution lawyer, Captain Collins, then for some reason thought it might be a good idea to bring my squad up. He started with BT. Hostile witness didn't even begin to describe how that went down. Collins wisely refrained from going any deeper; if he thought he was going to get something out of them, he was sadly mistaken.

Finally, I was called up. The desire to walk a few steps to my right and smack the back of Randing's head was nearly irresistible; oh the joy it would have brought me to watch his aristocratic nose bounce off the table. I wisely chose to get sworn in without incident. I made sure to work on keeping any anger Collins was bound to stir, in check.

"Lieutenant Talbot, can you state your name for the record?" Collins asked.

"Really? We're this far into this and nobody knows who I am or bothered to check?"

Bennington sighed. "Answer the question."

"My name is Michael Talbot; I am a lieutenant in what is left of the United States Marine Corps. I go out on exceedingly dangerous missions to help keep the rest of you safe and ensure your survivability while constantly endangering not only myself, but my squad."

"Colonel, could you please have the defendant refrain from adding to my questions?" Captain Collins asked.

"You can ask me that, I'm sitting right here."

"Lieutenant Talbot, I realize that taking these proceedings seriously is difficult for you, but if you could answer the questions as posed, that would be helpful," Colonel Bennington said.

I nodded.

"Verbal confirmation," he prompted.

"Yes, sir."

"Lieutenant, Major Randing has levied some serious charges against you, the first being that you disobeyed a direct order. Do you deny that?" Collins asked.

"I do."

"Anything more to add to that?"

"You just ratted me out to the colonel for giving too much of an answer and now you're saying I didn't give enough? I think you need to work on your litigation. Fine," I said before Bennington could say anything. "How is insisting on bringing dogs on a flight disobeying an order? That's the question that needs asking. Did I go above and beyond getting those scientists and their valuable information out of their lab and back to base? I did. Did I make sure the primary mission was a success by retrieving a lost package and making sure it was secured on the plane? I did."

Deneaux perked up at that; the scientists were no secret. Bennington made sure to release as much information as he could regarding what they were working on. It was a hell of a morale booster. The nuke? That he kept tight to the vest, and it looked like it was something Deneaux did not know anything about. I would imagine she would begin to work diligently to expose the truth. Bennington looked like he was trying to swallow his breakfast a second time.

"I lost a good man out there making sure that I obeyed the orders given to me. I don't consider Randing…excuse me… Major Randing telling me to not bring dogs that I saved, and that also saved me, on board a plane, an order. You going to tell me that you would have turned these two away?" I held up a small poster I'd made.

Bennington let his head fall a bit into his palm.

"Damn right!" BT stood up and clapped his hands together, loudly, twice.

"Gunney!" Bennington shouted.

"Sorry, sir." He sat back down.

This went on for a couple more hours. Randing really had nothing. It finally got to the point where Randing's lawyer was trying to prove how much contempt I had for the major. I didn't even feel the need to hide that; last I checked that wasn't a punishable offense. The further we went, the more agitated Deneaux became. I was certain she was going to ask the court if she could approach the bench. When she realized that this wasn't going the way she wanted, she and the entire civilian council up and left. Bennington looked over to me; I only shrugged.

"Prosecution rests." Captain Collins seemed exasperated.

"Captain Alomar, it is your turn to present your case."

Captain Alomar stood up, never moved away from the table. "The prosecution did a wonderful job presenting our case, sir. The defense rests." Then he sat.

The way Randing was looking at Captain Collins, I had to

figure the man was in danger of becoming the same rank as me by the end of the day. Though I couldn't imagine Bennington getting onboard with that.

"I've weighed all the evidence in this case. I do not need to retire for deliberation."

"Please stand," an MP off to the side directed.

"Major Randing, I understand your anger at Lieutenant Talbot; he has an uncanny ability to worm his way under your skin, moving quickly from a minor irritant to a fully enflamed, burning rash."

"Mm hmm. Amen to that," BT said loudly. I turned to look at my friend.

"Truth is truth," he replied.

"But with that being said, I do not see anything here that would lead me to believe he disobeyed a lawful order that pertained to the mission. In fact, Major, I question your ethos. Instead of swallowing a modicum of pride, you would have let those two magnificent beasts die upon the tarmac that day. If we demoted or pushed out of the military every person that questioned authority or groused and complained about command, I fear that we would have only ourselves left. Lieutenant Talbot."

I was beaming as Randing was getting called out for his pettiness. I was not ready for the Colonel's spotlight to shift toward me.

"You are not guilt-free in all of this. Don't." He held up a finger when he saw I was about to speak. "You have mostly won your case; don't screw it up now."

I wisely shut up.

"Most of my life, I wanted people to speak their minds, to not leave something unsaid. Then I met you, Lieutenant. You seem to have taken that to a whole other level."

"The truth will set you free."

"BT!" I turned. He had his eyes closed like he was in the middle of a rousing Baptist sermon.

"You've changed that for me, Lieutenant. I now want people to think very carefully before they speak, perhaps place a filter on their thought-to-speech translation, to avoid, at whatever cost, those cringe-inducing words. I can see how you could so completely incense Major Randing, and for that, I am going to levy some punishment, in the hopes that it will give you time to reflect on your actions and how you can improve upon them."

I looked back to Tracy; she smiled back, but she was nervous.

"For the next two weeks, Lieutenant, you and your squad will be prohibited from leaving this base. I remand you to the grounds. You will be required to wear civilian clothing for that entire time period." He stood and walked out of the room.

"Court is dismissed," the same MP said.

Randing was yelling at Captain Collins. BT came over gave me a big hug, then he started looking at my uniform.

"What the hell are you doing?" I asked him.

"Looking for the Teflon."

PFC Kirby came over; he looked pale. "Remanded to the grounds? What's that mean?"

"Means we're on leave," Corporal Stenzel told him. "Congratulations, sir."

There were smiles and handshakes and then I told them to head out and enjoy themselves. That if they had any problems, they knew where to find me. Lot of back clapping as they left.

My sister kissed my cheek before grabbing BT's hand.

"Good job, man." He smiled, then they left.

The entire courtroom was empty save me, Tracy and my kids.

"Geez dad...you can't even get time off from work without causing a big scene," Travis said.

"Even when he's on vacation, there's no telling what'll

happen." Justin was referring to the great Canadian border debacle.

"I see where this is going. The colonel starts the pig pile and you all hop on."

"I've got your back, dad," Nicole said.

"Got one on my side!" I wrapped my arm around her shoulders. "Let's get out of here before someone else thinks of a reason I should be in court."

Per Tracy's demands, I did seek out help—not the traditional route, though. I instead sought out an Army Chaplain. His name was Mulcahey, of all things. The problem was, he was so young he didn't know who I was talking about; hadn't ever watched the show. Didn't matter. The guy had seen enough to understand what I was going through. I saw him every day for those two weeks. The first couple of times, he had to pull words out of my mouth like a dentist might an impacted wisdom tooth. By the end, I think I was confessing transgressions I had done when I was six. I don't know if laying yourself bare is the answer to everything; but I suppose it makes it easier to examine the broken bits and where to apply some duct tape. I felt better for it. My night terrors had become less frequent and they lost a bit of their intensity. All in the nick of time before we headed back out into the wild.

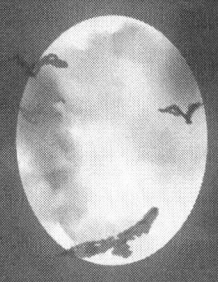

EPILOGUE

MIKE JOURNAL ENTRY 12

The Night of the Lord

We'd just come back from New York. Everything about that mission was still raw and now we were at it again.

"You look like shit, Lieutenant. You alright?" Colonel Bennington was sitting at the head of a large table; he stood as I came in. The table was packed with a cluster of shiny-lapeled officers.

"As all right as one can be after what we witnessed. Once I'm cleaned up, finished with my debriefing, I'm going home, then I think I'm going to drink an entire bottle of Jeff Daniels, and I hate the shit."

"Jeff?"

"Sorry, sir, I get the two mixed up. Long story."

"Have a seat. Tell us what happened."

After spending the next two hours recounting the entire mission and answering dozens of questions, I was finally about to be dismissed. About halfway through my recounting, a corporal came running in and quickly handed a piece of paper to the colonel. It looked urgent, but right now all I wanted was to finish out the day and hope the next was better. The colonel looked at the paper then at me before scribbling some hasty notes and sending the corporal on his way.

I stood up. "Hope I passed," I told the captain to my right, who had been taking copious notes. He looked up. I had expected some response, even if it was derision. That none of his facial features moved was somehow more disconcerting.

I was walking down the hallway of the command center after having finished my debriefing. My uniform was filthy, as was my rifle. I was shaking my head, attempting to get rid of the memories I had collected on the last mission. Life is strange; I realize by this point there shouldn't be much that surprises me, but there always seems to be something unique and terrible around every corner. I just wanted to get home and wash the stink of the last few days off me.

"Lieutenant Talbot…" Colonel Bennington had come out of meeting room and had called to me as I was leaving.

"Sir," I said, turning around.

"Listen, Lieutenant, I hate to interrupt your plans for what sounds like a stellar evening, but I'm going to need for your team to turn around quickly."

"Sir? His family should be…"

"I'll take care of it."

"No disrespect, but he was my man."

"None taken, Lieutenant, but you need to remember that all of you are my men."

"Yes, sir. You heard my debriefing, sir, you know we've been run ragged. I wouldn't doubt if all of my personnel were half in the bag or sleeping."

"I need you to check something out. I'd get another team on it, but there are none here."

My head sagged.

"I promise you, Lieutenant, it's close. And when you get back, I'll give your team a week's R&R."

"Unless, of course, something comes up." It was past my lips before I could even think to contain it.

"I'm going to let that one pass on by, Lieutenant, due to the rough nature of your last outing."

"I appreciate that, sir. We'll be ready to go in forty-five; going to need to restock everything."

"Already all set. There's a fully loaded Hummer right outside."

"Well, isn't it my lucky day, sir."

"Lucky I like you, Lieutenant."

"My wife says I've got an endearing quality. What are we checking out?"

"Eatonville, couple of towns over. Some brainchild has lit up the night sky with those industrial searchlights the auto dealerships use."

"Really? For what purpose?" I asked, the Colonel scowled. "Right…that's why you're sending us out there."

"Lieutenant be careful. If someone is willing to let the whole world know they are there, it's safe to say they are not too worried about anything."

"Or they're plain old crazy. Neither thing sounds good to me."

The colonel smiled. "See you soon," he said before heading back into the room.

I gave my rifle to the corporal who was sitting at the admittance desk. "Could you please get this to the armory?" I asked, placing the weapon on his desk. He looked down, horrified at the congealed blood that coated almost the entirety of it. "Don't worry, it's not mine," I told him before leaving. I had no sooner walked out of the building when BT, who had been leaning against the Hummer, pushed off and yelled.

"What the fuck, Talbot? Who'd you piss off now? You

realize we just got back, right? I bet you told the Colonel to go fuck himself with a frog or something like that. I was asleep! Some little pissant private came running in; I nearly choked him out. You know I hate when I get woken up."

"Did you get a shower?" I asked, stopping his diatribe.

"Yeah." He looked perplexed.

"How about a meal?"

"Of course."

"You get to see my sister?"

"Yeah, I did. What's that got to do with anything?" He was building back to surly.

"Substitute my sister for my wife, and I didn't get to do any of those things."

BT finally took a moment to look at me; the dried blood of the one we'd lost still on the uniform I was wearing. "I'm sorry, man, I just figured you had done something to get us on a shit list."

"Not a horrible or unjustified assumption, just not correct this time. There's no one else available for the job. Plus, the old man promised us a week of R&R once this is done."

"You realize that's horse shit, right?"

"Of course I do. Duty calls. At least it's close. Some idiot is playing with a huge flashlight over in Eatonville. Our job is to go check out why."

"Maybe he has a death wish," BT said as he got back into the Hummer. "Because I'm going to kill him."

I poked my head in; Sergeant Winters was driving. He nodded to me; even in the bad lighting it would have been difficult to miss the hollowness of his eyes.

"You up for this, Winters?" I asked.

"Tried to sleep, sir. That didn't go over so well."

In the back seat were my brother and Tommy. Gary, aka Gambo, was fast asleep. Tommy looked pensively out the window.

"Where's the rest?" I asked BT, as he was responsible for mustering the unit.

"The colonel only wanted one Hummer going in," he replied. "Figured we'd let the corporals and privates sit this one out."

In five minutes we were outside the gate and back into the unknown. The night was cool, though the day had been unseasonably warm. I knew what that meant: fog, and lots of it. Winters was leaning forward as he attempted to peer through the thick pea-soup that was rapidly forming.

I turned on the small flashlight I had and pulled open a manila folder that contained our mission parameters. "Gary, I need for you to be awake." I shook him.

"Come on, mom…no one wears rubbers anymore!" he shouted as he sat up. "Huh?" he asked, looking at our confused stares.

BT turned his considerable bulk around. "You had better clarify everything you just said."

"What did I say?" Gary had no idea.

"Something about your mother and rubbers, and I need for you to tell me that is vastly different from the half-dozen things going through my head right now. Go on. I'm listening," BT prodded.

"I don't know…oh, wait, yeah I do. Fifth grade…it was raining like crazy and my mother didn't want me to ruin my new shoes, made me wear rubbers. Instead of going to school, I hid under our back porch for the entire day."

BT turned his attention to me. "Mike, can you translate from crazy Talbot speech to English for the rest of us?"

"Oh yeah, I forgot about that story." I smiled. "Galoshes." BT still had a confused look on his face. "Rain boots made from rubber. You put them over your shoes so you don't get them wet."

"What kind of white bread shit is that? You put shoes over your shoes? Do all white people do that or only the insane ones? Winters, tell me you weren't in on this. Come on, man, I need someone on my side."

"They were a big thing on the East Coast," he said as a weak defense.

"You crazy fuckers should have been practicing more safe-sex instead of safe-walking. That way there would be less of you. People wearing condoms on their feet...were they called Toejans?" He laughed loudly at his joke.

"You done?" I asked him as I pointed out the front of the Hummer. Up ahead was a thick column of light piercing the fog-filled night sky.

"Shit," he sighed. "Yeah."

"We are only here to observe and call back in. Once that's done, we turn around and go home. If it gets hot, our extraction point is the town hall, which is about a klick away from where the light is coming from."

"Secondary extraction point?" BT asked.

"In this soup, my guess is there won't be a first," Winters said.

"There's a church on the far side of town, Our Lady of Perpetually Burnt Food. Head there."

"That a dig on my fiancee?" BT asked.

"Not at all. Not everything is about you," I told him. Gary fist-bumped me.

"I hate fucking Talbots."

"Mike, where's the comma in that sentence?" Gary asked

"It's best not to dwell on it," I replied.

"What, no fist bumps for me?" BT asked.

"Guess we know who's on point tonight," I said. "Winters, I don't want to get too close. I'd rather come in quiet. Let's make sure the ZADAR, zombie radar, is up and running too. I hate being in the fog, and I don't want anything sneaking up on us."

We stopped as soon as we saw the sign saying: "Welcome to the Town of Eatonville." The wooden sign was riddled with bullet holes and as Winters moved over to the shoulder, we drove over the skeletal remains of a half-dozen somethings. Most likely zombies, but I wasn't about to check if their heads had been shot. Best not to think on such things; all dead beings were zombies, that thought helped me sleep at night.

"Alright, let's set up a perimeter. Tommy, the ZAD is on you. Winters, could you help him, please?"

Winters nodded.

"All right Mr. T, Lieutenant, sir."

"It's fine, Tommy…the only one I want calling me Lieutenant is BT. He needs to know that the Marine Corps, in its infinite wisdom, decided that I should be his commander."

BT was in front of the Hummer with his weapon, scanning the area. He scoffed. "They promoted me first, dumbass. I just wanted to be part of your unit."

"He loves me; turned down a commission to be by my side," I told Winters.

"I promised your sister I'd look out for you," BT replied.

"Look out for me?"

"Remember, you're her little brother. She'll never stop thinking she needs to protect you. When in reality, we all need protecting from you. Crazy-ass," he said under his breath. "Talbots all be crazy. Never heard of no brothers wearing shoes over their shoes…hell, I was lucky I even had shoes."

"Yeah, because it was difficult to get them in canoe sizes," I said.

"I wonder if I can tell the colonel I reconsidered," BT said.

There was a loud series of beeps as Tommy fired up the ZAD.

"Sorry," he said as he immediately lowered the volume. I moved quickly to Tommy's side; the only reason the ZAD would give off beeps was if there was something beep-worthy, and unfortunately, we had a lot of beep-worthy entities. As far as military equipment used in the field goes, this stuff was pretty sophisticated. It had software that could render a three-dimensional image of our surroundings, including any beings within its range. Even had infrared capability which could penetrate buildings. The only downside was that the old school zombies who had first died and then were reanimated had a much lower body heat and hardly ever showed inside a building. So just because the ZAD showed a building as clear, we still had to take precautions. After all the shit we'd all been through, to be taken out by a first-generation zombie would be humiliating, to say the least.

It had pros and cons over the tech that Deneaux had brought us. We weren't limited by night or bad weather, but everything was in hues of green, and buildings were outlined in green lines, giving it a feel of video games from the eighties. Other than that, it was invaluable.

"There is a crapload of zombies around." BT was looking over my shoulder. "And bulkers." He pointed at the screen.

"You do realize that with those sausage fingers, you could be pointing to anywhere on half the display," I told him. "And it doesn't help that your gloves are the same size as the mitt I used to play baseball with."

"How do you think he stays so big, especially with our sister's cooking?" Gary asked.

"That's why he's so surly; only so many Eggos you can eat before you start to snap," I answered. "She burn those too, big guy?"

He looked angry, then relented. "If you put enough syrup on them they're palatable."

"Sorry, man," I told him. "Starvation is a slow and painful death."

"Can we maybe get through this so that I can find some real food? Looks like whoever set up the beacon got what they were looking for." The light showed up as a bright column on our screen and there was a bunch of zombies congregating around it.

"Yeah, but for what purpose? Distraction, maybe?" Winters asked.

"That looks like a football field," Gary said as we all looked at the screen. The fog was beginning to congeal; we couldn't see much more than ten yards. The nearest zombie was over a hundred yards off and moving away from us and toward the light.

"Must be a high school. We should check the field out, then this building. It has a large open floor; I'm thinking the gym."

"Yeah, and there's something in there." Tommy was looking intently at the screen. "Mr. T, there's something weird here."

"Listening," I told him.

"Look closer at the occupants in the gym."

There were two signals coming from the gym, and one of them was smaller like a shrieker. It wasn't moving, but the other blip was. It was a dark blip, and something about it made all the hair on my neck stand up.

"Vampire." I sucked the word through my teeth.

"Payne?" BT asked. We were instantly on high alert. Not that we weren't already ready, but the threat level had just been increased. "I know you know what I mean here, but I really fucking hate vampires."

"Understood," I told him.

When we had been shown the ZAD and had gone to a class on how it operated, Tommy and I had to always make sure we were on the "Good Guys" team. We wore a special pin that registered as a "friendly" on the ZAD so as to not show up as an anomaly on the special radar. We just glowed blue on the screen with our names and ranks displayed. That had been a stressful day; luckily, the captain teaching the course hadn't noticed just how adamant Tommy and I had been to be the "hunters." Once I had to switch with Gary; if the captain noticed, he said nothing.

"Shit. Now what? It looks like Payne is amassing an army," Winters said after pacing a few steps.

"I feel pretty good about the five of us against damn near anything, but I've got a vibe we might be in over our head," BT said. His words struck a chord; he was right. Something powerful was in that gym. I could feel the waves of energy vibrating through me.

"I take it we're going in?" Winters resigned himself to a fact he already knew.

"Of course he is because…"

"Talbots be crazy," Winters finished BT's thoughts.

"You know you're crazy when other people point it out." BT clapped Winters on the back.

"Winters, could you radio back to command that we are about to make contact with an unknown entity, and to maybe warm up our ride?"

"On it, sir." He moved closer to the Hummer and radioed in my message. BT and myself were going over the best approach to the building when Winters came back. "Birds are grounded."

"Shit." I looked up. "Listen, I realize I'm technically in command here by some strange twists of fate, but we're more than just a military unit; we're friends and family. And now that we've found out that help isn't coming should we need it, I'd rather put this up for a vote instead of making an executive decision and just ordering us in, because, you all know I want to go in. It's a character flaw of mine and I realize that, but I don't want anyone getting hurt just because from time to time I like to do a ball check."

"A ball check? You're calling the shit you do a '*ball check?*' And what the hell does 'from time to time' mean? It's every time. And, oh yeah, I'm in," BT said.

"You had to go through all of that shit just to say you're in?" I asked.

"Whenever there is an opportunity to give you a hard time, it's guaranteed I'm going to do it. *That's* in my nature."

"There's a part of me that appreciates when you do things like this, Lieutenant," Winters started, "but you're also the commanding officer here. I'm going to do whatever you say we're going to do. I'd rather not hear an option."

That was something I could understand. When you had choices, you could think yourself into circles about what was the right thing to do or whether you'd made a bad choice. But if you were told what to do, it took the responsibility off of your shoulders; it was actually easier, even if what you had to do was distasteful. Now don't get me wrong; I don't want anyone blindly following my lead or my orders, but yeah, there is something comforting about it.

"I'm your big brother; someone has to look out for you." Gary was a hundred percent serious, even added a bit of the Gambo inflection to make his point.

"Tommy?" I prodded; he was the only one that had been abundantly quiet.

"If we have an opportunity to stop her before she does anything cataclysmic, I'm all for it." He was staring at the screen, and though it was tough to discern because of the lack of light, I would say he was laser-focused on that off-color blip that signified Payne.

"Alright. BT, you and I are taking the direct approach. Winters, Gary, Tommy, I want you heading in here. This looks like a door–if it's not, make one. Let me know though, because I'll want to adjust our timeline. We need to be synched-up perfectly or she could escape. Let's do a radio check." I was paranoid about military equipment and always had my squad check that everything was functioning before I deployed anyone out. I almost lost one of my privates on our very first mission. Grimm had gone to take a crap in a port-a-potty away from where we had rallied. Not sure why anyone would want to use one of those this far into the apocalypse; it was highly likely that the second wave of death was going to spring forth from those blue devils.

Anyway, he had no sooner dropped his trousers and planted his ass on the seat when multiple hands had reached up and tried to pull him down. He tried to call us on his radio for help, but the unit itself was broken. If it hadn't of been for Springer following him over to take a leak, Grimm might have been dragged down into that portable cesspool and never heard from again. Not sure who had thought to dispose of live zombies in that stink-pudding quagmire, but if I ever found them, odds were I was going to sink them as well. All's well that ends well. Now Grimm always makes sure he takes care of his bodily functions either before we leave or real close to wherever we are, although, that's gotten a little old. It seems he always has to take a solid and usually moves upwind. Come to think of it, I might need to talk to him.

"Check, check." Winters broke me out of my tangential thought.

"Gotcha," BT replied.

"Ready?" I looked at everyone.

Terse nods all around, except for Gambo, who was busy putting black stripes on his face; they looked more like cat whiskers, but I wasn't going to wreck his psych-up. We moved quietly together for a little bit until the building came into view. With a hand signal, I motioned for the trio to move toward the back of the building. The football field ahead was glowing as the water droplets in the air reflected and refracted the plethora of light striking them. Our desire to see this giant searchlight increased as we got closer; I had an inkling of the dilemma moths must suffer. We stayed away, though; all that was there were zombies, and we'd seen enough of them for a few lifetimes. Although, if I'm being honest, I'd seen enough vampires for a few lifetimes as well.

"Found a way in," Winters said through my earpiece.

"How far are you from the main room?" I answered

through my throat microphone. The beauty of those was you could practically think your response and the person on the other end could hear you loud and clear.

"Twenty seconds. Fifteen if Sergeant Talbot finishes applying his make-up."

"Copy," I replied. BT was keeping tabs of the time elapsed on his watch, which would have looked like a clock on any of our wrists.

He tapped my shoulder when it was time to go. I turned the door handle; it made no sound. I had expected there to be some light inside, then I remembered the facts of our prey. I turned my flashlight on. The first thing it played across was a group of zombies in various stages of dismemberment. A slightly longer look made me think of a long-ago biology class in high school and television shows about autopsies.

"What the fuck?" came out involuntarily; at least it was quiet.

Three rifle lights illuminated from the other side. We had an effective lead sandwich; now we just needed some meat in between to make it complete. When I saw the zombie pile ahead of us, I had a flashback to Fritzy—if someone had jumped out of the shadows in a fucking catsuit I would have either gone shrieking into the night or unloaded all seven of my magazines into him. I tracked my light up onto the roof; no telling where Payne was.

"Mr. T…room off to your left." Tommy had the ZAD.

"Anyone else in here?" I asked before I attempted to move in on the other room.

"Nothing," Winters replied.

"Gary, you watch our six. Tommy, Winters, on us." As we went quickly to the door, rifles raised, we moved tactically, leaving plenty of room between us. Should she have a weapon or decide to attack, she could not hit more than one of us at a time. I knew in my gut we had eyes on us; something was watching our cautious approach. The only thing in question was, what was the outcome to be? We were in a semi-circle in front of that door; whatever came out was going to have a hell of a time getting past the barrage of bullets heading its way. Now came the tricky part: did we file in? I didn't like that tactic as we would shift the advantage Payne's way. Did I call out to her? What was the sense in that? Not like she was going to surrender; there wasn't a chance I was going to keep her as a prisoner. I had to entice her.

"Payne? 'Lot of fresh blood out here. You interested?" I asked.

"Seriously?" BT never looked away from the door as he questioned my words.

"You want to go in first?"

"Fresh blood?" BT echoed.

"Good evening." A disembodied, distinctly male voice spoke loud enough to echo slightly. "Can I help you gentlemen with something?"

Whoever was in there didn't seem overly concerned that four rifles were trained in his general direction.

"That's not Payne." This from Tommy; needed to remember to thank him for his incredible insight.

"There's no pain here," he agreed. "Well, none of any consequence. And no one by that name, either, in case you were wondering."

"Who am I speaking with?" I asked.

"Don't you use the magic word in this realm?" the voice asked.

"How about 'come the fuck out?' That magic enough?" I wasn't in the mood for games. My heart was thumping in my chest; whoever or whatever was in there wasn't human; my body knew what my head was unwilling to grasp.

"Strangely enough, the word 'fuck' or its linguistic equivalent is used as an intensifier in most of the languages I know," he mused, almost to himself. The man, and I use that word merely as a placeholder, stepped into the abundant shine our flashlights made.

"What the fuck. Everyone seeing the same thing I am?" I was looking at a person, standing in the neighborhood of six feet tall and very thin; that wasn't overly remarkable. What was, was the full body armor he was wearing—*really full;* helmet, pauldrons, gauntlets–the works. Add in two swords and a *cloak*, of all things, and there you have him. Not that swords are inappropriate gear for a zombie apocalypse, just extremely bizarre. In my opinion, he was sacrificing mobility, speed, and I would think, stealth.

"Do you think he raided an armor museum?" BT asked quietly.

I might have agreed, only it looked more like a dull, black plastic than metal. Maybe he ordered this from China back when the world was more normal. Probably showed up to his friend's Dungeons and Dragons games all decked out.

"What are we even doing here?" Not sure who I asked. My finger, having a mind of its own, was slowly applying pressure to the trigger. This wasn't right; he was too self-assured, like he knew something we didn't. As if he figured he could end this stand-off quickly, and with us on the losing end.

"You know, I've often asked myself that very question, Mike. When you think about it, what are any of us doing here?" He answered so nonchalantly. He moved to a bench. I got the feeling he moved slowly so as not to provoke a bunch of excited people with guns. Not out of fear, exactly, but maybe because he was used to it. Or, I don't know, maybe because he was humoring us. I didn't like the feeling at all.

"Great, he's existential." BT was not amused. "More specifically, what are you doing here in this gym, with these zombies? Any funny answers and I might start shooting so I can get home and eat some shitty dinner that this guy's sister, the woman that I love, prepares for me."

"TMI, BT," I said.

"I'm a little frustrated, man. I like my dinner. You know how many times she's stopped me from going to the Chow Hall to eat? The food there is like fine French Cuisine compared to the stuff she puts on plates. I have had to throw dishes away because whatever she tried to cook was permanently embedded within the ceramic or metal, depending. You're like the gift that keeps on giving, man. I already have to deal with you, and now I have to deal with your sister. It's more than any man should be exposed to. I fully expect Sainthood when my time comes."

Winters leaned back so he could look at me, his eyebrows arched. I shrugged a response. I would have swirled a finger near my temple if I hadn't been pointing my rifle at a potential hostile.

"Everything all right over there?" Gary asked.

I honestly didn't know how to reply. The person we were dealing with here was either extremely off his rocker or ultimately prepared. He didn't seem at all bothered. In fact, he leaned forward slightly, resting his elbows on his knees; he laced his fingers together and rested his chin on them. He seemed almost intrigued. I was glad I didn't have to make any judgment calls on him, as BT kept rolling.

"The chow hall eggs aren't bad. The hash browns are pretty good too, and the meatloaf is really good, and I missed that last time. Want to know what your sister made? She called it lasagna. Lasagna, Mike. It was green–and not because it was a vegetable lasagna, but because she boiled the noodles in green Jell-O water. Green Jell-O water, Mike! Why? What the fuck is that all about? I had to pretend that I thoroughly enjoyed a lime-flavored lasagna. Man, no one is that good of an actor! And then, instead of hamburger in the sauce, it was tofu. Said she was concerned about my cholesterol, even though *I told her* that my last physical came back *perfect*. She said she was thinking ahead. Want to know what tofu tastes like? Gooey snots. That's the best way to describe it. Man, look at me! I'm starving to death! I hoard candy bars when we go on these runs so I'll have something to eat when I get back. It's torture by Talbot!"

"Umm, right. Well, one problem at a time. And how do you know my name?" I asked of the stranger.

"Someone must have said it at one point."

I didn't think that was the case, but I wasn't one who could specifically remember everything that was said to them, though the lime lasagna noodles were going to stay with me for a good long while.

"Since we're on a first name basis, what's yours?"

"Oh! Terrible manners on my part; I do apologize. I've been a bit distracted by events. My name is Eric; I'm pleased to meet you." He stood up and offered his gauntleted-*gauntlets*, for fuck's sake-hand, taking a step toward me.

"Whoa, whoa, hold on there, Eric," I told him. "Don't come any closer." His reaction had caused me to stir, as it had all of us; I figured we were real close to having an incident, and I'd yet to determine if he rated a bullet or not. "We shoot you and then I have to do a bunch of paperwork explaining why we did, or, more likely, all of us here come to an agreement that we didn't come across anyone and then BT here can get to his raspberry eggs or whatever my sister cooks up."

"You're an asshole," BT said.

"Would it help if I say I have no interest in harming any of you?" Eric responded.

"Fair enough. Can you tell me what your intentions with the zombies are?"

"Mostly honorable," he replied, "although they don't seem to agree."

"Didn't quite mean it like that; I wasn't thinking you were taking them out on a date."

"I know. My sense of humor is a bit off; sorry about that. No, I've been examining the zombies you have in this world. I've never seen a biological zombie before, much less witnessed mutating specialist castes. Reminds me of ants," he finished, and shivered. The shiver was strangely reassuring. It meant he was afraid of something. Then it wasn't reassuring, because *he* was afraid of something, which meant there was something *worse*. The part of me that could sense these things kept telling me there *wasn't* anything worse, and I really wanted it to be right.

"This world?" Winters asked. "How many other worlds do you know?"

"I wouldn't even hazard to guess." Something like a low chuckle escaped him. "I mean, I know several personally, but I know *of* many, many more." He looked thoughtful, his eyes doing the thousand-yard stare for a moment. I had the strangest feeling he was…communing or something. Not talking to someone, per se, but something like it. Consulting his memory, maybe? He was a vampire; perhaps he had a lot of memory to consult.

"No, I don't have a definite answer for you. I used to keep a catalog, but it got lost, sort of. It's in the billions, in any case. By the way, speaking of things I've lost, I don't suppose you know where I might find a working FMRI machine, do you?"

I wasn't going to tell him we had one at the base, not until I knew a little bit more about who I was dealing with.

"You a doctor? Biologist maybe?" I asked.

"Mr. T, remember…he's like Payne," Tommy replied.

"Right, right," Winters chimed in. "When did humans become such a minority?"

"Probably at about the same time those flu shots rolled out," Gary said.

Eric was looking intently at Tommy and then his gaze shifted toward me. "Well, isn't that strange." He left it at that, for the time being, anyway. "Can we put the guns down now? I'm not a fan of getting shot. We're having such a lovely conversation, and pointing guns at people is usually considered rude."

"Forgive my manners," I said, "but you're a vampire who is rounding up zombies for what I must assume are nefarious, albeit honorable, reasons. For the moment, I feel better holding this weapon on you."

"The zombies, they have been getting smarter, yes? Yes." I felt like an explanation was coming as he answered his own question.

"Is that observation supposed to stop me in my tracks?" I responded. "Anyone who has lived this long realizes that by now."

"Hey, I think that's doing pretty good, especially since I've only been here…" he trailed off, and again I had that feeling he was…I don't know…*consulting*. Communicating. Almost *talking* to someone. "Eleven days? Curious. Time flies when you're doing your due diligence."

"Is any one else in there with you?" I motioned with my rifle toward the other room.

"Oh. No, there's no one in there."

"Who are you talking to, then?"

"That's a long story. It only makes sense in the extended telling; the short version makes me sound crazy."

"Try me."

"I have a psychic sword and an empathic horse, although the horse is usually a statue."

"A horse that's a statue?"

"Right now, she's a pickup truck. Her name is Bronze."

"Bronze?" I felt a headache coming. "Fine. Let's forget that for now. What are you doing with the zombies over there?"

"Ah. You don't believe in magic?" Eric asked.

"Not since I learned how David Blaine did the levitation thing on his shows."

His head tilted slightly. "Not an unreasonable view," he admitted. "Loved his shows, but I was always a Copperfield fan, myself. Let me take this in another direction. Some of these zombies aren't too physically capable, but they have a talent, a psychic ability. They scream into your mind, right?"

"Shriekers. We call them shriekers."

"Aptly named. And the hulking creatures?"

"Bulkers, then speeders; the slow ones, those that are left, anyway, we call them deaders. They were the first wave of zombies, corpses reanimated as the viral agent takes over. That quickly changed, and we got the speeders. They never truly died; their bodies were taken over before they went through the process of rigor mortis, thus keeping all their physical abilities, their speed. The bulkers were next; we figure they were adapting well to their environment. Once the speeders started dragging down everything in sight, people began to barricade themselves in their homes."

"Fascinating," he said, nodding. "And then these bulkers started showing up, breaking in through the barricades, yes?"

"That's about the way of it. Then came the shriekers to flush out those still remaining. Their signal seems to strike squarely in the flight response center of the brain. It's almost impossible to ignore the spike without some training in the matter," I explained.

"Your situation here is going to get worse," Eric said matter of factly. "I can't be completely sure without some dissection, some equipment, and perhaps a neurologist. What I *think* is happening is that another evolution of these beings is in progress; the development of a unified intellect; a hive-mind." He looked to us like he knew we suspected the same.

"I believe the shriekers can link telepathically with their horde, enabling the growth of a cohesive group. If it is not already in play, I suspect the next step will be their ability to link among themselves, which will form a collective consciousness that is much smarter than any individual zombie. Unlike normal evolution, these beings can learn unendingly from the deaths of their fellows, and thus adapt to threats without the need for a generation of weeding-out. It's difficult to guess what they might come up with once their intelligence is at its apex; indeed, humans may not live to see it." He shrugged his heavy shoulders. "Once the shriekers stop turning up food in large quantities, they'll have to adapt again."

I looked to BT. It had been our fear all along that as the zombies got smarter it was very likely they would begin to use tools and weapons, making them much more efficient killing machines. But a telepathic hive-mind?

"I also think…that they may be on the cusp of becoming self-aware," Eric continued. "This, I'm sorry to say, might be the worst thing possible. If they become smart enough to consciously direct their own evolution, there's no telling what specialized monsters they may become. Flying, bat-like things for bombing, multi-armed monsters with claws and carapace armor…or perhaps telepaths powerful enough to directly influence the actions of others. Your brains," he added, nodding at BT and Winter, "are capable of much more than you use them for. Intelligent shriekers would evolve them into much more potent weapons."

He sighed and sat down again, shaking his head.

"Sometimes I wonder how humans survived any of the zombie scenarios. In this case, though, there's a clear strategy in play. The shriekers are the brains, and that makes them the key. Neutralize them and you slow down the evolution of their entire species, prevent it from becoming purposefully developed. It won't stop the mindless hordes, of course, but it buys you time."

"Tommy, what do you think?"

"I think I wish we had a breatine," he replied.

"What's a breatine?" Eric asked.

"Small bug. It detects truth."

"Sweet! I could use one of those."

"Yeah, let's make everything even freakier," BT snapped. "A lot of weirdness going on Talbot; what are we supposed to do? I kind of just want to shoot him and go home."

"Yeah, I heard my sister was working on some seafood dishes; I can't imagine how she could screw those up." I could hear BT cringing. "So, Eric. Is all of this hypothesis, or do you have a plan to stop them?"

"Wait. You aren't buying into all this, are you?" BT asked.

"I don't know what I'm buying here, BT. I don't know what to do. Tommy says he's a vampire, he's a vampire. That doesn't mean he's inherently evil. Do we kill him to cover our asses? And I've never liked that–killing proactively, I mean. I'm definitely not bringing him back to the base. That's like bringing a bouquet of lit sparklers into a fireworks warehouse. So where does that leave us?"

"Tactical withdrawal, I hope," Winters responded.

"Look, I understand you're concerned," Eric offered. "I like to think I'm generally trustworthy."

"Generally?" I asked.

"Well, I've lied, stolen, cheated, killed, and occasionally been unkind, but I rarely do these things without some sort of justification. I prefer to consider them last resorts under exceptional circumstances. Of course, I may be biased."

"Is this one of those 'generally' times?" I was lowering my rifle.

"Mike, yeah, man. I would say this isn't one of those circumstances he was discussing, though." BT was not so ready to drop his rifle down.

"I'm listening, guys. If anyone has a viable option, speak up. Otherwise we hear him out. I'd feel more comfortable, Eric, if you put those swords you have over there."

"Firebrand? You want me to put Firebrand in a corner? Nobody puts Firebrand in a corner."

"Did he just kind of quote *Dirty Dancing?*" BT asked. Eric's face split in a grin.

"What?" I took my eyes completely off Eric to look at BT.

"Nobody puts Baby in a corner. *Dirty Dancing*, you know what I'm talking about, right?" BT was looking flustered.

"*Drink down that gin and kerosene!*" Gary started singing from across the gymnasium.

"*Light a match and leave me be!*" Eric sang back. Neither of them could carry a tune.

"This is not happening." Winters was shaking his head.

"Tell you what," Eric said, still chuckling, "come with me. I'll show you what I found out." Eric stepped to one side of the door he'd emerged from and swept his arm as if inviting us to go on.

"This a trap?" I asked.

"Talbot, I think you've finally snapped. Of course, it's a trap. You think he's going to tell you that?" BT said.

"Shall I go in first?" Eric asked.

"Not a chance." BT shouldered past all of us. "I'll take a look first." He was in there for about fifteen seconds, didn't hear any sounds of a struggle, then his voice came out of the room clear enough. "Listen, I know white people are touched, especially the ones I end up with but this is starting to border on the absurd."

"What's going on?" I lifted my rifle on Eric.

"He's got a zombie in here trapped by enough weights to sink the Titanic, plus it's wearing a football helmet."

"Go, please." I motioned for Eric to go in so I could follow. "Tommy, Winters, stay close to the door. Anything happens in there, shoot everything that's not a confirmed friendly."

I had my flashlight trained on the zombie, who looked, for lack of a better word, pathetic. Like maybe it was in massive amounts of pain, though as of yet I had never seen one display that emotion. Suddenly, I was struck with a profound new thought; not that I cared for its welfare, but I realized just to have that emotion meant it had to have feelings, and feelings came with higher intelligence. "Why the helmet, Eric?"

"It's one of your shriekers," he replied as way of an explanation.

"The helmet stops the shrieking?" I didn't believe that, but the thing wasn't calling out for help, so there had to be some explanation.

"Not exactly. The designs on the helmet are spells."

"Spells?" BT repeated.

"Okay, fine. It's magic."

"We're back to that?" BT looked about ready to kick puppies and shoo away rainbows.

"Alright, maybe the word 'magic' in this realm is more of the poo-poo variety. How about vampire powers?" He lifted his hands and wiggled his fingers.

"Better," BT said.

"Really?" I asked. He shrugged.

"I have a spell," Eric began, then caught himself. "...erm, I mean I have mystically...hmm." He held up a finger to beg a moment's wait while he thought. "Right, I think I've got it. Through technology so advanced as to seem magical, I have applied certain forces to the helmet. This causes her shriek to enter a feedback loop within her own head, with results as painful as you might imagine. She doesn't like it all that much." He shrugged. "Maybe she can learn some empathy; but all she's managed so far is anger."

"That's why she looks like her mom grounded her from going over to Suzie's party," I said absently as I looked down upon the zee.

"Yeah, Mike. I'm sure that's exactly what happened. Just want everyone to know that's my commanding officer right there. I wonder if they still do section eights? And you won't even need to wear a dress."

"What?" I looked away and to him.

"Bullshit! You don't know who Klinger is?" BT asked.

Eric answered with, "Corporal Max Klinger."

"Why are you talking about *MASH* at a time like this?" I asked.

"I give up." BT put his hand to his face and slowly shook his head from side to side.

"What's up with him?" I asked Eric.

"Beats me. None of your references make much sense; it is like listening to whales underwater when you speak to each other." Eric replied.

"Alright, Eric, I need for you to explain this in a way that I can understand and relay to others," I said.

"Sure. How basic do you need it?" Eric asked.

"Pretend you're talking to a first grader that somehow got his Kool-Aid mixed up with beer and got so drunk he threw up all over his Minion pajamas and married his favorite teddy bear, that basic," BT said. "Or a third grader that likes to pretend his paste is milk, that kind."

Eric was looking from BT to me, a confused expression upon his face.

"Really man?" I asked.

BT shrugged. "If the pointy cap fits, you wear it proudly."

Eric took that as his cue to interrupt before things got out of hand.

"Look, in a shrieker, large chunks of her brain activate during a scream," Eric stated as if I was supposed to know what that meant.

"I thought you said you needed an MRI machine?" I asked.

"To make more progress, yes."

"Then how do you know about chunks of brain activating?"

"I can't explain that without using words like 'psychic,' 'vampire,' and 'magic.'"

"Fine, we're listening. Winters, you make sure you recall everything he says," I said.

"Why me?"

"Because you have medical training."

"Yeah, as a medic, not a neurosurgeon."

"You'll be fine," I told him.

"Shall I continue?" Eric asked.

I motioned for him to do that. I wasn't completely convinced he didn't mean us harm, but it was easy enough to see at this moment he was much more interested in telling us what he had discovered rather than discovering how we tasted. I took note that Tommy made sure to stay in a corner of the room the farthest away, keeping a vigilant gaze upon him.

"Because of the…uh, the science-laden helmet I have applied to her head, I can tell the front of her brain performs tasks, while the echo of her scream activates areas closer to her brainstem. It seems to cause quite a bit of pain."

"Amen to that brother." Gary had come closer.

"This isn't a revival tent. Get back to your post," I told him.

I could hear him mumbling as he left. "I'm the older brother…who does he think he's bossing around? Wish I could tell dad."

Me too, I thought.

"I've only had experimental subjects for a couple of hours, but you seem to have psychic zombies. They can gather other zombies to them, can call out for help if needed, and obviously force people from safe hiding places by triggering the flight response. There are mutant ogre-types—sorry, I mean 'bulkers'—and your sprinters, er, speeders. It's almost like a hive with specialized workers, soldiers, and the like. It's worse, though, since they seem to be linking psychically to form a composite creature. Individual zombies die, but the creature learns and evolves."

"Preaching to the choir!" Gary shouted from across the gym.

"Gary! Do you want to lose a stripe?" I shouted back.

"Little bit of power and he lets it go straight to his head."

"The acoustics in this place are pretty incredible, Private!" I replied.

"It's Serg…forget it. I get it."

"What's next?" BT was done with the distraction as he looked to Eric.

"I can't tell for sure, not without studying them more or with some advanced machinery. I'm still thinking total consciousness isn't too far away for them."

I was happy when he didn't say "advanced spells" or something along those lines. It seemed strange in the times we lived in that I would be so anti-magic. I did not think I would ever get over that, not anytime soon.

Eric continued. "I think at some point, it will be safe to assume these screamers will get together, maybe a dozen at first, or a hundred, whatever the critical threshold is, and you'll have a group of zombies capable of *thinking*."

"Once that happens, we will find ourselves licking the stinky-pudding end of the stick," I said.

"Stinky-pudding? That mean what I think it does?" BT asked. "Forget I asked. Of course it does. Great, another visual." BT flipped me off. "Just fuck you, man. I love my pudding."

"These shriekers are the real problem," Eric went on. "They already possess a fair amount of intelligence…more than any of the others, anyway. It can register pain, for one thing, which implies it has a sense of identity. 'I' feel pain, but there has to be an 'I' to feel it, if that makes sense. This one stopped screaming because it hurts to do so. I'm not sure if she realizes the screams aren't going to summon help, but she *knows* screaming hurts."

"The group intelligence you're talking about…any idea the limitations?" Winters asked.

"Depends on how many there are. At first, you wouldn't have anything too bright, but once they realize they could get smarter by adding more members, they might also start evolving big zombie brains to act as central processors. The zombie horde could become more intelligent than any human simply because it would evolve faster than humans."

I took note that Eric did not seem to include himself within that equation and the more I looked at him, the harder it was to believe he had ever originated from humanity like myself or Tommy. What exactly was he and where was he from? For all I knew, he could be the vanguard of an invading force. He had direct knowledge of the zombies, maybe he was even now manipulating them so that they would be a more powerful adversary to us. So many questions. Good thing I had a shit ton of bullets on me. A significant part of me knew the safe play was to shoot him, but what if he couldn't die that way? I wouldn't want to piss him off. I'm sure we would find ourselves in a sinking vat of stinky-pudding in a hurry.

"The main thing in humanity's favor is this brainiac here," he nudged the shrieker with the toe of his boot, "doesn't appear to have a lot of memory. Firebrand has been listening; she doesn't seem to remember anything beyond the simple Pavlovian response level."

"Fire…your weapon? Your sword told you this?"

"My psychic sword," he reminded me. "You want me to go into it?" Eric asked, giving me a look.

"No, just continue," I sighed.

"Good idea. She knows enough that if she attacks, say, a red thing—"

"What kind of red thing?" Gary asked from across the room.

I put my palm to my head.

"It's just an example," Eric replied, nodding at me in sympathy. "How about we say it's a tank?"

"A red tank?" Gary asked.

"This isn't happening. Gary, you say one more thing while you're supposed to be watching our back and I'm going to call in to have you evac'd. Clear enough?"

"I've just never seen a red tank is all."

"Please go on." I turned back to Eric.

"Okay, so our shrieker attacks, for this argument and this

argument only, a red tank." He nodded over my shoulder to Gary whom, I would imagine, was beaming. "If this tank wiped out the entire group and this one were to survive, she might recruit another gang of zombies to attack. It's possible she could retain the memory—develop the conditioned response—that to attack a red tank only results in too many zombie deaths. She would be conditioned to avoid red tanks rather than attack them."

"That could be huge. We saw something like this early on, but if we could make them see humanity in its entirety as too difficult to attack, that could be the turning point."

"We're—that is, *I'm* not sure quite yet if it would be a true memory or a conditioned response. If enough get together to form a sentient entity, it won't matter. But yes, both could be quite useful."

He paused for a moment, as though listening again. I tried not to wonder about psychic swords and pickup-truck horses.

"Speaking of useful," he went on, eyeing me, "I can see you keep wondering what to do with me, Michael Talbot. Let me suggest that while you are uncertain about whether or not I am more valuable as an ally than I am dangerous as a potential enemy, what I am is a powerful unknown. As you suspected, I also dislike being shot. It annoys me dreadfully, and the only thing it will kill is any chance of me leaning toward ally."

"That's a lot of words to say not to fuck with you," I said.

"I thought I should share my viewpoint."

"I cannot bring you back to our base; there are too many unknown variables here. You say you're from another realm; do you mean harm here?"

"Nope. Just passing through, really, and wondered why the place seemed abandoned. Then I got curious about your zombies."

"Are you empathetic enough to see how strange this is for us?"

"Oh, hell yes. This is unusual even for me. I've never encountered nonmagical zombies before." BT bit his lip, but didn't say anything.

"How long you planning on staying? I don't want to be like the sheriff of every small town on a television show or movie who forces the outsider to the borders…"

"But," Eric said, he seemed to be bemused at the notion.

"Not going to lie, you and your research concern me. Like you're a giant hornet's nest a half mile from a school. Everything is all fine and dandy until one of them kiddies gets it in his head to throw a rock, then a thousand little hells pop loose. That make sense?"

"The analogy is not without merit."

"Umm…guys." Gary was moving away from the door.

"What did I tell you?" I was about to physically place him back at his post.

"You're going to want to see this," he told me.

Didn't need any magical scientific powers to know what was happening. "How many?" I asked before I got there.

"I don't know, maybe all of them."

"BT, Winters." I motioned for them to come with me. Neither Eric nor Tommy moved; I wondered which of them might start pissing first. Alright, so that wasn't so obvious, pissing contest, I mean. They looked like they were sizing each other up.

"That was fast." BT was looking through a two-inch opening on the door. The football field was covered in zombies and more were streaming in, beginning to cover the running track that encircled the field, and some were even in the stands as if they were waiting for the festivities to start.

"Lock that. What about the other exit?" I was heading to another door. I opened it only to have three, semi-inflated, red dodge balls roll out. "Supply closet. Great."

"I'll check the way we came in." Winters was gone for less than a minute. "Got close to fifty there. From the looks of it

I'd say they're circling up, checking out about a dozen used foil packs, not eating them just sniffing."

I turned to Tommy, who was looking through his pack. "I don't know how they fell out!"

"Shit," was my only response; all it needed to be, really.

"There are windows in the locker rooms we can fit through." Winters was in the doorframe.

"Anyone gauge how far we traveled to get here?"

"Fifty-one miles," Winters said. "Why?"

"How far can base artillery travel?" I asked.

"You insane…sir? Lucky for us, about eighteen miles. No way do I want people I don't know raining down shells that close to us."

"Just a thought."

"Don't let him upset you, Talbot. At least you had one. That's a rarity."

"Thanks, BT. I like it better when we're on-base, where all you assholes pretend like I'm in charge."

We were now standing in the hallowed girl's locker room, the beginning of many adolescent fantasies…though that ends abruptly in the face of reality. Whoever said girls were made of sugar and spice had never been in this site of stink. Adolescent boys didn't have the market cornered on funk.

The frosted windows were high up above a row of lockers, they appeared to only be for light, as I didn't see any hardware that would make them open. That wasn't the biggest problem; the biggest problem was standing next to me.

"You're not going to fit," I told him. Our host, Eric, was the most slender of us all, and he would have to wriggle his way through. I wasn't so sure I'd be able to get through, and the thought of my head sticking out for all to eat like a corn dog at a carnival didn't sit so well.

"Winters, give me the phone. Haven, this is Tribulation… repeat…Haven, this is Tribulation."

"Your call signs are getting worse," BT pointed out unnecessarily.

"At this point, we'll be lucky if they respond at all," Winters said. I gave him the finger.

"Go ahead Tribulation."

"Haven, we've found ourselves in a bit of a jam." Could almost hear the sigh from the other end.

"Tribulation, birds are grounded. We can't get you an extraction."

"Looking for a drone strike or two." He didn't respond for a few minutes and when he did, he told me to hold for a second.

"What the fuck does he think I've been doing, jamming my thumb up my butt?"

"Lieutenant Talbot, you probably want to keep your finger off the transmit button when you're not following protocol," Colonel Bennington said.

"Sorry, sir."

"What's going on?"

"We're stuck in a gym. No way out except through roughly seven, eight hundred zombies, sir. The majority are huddled around our beacon in the sky, in fact, striking that and only that would be optimum. Hopefully we'll be able to do clean up at that point."

"You safe?"

"For the moment, sir. They're amassing bulkers to assail our position at some point. Plenty of shriekers in the midst as well."

"And the light? Any idea who summoned the trouble?"

I was looking directly at Eric; how could I even begin to explain this.

"Sir, I'm not sure as to the who, but there's some whys. There are some zombies in the gym; looks like some experiments were being performed. Luckily, whoever was playing doctor left some detailed instructions."

"Anything we can use?"

"Does my answer determine if we get help or not?"

"Of course not, already authorized deployment. I'm told the ETA is fifteen minutes. Lieutenant, you're going to want to find some cover if possible; this one is armed with four Hellfires."

"Roger that sir. As for the notes, there's not a bunch of hard science, but some compelling theories. Some we're aware of, but some of the insight is new." At the Colonel's prompting, I spent the next five minutes going over everything Eric had told us. Bennington was a pragmatist; there was more than a decent chance that something would go south here and we'd never make it back. At least the information would survive, and that was the mission. Sure, none of us considered ourselves disposable, but that was never the case back at HQ. Mission first, safety third.

"Excuse me—not to interrupt," Eric asked, once I had my thumb off the button and we had a pause, "but am I to understand you're calling in an airstrike here?"

"Not here specifically, where the light is."

"I'm not sure the distance is sufficient."

"Well, maybe you should have thought of that before you set-up your little Frankenstein shop here. Don't worry too much; the drone operators are pretty good at their job." I told him.

"Sir, is it Andres or Verdan at the helm tonight?" Winters asked.

"Shit."

"What's shit?" BT asked.

"Verdan is my neighbor. Henry, for some reason, can't stand him or more likely his mode of transportation, keeps pissing on his motorcycle and has dropped a few deuces around it as well. Verdan has come into work a couple of times with Henry's offal peppered all over. The guy is actually pretty cool; I think it's that the machine is so loud it's disturbed some of Henry's naps."

"Your dog is tired after his naps, man, and because one of his siestas is disturbed, we now have to worry about getting pelted by Hellfires."

"I mostly smoothed it over."

"Sorry LT," Winters said. "I was there for one of your smoothing over sessions, smearing it further into his uniform with a wet paper towel doesn't count as damage control."

"It's the thought that counts, right?" I was looking for anything.

"Yeah, I'm sure that was exactly what he was thinking all day as he took whiffs of Henry's refuse," BT said.

"Well, if Henry dislikes Verdan now, what do you think the big dog will do if he offs his food delivery system?" I asked.

"That's a good point. I could see that dog dismantling his bike with that maw of his. Fuck, I do like when you make sense every now and again." BT clapped me hard enough on the shoulder I nearly pitched over.

"You realize that shit hurts, right?"

"Every time brother, every time. I consider it recompense for all the crap I have to go through with you."

"Alright people. We have five minutes. Gary, come on, I want everyone in the weight room."

I was keeping an eye on my brother as he crossed the gym floor, his gaze was down on his ancient walkman, as he must have been fast-forwarding through a song. I have tried repeatedly to get him to switch to a more updated mode of playing music, but he wouldn't hear of it, said the cassettes added character to the songs. He didn't care in the least that most music made from 2002 forward was not available in that format. He just said anything worth listening to came out between 1975 and 1989. Strangely specific span, but ultimately his call. Not sure if an mp3 player would have saved him anyway.

I called out to him just as his left foot came down in a wide smear of clear spinal fluid that had leaked out from one of the zombies. He slid for a good two feet before his balance was ultimately lost and he slammed down hard on his ass. He was more upset he had smashed his Walkman than that he had bruised his ass or that he was covered in goo. I had gone over to help him when the doors he had just left were slammed up against. Instantly I knew the sound for what it was: bulkers wanted in. The doors opened outward, but even a single bulker was completely capable of bashing the steel frame out of the cinderblock and concrete, given time-say, less than we had remaining before the drone strike. The weight room door was another steel door, but it might make the difference. I didn't like there wasn't any alternate way out once we shuttered ourselves in there, but if there was enough of a horde, I didn't see a choice.

We stood in a loose circle by the door, watching on the far side as those doors rattled. We bet on whether they would hold before the drone strike hit. Being from Boston, I knew better. They were going to give a good full minute before.

"You owe me a case," I told BT as the doors burst open.

He let his rifle express how angry he was. He'd opted for the heavier rounded 300 Blackout which worked considerably better than the 5.56 rounds the rest of us were firing. Still would've felt a ton better if he was hefting a fifty cal. BT knew better than to go for the armor-plated head, instead opting for the only real soft spot on the beast: the knees. The floor was bouncing up and down as three of the over-sized zombies lumbered toward us; though in no way does that imply that they were slow. The first bulker through the door thumped down to the ground once its right leg was infused with enough holes that it could no longer support the weight it was designed for. If you are an American football fan and happened to have had the displeasure of watching the end of Joe Theismann's career, you'll know what I saw. If not...the bulker's leg bent outward at a ninety-degree angle to the rest of his body. The echo of his head reverberating off the floor was immediately drowned out as his brothers passed him by.

"Inside, let's go!" As far as I was concerned, the main part of the gym was yielded ground. Eric stood next to me; his sword was out. As far as I was concerned, he had balls of steel if he was going to face a bulker with a bladed weapon. Not sure if he was technically an ally yet, but, enemy of my enemy and all that. Winters pulled the door shut and threw the bolt, stepping back just as the first of the bulkers slammed into it. Didn't bode well when three of the drop-ceiling panels fell free, one breaking over Gary's head and coating him in a fine white powder.

"Is this asbestos?" he yelled out, dancing around as if fire ants had crawled into his underwear. He was in far greater danger of knocking himself out running into a weight stack than he was of getting a lung disease.

"It's alright, man." BT was wiping the stuff off. "You're fine, just a regular panel, polystyrene, just polystyrene."

"How bad is it? Tell me!" Gary pleaded.

BT looked at me as if to ask how deep the crazy ran through the Talbots. He should already know; he was dating my sister. "It's a resin, a foam or something, it's fine." BT finally got my brother somewhat under control.

"Mr. T, the drone is here." Tommy had his head cocked to the side. I couldn't hear anything past the shuffling of feet and the pounding at the door. Only way I could have missed the missile strike, though, was if I was in a coma. The explosion was deafening, and if the ceiling tiles were old and indeed made from asbestos, we were screwed, as nearly all the rest of them came down. Looked like we'd been in a baby powder factory after an industrial accident. The drone swung by overhead and fired another missile. I was going to wait until it dropped its entire payload before I committed to a course of action.

The missiles would rip giant holes in the carpet of zombies, but then any of them that had yet to join the party would be coming to investigate. We had an escape window we needed to hit.

"What the hell is taking so long?" I asked when we didn't hear any more explosions.

"Hear that?" This from BT.

Just on the outer range, I could hear a high-pitched whine.

"Get down, get down!" Winters yelled. "Drone engine is failing!"

I think he finished the sentence, tough to tell as the machine blasted into the gym. I, along with everyone else, was tossed around like kids in the back of a pickup. Heavy steel weights were tumbled in the mix; if we did get home, we were going to be dealing with multiple contusions.

"Verdan fucking hates you, man," BT grunted as he stood, helping me up.

Thankfully, the relentless assault on the door had stopped, but we had other problems; smoke was beginning to creep in around the frame.

"The door...BT, get it open. I'll cover you." Zombies are one thing, but there was no way I was going to die by asphyxiation.

He grabbed the handle. "It's warm." He tried to push it open, then he placed his shoulder against it. "Not moving." He had his full weight and considerable muscle attempting to do so.

"Tommy, help him." I was worried that when it opened they would spill out onto the floor and be completely vulnerable. The smoke inside was beginning to thicken up.

"Wedged, Talbot." BT was using all of his considerable resources to try.

"Stand back! I'll shoot it." Gary was aiming his rifle.

"Yeah, hold a sec on that idea. It's wedged in the frame."

"Stand back," Eric said. "Shield your eyes."

"What the fuck?" BT asked.

"I'm not going to ask you to trust me," Eric replied, placing the point of a big-ass sword against the door, "but just chant 'The enemy of my enemy is my friend,' and you'll feel better. I'm not going to be ripped apart by zombie hordes if I can avoid it, and I'm pretty sure I can. Being a decent sort, I'll also bring you with me as we leave. Can't ask for a deal more fair than that." His eyes narrowed and something totally weird happened. The sword was a big monster of a blade, thoroughly medieval, with an ornate pommel in the shape of a dragon's head with tiny jewels for eyes. I swear to God, despite the obvious risk I take in doing so, the damned thing *winked at me*.

I instinctively looked to Tommy. Even he seemed out of his element with this one.

"I'm getting something but it's garbled, kind of like distorted images I might see at the bottom of a dirty pool," Tommy said. I honestly didn't know what he was even referencing. Later, I would find out more about Bronze, the statue, the psychic link, and the possessed truck, but at the moment I was close to flying blind. This stuff is beyond my capability to make up, and there was no way I was ever going to tell anyone about it when I was debriefed. And if any of those with me mentioned this, I would, as their superior officer, recommend that they go through a few days of a psych eval.

I backed up as I watched the edge of the blade begin to glow, then I got closer, making sure it wasn't a trick of my eyes. It wasn't. The light grew brighter as the whole length of the blade caught fire then narrowed, focusing down to a star-hot line of fire along the edge. He pushed it through the door while everyone shielded their eyes. The damn thing cut through the steel fire door like a plasma torch.

"Any chance I could get one of those?" I asked him.

"I don't have a spare dragon," was the cryptic answer, "and you might want to step away."

"Can I try it?"

He turned his head, lifted his visor and looked at me. In the searing light from the blade, his face seemed different, especially the eyes. They didn't look like human eyes. There was something deep and dark and terrible in them, something ruthless and savage. Even so, maybe there was also something a little sad. I backed up a step. I moved farther back when he returned to the task at hand.

"That's like a tiny acetylene torch, right?" BT asked me.

"Where? In the hilt? It would already be exhausted," I whispered.

"I know you hate the concept, but it is quite definitely magic," Eric seemed slightly perturbed. "It's got a dragon spirit inside of it, and you'd better get used to the idea of spirits inside things, because they're going to save our collective asses."

I wanted to tell him "bullshit," but how do I tell someone that while they're cutting through a steel fire door with the edge of a burning sword?

"A dragon?" Winters looked distraught at the thought. "Lieutenant, what did you get us into?"

"I really don't think this can be laid at my feet."

"Come on man," BT started. "I guarantee that any other team came out on this bullshit run, they wouldn't have encountered any of this weird shit. There'd be, like, a discarded flashlight in the middle of the field and one old toothless zombie gnawing on it. Eric here would be a scarecrow in a cornfield."

"Hey!" Eric called, not stopping in his slicing. He wore two swords, the other one was more like a cavalry saber. What the hell did he need it for when the greatsword was a cutting torch?

"Sorry. I'm just saying, Talbot, you're like a magnet for

this type of shit. One of those special rare-earth magnets but instead of metal, you attract crazy–a fucking super-conductor for insanity. Why do I decide to stay with the guy that's a few cushions shy of a couch?"

"What?"

"No insulation in the attic," he continued, nudging Gary. "Probably put your shoes on before your pants, you crazy bastard."

I think he would have gone on until we all choked to death on smoke, luckily, Eric spoke.

"The door will go with a good kick," he said as the light and fire died around the blade. "Are we going to pick on Talbot some more or run like hell?"

BT nodded, we all raised our rifles.

"I'll rush the door and take it out. Bronze is waiting for us."

"The statue? The statue is waiting? How fast does it go? Can we all fit on it? It's a statue of a horse, right?" Gary wanted to know; hell, I wanted to know.

"Not exactly how it works. Just pile in and we'll sort it all out later, okay?"

Eric pushed the cut-out door over. The two bulkers that had been trying to force themselves into the gymnasium were running around the gym ablaze, could hear the vast fat stores sizzling as they did so. Occasionally, large droplets would fall from them and continue to burn.

"Well, that's fucking gross. Don't shoot them; let's try to get out of here without making any more noise," I said.

The gym was burning; easy enough to see the origin of the blaze. Verdan's drone had punched a hole right through the roof. I was not thrilled when I saw the tips of two missiles pointing directly toward the weight room.

"What aren't you telling us?" BT asked. "This is about more than just a couple of shitty uniforms. You run over his pet turtle? Maybe put your trash out too early?"

We were moving quickly to the only exit afforded us. We could hear the throaty roar of a V-8 not too far off; I looked over to Eric, who was smiling. Verdan might dislike me immensely, but he had done an admirable job with the gaggle of zombies. There were two large craters on the football field; The Eatonville Eagles would not be playing a home game anytime soon. The zombies that had not been completely obliterated were in complete disarray. Safe to say they were not fans of fire, maybe not the crazed affliction Frankenstein's monster suffered, but they were staying away from the secondary blazes. We had to clear a couple of them away from our general area, but nothing too taxing. We rounded the corner of the building to where Bronze was parked. *Hesitant* to get in was an accurate statement, maybe not strong enough to truly imply how I felt.

"It's not going to turn back into a statue, is it?" I asked as Gary piled in.

"That's not how it works," Eric responded. "It's a perfectly normal truck." The engine surged twice, like a laugh. "Mostly normal," Eric amended. "It's just…possessed. Get in."

BT looked over at me. "Hummer isn't that far away." He had the same misgivings I did.

"You mean the one behind all those zombies?" Eric asked, standing in the bed of the truck and looking toward our vehicle. "Think we can clear them, get it going, and get away before the rest get their act together?"

"Huh?" was my thoughtful answer. My gaze did not waver from the truck; I had poked my head in to see if perhaps this whole magic thing was a ruse and there was a driver, albeit a small one, in there operating the controls. Even when I proved that hope false, I was thinking this could maybe be remote controlled; that was a much more valid notion than a self-aware statue that could inhabit vehicles, right?

A shrieker was barely visible behind what remained of the visitor's bleachers; its head was thrown back and its mouth was wide open. Neither I, nor anyone with me, was suffering the effects of its yell.

"Oh, wonderful," Eric and Tommy said in unison. They traded glances and Tommy added, "It's summoning."

Even though I hadn't picked up on the psychic signal, the effects would have been difficult to miss. Zombies who were, only moments before, confused individuals were beginning to coalesce around the shrieker and as they got closer to him, it appeared that they were receiving a secondary message as they would turn to us and start moving as fast as they could. I entertained thoughts of standing and fighting, but there were too many and more were coming.

"Oh well, I guess I can always tell my grandkids I rode inside a magical statue; pretty sure they'll just commit me at that point, but what the hell." I waited until everyone was in before joining them. The engine thrummed; the reverberations were loud inside the cab as it left a trail of rubber some twenty feet long as we fishtailed it out of there. Eric said nothing, riding in the bed and holding on to the headache rack with one hand as the driverless vehicle barreled down the highway.

"Don't you want to get in?" I shouted.

"Swords," he replied over the engine roar and wind. "This truck doesn't have the sword rack option installed."

I would have felt much better to see someone driving. The wheel turned, the pedals moved, the whole thing ran like a machine possessed, which I guess it was. I swear it was fucking with me as it would drift around, coming dangerously close to debris or other stalled cars along the road, then swerving clear at the last possible moment. I winced or involuntarily bunched up each time, and it seemed to be getting its jollies from the entire affair. I was smart enough to wait until we were stopped and all out before I told Eric his statue was an asshole. I flipped it off, too. The engine backfired, spitting a black cloud of smoke. Same to you, buddy.

"She's just playful."

"The Hummer is one street over." BT was looking at his GPS.

"See? She can be nice," Eric pointed out.

"What now?" I asked him.

"I think I'm going to move on. Too many zombies, not enough magic, and I doubt anyone is interested in taking up a collection to keep me fed. Don't misunderstand. I'd be willing to help, but I suspect your superiors will start poking their noses into things better left unpoked. I might be forced to do some unsavory things in response to their prejudice. I'm sure you understand."

"Yeah," I agreed, because I did.

"All in all, I think we should end on a high note. Don't you?"

"This is a high note?" BT asked. "I'd hate to see your aria."

"The Queen of the Night's got nothing on me," he replied, smirking. I caught the joke. "It's been interesting," he went on. "I doubt we'll see each other again, but I've been wrong before. Entirely too often, in fact." He seemed to be scanning a memory.

I stuck my hand out, wasn't sure what else to do. Eric tugged off a gauntlet and shook it. His grip was firm and dry, but his hand was cold, very cold.

"Thanks for...I'm not sure what," I admitted.

"You are most welcome...Michael Talbot, Lawrence Tynes, Gary Talbot, Thomas Van Goth, and Jake Winters. Good luck with the zombies! With those, the shriekers are the key."

"Oh, we got it," BT agreed.

"As for the humans," he added, "I wish I had an answer for you."

"What's that supposed to mean?"

"Observe humans for a thousand years and see if you still need to ask."

We all watched as Eric mounted up on his V8 steed and took a grip on the headache rack. It roared to life with the cab still empty. The headlights came on and one of them blinked off for an instant, like it winked at me. The whole truck darkened from a coppery color down to a dull black before it spun through a tight turn and roared off into the night.

"Are we gonna check out where he goes?" BT asked.

"Not a fucking chance," I said as I turned and was heading to our ride.

"What are we supposed to say in our debriefing?" Winters asked.

"Everything, exactly like it happened, just without Eric, magic swords, possessed trucks, and all the other crazy-ass bullshit. Should make it simple enough," I told him.

The drive home was quiet except for Gary's humming. We were all trying to process what had just happened, or at least assimilate it into our new reality. Luckily, I was the only one Bennington met with and after an hour of telling him all I wanted him to know, he dismissed me. I had stood and was heading for the door, thankful he'd not delved too deeply.

"Oh, Lieutenant, the next time you don't want to tell me something, I suggest you work a little longer on your delivery."

"Sir." I turned back. "What I saw, what we all saw…I don't even think I believe it. I wouldn't even know how to explain it. The intel is good, the anomaly is gone; if you still want to know, give me a day or two to formulate some thoughts."

"If you think I need to know, then you know where to find me. Otherwise, good job, Lieutenant. Enjoy some downtime."

"Thank you, sir."

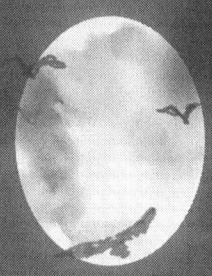

POST EPILOGUE

Post Episode:

I WENT BACK a couple of weeks later, alone. I wandered around the burned-out gym and the destroyed football field. Don't know why I felt the need to do what I was doing. Thanks to Eric, we now had people back at the base working on something like noise-canceling headphones. They were big and bulky and right now, I didn't see how they could be used in a tactical situation. But I was told these were early prototypes and soon they would have something that fit into our gear and weighed under a pound—we'd hardly notice it. I believed that as much as I believed in war rabbits. Errant thought, but true, nonetheless. I'd been in the military long enough to know it would probably weigh more than fifteen pounds and have to be mounted on our chest or some such shit, but it was a start. I thought on Eric a lot and the more I did so, the more I came back to the realization I didn't believe him to be human, or to have ever been human. The demon truck was just a small piece of it; I dwelt on his line about watching humanity for a thousand years. Who says something like that and then leaves? Yet, through all my doubts, here was an ally, potentially. Tough to gauge someone whose thoughts were probably very alien to my own, but there I was. Humans, as a species, were on the ropes and getting burns on our backs as we quickly slid down them; we could only hope there wasn't a noose waiting at the end. If help was out there, in any form, I was going to do my best to secure some. I wrote a note and stuffed it into a large manila envelope which I emblazoned with block letters that spelled out his name. That should keep anyone else away. I used a liberal amount of tape and adhered it to the front of the high school. The odds he would ever come across it, I pegged at a billion to one. About the same odds of there being a zombie apocalypse, so yeah, stranger things could happen.

I wrote:

Hey Eric, it's Michael Talbot. First off, thank you for getting us out of that jam. Wait, now that I'm writing this down, if it weren't for you setting the whole thing up, we would have never been in trouble. Almost a self-fulfilling prophecy at that point. Forget it. A simple thanks is what I'm shooting for. Ultimately, I don't know what your motives are, but if you're in the neighborhood and humans still exist, I wouldn't turn down your help, and I'll even offer you a beer.

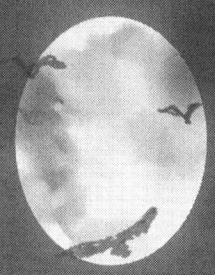

14

TALBOT-SODE ONE

I WAS SITTING in the living room. Wesley and I were discussing the merits of Duplo blocks over traditional-sized Legos. He was young, so it was mostly a one-sided affair, though every once in a while he would let me voice my opinion. When he was done building his masterpiece and destroying mine, we went to sit in my chair so I could read him the Lion King for who knows how many times. Can we go back to the blocks for a moment? Funny little quirk about the boy. For whatever reason, no matter what I built, wall, house, plane, spaceship, he had to destroy it. Now I'm not talking the normal, taking his matchbox car and slamming it into the side like we all have, destroy it; I'm saying he dismantles it down to the block, almost as if to erase the fact the structure ever existed. Strange; I'm sure there's more to it, but for now, it's just one of those things that makes me scratch my head. Okay, where was I? Ah, page one of the Lion King. I was rapidly getting to the point where, if I was in this story, I would kill Mustafa, Mufasa or whatever his name is, just to get it over with. Maybe mow down the entire pride.

"That's cynical even for you, Talbot," I said aloud. I cleared my throat and began the narrative. It was something I could now do from rote. Which, in this case, was not a good thing as it gave my mind a chance to freelance. I'd been having a reoccurring dream lately, vivid enough that I was more than convinced it had happened. Not in this life-line, maybe, but in one of the others. I did not envy that version of Mike, even if it seemed his world was devoid of zombies. It goes something like this…(if this were a movie, you'd see the wavy lines on the screen indicating a reality shift right about now).

"I can't believe I gave up a day off to be with you," BT groused as he pulled a large toolbox out of the back of my Jeep.

"What are you bitching about? I'm paying you for this. Can't you grab the other box too?"

"What are you going to carry?"

"I'm the foreman! I've got the pencil."

"You sure this is the house?" BT had put the box down on the dilapidated front porch, stepped back and was looking up at the gray Gothic structure.

"Yeah, 1282 Raven's Head."

"Mike, there's a Giovanni and Sons sign out front."

"Yeah? So?"

"They're famous for flipping houses. Do all the work themselves. They make a fortune doing this type of thing; why would they call your little handy-man business?"

"Maybe they're overwhelmed."

"Maybe that's the case, but, and I don't mean this in a hurtful way, but how far down on a contractor's list do you think they had to travel before they got to your name?"

"Don't mean to be hurtful? Maybe next time punch me in the throat. At least I'd be out cold while I nursed my injury."

"You know what I mean. They must have tons of contacts in the field, workers they've used for years. You've been doing this for two months, and only on the side."

"Don't know, don't care. They're paying me a shitload to

demo a kitchen. Eight hours of work and I might be able to retire."

"Exactly how much are they paying you? Because you told me all you could afford was twelve bucks an hour, which isn't shit! I'm doing this as a favor to you."

"Shitload was a figure of speech. We should get started while we have light; there's no electricity inside."

"Are you kidding? What about heat?"

"Not likely."

"It's going to be freezing in there! I hate that empty house cold feeling; it seeps into your bones."

"Well, if you work hard and start earning your pay you won't even notice." I grabbed a sledge and used the key I'd been given to head in. The house was a mess; it was tough to even tell what style it had been in before the demolition had started. It never even dawned on me why it had not been finished.

"There's shit everywhere…even tools. What gives? A contractor worth a shit would never leave his gear behind."

"Most of this stuff is DeWalt; think anyone will miss it?" I asked as I picked up a drill that, on my best day, I couldn't afford. Don't get me wrong; my Black and Decker worked just fine, but a DeWalt was like the Rolls Royce of power tools.

"You start tossing other people's tools in your Jeep and I'm out of here. I'm a cop, Mike, people already think I'm corrupt. I'm not going to give them any concrete proof."

"I would think this would be right up your alley," I told him as I reluctantly put it down. "Want a hit?" I pulled out a joint.

"You are absolutely kidding me."

"What? We're in Colorado. It's legal."

"So is Scotch. That doesn't mean I'm going to pull out a decanter while I'm working."

"Suit yourself." I took a quick toke. I was hoping it would quell some nerves that were beginning to make themselves known. Besides the bone-chilling cold BT was complaining about, this house just felt…off. But if I thought a hit or two of some Mary Jane was going to do anything to dispel that feeling, I was sadly mistaken. Chalk that up with all the other poor choices I had made through my life; soon I was going to need another notepad to keep track.

I turned the corner and headed into the kitchen, then paused for a second to look around. The rest of the house looked as if it had been attacked by steroid-fueled workers; in contrast, the kitchen was immaculate, everything was pristine. A light gray granite counter-top sat upon beautiful cabinetry. The oven was a Southbend antique stove; somehow the hundred-year-old appliance looked like it had just come out of the box. It looked more like a piece of art than something used for such pedestrian purposes as cooking a meatloaf. The floor was hardwood, possibly oak; it had a brilliant shine to it. BT had to push me out of the entryway as he hefted the tools in. He set it all down then stretched and popped his back.

"What the fuck have you got us into?" He had walked to the cabinets and opened one of the top ones up. "This is Royal Doulton." He flipped a gold-rimmed teacup over. "This stuff is worth more than you." He opened up a drawer. "Silver. These utensils are silver. I'm not trying to be a dick, Mike, but this kitchen is worth more than your townhome. There's no way someone wants it gutted. That stove itself is close to ten grand in that condition. The cabinets are American Chestnut; you can't even get this wood anymore." He was longingly rubbing a hand across the smooth, pale-grained finish.

"What?"

"Some idiot brought Asian chestnut trees over to the states back in the early 1900s. Huge blight pretty much wiped out the entire species; they only grow for a few years then die. Never big enough to harvest any wood from. I can't even begin to put a price on what something like this might cost."

I fumbled through my jacket, pulled up a mostly folded but somewhat wadded piece of paper. I reread the signed contract before handing it over to BT. He took a second to look at it before handing it back.

"I'm not doing it. I can't. This is like breaking into the Louvre and trashing the Mona Lisa."

The job paid twelve hundred bucks. There was a dumpster onsite, which meant I didn't have to rent a truck or pay a disposal fee at the local landfill. After I paid BT, I was going to clear around nine hundred. Unbelievable pay for eight hours of demo work, and with the holidays rapidly approaching, it was an infusion of cash the Talbot family could use.

"Shit." BT knew we were hurting for money; that's why he was even here, helping out a friend.

"They want you to just tear this shit out and throw it away?"

"That's what it says."

"What if we take it down gently and salvage it?"

That got me thinking. I'd have to rent a truck, but if we sold even half this stuff…I let the thought trail off.

"I'll split it twenty-eighty," I told him.

"Fifty-fifty."

"Twenty one-seventy nine."

"Talbot."

"Fine, fine. Going to take a lot longer than we thought; might as well get started. And not for nothing–how are we planning on moving that stove? It looks like it could be heavier than my car."

"Worry about that when we get to it. We're not going to be able to save the granite. Let's get these top cabinets down and we'll work on that."

I handed him my drill. He pressed the trigger a couple of times, something every male that ever grabs a tool is wont to do. Whirred and spun just like it was supposed to, right up until he put it inside the cabinet and against a screw. I could hear the tell-tale *click* as he pulled the trigger, but nothing else.

"Come on, man! You didn't charge the batteries?"

"Did it last night."

"Whatever." Safe to say he didn't believe me. "Give me the spare."

After he switched them out, he once again tested the drill. Worked fine again, right up until he placed it in the cabinet.

"I'm telling you, I always charge them up before coming out on a job." I left the kitchen and grabbed the DeWalt. I gave it a couple of pulls; it lit up and spun. I handed it over to BT. He checked it too, because I can't be trusted. This time, I was right behind him, watching, seeing if he was somehow doing something wrong. But a two-year-old with decent dexterity could pull off running a drill. The guide light came on for the briefest of moments, dimmed, and then went completely out. I took note that I could now see his breath.

"Can't even charge the things." BT angrily put the drill on the countertop. I was getting the sneaking suspicion that even if we had electricity, an electrically powered drill wouldn't work. Money be damned. I was thinking that maybe just forgoing this job might be the best idea. I had a couple of other small jobs lined up that could help with the bills. There was Mrs. Jonniker, who paid me twenty dollars a month to come over and change out her burnt-out light bulbs, whether she had any or not. Generally, this cost me two hours of my time as she would invariably talk my ear off, but she did make great cookies. Then there was Benny DelForte. He wanted his closets painted; so far not too strange, but this is me, so you know there's a twist.

He wanted them brown, or a color he called "sexual chocolate." Sure, whatever, the kicker, though, was he would pull up a chair and watch me as I worked. You can go anywhere you want with that information. Personally, I do my damnedest not to think about it. Oh, and did I fail to mention he had three parrots who, if they weren't screeching, constantly sang *It's Raining Men*. I surcharged the shit out of that job in the hopes he would not pick me to do it, but he always did. I shook my head, letting the thought slide away.

"Maybe we should just go," I told BT.

"No way. Some other crew is going to come in here and ruin these. This stuff should be in a museum, not at the bottom of a trash heap." He was fumbling around inside the toolbox for a screwdriver.

"Maybe forget about preserving the cabinets and think about preserving us," I said. Seemed random enough; and I'm not entirely sure why I said it, though there was a ring of truth to the words.

"That's dramatic even for you," BT said as he leaned into the cabinet. "Hey, can you shine the flashlight inside here so I can see what I'm doing?"

I pulled a light off my tool belt. "This is a 3500 lumens light; can almost start a fire with how bright it is. Last night, I put four fresh, triple-A batteries in it because I knew this house had no electricity."

"Why are you telling me this?" he asked just as I turned the portable lighthouse on.

"If this does what I think it's going to, I want to leave." I moved closer to the cabinet; the inside shone brightly for all of three seconds before dimming and becoming dark again.

"Real funny. I'm serious–keep the light on."

"It's dead." To me, those words seemed mighty ominous. But BT wasn't quite ready to pack it in.

"Give me that." He swiped it from my hand. Clicked the button two, maybe three hundred times. "You break it?"

"Batteries are dead."

"You said they were brand new."

"I've watched enough ghost shows to know that spirits attempting to gather energy to manifest can sap power from batteries and it seems like we've brought them a portable charging station."

"You sure are dramatic. Should have been a Theater major."

"Yeah? What's that then?" I was pointing to the far side of the kitchen where a pantry door had, of its own volition, opened outward. Could have blamed that on a lot of things, wind, tilted house, a door not hung correctly, all valid enough reasons. Explaining away the thick, black mist that poured forth was going to be a lot more difficult.

"This some sort of prank?" BT looked tense and held the screwdriver out in front of him like one might a knife to a threat.

"No." There was a tremor to my voice. I think BT was confused when I didn't protest with some measure of sarcasm. To be honest, I was too terrified. I was worried that if I tried to run I would find that my legs wouldn't work correctly or they'd be bogged down by some invisible goo. What happened was far, far worse.

"I think we should go." Even as BT was saying it, I was buttoning the toolbox back up. With as much adrenaline as was coursing through my system, I barely felt the weight of it.

"Ready when you are," I told him.

It's difficult to explain the sensation that flowed around and through me, and I'm sure BT as well, as we crossed the threshold or attempted to cross, I should say. There was a loud *whooshing* through my ears, like I was being thrashed around in some heavy surf. My vision darkened to the point I couldn't see; I caught a whiff of something sickly sweet, like decaying strawberries, and my mouth tasted like I was sucking on pennies, or blood–coppery–if that makes sense.

All of my normal senses, save one: touch, were being assailed. I would bet that if I had reached out to run my hands over something, I would have felt the bracing chill of the specter passing by, thus forever altering every way I interacted with the world going forward. The more steps I took toward where I figured the door was, the louder the sound, the darker my vision, and the worse the taste in my mouth. It became a crescendo where I did not believe I would be able to take much more. Then, as suddenly as it had started, it stopped.

"What the fuck?" was all I could manage as I looked around at the kitchen I thought I had vacated.

"Bullshit!" BT said next to me. "Come on!" He grabbed at my shoulder as he made a run for the door. His hand slipped off as I did not follow, not willing to again go through what had just transpired. What happened next defies a normal explanation. For a split-second, it looked like he might escape the pull of this surrealist nightmare; then, without warning, his momentum just halted. His legs were still moving, but he was doing what looked like the perfect version of Michael Jackson's Moonwalk. In seven steps, he was again back and next to me. I was speechless as he shook his head and looked over to me. He was breathing heavy, like he had sprinted a few hundred yards. He was looking like he was going to give it another go; I touched his shoulder and shook my head.

"Won't work." I knew that instinctively.

"You got me in here—you get me out."

The only other egress from the kitchen was a door next to the fridge. You didn't have to be a writer for a horror movie to know it led to the cellar; that was a given.

"I think we can get out that way." I feel like I should be ashamed to admit it, but I was hoping BT would go first. When he didn't move, I walked the few steps over and grabbed the door handle. It was simultaneously hot and cold to the touch. It turned effortlessly; again, that was to be expected. I opened the door cautiously. Dark is a word I could use as I peered down, maybe "fucking dark" would be more accurate. The walls were old foundation, made from rocks cemented together. Wooden steps descended into madness. Maybe BT was right, maybe I was too dramatic. All I know was that the final third of the staircase could not be seen as it was swallowed up by the all-encompassing blackness, and I could feel some vague presence at the bottom. BT was looking over my shoulder.

"You want to go down there?"

"Want to? Not so much," I told him.

"What about the window?" he asked as we looked back at the frosted panes residing above the sink.

"My guess is it won't open, then we'll try to smash it with a hammer and it will be like hitting a bank vault door. And, if by some miracle it does open, it will be much like the other exit."

"So we just go down the stairs?"

"I've got a feeling that's what we're meant to do."

"Yeah? What if there's a gaggle of clowns down there?"

"First off, that's a real shitty thing to say. And secondly, a group of clowns is called a *shudder*, for obvious reasons. You coming with me?"

"Twelve dollars an hour. I'm going to die making less than minimum wage in most states. You're the crappiest friend a man could ever have."

I was two steps down when he finished his mini-diatribe. Four, by the time he touched down on the top one. By the time I was halfway down, the shadow below was creeping up to meet me.

"That can't be right," BT said as he watched the phenomenon.

I was hesitant to go any further. The darkness, which held no shape, rolled over the step right below where my feet were. It pooled and swirled there, waiting expectantly for me to immerse myself in it. My labored breathing was the only thing I could hear for long seconds before BT spoke and made me jump.

"You sure about that?" he asked as my foot hovered above the step.

"I think we're supposed to go down there."

"Says who? The voices in your head or this house?"

"Could be the same thing."

The swirling dark mist was piling up so that it was directly below the sole of my boot, like there was a slight magnetic attraction between it and me. I stepped down, expecting that the darkness would splash away much like fog might when disturbed. Instead, it clung like dirty water.

"Maybe this wasn't a good idea," I said as I tried to lift my leg and was met with resistance. I pulled free with an audible squelch. The wet mist snapped back like a rubber band, then once again began to pool up.

"First smart thing you've said in nearly a month."

"I'm still going down."

"Why? To look for the bodies of the other poor bastards that came here before us?"

"That would explain all the tools upstairs."

"Again, valid reasoning which makes your desire to continue on this path not reasonable."

"Agreed. This is super freaky and I'm terrified, BT, but so far nothing bad has happened. We haven't heard some menacing spirit tell us to get out…or redrum chanted over and over," I said, wiggling my finger like that poor kid Danny in *The Shining*. I, however, did not use his creepy voice, as that would have been way too scary and over the imaginary line I'd drawn.

"If you haven't noticed, it won't let us go. Who the hell knows why it wants us."

"I don't think it means us harm."

"Forgive me for not trusting your judgment, but aren't you the same guy that just last week told your boss that there were a series of Widespread Panic concerts coming up and you would appreciate being taken off the random drug testing roster?"

"I'm a good employee. I would like a little leeway when it

comes to my recreational use of illicit substances during special occasions."

"Mike, you know I'm a cop, right?"

"Yeah, the same cop that was over at my house last month taking bong hits with weed he confiscated."

"Bong hits? I took two tokes off a joint. Hardly makes me…" He paused. "You."

"Fine, but I think we need to go downstairs anyway." I took another step down. My right leg was submerged, maybe "engulfed" is a better term, all the way up to my knee. The mist had a gravity to it, a weight I could feel pulling on my leg. Not in a cloying manner, but rather a gentle pressure, maybe akin to a swaddling. Although, just the mere thought of swaddling made me feel claustrophobic. I moved my left foot down and into the darkness; the blackness was creeping up toward my hips and waist. I can't say I was looking forward to this spectral visitor moving any farther up. Would I be able to breathe once it covered my mouth and nose?

"Mike?" BT asked as he pointed to his boot and the mist swirling up and over it.

"Is that you?" a voice rose from deep inside the basement. Going to freely admit, I was happy it wasn't a little girl. For some reason, small children, girls in particular, tend to make the scariest ghosts, demons, vampires, whatever. Makes sense though, because as teenagers, they can strike fear into the hearts of any father. Go on, have one. You'll see what I mean.

"You hear that?" I asked BT.

He nodded. "Yeah, was making sure you did too before I admitted it."

"Who are you looking for?" I shouted, much too loudly.

"Michael Talbot." My heart skipped a beat from the answer, but it was tough to take it seriously as the voice (which was distinctively male) added a bunch of fake ghostly sounds like *awhoooo* and drawn out *boooos*. "And that other big fellah who's usually with you." There was a snapping of fingers like he was trying to remember names. "KP? BJ. Nope, nope… BLT! That's it."

"You know this fool?" BT had instantly shed his fear and was rapidly moving to anger after being called a sandwich.

"Yes. I frequent haunted houses all the time."

"This place is haunted?" the voice drifted up.

"You live here. I would think you would know, crazy man," BT shouted past my ear.

"I'm just visiting," the disembodied voice informed us.

"In the basement of this house that's being renovated? You a squatter?" I asked. I was even more hesitant to go down now that I thought there was a person there, as opposed to only whatever was in control of the peculiar happenings occurring. Getting stabbed in the neck with a broken beer bottle by a squatter was not high on my bucket list items.

"I've squatted from time to time, you know, when the mood strikes and you have to go but you find yourself at a music festival with far too few plastic poo potties. A bit of advice, if you decide to eat seven bean burritos in the morning, make sure you remove your pants from at least one leg when you go or you're liable to leave yourself a stinky present or two in your underwear, and let me tell you, it's no fun when you pull your pants back up."

"What is this crazy person talking about? Do you think the house did this to him?"

Logical thinking on BT's part. Now I was left wondering if we should keep descending; it was anyone's guess how far we would go.

"I'm still alive…we're still alive," he corrected himself.

"Who are you?" was all I could think to ask.

"What world is this?"

"Mike." I was sure BT was going to haul me out of there and make another stab at the front entrance; instead, he was pointing to the mist, which was now halfway up my chest, though I had not taken another step.

"I wouldn't stay in that stuff too long," our host offered.

"Then why are you here?" I was watching in fascinated horror as the inky mist crawled up my shirt with a mind of its own.

"Ponch, I tried. I tried to save them all."

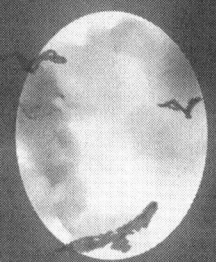

15

FADE TO A SEMI-AWAKENING

THE DREAM WAS SAVAGELY real to me, and the duality of it was conflicting. The Mike swathed in darkness had no idea who the voice was or what he was saying, but the sleeping voyeur knew exactly what was happening, and even asleep I could feel the sob building deep in my chest. "Trip? You're alive?" This I said aloud; Tracy bore witness to it, sleeping next to me as I'd awakened her with my calling out.

"Ponch? Is that you?" I nearly started awake. I was no longer watching from a safe vantage point, I was an active participant. The BT in the dream had heard something and was looking around. The strata of strangeness going on at this very moment was overwhelming. Dream Mike and dream BT were in very real danger; I could not be sure if it was happening right this very moment or already had, and truth be told, what the hell was I going to do about it? He'd already broken the cardinal rule of every horror movie everywhere by going downstairs, I thought I had taught him better. At least he went with a friend.

"Where are you, Trip?"

"I'm not sure; I was pretty wasted last night while Stephanie drove the tour bus. I do know it snew last night."

"Snew? What the fuck is a snew, Trip?"

"Middle English dialectal, past tense for snow."

"Wha…?" I was shaking my head in my dream. I had gone from overseer to first-person shooter perspective. I was in the basement; luckily, I was not dealing with the mist. I was staring at a shimmering doorway; it was slightly better than a glass privacy door in a shower, but not by much. I was thankful that Trip appeared clothed; with him, nothing was a certainty. My heart surged with the idea that some of them had made it…including the crazy bastard.

"Stephanie says we're out West somewhere; our paths will cross soon. Be careful, man. We have company." And just like that, the doorway began to lose its translucence. "BYE, Bye, bye, b…." Trip had not moved; he was just saying each word softer and softer to give the effect that he was backing away.

"Still here, Trip."

"I was going for flare, Ponch."

"I think showing up in my dream was enough flare."

"Just remember Payne…."

"Wait, what about her!?" Of course, this was when he really did fade out. Had a conversation about snew, but couldn't be bothered to tell me about Payne, a vicious vampire.

"And Iggy!" drifted back.

"The gorilla?" I let barely escape my lips after pondering the name for a minute.

"What gorilla?" BT, on the stairs, asked.

"What are you talking about?" other Mike asked.

This was going far past the realm of delusion, I don't know what the word for that would be, but I was living it. I had every intention of pinching myself and extracting my consciousness from whatever this was. That was right up until I saw the three men against the far wall in the basement. They were all in heaps near each other but not touching. They were unmoving in that particular way; I knew they were dead, and that wasn't the worst part. There were deep scratches in the rock and cement behind them that were outlined in crimson. On closer inspection, I would have been able to tell without a doubt that they had been attempting to claw their way out and had died from the effort. This Mike and BT were very much in danger; what kind of shadowy presence would I be if I didn't help them?

"Bulkhead! There's a bulkhead over here!" I screamed, making sure I would be heard. Funny thing about whatever this place was, the louder I spoke, the less they heard. Damn near gave myself an aneurysm before I figured that little tidbit out. "Bulkhead. There's a bulkhead straight ahead." This, not much above a whisper.

I noticed that Other Mike was now completely covered, and BT was nearly so.

"I can't see anything…breathing is getting difficult." Other Mike was laboring.

"We need to go back." BT's voice was rising in alarm. What would a good haunted house be, if not determined? The basement door slammed shut, cutting off what little light had been able to filter down.

I wasn't sure if the bulkhead was a viable option for escape, but there were no windows, and scraping through rock had proved ineffective.

"The door out is straight ahead and slightly to the left when you get to the far wall." I could see Other Mike and BT struggling to get through the murkiness, their hands outstretched, feeling for obstacles, eyes opened wide and unblinking in the hopes some errant ray of light would find its way to them. As for me, I was cloaked in that preternatural greenish-brown color that often happens in nightmarish dreams. While I most likely could not read a book by it, I could still see perfectly well. Shadow figures began to peel themselves from the darker recesses in the basement. One took note of me as it passed by, but I, for some reason, was untouchable to it in this realm. O.M. and BT seemed to be fair game though.

"Something's coming," I whispered, afraid if I said it any louder the thing would find a way to cross realms.

"Could you be a little more specific?" O.M. asked.

"You are not talking to the disembodied voice, are you? It could be a trick." BT frowned at O.M. and shook his head.

"Got any better ideas? We're already trapped; seems like no point in adding further insult."

"Guess you don't understand the minds of psychopaths then. They thrive on that shit," BT answered.

"Been called a lot of things but not…wait, scratch that. I had an old girlfriend in high school call me that, but in fairness, she was REALLY pissed I had fooled around with her friend, and I don't think she used it in the right context," I said aloud.

"Cathy Gregory," O.M. replied. "I could never get over the fact her nickname was Gregs; just felt weird to be kissing someone with a masculine name."

"You let homophobia wreck a relationship?" BT asked.

"I was seventeen. Wasn't like it was going to last, and I was a lot stupider back then."

"Back then huh?"

"Guys…they're moving slow but not that slow. Get your asses moving!" I whispered a shout. It worked.

"We listening to that voice?" BT asked.

"You'd better," I told him.

Other Mike and BT had finally got to the last step and stepped onto the floor, both had their arms out, making sweeping gestures with them. "I don't know how, BT, but that voice is mine."

"Fucking great. World isn't screwed up enough, now there are two of you."

"Gonna have to trust me on this. The far side is twenty-five feet ahead; keep your arms to your sides and move quickly," the me having the dream said. (This was confusing for me...can't imagine what this is like for those reading my journal.)

The shadows were converging; I didn't know what would happen if they touched O.M. or BT, but I got the feeling it wouldn't be good.

"NOW!" O.M. jolted at my command, but did as I asked. "BT, keep your goddamned arms to your side!"

"I don't like you, and I don't like you," BT referred to us both.

O.M. and BT had passed by three of the four specters, one so narrowly I saw BT shiver from the near contact. The fourth had parked itself directly in their path.

"Quick left for five feet!"

O.M. was slow to react; BT nearly took him out, but made sure to keep him on his feet as he grabbed his shoulders and heaved up.

"Turn right. Ten feet dead ahead."

"Really?" BT asked, questioning my wording. "Now I know it's you."

"Steps," I warned them a fraction of a second too late. O.M. went down hard; BT almost made sure O.M. never had any more kids or sex, as his foot came down dangerously close to the other's crotch. Again, he picked him up by the shoulders and deposited him down. "Bulkhead." Again I was too late in warning, but this time it was on O.M., I had told him there was a bulkhead; what did he think was going to happen? As he climbed the stairs, there was a resounding *gong* as his head smacked hard into the slanted metal doorway.

"Fuck! I think I got a stinger!" he shouted, his head bent at an angle that was hurting me just looking at it.

"Hey! Other pain in the ass! Where's the handle?" BT demanded.

"Above your head to the right," I told him. I could see him fumbling around for it, then I lost sight of them both as four spirits floated in and were now between me and them. One turned; an unnaturally long finger first pointed at me and then dragged across its neck. Didn't need a demonology dictionary to decipher that. "Hurry up!"

"Like I'm taking my sweet ass time," BT grunted. "Frozen." I heard the tinkle of metal parts as they cascaded down from the door and onto the cement steps. Then I had to turn my head from the brilliant light that shone through. BT had pushed the doors open so hard, one had completely become unhinged and hung off to the side. He and Mike were through, and to what I hoped was safety. I was also going to vacate the premises, as my neck dragging buddy turned back to me. I also showed him a finger, different gesture, though, as I pulled myself free from whatever the hell that was I had been in.

I SAT UP. I was bathed in sweat. Tracy had just come out of the bathroom; she'd been getting ready for her day at school. "You all right?" she asked, concerned.

"Trip's alive!" I let the rest of the dirty remembrance fall away from me. To her credit, she didn't question me on how crazy that sounded or how I could possibly have known. "Now I just have to find him."

16

TALBOT-SODE TWO

I'M sure you've heard that there are no atheists in a foxhole. First off, it's called a "fighting hole." I once asked my DI where he wanted me to dig my foxhole; he smacked me so hard up the side of the head I remember seeing Tuesday. Then he calmly explained it's a fighting hole. Lesson learned. I was in the mountains of Afghanistan a year or so after that instance; Sam Brannison and myself were assigned a forward outpost position. Not sure what he'd done to be on the shitty end of the stick; I had been caught trying to ferment mouthwash into something passable as alcohol. Didn't work. Still got in trouble as if it had. Want to talk about the injustice of it all? The lieutenant that passed down the field judgment reeked of whiskey. Whatever. Now I knew where to liberate some stock when I got back to base.

So Brannison and I are tasked with digging a fighting hole. I don't know how many of you are familiar with the standard Marine Corps issue tri-fold shovel. It's roughly the size of a toy you would buy for a child, and Afghanistan, well, it's comprised mostly of cement. Natural cement, in the form of granite-like dirt and boulders the size of tires. On a good day, we'd be able to scrape a few inches of earth to hide in. The enemy was active in this area, and we weren't feeling overly confident in our ability to make it through the night.

Typical talk of all fighting people everywhere revolves around food, home, and invariably, members of the opposite sex. We covered all those topics just as the sun went down over the horizon. Once the night settled in, the conversation became more somber. Not how I would normally while away an evening, but we moved on to religion. Yeah, I went to services on Sunday, but mostly because it got me out of the sand and into an air-conditioned tent. And in the off-chance there was a Maker, I wanted to make sure the lines of communication had been kept open. I had my doubts about the presence of an omnipotent, omnipresent deity, but again, what harm was there in playing all the odds? Brannison was Methodist, not that this made the slightest difference to me, just part of the narrative.

"I think guilt is the primary weapon favored by Catholicism," I told him. "My mother got an advanced degree in its use."

"Not too late…you could convert. As a Methodist, you would learn that we toss food around instead of shame."

"I like your religion better; guilt weighs way more than food."

"Ain't that the truth," he responded as we toasted with our canteens, which, unfortunately, were filled with water and not sacramental wine.

Brannison and I were friends in the Corps; can't say we would have been close outside the confines of battle. He was entirely too straight-laced. But he was a good guy and a great shot. Plus, right now he was watching my back; all of that equated to us being best buds. We made it through the night with only one report to make. Two weeks later, parts of Brannison were sent back to the states after an IED on the side of the road blew up the Hummer he was riding in. I think of him often and even went to a few Methodist services to see, and yeah, they like their food.

17

TRIP'S LOST ESCAPE

"I don't like it in here." Stephanie was shaking.

"It's all good, I have snacks," Trip said as he pulled various half-eaten cellophane bags from his pockets. Stephanie winced at the excessive sound he was making.

Porkchop, Mark, and Sty looked longingly at the chip bags. Trip looked at the boys then slowly began to put them away.

"John," Stephanie urged.

"Yeah?" He never took his eyes off the kids as he tucked all the snacks away.

She nodded her head to the boys.

Trip did the same thing. "What are we doing?" he asked her.

"I'm telling you to give the boys the chips without having to *tell* you to give them the chips."

"How's that working out for you?" he asked.

"Not so good."

"Didn't think it would," he told her then turned away.

"John!"

"What?" He snapped his attention back to her.

"Give them the chips."

"Why didn't you just say so?" He pulled some bags out and handed them over.

She looked fairly exasperated.

"We should have stayed with Uncle Mike," Mark said as he took a bag that Trip was reluctant to let go of.

"He thought we'd be safer here sweetheart," Stephanie told him.

"Uh huh."

For every snack bag Trip doled out, he grabbed something from the shelter's ample food supply and replaced the emptiness. It was irrelevant what he grabbed; power bar, bag of beef stew, napkins, he didn't care. Just as long as he had something in place. As if his pockets abhorred a vacuum.

"Shh…you hear that?" Porkchop asked.

"Can't hear anything over your munching," Sty ribbed him.

The bunker was a lot of things; airtight was not one of them. A malignant odor drifted in. It was so thick, Porkchop put his bag down, even went so far as to let it drop to the ground, but that had more to do with fright.

"You lost your mind?" Trip whispered as he bent down to pick it up. Trip threw his head back, as the first of the screeches ripped through his brains. When it stopped, Trip turned to the side. He was breathing heavily and his eyes were open wide in a wild, animalistic stare. Zach was screaming his lungs out; any chance they had of going undetected had long since slipped by.

A rhythmic thrumming began on the door. One of the zombies that had not yet climbed up the evolutionary ladder was using its skull to knock.

"What are we going to do?" Porkchop asked.

"We're going to stay right here," Stephanie said as calmly as she could manage. She was attempting to get Zach to stop crying; she'd been close to succeeding until another burst shot across their minds.

When it stopped, Trip had his head against the wall. Blood was flowing from his nose. "Going to rip our minds in half," he breathed out with difficulty.

"Nonsense," Stephanie said without conviction.

"Come out."

Trip's head first swiveled to the door, followed by the other inhabitants of the shelter. They had all heard it, and he didn't know if he was sad or relieved.

"Do you think my uncle will come back?" Mark asked.

"Right now we are all we have," Stephanie told him. Except for Zach, they were all armed, but what good was that? Trip preferred his slingshot, and she was reluctant to fire her revolver while holding the baby. That left three barely pubescent boys to do all the heavy lifting. She became irrationally angry at Mike for leaving them this vulnerable, even if he'd thought it was for the best, and so had she at the time, but things had changed, and so had her mind. It wasn't fair to him, but this was their lives hanging in the balance; fair was out of the equation now.

Trip began to click his tongue. Stephanie looked over to him, his eyes were closed. He'd been skirting the edge of insanity for so long she figured the shrieker had finally finished off what traveling through realms and ingesting enough drugs to sedate a third world country had begun.

"Oh no, no, no, honey." She reached up with her free hand to caress the side of his head.

"Echolocation," he told her before resuming his clicks.

"What?"

"Shh…I'm figuring out where the asshole is at."

Mark twirled his finger by the side of his head; Porkchop wasn't so sure, though he wondered how the man was getting any return signals through the door.

"There's ten of them; asshole is fifteen feet to the left." Trip finally opened his eyes.

"No," Stephanie told him. "You can't possibly know that, and we're not going out there."

"Only ten?" Sty asked.

"No," Stephanie admonished him.

"They'll get more if we don't," Mark observed astutely.

"You're not a dolphin!" she said to her husband.

"I watched *Flipper* when I was younger," he offered as way of an explanation.

"We take them before they get a bulker," Porkchop said.

"You too?" Stephanie seemed lost. "Is that what having testosterone is like? We have a baby here."

"Lady, what do you think that shrieker is doing to his little baby mind?" Sty asked.

Trip was digging in his pockets for steel ball bearings. He grabbed the largest one splayed out in his hand; it was roughly the size of a super ball, but weighed significantly more.

"This'll do, rabbit." He held it up to the small flickering ceiling light, the batteries of which were starting to die. Stephanie could not help but think it was doing its utmost to mirror their own lives.

"Are you sure?" Stephanie asked Trip.

"About what?" His look of confusion only added to her fears. "Check your rounds and make sure your safeties are off, boys! The charge of the light brigade is about to begin."

"Hold on." Stephanie ripped part of her shirt off and wrapped it around Zach's ears as many times as she could. "I love you, John, but I'm not relying on a slingshot to get us out of here."

"Oh, it won't, they will," he whispered pointing to the boys.

Porkchop gulped heavily, a sour mash of taste rising from his stomach. He wished he'd not eaten any of the salty snacks he had received from Trip, as they were now blistering his throat with acid reflux.

"We've got this." Sty was trying to psyche them all up; it wasn't even working on himself.

"Steph, I need you to open the door then step back. Mark, Sty, there will be two very surprised zombies standing there; one is most likely going to fall right in."

"The knocker," Porkchop said.

Trip touched his knee like one might their nose in a rousing game of charades.

"There will be no shooting until my blushing bride is completely out of the way, is that clear?" Trip made sure to look each boy in the eye. When he was satisfied with their non-verbal affirmation, he continued with his plan. "With those two down, I am going to put this giant metal ball straight into the eyeball of the shrieker; I plan to give him some karmic justice–firstly, and hopefully, not lastly." He quickly produced a half-smoked joint and a match.

"Not this close to the baby or the boys," Stephanie protested.

He eyed her, his left eyebrow arching high. "Fine, edibles it is," he said as he swallowed it down.

"That's just gross," Sty said.

"Now we wait," Trip replied.

"Wait for what?" Porkchop asked.

"Takes about twenty minutes for that to kick in. If I should fall, I'm not going down unstoned."

"Unstoned? You mean straight?" Mark asked.

"Straight is for squares." Trip drew a circle in the air. "Whoa, maybe that kicked in quicker than I thought, or maybe the quaaludes weren't quite done." Trip exhaled a big breath of air while also leaning back. "Let's get this done."

"Right now?" Sty asked.

"Trust me, this is the best time," Stephanie said as she moved nearer to the door. "Boys?"

"Yup," Mark said.

"Shit," was Sty's reply as he fumbled with the safety.

The door opened quickly, and just as Trip predicted, the head banger fell straight in, the top of its head landing squarely on Mark's boots. Sty had jumped back and Mark was busy placing three hastily shot rounds into the other zombie who had not yet, nor ever would, move into the shelter. Porkchop picked up the slack as he placed the muzzle of his small caliber pistol up against the fallen zombie's skull and pulled the trigger hoping that the bullet didn't go from skull, squishy stuff, skull, boot, to more squishy stuff, thus rendering Mark unable to move quickly. Mark, after killing the zombie directly in front of him, moved away just as Porkchop finished off the one at his feet.

Trip had moved with a quickness not normally attributed to him; the smoke had not stopped coming from Mark's barrel as he stepped out of the enclosure. He raised the ball bearing-laden slingshot as he did so. The shrieker, seeing that his life was in jeopardy, was preparing for his aria just as the ball struck his eyeball at high-velocity. The gelatinous mass ruptured completely; eye fragments blew out to the sides as the ball dug further in. The shrieker's head snapped back as the ball broke through his orbital socket and splintered the optic nerve. From there, the ball traveled another two inches, lodging deep into the frontal lobe and pressing hard on the temporal lobe. But none of that mattered, least of all to the shrieker, as he fell over, dead.

"That'll teach you to try and screw with this brain!" Trip was touching his jaw. Stephanie came up beside him, her revolver roaring as she fired.

"Boys! Come on!" Mark and Porkchop were quick to follow. Sty had frozen in fear and indecision, not daring to come out.

"No!" He was shaking his head back and forth; Stephanie had thought he'd finally relented as he moved quickly; she thought to catch up to them as they moved and continually fired, taking care of the majority of zombies inside the house. Instead, he shut the door and threw the lock.

"Sty!" Stephanie begged.

"Mrs. Trip look!" Porkchop pointed to a window that looked upon a scene that would have been difficult to miss. A murder of zombies was coming down the road after hearing the shots.

"Sty, open the door!" Stephanie begged.

"I'm, I'm so sorry…I can't!" She could hear him crying.

"Get out here!" she urged. She could hear him whimpering and possibly shuffling backward, though it was impossible to tell. What he wasn't doing was opening the door and any avenue of retreat was quickly fading.

Trip looked at her solemnly. "Backdoor," he told her.

"We can't leave him here."

"We can come back. We need to get away first."

Her husband was withholding some information, but none of them had the time for her to decipher exactly what it was. He was right, and she was pissed about it.

"We're coming back!" she made sure to point out.

"Of course we are," he told her as they dashed for the kitchen and the door to the backyard. They quickly scaled the six-foot privacy fence, Stephanie handing Zach over before joining the rest of the small group. They found themselves in a small, but well-landscaped, yard that had a beautiful rock wall and a koi pond which had long since gone green. A swimming pool dominated the rest of the area; five zombies bobbed around in the now viscous-looking swamp. They watched with hungry eyes as the group inched away from them and around the other side. A small, female zombie puzzled out that she would not be able to get at them from the deep end, so headed to the shallows where the scalloped steps led out.

Porkchop had moved toward the house and the gate by the side; he opened it a few inches before closing it quietly. "Zombies," he whispered. They were not only surrounded, they had some within the perimeter. Shooting the ones here would only bring the rest down upon them. The small female's progress had slowed as she got into the shallower water and had nearly halted as her foot came down upon the first step. The rot and ruin below her head was not a sight any of them would soon forget. Brownish-black muscle shown through her translucent skin, where there was skin at all. Some of the muscles in her arms and legs had detached from the tendons that held them in place, hanging loosely against her body as if she were wearing a macabre gown of streamers. She could not raise her right arm at all, and her legs did not appear to be able to support her weight. Still, she tried to make it out of the pool.

She gripped the metal handrail to keep from slipping and left a trail of bloody mucus from the contact. On her next step ahead, she pitched forward, her jaw smacking loudly onto the concrete edge. Chunks of teeth rattled away like hard cast dice. Two of the zombies in the pool with her, after hearing the noise, chose to investigate.

"I don't think I can watch that again." Stephanie's voice quivered with horror. They were spared the sight as their attention was diverted; heavy gunfire was happening off to the east. It was getting closer and hope surged in her heart as she thought help might be coming. Then, as high as her thoughts had gone, they crashed down doubly far as the sound began to trail off and stop completely. There was a loud crashing sound immediately to their rear. Try as she might, she could not shake the knowledge of what it was. A bulker had broken through the doorway to the house they had just vacated; Sty's refuge was next. She thought she might go mad with the knowledge of it.

"Come." Trip had gently grabbed her shirt and was urging her toward the garage. Porkchop took hold of her other sleeve and got her moving. She knew they were going to lose one, but she had to look out for the other four. She unwillingly went with them. "I…I think we were meant to be here."

There was a tear in Trip's eye as he looked at the restored VW van sitting parked in the garage.

"Have you already forgotten about Sty?" Stephanie cried.

"I will never forget about him or his sacrifice. If not for that boy, we would not have had the opportunity to escape." He said it so tenderly and so heartfelt, she could not doubt the sincerity of his words. "You need to drive; I don't want to get another DUH," he told her.

"A duh?" Porkchop asked.

"Driving under hallucination," Trip explained.

"What about the keys?" she asked as she got in.

Trip opened the glove box. "That worked?" he asked as he pulled a small key ring out.

Stephanie turned the ignition; the vehicle backfired once and started. She took note that the fuel level hovered at three-quarters full. One small bright spot in a day filled with bleakness.

"I've got it. Just get ready to go." Mark was looking out the garage door window; he had pulled the electric opener handle, releasing it from the machine's engagement. He had one hand on the garage door handle and was going to open it fast then dive for the van. Porkchop was manning the sliding rear door to shut it as soon as the other was inside.

Stephanie put the van in reverse and nodded to Mark, who was watching her through the side-view mirror. He pulled the door open and could not help but notice the trio of zombies coming to investigate the small explosion that had happened. He spared them not a second glance as he turned and climbed inside. Porkchop immediately closed and locked the door. Stephanie gunned the van backward, she and the passengers bouncing about wildly as she did so. There was one agonizing moment as she reached the roadway and threw the transmission into drive; the car sputtered and nearly stalled. And then they were off. West; they were heading west.

ABOUT THE AUTHOR

Visit Mark at **www.marktufo.com**

Zombie Fallout TV Trailer
https://youtu.be/FUQEUWy-v5o

For the most current updates join Mark's newsletter
http://www.marktufo.com/contact.html
I love hearing from readers, you can reach me at:

email
mark@marktufo.com

website

www.marktufo.com

Facebook
https://www.facebook.com/pages/Mark-Tufo/133954330009843?ref=hl

Twitter
@zombiefallout

For information on upcoming releases please join my newsletter at:
newsletter sign up

Zombie Fallout book Trailer
https://youtu.be/FUQEUWy-v5o

All books are available in audio version at iTunes Audible and Barnes and Noble.

DevilDog Press LLC

If you enjoyed the story please take a moment to leave a review. Thank you.

ALSO BY MARK TUFO

Zombie Fallout Series

Lycan Fallout Series

The Book Of Riley Series

Timothy Series

Indian Hill Series

Dystance Series

The Spirit Clearing

Callis Rose

Demon Fallout

Devils Desk

ALSO FROM DEVILDOG PRESS

Zombie Fallout by Mark Tufo

Caldera Book 1 By Heath Stallcup

All That Remain By Travis Tufo

From The Ash by Dave Heron

Mossy Creek A Maggie Mercer Mystery By Jill Behe

The Monster of Selkirk by C.E. Clayton

Prey: Blood of The Ancients by Tim Majka

CHLOE AND HOLLY

Made in the USA
Columbia, SC
09 July 2025